Unseemly Ambition:

A Concordia Wells Mystery

K.B. OWEN

Author of *Dangerous and Unseemly* and *Unseemly Pursuits*

Unseemly Ambition

A Concordia Wells Mystery

To my parents, Steve and Agnes Belin,

who nurtured my love of reading

and taught me to be daring in my ambitions.

Thank you.

Acknowledgments

Many people have had a hand in bringing this book into being, and I want to express my sincerest thanks to them here. Among those who helped were several scholars and experts. Any errors found are solely mine, not theirs.

To Pamela Mack, Ph.D., at Clemson State University, who generously provided information about women engineers in the late-nineteenth century.

To the academic scholars of Victoria List (Victoria@list.indiana.edu), who furnished me with a wealth of information about nineteenth century anarchists.

To Jay Holmes, for his expert and ever-patient answers to my questions about nineteenth-century bomb-making.

To author Mary Morrissy, who helped me make Mr. Flynn's dialogue more authentic. At last, the Irish are gettin' a look-in.

To Margot Kinberg, Kassandra Lamb, and Rachel Funk Heller, the best beta readers a gal could ask for. Thank you for your thoughtful feedback. Your suggestions helped immensely.

To fellow Misterio Press author Vinnie Hansen, who provided invaluable editing in the novel's final stages, and Kirsten Weiss, for her meticulous formatting. For the latest mysteries by these and other authors at Misterio Press, please visit http://misteriopress.com/misterio-press-bookstore/#all.

Speaking of formatting, I'd like to thank Debora Lewis for her formatting of the print version. You truly make these words a thing of beauty.

To artist Melinda VanLone, who never fails to create such wonderful covers. I am grateful for her time and talents. Melinda can be reached at BookCoverCorner.com.

To Kristen Lamb, Piper Bayard, and the generous community of fellow writers known as WANAs, for their advice and support. We are truly not alone.

To my parents-in-law, Steve and Lyn, and the extended Owen clan of wonderful sisters- and brothers-in-law, nieces and nephews. You continue to read my books and cheer on my milestones. Thank you!

To my young niece Isa Owen, who motivates me with her own love of writing. I look forward to reading your books someday.

To my parents, Ag and Steve, to whom this book is dedicated. I love you.

To my sons, Patrick, Liam, and Corey, who have been so supportive of my writing efforts. Corey—thank you for keeping me well-supplied with cheese and crackers.

Most of all, I want to thank my husband Paul for his boundless encouragement and love. I would not be the author I am today without you.

K.B. Owen
October 2014

Chapter 1

Week 2, Instructor Calendar
Valentine's Day 1898

Why must fancy shoes inevitably pinch during long speeches? Professor Concordia Wells pondered this and other unanswerable questions as President Langdon droned on in front of a crowd in the Sycamore House dining room. At least today Langdon was droning on about her dear friend and cottage-mate Ruby Hitchcock, so the discomfort was worth it.

Concordia, not blessed with tall stature, stood on tiptoe to better see President Langdon, Lady Principal Pomeroy, and Ruby on the platform. The guest of honor looked lovely today, beaming and dressed in her best Sunday-church outfit, a soft white pleated shirtwaist with a two-toned tweed skirt of fawn and navy.

"Today we give Ruby Hitchcock this Outstanding Staff Member Award for her more than twenty years of faithful service to Hartford Women's College," Langdon said. His smile reached his eyes, soft with paternal sentiment. "But our Ruby is not simply the matron of Willow Cottage, keeping house and acting as chaperone to the students who live there. She, along with Miss Wells, are the heart and soul of that little domicile, acting as surrogate mothers to the girls in their care, fostering kindness, cooperation, and refined womanly behavior."

Ruby looked across the room at Concordia and rolled her eyes. Concordia grinned, then glanced back at Miss Smedley and Miss Lovelace, the two Willow Cottage girls assigned to help serve the refreshments today. Each girl stood as far from the other at the dessert table as she could manage, exchanging unladylike scowls. Concordia wished that "kindness, cooperation, and refined womanly behavior" would assert itself soon. It might make it easier for the two to share living quarters.

Concordia turned her attention back to Ruby, who was extending a gloved hand to accept the plaque and envelope. After a hearty round of applause, the room fell quiet, waiting.

"Ah, um...." Ruby hesitated. A dusky flush crept up her neck.

Concordia hid a smile behind her glove. How ironic that a woman perfectly at her ease when dressing down a wayward student in her charge should find it daunting to address a crowd of teachers, administrators, and trustees. Perhaps the presence of the newspaperman jotting notes made Ruby nervous.

"This is right kind of you, Mr. Langdon," Ruby said finally. "Thank you."

The reporter raised a hand.

"Yes...Mr. Rosen." Langdon pointed with a pudgy finger.

"How do you like your job, Mrs. Hitchcock...it *is* Mrs, isn't it?" the man asked, pushing his bowler further up his head as he checked his notes. "Widowed, ma'am?"

Ruby stiffened and her right hand twitched. Concordia remembered the milkman's boy had gotten a sound cuff on the ear last week for asking how old the matron was. Luckily the reporter was out of range.

"Yes, her husband died in the war, more than thirty years ago," Langdon added quickly.

"Ah. My sympathies." He made a note. "So what can you tell me about cottage dormitory life?"

Ruby took a deep breath. "We-ell, them girls can be right mischievous. I have my hands full keeping up wi' them."

Concordia glanced again at Miss Smedley and Miss Lovelace. They now stood beside each other, and close proximity between those two rarely ended well. Miss Smedley appeared to be re-positioning the cups and cutlery, while Miss Lovelace gripped one lone spoon in her white-knuckled fist, either to thwart the other girl's arrangement or to shove it up her nose...it was difficult to tell.

Right mischievous, indeed.

"But they're good young ladies all the same," Ruby added hastily, watching the reporter scribble on his pad.

"What do you like best about being here?" he asked.

"I suppose the girls keep *me* young, too." Her eyes softened. "I remember them all. I've even bounced some o' their babes on my knee, when they've come back to visit." She cleared her throat awkwardly.

Satisfied, the reporter tucked away his notepad. "The story will be featured in the paper's *College Miscellany* section this Friday," he said.

Langdon beamed his approval, then gestured to the back table. "Everyone, help yourselves to refreshments."

Ruby breathed a sigh as she and Concordia moved to a buffet table laden with a bounty of sweets: madelines, scones, linzer tarts, meringues. The sharp tang of raspberry reminded Concordia of summertime on this blustery winter day. She offered Ruby a cookie plate. "Here, try the jammy ones, they're delicious."

Ruby shook her head. "I'm jes' parched, miss. I could do wi' a cup of tea. Can we go home now?"

"Not quite yet. The lady principal said something about posing for a picture. But I'll get you that tea in the meantime. Why don't you find us seats?" The matron was looking pale. Concordia wasn't so sure this award business was doing her any favors.

Concordia reached the tea table, a visual confection of lace and the thinnest, gold-rimmed bone china. As every surface was spoken for, she struggled to pick up the teapot while balancing plate, cup, and saucer. Randolph Maynard, the school's dean, watched her across the table. "Mr. Maynard, would you mind?" She inclined her head toward the teapot.

The dean raised a heavy black eyebrow. "I'm not on the wait staff, Miss Wells," he growled in a deep voice.

Concordia bit back the impertinent retort that sprang to mind. It would not do to squabble with the administrator, difficult though he was. Despite being at the school for a year now, Maynard remained stiff and distant, even downright grumpy. He got along better with the horses in the school's stable, where he spent much of his free time.

"Speaking of which," Maynard continued, his scowl deepening, "where are your students? Aren't they supposed to be helping here at the table?"

Oh, no. She had seen them just a few minutes ago. Concordia turned away to look up and down the dining room, praying the girls weren't off in a corner quarreling. Miss Lovelace and Miss Smedley were nowhere to be seen. Why had they abandoned their posts? When this was over and she returned to the cottage, she would give them an earful.

"Here, miss, let me help you with that," said a voice at her elbow. Mr. Rosen picked up the heavy pot and poured the tea.

"Oh!" Concordia was more distracted than she realized. "Thank you."

Rosen dropped his voice. "I haven't seen you since that...unpleasantness last year. You know, with Colonel Adams' death."

Concordia frowned. "Of course I remember. But that's long past. Best not to bring it up again." She glanced in Dean Maynard's direction. He was scowling into his cup, mercifully oblivious.

"I couldn't help but notice your role in solving the case, Miss Wells," Rosen continued.

Concordia waved a dismissive hand. "I'd say you played a more significant part in helping Lieutenant Capshaw track down the culprits than I."

Rosen beamed. "I got quite the scoop out of it. Certainly a feather in my cap at the *Courant*. But I was wondering...could I interview you about your experience?"

"Me? There's hardly anything to tell that you don't already know."

"But it's a terrific angle," Rosen said enthusiastically. "You know, the *lady sleuth*, and all that. I understand there had been another incident at the school, a semester earlier. I only just learned about it. Lots of material there. My readers love that sort of thing."

To Concordia's dismay, she noticed Maynard, on the far side of the table, had taken on a posture of attentive stillness, which typically comes from trying to *look* as if one is not eavesdropping. Time to squash this, before the dean heard more about her past as a *lady sleuth*.

"Certainly not, Mr. Rosen," Concordia said. "I have no interest in that sort of self-aggrandizing. If you'll excuse me." She turned away, awkwardly balancing the teacups and plate.

Rosen slid his card under a cookie. "In case you change your mind. And if there's ever anything you need, feel free to contact me."

Concordia found Ruby seated on an ottoman beside the window. "Quick, take something before I drop it all."

Ruby grabbed the topmost cup. After setting everything down, Concordia collapsed into a wing chair. She looked over at the matron and smiled. "How does it feel to be the guest of honor?"

Ruby pursed her lips as if tasting something sour. "A lot of folderol, if you ask me. I prefer a clean kitchen and a quiet spot by the fire. O' course, I don't get much in the way of clean and quiet at the cottage, either."

Concordia laughed. All too true. "At least the reporter didn't keep you long with a lot of questions." She passed Ruby a napkin.

"Mighty nosy, all the same." Ruby snorted. "Wot does he care if I'm a widow or not?"

"I suppose they get carried away. Asking questions is their business, after all. I hope it didn't bring up bad memories."

Ruby shook her head. "No, it's not that. Land sakes, that was more'n thirty years ago. I was a new bride when Johnny went off to war. After he died, it was hard to make a living. But I managed, even though the widow's pension was pitiful."

Concordia nodded. Ruby's hobbling gait, graying hair, and short stature implied a frail old lady, but the matron was far more resilient than her appearance let on.

"Now that we're talking 'bout brides," Ruby said, dropping a sugar cube in her tea, "when is your friend Miss Adams getting married to that policeman?"

"Next week," Concordia said. "I'm grateful for your help in hemming my dress. Now it's perfect."

Ruby smiled. "You'll make a lovely maid of honor. Will Mr. Bradley be there, too?"

Concordia nodded.

Ruby's smile broadened. "Then you might want to tuck away those spectacles of yours before the ceremony."

"I happen to be fond of seeing where I step, thank you very much," Concordia retorted, self-consciously adjusting her glasses.

"With a man's arm to hold onto, who needs to see?" Ruby asked mischievously.

Concordia blushed. "That will be quite enough of *that* sort of talk."

They looked up to see Lady Principal Pomeroy approaching. "Ruby," she said, in her high-pitched, breathy voice, "the photographer is ready for you."

"Um, Miss Pomeroy…." Concordia gestured toward the lady principal's frizzy brown flyaway hair, coming out of its bun.

"Oh!" Gertrude Pomeroy reached up to anchor the straggling pins. "Thank you, dear." She gave a wink, her eyes bright blue behind crooked spectacles.

Ruby stood and tugged at her cuffs. "Let's get this over with."

"I'll wait for you," Concordia offered. "We can go back to the cottage together."

With a nod, Ruby followed Miss Pomeroy toward the platform.

Concordia sipped her tea. Over by the French doors, Miss Jenkins, the school's infirmarian and physical training instructor, conversed with Bursar Isley and his wife, Lily.

Concordia found her attention drawn to Lily Isley—an attractive woman, though on the nearer side of fifty. Today her elegant figure was shown to great advantage in a godeted skirt of deep-red velvet, which drew a number of admiring glances from the men in the room. No doubt Mrs. Isley was accustomed to such looks from her days as a stage actress.

Though Mrs. Isley had obviously abandoned the footlights since her marriage, Concordia hoped she could be coaxed to take over the senior play. It had by default become Concordia's responsibility once again this year.

Miss Jenkins detached herself from the group and poured herself a cup of tea. Concordia caught her eye, gesturing to the rocking chair beside her, and Miss Jenkins crossed the room.

"Whew!" Miss Jenkins settled into the chair. "Between the warm room and the non-stop talking, I was beginning to feel as if I were on the basketball court with my students."

Although Hannah Jenkins was getting on in years—her white hair and deeply-lined face from hatless years of outdoor activity made that clear—she carried her trim figure with an ageless vigor that astounded her colleagues. Concordia, decades younger, couldn't imagine keeping up with a gymnasium full of students day after day.

"I thought you kept the girls running around too much to have breath for chit-chat," Concordia said with a grin.

Miss Jenkins pursed her lips. "You'd be surprised. If mindless chatter were a school subject, these girls would pass with flying colors."

"What were you speaking to the bursar and his wife about? It seemed a lively conversation."

"It was entirely one-sided, I can assure you," Miss Jenkins said. "First, Isley complained about the cost of this reception, but of course it's not surprising that he'd been overruled. One cannot come between ladies and their sweets. I'm surprised all his years of marriage haven't taught him that."

Concordia smiled. "He's quite near with a dollar."

"*Stingy* is more like it," Miss Jenkins retorted, setting her empty cup aside. "Oh, I'm not saying the college's financial condition hasn't improved considerably under his tenure, but when the president of the school can't even get a new buggy to replace the old one that's beyond repair, it gets ridiculous."

"But I heard we *are* getting a new buggy, and that you had something to do with it," Concordia said.

Miss Jenkins smiled. "It wasn't easy. A friend of mine works for the Hartford Carriage Company, and I was able to wheedle a college discount on last year's Buckeye buggy. The model didn't sell as well as expected. The deep discount swayed the bursar in the end." She sighed. "The sight of Edward Langdon riding to town in the custodian's farm cart should never be repeated."

Concordia smothered a laugh, remembering Langdon's expression of painful dignity last week as he rode through the front gate on the rickety old wagon.

"Then our conversation shifted to politics," Miss Jenkins went on, plucking a meringue from a nearby tray. "I didn't realize how active the Isleys are in the state senatorial campaign. Particularly Mrs. Isley, which was a surprise."

Concordia raised an eyebrow. "Really?"

"Regrettably, I couldn't shift the topic to women's suffrage, so that's when I—" Miss Jenkins hesitated as Ruby approached them.

"All done with the photographer?" Concordia asked Ruby.

The matron nodded. "And more'n ready to go home."

Concordia checked her lapel watch. "My, yes, it's getting late." She stacked their dishware, giving a little nod of goodbye as Miss Jenkins turned to leave as well.

"Wot's this?" Ruby asked, pulling Mr. Rosen's card off the plate.

"What *is* that, indeed?" a testy male voice chimed in.

Concordia's heart sank as she turned to see Randolph Maynard's tall figure looming over her. The dean's imperious tone had attracted the attention of others standing nearby: Lady Principal Pomeroy, President Langdon, and the Isleys.

Maynard glanced at the card Ruby clutched. "Hmm. What does a *newspaper reporter* want with one of our teachers?" He raised an eyebrow. "Or do you prefer 'lady sleuth,' Miss Wells?"

Chapter 2

What, have you lost your wits?

Othello, I.i

Week 2, Instructor Calendar
Valentine's Day 1898

Concordia slipped the card from Ruby's grasp and tucked it into her skirt pocket. "If it's all the same to you, Mr. Maynard, I have themes to grade," she snapped. The nerve of the man, holding her up to ridicule in front of everyone as if she were an errant schoolgirl.

Maynard's lip curled. "One would hope so, Miss Wells. That *is* what we are paying you for."

Concordia turned away without another word, remembering on her way out of Sycamore House to retrieve her coat. And a good thing, too: the snow that had been threatening all day was coming down in earnest. Several inches covered the ground already.

Ruby followed right behind. "Too big for his breeches, that one," she huffed. She wrapped her scarf more securely around her head and planted her feet in Concordia's tracks in the snow.

Concordia nodded miserably as she thrust her hands deeper in her pockets. What a horrible man. It would be a relief to get back to the cottage and work in peace and quiet.

Peace and quiet were not to be had at Willow Cottage, however. After nearly three years of living and teaching at the school, Concordia should know not to expect *that*. She and Ruby returned to a cottage filled with chattering girls. They had made a banner: *Congratulations, Ruby!* decorated in Valentine's

Day style, with pink and white lacy hearts around the border. The students greeted the matron with hugs and an avalanche of questions:

"How much money did they give you?"

"Were you nervous?"

"Let's see the plaque...did they spell your name right?"

"Ooh, what a pretty skirt you're wearing today!"

"What did the newspaper man ask you?"

"What sort of food was there?"

Ruby turned a flustered red and held up both hands in surrender. "Enough!" she cried. "You'd think I was the blinkin' President of America, the way you all are carrying on." Her expression softened at the sight of the banner. "I'm real grateful for the trouble, lambs, but there's work to be done around here, and this parlor i'n't going to clean itself." She gave one of the freshmen a meaningful look, and the girl hurried to get the duster.

"You heard Ruby," Concordia said. "You all have chores and other things to do, so go on, let the poor woman catch her breath. Anna, take the broom out to the porch and clear off the snow. Has anyone seen Miss Lovelace or Miss Smedley?"

"I haven't seen Alison," one young lady volunteered, "but Maisie came in to change and then left again. She said she was going coasting on Rook's Hill with a couple of the other girls."

Concordia looked through the window. With the snow coming down at this rate, she had no intention of chasing after Miss Lovelace.

Ruby frowned at Concordia. "Somethin' going on with those two again?"

Concordia pulled her away from the girls. "They left the reception much earlier than they were supposed to," she murmured. "The dean was the one who pointed it out."

Ruby sighed. "Land sakes, of all people to notice. I think some extra chores are in order, once they show up."

Concordia nodded.

"When will we get to read the valentines?" one girl asked, motioning to the hall basket, filled to overflowing with homemade cards and small, tissue-wrapped packets.

"You know we distribute them after dinner, and not before," Concordia said firmly. "Go on, now."

The girls pouted but shuffled off to their tasks.

At that moment, Alison Smedley walked in. She hesitated at the sight of Concordia and Ruby.

"Oh. Miss Wells…" she began.

Concordia gestured to the girl's sodden boots and coat. "Hang up your things to dry, then join me in my quarters." She looked over at Ruby. "I'll take care of it. Why don't you rest for a while?"

Ruby gave her a grateful look as she headed for the kitchen.

Concordia regarded Miss Smedley in silence as the young lady perched uneasily on the only other chair in Concordia's study, nervously smoothing back her pale hair in its bun and settling the folds of her burgundy-velvet-trimmed cashmere skirts.

Concordia knew that Alison Smedley came from the Philadelphia Smedleys, a family of blue-blood wealth with powerful ties to steel and railroad magnates. Here at Hartford Women's College, Miss Smedley enjoyed a bevy of admiring girls who sought her favor. When it suited her, she could be a pleasant young lady. It did not always suit her. Particularly where her roommate was concerned.

"I know what you're going to say," Miss Smedley said, breaking the silence. "I was supposed to help during the entire reception, and I didn't stay."

Concordia waited for more. "Why did you leave?" she finally asked. It was like pulling teeth.

Miss Smedley gave a dramatic sigh. "Maisie was useless. If she wasn't staring out the window at the snow, she was rearranging the table, and I'd have to change it back. I worked hard to get it just right. The spoons should never go to the left of the saucers in a proper afternoon tea configuration, nor should the cups be *stacked*." She rolled her eyes.

"So that's why you left?"

"No," Miss Smedley said through gritted teeth. "Maisie abandoned me first. To play in the snow. I suppose one can't expect much from such an ill-bred girl. I left after that. After all, why should I stay and do all the work?"

"Because we were even more short-handed, and needed you," Concordia retorted.

The girl shrugged.

They were getting nowhere. Concordia stood. "I will have a list of chores for you in the morning, Miss Smedley. You may go."

Miss Smedley raised an eyebrow in surprise, no doubt expecting a long-winded lecture. "What about Maisie? She should get *more* chores."

"There will be plenty of work for both of you," Concordia assured her.

After dinner, two dozen excited girls gathered in the parlor of Willow Cottage. Ruby took a quick count. "We're missin' a few sophomores."

"Miss Lovelace and her friends promised to be back in time for the valentines," one of the students said. She paused. "I think I hear them now."

Sure enough, the door swung wide as two girls stepped in, bringing a swirl of snow with them.

"*Brr*, get that door closed," Concordia said. "Where's Miss Lovelace?"

"She's stowing the sled," one girl answered, shaking snow from her scarf.

"You're getting water on the floor," Concordia said sternly. "Go hang those things by the kitchen stove to dry, and mop up this mess. You know better."

They gave her a sheepish look and hurried to the kitchen.

Concordia threw on a shawl and stepped out to the porch to see what was keeping Miss Lovelace.

What on earth?

A snow-encrusted Maisie Lovelace was grappling with an enormous sled, obviously homemade and painted a gaily-hued red.

"Let me help you with this…leviathan," Concordia said, grasping the rope.

"Thank you, Miss Wells," Miss Lovelace said, pushing the sled from the back. "It *is* rather big, isn't it?"

"Why didn't your companions stay to help?"

"We were running late, so I sent them on ahead so the other girls wouldn't be anxious, waiting for their valentines."

"After we're finished with the valentines, I want to have a little chat with you," Concordia said.

Miss Lovelace paused, grimacing. "I know. I'm sorry I left the reception early. I cannot abide that girl, and to have to live with her, too…." She shrugged. "I saw it was snowing, and I wanted the chance to try out the sled."

"Well, you're going to have to make up for your lapse. You know better than that. I'll be assigning you additional chores." Concordia looked down at the sled. "Where on earth did this come from?"

"The other girls and I made it ourselves, during the winter recess," Miss Lovelace explained. "We modified the lever-driven steering mechanism, widened the runners, and added a strong suspension for bumpy slopes. It worked beautifully on Rook's Hill."

"Impressive. I only wish you hadn't made it so…" Concordia grunted as she tugged at it again "…large."

Miss Lovelace chuckled. "We wanted it big enough to carry all three of us. I hadn't thought of the problem of storage before now, though. It's been in my uncle's shop. He brought it over this afternoon."

As they propped it against the porch railing, Alison Smedley poked her head outside. She scowled at Miss Lovelace. "We have better things to do than watch you cavort in the snow. You are holding us up."

Concordia suppressed a sigh. *Here we go again.*

Miss Lovelace glared back at Miss Smedley. "Go on without me. I don't care."

Miss Smedley tossed her blonde head and sniffed. "No, I suppose not. I doubt you'll have any cards to open, anyhow." She cast a disdainful eye at the sled. "You'd better not be bringing that hideous contraption into *my* room."

"It's *our* room," Miss Lovelace muttered. She brushed the snow from her coat, looking at her roommate with a mischievous gleam in her eye. "Actually, once the sled is dry, I plan to bring it up to our room for safekeeping. Maybe you can give me a hand?"

Miss Smedley sucked in a breath. "Miss We-ells!" she wailed, looking plaintively at the lady professor.

Concordia raised an eyebrow in Miss Lovelace's direction. The girl laughed. "Don't have a conniption fit, Alison. I was only joking."

Concordia collected the basket from the hall table, noticing that last-minute contributions had made their way in. It certainly was heavy.

The young ladies perched on the edge of their seats, leaning forward, looking over one another's shoulders as Concordia distributed them.

In the interest of fairness, Ruby and Concordia had written valentines of their own to each girl so no one would feel left out. During her Christmas holiday shopping, Concordia had snapped up a spool of lacy peach ribbon from the sales tables. From it, she had cut lengths of the ribbon and tied one to each card, knowing the girls could use it later for a brooch or hair adornment.

"Ooh, so pretty, Miss Wells!" one girl exclaimed, holding it up. "Thank you!"

Looking at the stacks of cards beside each young lady, it was easy to see who among them was the most popular: Miss Smedley, of course, along with the ever-vivacious junior Miss Yarrow, who was also the lead culprit in much of the illegal cooking that went on.

Concordia was getting to the bottom of the stack now. She had a fair number of missives with her own name on them, one of which bore David Bradley's handwriting. She blushed when a student noticed her tucking that one in her pocket.

"Ah-ha, Miss Wells has one she doesn't want us to see!" the girl teased. "I wonder who it's from?" Of course, they all knew Mr. Bradley, a frequent visitor to Willow Cottage.

"Never you mind, young lady," Ruby admonished. But she gave Concordia a wink that made her blush even more.

Later, in her own rooms, she pulled out David's valentine. Inside was a sketch of a lady perched on a bicycle. Rough as it was, Concordia recognized herself as the woman in the picture. *Remembering the first time we met,* he wrote, adding: *Never thought I would be so happy to be run down. Happy Valentine's Day.*

Concordia smiled at the memory. She had, indeed, nearly collided with him, when her thoughts—and the machine—had strayed on a beautiful spring day almost two years before.

Through her partly open door, she heard two students talking in the parlor.

"It's nice that he gave Miss Wells a valentine. Do you suppose she'll marry him?" one of the girls said.

Concordia dropped the card into her lap and shamelessly listened.

"Probably," another said. "Mr. Bradley is quite handsome and really nice, especially for a Chemistry professor. Not like that gruff old Professor Grundy."

"What will happen if she leaves?"

"They'll simply assign another teacher. But I know what you mean. I'll miss her, too. She's a good egg."

"Couldn't she still stay after she gets married? To be our teacher, I mean. I know she couldn't *live* here anymore, but—"

"Don't be a ninny. Married women don't teach. The school would never allow it."

"But there are male teachers at the school who are married. They just go home each day after classes, rather than live here."

"But they aren't the ones in charge of the household and the children, silly—"

The voice broke off at the rapid approach of another student.

"Has anyone seen my scarf?" a girl asked urgently. It was Miss Lovelace.

"No. I think you took it off on the hill. You got too hot, remember?"

Concordia checked the clock. Almost ten. Time to break up this little chat. She opened her door and crossed the hall to the parlor. "Shouldn't you ladies be getting ready for bed?"

One of the few steadfast policies of the college was the "ten o'clock rule": students in bed, lights out, by ten o'clock.

Miss Lovelace turned to Concordia, eyes pleading. "I know it's late, but can I go back and get my scarf, *please*? I'll run very fast."

"In the dark?" Concordia said skeptically. "That would be foolhardy in the extreme. It's not going anywhere, dear. It can wait until morning."

The girl bit her lip.

"Miss Wells," one of her friends said, "it's the scarf her grandmother made her last Christmas. It's very special." The young lady's voice grew subdued. "Her grandmother died only a few weeks ago."

Concordia threw up her hands in surrender. "All right, but *I'll* go. Tell Ruby I'll be back shortly. And *get to bed*."

Miss Lovelace nodded her thanks. "You can't miss it—it's bright red wool."

Well, apparently it *could* be missed, since the heedless girl had failed to bring it back with her, but Concordia was too tired to argue the point. She bundled into her jacket and brought a lantern, setting out for the path to Rook's Hill.

The air was bitterly cold. Thankfully, it had stopped snowing and a nearly full moon had risen, making it easier for her to search as she trudged up the hill. *Ah*, there it was, huddled beside a shrub. She picked up the scarf, stopping a moment to catch her breath.

A moving shadow caught her eye. Looking up, she saw the silhouette of a man walking along the crest of the hill.

The figure was of medium height and a slender build. A youth, perhaps? Concordia couldn't see his face, as he was wrapped up in a thick muffler. He walked at a brisk pace, pulling his collar more tightly against the chill air. Suddenly he stopped and bent down to look in the snow at his feet.

Concordia's mouth set in a grim line. Strange men shouldn't be strolling the grounds of a women's college. How had he gotten past the gatekeeper?

"Hello? Who are you?" she called out, with as much breath as she could muster. She puffed up the hill toward him, avoiding the slick coasting tracks.

The figure turned toward the sound, hesitated, then ran.

"Wait!" Concordia called out, trying to run after him. However, racing up a snowy hill in full skirts does not allow one much speed—or solid footing. Soon she went sprawling, landing on her stomach with a decided *oomph*.

Drat. She hastily got to her feet and clambered to the top of the hill. She looked around, but even with the moonlight on the snowy landscape, the man was nowhere to be seen.

What had he been looking for? She crouched down in the snow, probing with mittened hands. Then she felt something. The moonlight picked up the sheen of a brass pin, though she could see little else in this light. She stuck it in her jacket pocket to look at later, and trudged back to Willow Cottage.

Chapter 3

I am bound to thee for ever.

Othello, III.*iii*

Week 3, Instructor Calendar
February 1898

Concordia's first impression, when she peeked through a side door into the nave, was that of a profusion of blooms. Sophia's family must have raided every hothouse in Hartford. Lilies, oleander, and chrysanthemums spilled over from vases tucked into alcoves, beside doors and windowsills. While beautiful, the sheer volume of floral sweetness was overwhelming. Concordia held a gloved finger under her nose to hold back a sneeze.

She had left a restless Sophia in the anteroom. Although Concordia had never before been a maid of honor—and hoped never to be one again—she knew Sophia well enough to see that her friend craved solitude before the ceremony. After all, marriage was a big step for any woman, but especially one such as Sophia, who had carved out an unconventional life as a tireless advocate for women and the poor at Hartford Settlement House.

So, once Sophia was dressed and ready, Concordia ushered Sophia's stepmother and little sister out of the room and left her alone.

Concordia checked her watch. Just a few more minutes. From her vantage point, she saw several women from Hartford Settlement House being escorted to their seats by David Bradley. The church was getting crowded now. Someone had pulled open several windows to dispel the stuffy air.

David looked quite dashing today. Instead of his customary lumpy-pocketed houndstooth jacket with the worn elbows, he wore a tailored morning coat and pinstripe trousers, with a crisp white shirt that set off his dark eyes and wavy black hair. His hair curled just at his collar in a way that made her want to smooth it with her fingers. She smiled. *Land sakes,* weddings were rife with romantic impulses.

As she surveyed the congregation, she saw that Mother and her escort were seated near the front. Concordia craned her neck for a better look at the man. She didn't know much about Robert Flynn, except that he was a native of Ireland, worked as an attorney for the prestigious law firm of Barrows and Hodge, and was younger than her mother. His exquisitely-tailored jacket fit him beautifully. His neatly-trimmed mustache and beard, heavy eyebrows, salt-and-pepper hair and steady gray eyes bespoke intelligence and reliability.

Mother had only recently told her about Mr. Flynn, describing him merely as a friend who accompanied her to various social functions. Concordia hoped she could learn more about his intentions. Her mother was an attractive widow, though only of modest means. Still, one could not be too careful.

Concordia became aware of movement in the chancel. Opening the side door a bit wider, she recognized the tall, gaunt figure of the groom: police lieutenant Aaron Capshaw, his bright red hair and mustache unmistakable. Gone today was his perpetual gloomy expression, and his habit of walking with a slight stoop, as if looking for clues he had missed. Instead, his carriage was ramrod straight, with a spring in his step. He took his place next to the minister and his best man, eleven-year-old Eli.

The boy looked exceptionally presentable today, although one stubborn cowlick refused to stay slicked down in his wavy hair, and his wrists and ankles showed beneath the ill-fitting borrowed suit. He looked across the nave, smiling when he noticed Concordia. She gave him a little wave before he turned back to Capshaw with luminous eyes, waiting to respond to any direction he'd give.

Concordia scurried down the hall and rapped on the anteroom door. An anxious Sophia poked her head out. "Is it time?" she whispered. "Thank goodness."

Concordia grinned and gave her a careful hug so as not to muss her dress. "You look beautiful, dear."

More than beautiful—radiant, she thought, admiring the short-trained gown of elegant ivory satin overlaid with antique lace. A simple circlet of pearls adorned Sophia's light hair, and she carried a bouquet of orange blossoms.

With no father living, Sophia had decided to keep the procession simple, with Concordia preceding the bride as the organist played the Wedding March. Concordia was glad she wasn't the center of attention; it was a bit unnerving to have so many eyes fixed upon her merely in passing. She concentrated on not tripping over her hem.

As they got to the chancel steps, Concordia caught a glimpse of a patchwork-colored tail swishing behind a vase. *Oh dear.* Eli's cat had decided to join the wedding party. Wherever Eli was, the cat was sure to follow, Concordia knew. But she had to admit, the creature had been the saving of the boy—and herself—last year. She could only hope it wouldn't wreak havoc today.

The bride and groom hadn't noticed. Sophia only had eyes for Capshaw, who stopped shifting his long legs to take in the sight of his bride. Concordia realized she had rarely seen an out-and-out grin on the typically somber-expressioned policeman. She felt as if she had intruded upon a private moment between the two as she stood so close to them.

Her throat prickled with a mix of emotions: joy for her friends, awe at the union between them, and uncertainty for herself. Would she ever feel that way toward a man? She stole a sideways glance at David Bradley, sitting in the front row between Sophia's stepmother and sister. Or did she *already* feel that way? If so, was she willing to sacrifice her independence for love?

As if aware of her gaze, David turned to Concordia with softened eyes. Oh, this was trouble. The man was getting ideas.

A loud *crash* made everyone turn to see Eli's cat bolting through the debris of flowers, water, and the ceramic shards of what was once a large vase. With a final acrobatic leap, balancing briefly upon the enormous hat of a shrieking lady, it fled through a window.

Several men rushed forward to help as the unflappable minister observed the event with nary an "oh my." Sophia had a gloved hand to her mouth, doing her best not to laugh. Eli looked aghast, and Capshaw pulled him away from the cleanup.

"No matter, son," he said, keeping a firm grip on the boy's shoulder. "Your place is here with me. You're my best man, remember?" Eli gulped and stood up straighter.

Capshaw really has a way with the child, Concordia thought. She wondered if he and Sophia might adopt him. That was a happy ending she'd dearly love to see.

At last, the mess was cleaned up, the vows were spoken, and the ceremony was over without further incident.

Concordia stood to Sophia's left in the receiving line as the happy couple greeted their well-wishers.

Soon David Bradley appeared at her elbow, followed by several ladies Concordia recognized from the settlement house. She made the required introductions.

"Are you acquainted with Mr. Bradley? He's a childhood friend of the bride, and godfather to Sophia's little sister."

The women nodded politely.

David gave a courtly bow. "Have you found a replacement for Sophia?"

The ladies exchanged blank looks.

"Now that she's a married woman," David added.

"Oh, no, indeed, Mr. Bradley," one woman huffed. "Sophia is irreplaceable. We would be lost without her."

David's brow wrinkled in confusion. "But she has other responsibilities now: a husband, a home to run...later, a family."

Concordia plucked at the folds of her gown to hide her irritation. Although she understood how impractical it would be—absurd, even—for a married woman to have an independent life outside of the home, it rankled that a lady would be expected to abandon her former life like last year's worn jacket. Was any endeavor taken up during one's single years simply a way of marking time until a marriage proposal came along?

"Miss Wells?"

"Hmm?"

"What is your opinion of Sophia working once she's married?" the head of the settlement house, Martha Newcombe, demanded.

David looked at her expectantly.

Drat.

"We-ell, I'd say it should be decided between the couple," Concordia said.

David waited for more. Concordia turned away slightly, giving her attention solely to Miss Newcombe.

"We know she won't be living at the settlement house, naturally," Miss Newcombe was saying, "but Sophia has told me she intends to remain in charge of the kindergarten program, make her usual rounds of the Colt factory workers' housing, and speak at the occasional suffrage rally."

Concordia glanced back at David. Judging by his expression, he was either wincing at the thought of suffrage rallies, or he'd caught a pebble in his shoe.

"She certainly has a talent for the work," Concordia said, smoothing her skirts and looking around.

And with that, David and the ladies moved down the line to congratulate the Capshaws.

Her mother and Mr. Flynn—the man was taller and leaner than Concordia had realized while he was sitting down—came along next.

"Concordia dear, your dress is absolutely lovely," Letitia Wells said, admiring the duchesse satin of soft myrtle green, adorned with pale green tulle rosettes at the sleeves.

Concordia smiled. "Thank you. Sophia helped me pick it out." And thank goodness for that. Rarely could Concordia find a shade that suited her green eyes, unfashionable red hair, and pale, freckled complexion. Fortunately, she didn't have much need of ball gowns and other fripperies at the college.

Her mother nodded in approval. "So much nicer than those plain skirts and horrid shirtwaists you usually put on. And you've done your hair differently. You should wear it that way all the time." She turned to Mr. Flynn and shuddered. "She inevitably has a pencil stuck through a topknot."

Concordia bit back a retort and said instead, "Mother, why don't you introduce me to Mr. Flynn *before* informing him of my customary manner of dress and comportment?"

Mr. Flynn laughed aloud. "Ah, Miss Wells, 'tis grand to make your acquaintance at last. Robert Flynn, at your service." His voice had a melodic, Hibernian lilt that Concordia found mesmerizing. He took her hand and made a gallant bow over it. "Your ma's after talking about you so much, I feel I know you already."

Mrs. Wells flushed. Concordia nodded politely. "The pleasure is mine, Mr. Flynn. Have you lived in Hartford very long?"

"So I have, a number o' years now," Flynn answered. "'Tis a fine town, though a shame it is that I didn't meet this lovely lady all the sooner." He gazed warmly at Letitia Wells, which made the woman blush more deeply and shake her head.

"You see how Mr. Flynn turns on the Irish charm," Mrs. Wells said in mock severity. "Don't encourage him."

With a nod, Concordia's mother and Robert Flynn moved on to speak to the Capshaws.

The line had thinned as guests climbed into carriages for the reception.

Mr. Flynn, now on the outside steps conversing with Capshaw, turned his head abruptly toward the far side of the street. Concordia, Sophia, and Capshaw followed his glance.

A woman in her late twenties, standing on the periphery of the crowd, was staring at them.

"Do you know her, Robert?" Mrs. Wells whispered to her companion.

Flynn turned away with a shrug. "I cannot say she looks familiar. I suppose something about her caught my eye."

Concordia didn't have to wonder at that. The woman was ordinary enough in appearance, thin and slightly-built, bundled in a shabby gray wool coat against the February chill, but the intensity of her gaze made her stand out. She interacted with no one, a still pebble in a stream of people.

"I don't recognize her, either," Capshaw said.

Concordia felt a vague uneasiness as she realized that the woman seemed to be staring at Eli in particular. When the lady noticed the group was watching her, however, she quickly turned on her heel and hurried away.

"Does *anyone* know her?" Sophia asked. She stooped to point her out to Eli, but when they turned back, she was out of sight.

"How odd," Capshaw said.

Chapter 4

Week 3, Instructor Calendar
February 1898

Concordia lingered at the Adams' house as the reception came to an end. After the other guests had left, she went looking for Sophia. She found the new bride in the sitting room. She was slumped upon a chaise, shoes tossed aside and stockinged feet tucked under her. Concordia grinned at the sight.

"Getting a respite at last?"

Sophia grimaced. "You have no idea how my feet hurt. And I am tired of talking. Who knew these functions could be so exhausting? I'd rather address a hostile auditorium of people who think women have the intelligence of dairy cows than chatter on with genteel society over punch bowls and cheese plates." She closed her eyes.

Concordia remembered the early demands of her sister's marriage. "You'd better get used to it," she said mildly.

Sophia opened her eyes briefly and waved toward a chair. "You should sit, too. Your shoes don't look any more comfortable than mine."

Concordia didn't need a second invitation. She set down the plates she'd collected and sank gratefully into a padded chair. Neither spoke for a few moments.

"Have you seen Aaron?" Sophia asked.

"He and Eli are out looking for the cat. The animal hasn't been seen since it bolted from the church."

"It's as good an excuse as any to get some fresh air, I suppose," Sophia said.

Concordia nodded. Although fresh air in mid-February was bound to be quite bracing, she knew young boys could get restless at public functions. She noted the lengthening shadows outside. "I hope they return soon."

"I know Eli's attached to the animal," Sophia said, "but I'm not looking forward to sharing quarters with it."

Concordia sat up straighter. "You've decided to adopt Eli? How wonderful!"

Sophia smiled. "Once we're back from New York, we'll get the process started."

"The ladies at the settlement house are under the impression that you'll still be working there," Concordia said. "Is that true?"

Sophia nodded wearily. "Aaron and I have had several discussions about it. I *must* continue my work." This was accompanied by that characteristically-stubborn tilt of her head.

"What did he have to say to *that*?" Concordia asked.

Sophia sighed. "It took a little persuading, but he understands that my work is just as valuable as his. He gets called out at all hours, investigating cases. Why should I sit at home alone, of little utility, when I'm needed as well?" She gestured toward the darkening windows. "Would you mind drawing the curtains?"

Concordia crossed over to the windows, lost in thought. Capshaw's willingness to adapt to such an unconventional arrangement was surprising to say the least. In the two years Concordia had known the man, she'd lost track of the number of times he would sigh, shake his head, and claim not to understand the unorthodox ways of "college people."

"I hope he knows how to cook his own supper," Concordia said over her shoulder as she tugged at the draperies.

She turned back from the window. "But seriously, Sophie, how will you manage a child, a new marriage, and your settlement work? That seems a formidable challenge."

"Not that it's any concern of yours how I run my life," Sophia answered tartly, "but Eli will have his lessons along with Amelia, here at my stepmother's house. He can stay here whenever Aaron and I both have to be out. We've found a brownstone a few blocks away that we can afford."

"I see." Concordia sat down again.

The silence lengthened. The mantel clock sounded unnaturally loud in the stillness.

"I'm sorry," Sophia said.

"I know, dear."

Sophia got up and began to pace the room. "It's all so nerve-wracking. I cannot believe I'm...*married*. I love him; I couldn't imagine ever walking away from that. But so many changes.... I should be braver than this."

"You're the bravest person I know," Concordia said firmly, "but you cannot pretend this isn't going to profoundly affect you. Your life will never be the same."

Few among us heartily embrace change, Concordia thought, even when we know it's what we want. We cling to the familiar. Even those like Sophia, who crusade for change. Because when it's your own life, it's different.

The parlor door pushed open and Capshaw walked in. He smiled briefly at Concordia, but made a straight line for Sophia, joining her on the chaise and planting a kiss on her forehead.

"I should go," Concordia said, starting to get up.

Capshaw waved her back into her chair. "I need to speak with you."

Sophia sat up. "Where's Eli?"

"At the settlement house. We did find his cat—finally. But it was getting late, so I brought him back there first."

"Sophia tells me you two are going to adopt Eli," Concordia said. "Congratulations."

Capshaw smiled. "He's a wonderful boy, and deserves a family of his own."

"What did you want to talk to me about?" Concordia asked.

"I have a favor to ask you," Capshaw began, hesitantly. He glanced over at Sophia. "When Eli and I went out, we saw that same stranger—the woman who was staring at us after the ceremony, remember?—lingering near the side gate. When I approached to find out her business, she ran off."

"That's certainly disturbing," Concordia said. "What do you want me to do?"

"We leave by the nine o'clock train tomorrow morning, and don't return until next Saturday," Capshaw said. "I'm uneasy about Eli during that time. My impression is that the woman is interested in *him* in particular. It will be difficult to reach us in a timely way. Since Sophia's family will be gone this week as well, I told Martha at the settlement house to contact you if there's a problem." He gave her a small smile. "You're the only family we'll have nearby."

Concordia was touched. "I'd be happy to help. Did you tell Martha about the woman?"

Capshaw shook his head. "I didn't want to alarm her unnecessarily. I merely asked her to keep an eye on Eli. He may feel lonely with us gone. And I told the boy to stay close to the settlement house in the meantime, and not wander off."

Sophia's brow creased. "Should we cancel our trip?"

"I've asked the district patrolman to keep an eye on the settlement house," Capshaw said, "and I'll send a note to Sergeant Maloney before we leave, to see if he can find out more about this woman." Capshaw patted Sophia's hand. "Eli will be fine."

Chapter 5

Upon malicious bravery, dost thou come
To start my quiet.

Othello, I.i

Week 3, Instructor Calendar
February 1898

Concordia was enjoying a rare opportunity for quiet reading in her quarters at Willow Cottage. The girls were off at their various pursuits, with Literature Club, basketball, and ice skating being the most popular at the moment.

She relished the peace—no thumping over her head, no illegal cooking, no screeches. Just silence. Even Ruby was out shopping. The steam heat radiators and the bedside clock were the only background sounds; so soothing....

She was startled awake by a banging on the front door. *Mercy*, how long had she been asleep? She sheepishly smoothed her skirts and adjusted her hairpins as she hurried to the front door.

"May I help you?" Concordia asked the short, stocky man on the porch.

"Ahm lookin' fer Ruby," he said, sucking at a toothpick between his teeth.

"Who are you?" Concordia couldn't imagine Ruby having dealings with such a man. He was decidedly unkempt, his barrel chest straining the buttons of his grimy pea-coat, his bushy gray beard untrimmed and harboring the remnants of his last meal. Concordia felt a twinge of sympathy for him, though, noting the deep scars across his balding head and the missing left ear lobe.

Thank goodness the students weren't around to see. Why hadn't Clyde stopped him at the gate?

"Ne'er ye mind who I am, li'l miss," he sneered down at her. Concordia's eyes watered at the stink of cheap liquor on his breath. He waved a scrap of newspaper under her nose. "Jes' tell the *famous Mrs. Hitchcock* that I's come back. She'll know."

Concordia couldn't imagine how the man had gotten past the usually-vigilant gatekeeper, but she couldn't allow him to run around loose on campus.

She had an idea. "Are you hungry? We're serving dinner shortly, in the dining hall."

The man wobbled a bit, but grinned. "Lead the way, li'l lady."

Concordia grabbed a shawl from the coat rack and wrapped herself in it. The air was bone-chilling cold, but with any luck, she wouldn't be out long. After latching the door, she took him back over the paths, but instead of the dining hall, she led him to the gatekeeper's cottage.

"Hey! Wot's this?" the man demanded as Concordia knocked on Clyde's door.

Clyde stepped out. "Yes, miss?" His look swept over the drunkard in alarm. "How'd ya get in here? I told ya to get lost!"

"Can you please show this...gentleman...out, and make sure he *stays* out?" Concordia asked.

Clyde showed a gleam of gaping teeth beneath his bristled mustache, and put one burly arm around the man's neck, twisting his wrist behind his back with the other. "Let me show ya where the trolley is, my good sir."

As the stranger was being marched toward the gate, he glared over his shoulder at Concordia. "This ain't over," he growled. "I'll remember yer conniving ways. I ain't gonna be bested by a bitty thing like *you.*"

"That's enough outta ya," Clyde growled.

Concordia shivered and wrapped her shawl more firmly about her as she walked back to Willow Cottage. She had some questions for Ruby.

Ruby barely returned in time to help escort the students to the dining hall that evening. She rushed in, arms full of parcels. "Lemme jes' put these away; I'll be right out," she said breathlessly, scurrying down the hall.

Concordia and the girls waited patiently until Ruby re-emerged. "Sorry," she said, smoothing her hair back. "I'm ready now." She grinned. "Wait 'til I show you the bargains I snapped up at Sage Allen's white sale."

As the girls walked briskly ahead on the path, eager to get to their suppers, Concordia touched Ruby on the arm. "A man came looking for you today."

Ruby frowned. "A man? I weren't expectin' anybody. Who was he?"

"He didn't give his name, but he asked for you specifically."

"*Me?* Wot did he want?"

"He said to tell you he was *back*, and he waved a scrap of newspaper at me, referring to you as *the famous Mrs. Hitchcock*. I think he was referring to the newspaper article about your award."

Ruby shook her head. "I never did like the idea o' that newspaperman writin' about me. Wot did the man look like?"

"He was a rather disagreeable character. Drunk and ill-mannered. I'm not sure about his age, but close to sixty, I'd guess. Short, broad-shouldered, bushy gray beard, blue eyes. Large hands. He was nearly bald, with a big scar across the top of his forehead."

"It don't sound like any man I know, thank goodness," Ruby said, her face growing pale.

The girls were holding the dining hall door open for them. Concordia and Ruby walked briskly to catch up.

"Oh, and one other thing I noticed about him," Concordia added, "part of his left ear lobe was missing."

Ruby hesitated at the door, stiffening. "Ya don't say? Well, let's hope Clyde stops him at the gate next time. It don't sound like a man I want to know." Without a backward look, she went inside.

Chapter 6

There are many
events in the womb of time which will be delivered.
Othello, I.*iii*

Week 3, Instructor Calendar
February 1898

The next morning brought the usual bustle of students dressing for classes, and a time-pressed Concordia gathering her lecture notes and graded themes. *Drat.* Where were her pages on Elizabethan drama?

There was a tap on her door.

"Enter!" she called. She hoped it wasn't someone with a problem.

One of the students stuck her head in. "A lady to see you, Miss Wells. I know you're leaving, and I told her so, but she was most insistent."

Concordia grabbed her satchel and followed the girl into the hall, where the head of Hartford Settlement House waited.

"Martha, what a surprise!" Concordia exclaimed.

The woman's worn face seemed more deeply lined than usual. "I understand you're on your way to class, but it's about Eli, and with Sophia being away…." Her voice trailed off.

Concordia's stomach clenched. "Is he hurt?"

"No, no," Martha assured her, "but—"

"Can you walk with me?" Concordia asked.

As they passed clumps of student groups on the paths, Martha explained. "A woman came to see us yesterday. At first, I thought it was someone in need of our services. She was so thin and pale, and seemed quite apprehensive, looking over her shoulder, shifting in her chair...but what she had to say was a complete shock to me."

"What was it?" Concordia asked, sidestepping a slushy pile of snow.

"She says she's Eli's mother. She wants to take him."

Concordia stopped dead on the path, causing several students to bump into her. "Sorry," she muttered. She stepped out of the way and dropped her voice. "His *mother*? Are you sure?"

Martha pulled at her lip, troubled. "No, I'm not. She has the same coloring as Eli, but that's no way to tell. He doesn't recognize her at all, says she looks nothing like the mother he remembers, whom we've never been able to find and assumed was dead. This woman claims to be on speaking terms with the settlement house's primary benefactors, and has threatened to complain to them if we don't give him up. I don't know what to do. Could *you* talk to her?"

Concordia took a deep breath. "I'm not sure how persuasive I can be, but I could at least get more information. What's her name?"

"Florence Tooey."

The bell rang. Concordia touched Martha's arm in reassurance. "I have to go. I can come to the settlement house tomorrow at noon. Just get her and Eli there, and I'll see what I can do." Martha nodded as Concordia hurried into class.

Chapter 7

By heaven, I'll know thy thoughts.

Othello, *III.iii*

The trolley ride from Hartford Women's College to the Main Street stop near Hartford Settlement House gave Concordia the chance to think, but it didn't seem like nearly enough time to come up with a plan. Who was this woman? Where did she come from? And why had she come for Eli *now*? Without any real information to go on, Concordia would have to innovate as she learned more. If the woman were indeed Eli's mother, would she not care enough about his emotional well-being to refrain from abruptly uprooting the child?

Concordia walked the last few blocks to the settlement house and up the stone steps, dodging the children playing hoops near the entrance, her steps and her heart heavy.

She'd known Eli more than a year now, from the time he'd arrived as a homeless, raggedy ten-year-old who couldn't read or write his own name. But he was thriving here at the settlement house, going to school, settling into a routine.

Concordia approached the young girl at the front desk. "I'm here to see Martha."

"Ah, yes, Miss Wells, she's been expectin' you," the girl said. "This way, if you please."

Concordia stepped into the office, where Martha, Eli, and familiar-looking woman waited. *Of course*—the stranger from Sophia's wedding, the one who couldn't stop staring at Eli.

Florence Tooey was a woman of petite stature. She was plainly attired in a dark worsted dress, worn gray coat, and water-stained shoes. Her soft, wavy dark hair framed a face made gaunt by some unknown strain. She had the same piquant chin as Eli's, and the same luminous eyes.

With a drop of her heart, Concordia knew she was looking at Eli's mother.

Martha stepped forward to make the introductions. "Miss Wells, this is Mrs. Tooey."

"Call me Florence, please," the woman said, her voice quiet, the accent refined. Concordia was startled; this was no servant who had gotten herself in trouble and had to turn to the streets to raise a child on her own. And yet she was dressed in a shabby coat and worn shoes. Who was she?

During this interchange, Eli eyed the adults, limbs shaking, mouth quivering. He sidled up to Concordia and grasped her hand. "Please, miss—doan' let her take me away."

Concordia's heart lurched at the sight of Eli's pale face. He had saved her life last year. Although the scars on her wrists had long healed, the bond she and Eli shared remained irrevocable. She must save him now.

Concordia patted Eli's hand. "Let me talk with Mrs. Tooey alone. We'll work things out." She tried to make her tone sound as reassuring as she could, although she felt less than confident.

Martha put a hand on Eli's shoulder. "We've got some bread and jam for you in the kitchen, okay?"

Eli gave a dejected nod and followed Martha out.

Concordia sat and motioned the woman into the other chair.

"Can you tell me a little about yourself, Mrs. Tooey? Where do you come from? How did you come to be separated—" she was careful to avoid the word *abandon* "—from Eli? You can see he's in very good care here, and Martha wants to be sure to do what's in the boy's best interests."

Mrs. Tooey bristled. "It's in his *best interests* to be with his mother, not in some charity ward. Obviously, not being a mother yourself, you wouldn't understand. I'm determined to take him, and I'll go to your sponsors if I have to. Where will your precious settlement house be without funds?"

Concordia ignored the threat. "It doesn't take a mother to know that Eli is much better off now than when he was found—dirty, hungry, and alone—trying to fend for himself in the world. What mother would put him in such a position?"

"That was not in my control at the time," the woman shot back.

"Which brings us back to my original question. How did Eli come to be alone? He told us that his mother had disappeared. He certainly doesn't recognize you as that woman. Surely you can see why it is necessary for us to understand this tangle, before we could consider turning him over to your care?"

Mrs. Tooey pressed her hands together until the knuckles were white. It was the closest Concordia had ever seen to someone literally wringing her hands in distress.

"When he was just a baby, he was kidnapped. His nurse had charge of him at the time, and had wheeled him in his carriage to the park for some fresh air. She sat on a bench and fell asleep, careless girl! When she awoke, the perambulator was empty, the baby gone."

"But that must have been...nine or ten years ago," Concordia countered skeptically. It sounded like a penny dreadful one would read on a train. "Why did it take so long for you to find him? And how do you know Eli is yours? Babies change a great deal as they grow up."

"He has a strawberry-colored mark on his left wrist," Florence said. "We made a thorough search when he disappeared, of course, but discovered nothing. Then, a few weeks ago, a friend of mine living in this area noticed the boy's resemblance to me—he was running an errand for her. She knew about the birthmark, and there it was. I came as soon as she wrote to me."

Concordia had noticed the mark on Eli's wrist, so that part rang true. Yet the story sounded far-fetched. If Lieutenant Capshaw were here, he could easily check it.

"Where is the boy's father? Is Eli a natural child?" Concordia asked.

"I'm not interested in giving you my life story—it is not your concern," the woman snapped.

"Perhaps not, but what sort of home will you be giving him? A couple wants to adopt the boy—the Capshaws. They and Eli share a mutual affection. Would you be so selfish as to snatch that from him?"

Florence's lip trembled. "Eli's father is dead. The child is all the family I have left."

Concordia realized with a sinking heart that for this woman, Eli was a memento, a piece of something she'd lost, rather than a child with needs. There had to be a way to stop her, but she needed help to do it.

She stood. "I'll be back in a moment."

Concordia found Martha pacing in the hall. "Any success?" Martha asked eagerly.

"I'm afraid not. Mrs. Tooey seems determined to take him."

Martha's face fell. "I'd hoped you could persuade her."

Concordia smiled ruefully. "It seems my powers of persuasion don't run that deep."

"What are we to do? Eli's threatening to run away rather than leave with that woman."

"I have an idea," Concordia said. "We can stall for time until the Capshaws return. Then the lieutenant can look into her background and find out more. Her story sounds...melodramatic."

Martha's face brightened. "We could even offer her room here, to stay while she waits."

Concordia shook her head. "I don't think that's wise. She may put pressure on Eli and cause him to do something rash. Do you have any money? I only have a little with me. But perhaps between us we can give her enough to rent a room at Mrs. Hofferman's boarding house for the week. Once Sophia and the lieutenant are back, they'll know what to do."

Martha went to the lock box and checked. "I think this should be enough; let's see if she'll agree."

When they returned to the room, Florence was buttoning her jacket. "I want to see Eli. Alone."

Concordia held up a hand to interrupt whatever Martha was going to say. "Very well, on one condition; that you do not take him away with you until the Capshaws have returned next week. We'll pay for your room and board at respectable lodgings nearby."

Florence locked her brown eyes upon Concordia, staring at her shrewdly. "What sort of lodgings?"

"Oh, Mrs. Hofferman's is very comfortable," Martha interjected quickly. "It's along a quiet street, out of the way of traffic. I can have one of our girls show you."

Florence glanced down at the bills in Martha's hand, then relented. "Very well. But I want to talk with Eli *now*."

A trembling Eli was brought in. With some reluctance, Concordia and Martha waited outside the door.

"Why do you suppose she wants to see him alone?" Martha asked.

Concordia shrugged. "Perhaps she thinks she can persuade him to go with her? If so, she's sadly mistaken."

After about ten minutes, Eli and Florence came out of the room. Florence hugged Eli's stiff shoulders, then fixed a steely gaze on Concordia. "One week."

Martha gestured to the girl waiting to escort Florence Tooey. She passed her the bills. "Give my regards to Mrs. Hofferman." The girl nodded, and Florence followed her out.

"Are you all right?" Concordia asked Eli.

He held up a pocket watch. "She gave me a present. That's nice, but I still ain't goin' with her."

"Don't worry," Concordia said, ruffling his hair. "We'll figure out something." She hoped she was right, especially when the boy turned a trusting, relieved face in her direction.

Chapter 8

To mourn a mischief that is past and gone
Is the next way to draw new mischief on.

Othello, I.*iii*

Week 4, Instructor Calendar
March 1898

Concordia loathed Glove Night, with a passion typically reserved for war, famine, and pestilence.

She reluctantly groped her way up the stairs in the early morning light, toward the sounds of freshmen wailing overhead.

The sophomores never seemed to tire of their pranks on the freshmen, and Glove Night was their favorite. It was astonishing to contemplate the organization required for sophomores from all six cottages on the same night to slip into freshmen rooms, steal their gloves, hide them throughout the grounds, and return to their own beds without detection. If only they would apply such cunning and forethought to their work.

The upstairs corridor was crowded with freshmen girls in various states of distress and dishabille. A nightrobe-clad, felt-slippered Ruby was trying to usher them back to their rooms. "There now, no need to tear the rooms apart. You know the gloves won't be here. You can search the grounds after chapel and breakfast."

Ruby's unfortunate mention of *chapel* provoked a round of fresh wailing. Though the sound set her teeth on edge, Concordia could sympathize. For a lady, going about bare-handed was akin to walking bare*foot*. It was simply not done. Attending chapel without one's gloves was particularly frowned upon. The administration, of course, would exercise leniency while the freshmen hunted for their gloves.

And *hunting* was often required, as the sophomores looked on and snickered at the hapless "freshies." It seemed no place was out of bounds for the gloves: the fountain (drained in winter, mercifully), the library, the arboretum, and once even dangling from the beams of the chapel. This year, Lady Principal Pomeroy had extracted a promise from the sophomores that they not hide any gloves in the stables. For some reason, it spooked the horses.

"But Miss Wells, I was ever so careful. I don't know *how* they found my hiding place," one freshman girl complained, as Concordia coaxed her back to her room.

"Don't worry, dear," Concordia soothed, "we'll find them." And quickly, she hoped.

By the third day, nearly all of the freshmen had recovered their gloves. Peace was once again restored in the cottages, without the horses being traumatized this year.

The single gloveless exception was Willow Cottage's Miss Carey. Concordia strongly suspected Miss Smedley had something to do with that. She had noticed glances exchanged between Alison Smedley and her sophomore cohorts each morning before chapel, as if enjoying a private triumph.

Concordia could have lent Miss Carey a pair of her own gloves, but that wouldn't solve the bigger problem. She had an idea. That afternoon, when Miss Smedley was out of the cottage, she called Miss Lovelace to her quarters.

"Yes, Miss Wells?" Maisie Lovelace sat primly in the hard back chair, her hands neatly folded in her lap.

"Does Alison Smedley have Miss Carey's gloves?" Concordia asked bluntly.

Miss Lovelace scowled. "I don't know that for a fact, but it wouldn't surprise me."

Concordia raised a skeptical brow. "I find it hard to believe, as a sophomore yourself, that you didn't participate in the prank."

"Well, it's true," the girl said defensively. "I intended to, but Alison put herself in charge of the whole thing. I stayed out of it."

"I see." Concordia hesitated. "I need to ask you a favor, but it violates the roommate code of ethics. You are free to decline."

Miss Lovelace's eyes widened, but she waited.

"I need you to search Miss Smedley's belongings—discreetly, so that she is unaware it has been done," Concordia went on, firmly squashing a twinge of guilt. "Would you recognize Miss Carey's gloves if you saw them? Yes? Good. Give them to me and tell me where they were hidden. But say nothing to anyone else."

Miss Lovelace shifted uneasily. "Are you going to give them back to Miss Carey? Alison will know I took them. Things are tense enough between us."

"Actually, *she* will give them back. Leave that to me. Will you help?" Concordia asked.

Miss Lovelace grinned. "Give me a few minutes."

The next morning, the fourth day after the prank, the young ladies of Willow Cottage were dressed and waiting by the door when Concordia joined them. "Everyone ready?" She turned to Miss Carey, whose hands were thrust in her jacket pockets. "No gloves yet?"

"No, miss," Miss Carey whispered, close to tears.

"Don't worry, dear, I'm sure they will turn up." Concordia turned to Alison Smedley. "Miss Smedley, lend your gloves to Miss Carey in the meantime, if you please."

Miss Smedley started, involuntarily looking down at her fashionable—and quite expensive—white kid leather gloves trimmed in pearl buttons. "I'm not giving these to that...freshie."

The girls had stopped talking and stared. Ruby looked on in interest.

Concordia leaned in close to Alison Smedley. "You will give her your gloves, or find the missing ones yourself. Right *now*."

Miss Smedley stared at the stern-eyed professor for a long moment, open-mouthed. She glanced around at her fellow cottage occupants. They waited silently. She would get no help from that quarter.

"*Now*," Concordia repeated.

Miss Smedley ran up the stairs.

The girls murmured among themselves as they waited, but all listened to the sounds overhead in the room Miss Smedley and Miss Lovelace shared: drawers being slammed, a trunk lid flung open, a stool pushed aside. Then silence, before they heard the young lady coming back down the stairs.

"Well?" Concordia said.

Wordlessly, Miss Smedley handed Concordia a pair of plain gray cotton gloves. Concordia held them up. "Are these yours, Miss Carey?"

"No, they are *not*," Miss Carey said, glaring at Miss Smedley.

"I couldn't find them," Miss Smedley said in a subdued voice. She gave her roommate a sharp look. Miss Lovelace raised an innocent eyebrow.

"How unfortunate," Concordia said.

"These are my spare pair," Miss Smedley said. "She can wear them."

"No. Take off your gloves, Miss Smedley."

The girl's eyes widened. "But I just said that she—"

"—and I *say* that *you* will wear the cotton gloves, my good miss, and Miss Carey will wear these nicer ones," Concordia interrupted. "That should afford you plenty of time to look further for Miss Carey's own gloves, and to reflect upon the ill-spirited nature of your actions."

Flushing an angry red, Miss Smedley pulled off her gloves in short, jerky movements. Concordia passed them to Miss Carey.

Ruby opened the door. "All right, let's go before we're late to chapel. Come on now."

As the girls filed through the door, Concordia murmured to Ruby. "I'll catch up in a few minutes."

Ruby gave an appreciative nod. "Nicely done, miss."

Once the door was closed behind them, Concordia ran up the stairs to Miss Smedley's room. She pulled Miss Carey's gloves out of her pocket and returned them to Miss Smedley's trunk, where Maisie Lovelace had said they'd been hidden. With a sigh, she put on her coat and gloves and hurried to catch up with the others.

After chapel and breakfast, Concordia set off for a meeting with the lady principal to discuss the senior play. She hoped it was good news. Directing the play was a substantial drain on her time, and there were usually problems aplenty. Concordia was a teacher, not a stage manager.

But perhaps this year would be better. Miss Pomeroy had said that Lily Isley was indeed interested in helping. Perhaps Mrs. Isley would take complete charge of it? After all, the stage came naturally to that lady.

The lady principal's office was a familiar place to Concordia, as it was just down the hallway from her own. She'd had many occasions to visit it for some college business or other. Each lady principal had placed her own style and stamp upon the quarters. In Miss Pomeroy's case, it wasn't so much a stamp as a wading through of books, papers, and assorted knick-knacks, as the lady principal was...well, rather slovenly.

Miss Pomeroy glanced up briefly from her work and waved Concordia into a chair. "Just a minute, dear. Let me get this down while I'm thinking of it."

Concordia found a chair beneath a stack of translations of *La Chanson de Roland* and sat with the pile in her lap, for want of a better place to put it.

Besides serving as lady principal, Gertrude Pomeroy had taught at the college as one of its foreign languages professors for nearly twenty years. The lady was a brilliant, well-respected scholar, fluent in six languages, with a sharp memory of every text she had translated. The position of lady principal had been unexpectedly thrust upon her last year, with the unfortunate retreat of her predecessor.

She'd accepted the change with good grace; however, her absent-mindedness and indecisiveness were qualities ill suited to an administrator. Concordia could see it was a struggle for her to adjust.

Miss Pomeroy eventually set aside her pencil and looked up at Concordia, her eyes china-doll-blue through her wire-framed spectacles. "So glad you came, my dear, we need to get this play underway...now where is my...."

"Is Mrs. Isley joining us today?" Concordia asked.

The lady principal leaned forward, spectacles perilously close to the end of her nose. Concordia resisted the impulse to push them up the lady's face. "Indeed, yes! Mrs. Isley wants to direct the play. We'll still need you to help, of course, since she's new to the school...not really part of the faculty, either...." Miss Pomeroy's voice trailed off again.

They were interrupted by a knock.

"Yes?" Miss Pomeroy called out.

Mrs. Isley entered in a wake of lavender fragrance.

"A pleasure to see you again, Miss Wells," Mrs. Isley said, extending a delicate gloved hand in Concordia's direction.

The woman tugged upon her double-breasted jacket of buffalo red melton and adjusted the fox fur stole draped over her shoulders. Rather than sitting, she paced the cluttered confines of the room – no easy feat, given the obstacles in her path – turning with a self-conscious grace to face one or the other occupant. "I am happy to be of help in my own little way," she added.

"I'm sure it will be more than 'little,' Mrs. Isley," Concordia said. At least, she hoped so. The more work the lady could take on, the better.

"Oh, please, call me Lily."

"Then you must call me Concordia."

"Ah! *Concordia*...what a charming name. After the Roman goddess of harmony, is it not?" Lily inquired.

"Few people are aware of that," Concordia answered, surprised.

"I am conversant in all of the mythologies and classical stories of our age, my dear Concordia. As you know, I was a student of the stage before I married. Classical theater was my playground: Shakespeare, Cowper, Molière, the Greeks—they were all my playfellows!"

Concordia could tell that, while Lily may have left the stage, the stage had by no means left Lily. She suppressed a smile. "Indeed?" she said.

"Oh my, yes," said the lady. "I studied with some of the greats of our time: Irving, Bernhardt…at the risk of seeming immodest, I must say that my performances drew adoring crowds. Had I not retired early from the stage, I would have had a marvelous career. Nothing could keep me from my Barton, of course, although I do miss the footlights at times."

"I can imagine," Miss Pomeroy put in absently, her glance straying to the stack of papers in Concordia's lap.

"So you see, my dears," Lily continued—Concordia almost choked in laughter at the *my dears*…did all stage people speak in such an extravagant fashion?—"I would be *privileged* to produce this little college play. And I have so many ideas! But I was wondering…perhaps there would even be a part for me?"

Concordia was willing to give Lucifer himself a part in the play in exchange for less work and aggravation. "Absolutely." She turned to Miss Pomeroy. "The play is *Othello*, is it not?"

"Hmm?" Miss Pomeroy came out of her daydream. "Oh, yes, indeed—it's *Othello*."

"Well, then, I'd imagine you would be perfect as our Desdemona," Concordia said recklessly. Whatever senior had dreamt of having that part, a pity. Besides, Desdemona gets smothered in the end, and Concordia couldn't wait to see their theater expert handle *that*.

"Excellent!" Lily exclaimed, clasping her hands together in excitement.

"Well then, we are agreed," said Miss Pomeroy, who promptly reached for the stack of papers in Concordia's lap and shooed them out.

Chapter 9

I pray you, sir, go forth,
And give us truth who 'tis that is arrived.

Othello, II.*i*

Week 5, Instructor Calendar
March 1898

At last the Capshaws returned from their honeymoon. Although Martha had no doubt left them a message, Concordia wasted no time. As soon as she finished with classes for the day, she hopped a trolley and got off at Retreat Avenue, walking the last few blocks to the Capshaws' new residence on Alden.

It was a working class neighborhood, quite different from the nearby Governor's Row section of wealthy families in which Sophia had grown up. However, it wasn't run-down or crime-ridden, as some poorer neighborhoods could be. Here, a mixture of children, languages, and walks of life were plentiful; merchants ran small shops and kept their sidewalks well swept; people smiled and greeted each other as they passed. Not a bad neighborhood at all to start a life together, Concordia thought.

Soon she found number fifty-nine and rapped on the worn brass knocker. A young girl answered it promptly. She was clean and presentable, but her apron was too large for her thin frame, and her cap was crookedly perched on her head. Concordia smiled when she recognized Sadie from the settlement house.

Sadie's eyes lit up when she saw Concordia, but she maintained her role.

"Yes?" the girl asked politely.

"Are the Capshaws at home?" Concordia asked.

"O' course, Miss Wells," she said, opening the door wider and stepping aside. "Let me take your coat for you."

"This way," she said, turning down the narrow corridor. Concordia followed, looking around curiously as she passed. This was the first time she'd been in Sophia's new home. The bare hallway, cramped rooms and peeling wallpaper were a stark contrast to her friend's childhood house of wealth and privilege. And yet the creaky wood floors had been well-scrubbed, and not a cobweb or speck of dust was anywhere to be seen.

The parlor had a good fire going, a welcome sight after the chilled walk from the trolley stop. Concordia sat and stretched out her hands.

Sophia came in soon after. "Concordia!" she exclaimed. "It's so good to see you."

Sophia was naturally tall and angular of figure, but her angles seemed to have softened. The new bride wore her hair in a relaxed chignon at the nape, instead of her usual no-nonsense topknot. Her face was glowing, her brow relaxed.

"Look at you," Concordia said with a smile, "you are simply beaming. Marriage suits you."

Sophia blushed as she joined Concordia beside the fire and gave her a hug. "I'm so happy. I'd recommend it to anyone."

"Where's the lieutenant?" Concordia asked.

Sophia smiled. "I think you can call him *Aaron* now. You're family to us."

Concordia grimaced. "We'll see. I'm not sure I can get used to that. Is he home?"

Sophia nodded. "He's finishing a staff interview. Our funds are small, as you might imagine, but we're hiring a woman from the settlement house who'll come in to clean and cook. You saw that Sadie's here already. It helps all of us that way. They will develop a respectable work history and references when they are ready to move on, and we get affordable help from women we know."

"It sounds like a wonderful arrangement, Sophie, but I'm actually here on an urgent matter," Concordia said. "You haven't checked your correspondence since you've returned? Talked with Martha?"

Sophia shook her head. "We were back so late last night; there's been no time. We haven't even seen Eli yet. But what is it that's so urgent? You look worried."

"Something happened while you were gone, but I'd rather wait until L—Aaron comes in, so I can tell you both—"

"Tell us what?" Capshaw walked into the parlor. "It's good to see you, M—Concordia." He sat beside Sophia. "What's happened?"

Concordia perched on the edge of her chair and told them about Florence Tooey, her claim to be Eli's mother, and her determination to take Eli with her.

"She has reluctantly agreed to wait until you were back from your trip." Concordia turned to Capshaw. "We need to find out more about her."

"Which I certainly will," Capshaw said grimly. Sophia had paled during Concordia's narrative. He placed a reassuring hand on her shoulder. "Don't worry. We'll get to the bottom of this." He turned back to Concordia. "Where is she now?"

"Staying at Mrs. Hofferman's boarding house. We couldn't get any useful information from her. She was spinning stories the whole time."

"We'll see what we can do about that," Capshaw said mildly, although Concordia recognized a steely glint in his eye that didn't bode well for Mrs. Tooey.

"Can we go with you?" Sophia asked anxiously.

Capshaw hesitated and looked at Sophia. "I don't suppose I could stop you, even if I were to refuse?"

Sophia smiled and turned to Concordia. "You see how smoothly a marriage can proceed when a husband and wife have an understanding?"

Chapter 10

Put out the light, and then put out the light.
***Othello**, V, ii.*

Week 5, Instructor Calendar
March 1898

Although the trip was only six blocks, the Saturday afternoon shopping traffic slowed them down. Concordia perched on the seat's edge the entire time, anxious to get this over with. At last, they reached the boarding house.

"We'd like to see Mrs. Tooey," Capshaw said to the maid.

She escorted them to the visiting parlor, where the landlady allowed her boarders to receive company. "I'll let 'er know yer here."

They waited. What was taking so long, Concordia wondered, checking her watch.

The maid returned. "I'm sorry, but she's not answering, and 'er door's locked. I suppose she's out." She pursed her lips. "Funny, though. She said she was goin' to lie down 'cause she weren't feeling well. I was sure she was still here."

Capshaw's brow creased. "Fetch Mrs. Hofferman."

Soon the landlady came in, wiping her flour-dusted hands on her apron. She eyed the group suspiciously. "Wot d'yer want?" she demanded. "I'm all full up; no rooms to let."

"We're not here for rooms," Concordia said, interrupting Capshaw before he could identify himself as a policeman. "We want to talk to our friend, Florence. The maid thought she was in her room, but she's not answering the door. Please, we're very concerned for her. Lately she has been—unwell. Could you unlock the door, just so we can make sure she's all right?"

Mrs. Hofferman's face softened. "Ah, well, I suppose. As long as you don't go in without me there, mind." She pulled out a ring of keys. "This way."

They followed her up two flights of narrow wooden back steps, probably what was originally a servant's staircase in the days when this was the affluent part of town. Reaching the second door of the hallway, she tapped on it.

"Missus Tooey? Visitors for ye!" she sang out. No answer. Capshaw nodded to the woman, who reluctantly unlocked the door.

With a murmur of thanks, Capshaw pushed open the door and went through first, Sophia and Concordia right behind him, as the landlady brought up the rear.

Concordia gave a small shriek as an all-too-familiar furry animal darted through her skirts and ran out the door. *Eli's cat?*

"Land sakes!" the landlady exclaimed, putting a hand to her mouth and pointing with the other toward the bed.

Concordia turned and gasped.

Florence Tooey lay on her back across the thin mattress.

It was painfully obvious—by the purple of her face, the open eyes staring at the ceiling, and the mark of a red livid line around her neck—that she was dead.

Capshaw promptly pushed the ladies out the door. "Do you have an errand lad here with quick feet?" he asked the landlady. "Good. I'm a policeman—Lieutenant Capshaw." He pulled out his identification. "Send your messenger to the Pratt Street station right away. Ask for Maloney. Tell him Capshaw needs him, now." He took in the sight of Concordia and Sophia, each pale and gripping the other for support. "You two go back to the parlor and wait for me. I expect a good strong cup of tea would do you all some good, Mrs. Hofferman. Would you mind making some?"

The lady scurried off, while Sophia and Concordia found their way back to the parlor.

"Who do you suppose did this? And why?" Sophia asked, her composure returning as she and Concordia sat in the visiting parlor. Maloney had come within a few minutes, and he and Capshaw were going through the murdered woman's room. Concordia shook her head. "I could get very little from Mrs. Tooey when I spoke with her last week. My impression was of a woman with a troubled past. Perhaps that past caught up with her?"

"If so," Sophia said, "why now? And why here?"

That's what worried Concordia. *Why now? Why here?* The only variable she knew of was...Eli. She set aside her cup. "I think we should talk to Eli."

"Now? Why not wait for Aaron, and go together to break the news to the child?" Sophia asked.

Concordia shook her head. The more she thought about it, the more uneasy she became. Why was Eli's cat in the room with the dead woman? Something was wrong, and she had a strong feeling that Eli was about to get caught up in it. "I want to make sure he's safe."

Sophia gave her a wide-eyed look. "The cat. This is somehow connected to Eli," she whispered.

"I don't know, but sitting here isn't going to find that out for us," Concordia pointed out.

"You're right," Sophia said, with a decisive tilt of her chin. "Let's go."

After scribbling a note for Capshaw and leaving it with a puzzled Mrs. Hofferman, Sophia and Concordia made the brisk walk to Hartford Settlement House.

Chapter 11

Week 5, Instructor Calendar
March 1898

"Miss Adams! Er, I mean, Mrs. Capshaw—it's so nice to see you back," the girl at the front desk said eagerly. "I know Martha will be glad. Did you have a nice trip?"

"Can you get Martha for me? And Eli, too?" Sophia said, urgency in her voice. There wasn't time for pleasantries.

The puzzled girl hesitated, then hurried down the corridor.

It seemed an agony of waiting before the girl located Martha, who greeted Sophia with an enthusiastic hug. "Welcome back!" She turned to Concordia. "So good to see you, too, dear. Now we can take care of that little problem—"

"Unfortunately, Martha, Mrs. Tooey is dead," Concordia interrupted. "We went to the boarding house to speak with her about Eli, but found her…strangled."

Martha paled and put her hands to her bosom. "Dear heaven."

"Here, sit down." Concordia helped Martha onto a hall bench.

"I'm all right," Martha said, taking a deep breath. "But how horrible. Do they know who did it?"

"It's early yet," Sophia said. "Aaron's investigating now."

"That poor woman," Martha murmured to herself. "I suppose we should tell Eli. As distressing as the death might be to the child, at least he'll have some peace of mind in knowing he isn't going away with her." She stood and gestured to the girl at the desk. "Can you fetch Eli?" She checked her lapel watch.

"Let me think...he should be in carpentry class. We'll wait in my office." She nodded to the girl, who took off.

"We'll be more comfortable—and private—in here," Martha said, with a quick glance at the cleaning woman who had just entered the hall with mop and bucket.

Once they were settled, Concordia asked, "Had Eli seen Florence at all this week?"

Martha's brow puckered in thought. "I don't believe so," she said, "but that boy comes and goes at will, more than I'm happy with. Even after a year of our care—and our rules—he can't seem to shake his harum-scarum habit of just going where the mood strikes. He hears about a job delivering extra papers, or taking over a shoelace stand for a sick boy, and he's on it like a flash. Not that I don't admire his hard-working, entrepreneurial spirit, but his studies are erratic, and he seems quite restless. Lately, I've attributed that to the stress of having a mother he never knew come back to fetch him." She sighed.

Concordia sympathized. Managing wayward children and unstable families on a thin budget was no easy task. Funds, room, and time were all out of favor in such an endeavor.

The girl came back. "Master Bernard says Eli never showed up, miss."

Concordia sucked in a sharp breath. "Has anyone seen him today? It's very important we find him."

The girl pursed her lips and thought. "I can ask Madge. She was at the front desk early this morning, and might a' seen him."

"Ask *everyone*," Sophia urged. She had paled again. Concordia wished she had smelling salts.

"Yes, miss," the girl said, and ran out the door.

The three women looked at each other. What could they do now?

Their unspoken thought was answered when there was a brief knock and Capshaw walked in, red-faced. "I thought I told you both to stay put," he growled at Sophia and Concordia. "I don't need to walk all over creation to find you."

"But we left word as to where we would be," Sophia said in mock-meekness, earning her a sharp glance from her husband.

Maloney came in and stood by the door, waiting.

"What did you learn?" Sophia asked.

Capshaw shook his head. "Not much. She was strangled with a garroting wire." He ran a distracted hand over his head, making tufts of red hair stand on end. Concordia was reminded of a Pomeranian with its hackles raised. He turned to Martha. "Where's Eli?"

"We're looking for him," Martha said.

"The presence of his cat in the room can only mean that he was there recently," Capshaw said. "More worrisome is that he left without the animal."

"What does it mean? Do you think he witnessed the murder?" Concordia asked. She stood, too restless to sit.

"I don't know, but I want to find Eli and be assured he's safe." Capshaw fingered his mustache. "I have a bad feeling about this. Whatever this woman's past, her attempt to take Eli with her seems to have spurred someone to act."

"So Eli could have been taken by whoever killed Florence," Sophia said in despair.

The girl from the front desk came in at that moment.

"Ma'am," the girl said nervously, "no one's seen 'im since this morning. And no one knows where he was going. Should I keep asking?"

"Yes, dear," Martha said. "It's urgent that we find him."

Capshaw turned to Maloney. "Check the grocer's, the women's college, and the newspaper stand on Main and Church. Those are his usual places to earn a nickel. Take a couple of patrolmen to help you search. Also check the infirmaries nearby, just in case. The boy is about so high—" he held his hand up to chest-level "—black curly hair, pale complexion, freckles. Thin." He turned to Martha. "Do you know what clothes he was wearing this morning?"

Martha mutely shook her head.

"Ah, well, that should be enough to start. Find him, sergeant," he said to Mahoney. "I'm personally counting upon you."

With a quick nod, Maloney left.

Chapter 12

What, in your own part, can you say to this?

Othello, I.iii

Week 5, Instructor Calendar
March 1898

Not even the busy routine of campus life was enough over the next few days to distract Concordia from her worry over Eli. Sophia sent her daily messages, but there was little news to report.

Concordia tried pushing her fears to the back of her mind as she spent the evening grading student essays on *Paradise Lost*. She clucked her tongue at some of the silliest opening sentences that she had seen in a long while.

> *Milton was a blind poet, which made it quite difficult to write* **Paradise Lost**, *even though he asked for sight in the beginning of the story.*

> **Paradise Lost** *is about Satan being happy in hell, and trying to get Adam and Eve to join him. He does so through the weaker of the two, Eve.*

Really? Concordia rolled her eyes. These ninny answers came from the young ladies of Miss Smedley's social set, who had apparently taken her cue in neglecting their work.

Concordia re-read the all-too-brief entirety of Miss Smedley's essay:

> *The most compelling character in **Paradise Lost** is that
> of Satan, which I hardly think was Milton's intention. It's as if
> the allure of evil was too great even for the author himself. After
> Adam and Eve ate the apple and Satan was banished, the story
> ceased to be interesting. I stopped reading after that.*

Miss Smedley had an intriguing idea, but Concordia was
disappointed that she simply gave up and didn't finish. If the
girl only applied herself, she would be a promising student. But
Miss Smedley's enthusiasm for the pages of *Harper's* fashion
plates did not extend to the pages of Milton or Chaucer.

Concordia took off her spectacles and rubbed her eyes.
Time for a tea break. She pulled out her pot and headed to the
kitchen.

The kitchen was empty. Where was Ruby? Concordia
frowned over the dirty cups and spoons in the sink. Ruby could
not abide unwashed dishes. Perhaps she wasn't feeling well?

Concordia pulled an apron from the hook. At least she could
wash up and tidy the kitchen, then check on Ruby afterward.

She had just dried her hands when the kitchen door opened
and Ruby slipped in quietly.

"Oh!" Ruby jumped. "You scared me to death."

"I'm sorry," Concordia said, filling the kettle and putting it
on the stove. "I thought you were lying down."

Ruby took off her coat and hung it up behind the door.
"Uh, well…I thought I heard a couple o' tomcats tussling
outside."

"Oh?" Concordia hadn't heard anything. She'd been in the
kitchen for at least ten minutes. How long does it take to look
outside?

But Concordia wasn't responsible for the matron, and had
no right to pry. Instead, she reached for the tea canister and said
nothing more.

Ruby turned toward the sink. "Let me jes' finish these—oh!
Did you wash the dishes?" She flushed. "Thank you, miss."

"No trouble. I'd better get back," Concordia said, clutching
her now-full teapot. "I have more grading to do."

As Concordia headed back to her rooms, she wondered what the matron had really been up to.

Chapter 13

Week 5, Instructor Calendar
March 1898

"*So will I turn her virtue into pitch, and out of her own goodness make the net that shall enmesh them all.*"

"Very good," Concordia said, reading along from her copy, "now, I want you to look at the last eight lines of that speech, and recite them aloud. With feeling."

As the student performed the lines, Concordia fumed. Where was Mrs. Isley? She was supposed to be in charge of the play, particularly these time-consuming auditions.

It seemed as if everyone wanted to be Iago. There were a fair number of seniors to get through yet, and Concordia didn't want the decision to be hers alone. She had a feeling that, although Mrs. Isley liked to be in charge, she wasn't over-fond of putting in the time involved.

They were nearly finished when Mrs. Isley arrived.

"My dears! Oh, how sorry I am to be late!" Lily Isley sashayed in on a cloud of rose-water scent that made Concordia sneeze.

"Concordia, you'd better mind that cold before it becomes something more serious," Lily advised, taking a step back, "we don't want to infect the players, now, do we?"

"Certainly not," Concordia answered through gritted teeth.

"So, how are these charming young ladies faring? Have we found any dramatic prodigies yet?" Mrs. Isley paced up and down the apron of the stage, looking over the girls, who tittered nervously. "My, my, such fresh young faces! We will have our work cut out for us with stage makeup, to make them look battle-weary...or evil."

Concordia motioned toward her clipboard. "I've seen several promising students, Mrs. Isley…."

"Wonderful!" Lily came over to look.

"I was thinking that these three—" Concordia pointed to several names and nodded toward the girls "—would make good candidates for Iago."

Lily clucked her tongue and glanced over the assembled girls. "Oh, my dear, they simply do not have *the look*! No, no, they won't do at all."

"We can adjust the *look*; isn't it more important that they can *act*?" Concordia said, working to keep the sarcasm from her voice. How long had it been since Lily had performed in the theater, anyway?

Lily gave Concordia a pitying glance, and turned toward the door, where Millie Carver, one of the quieter seniors, stood. Concordia hadn't even auditioned Miss Carver, as that young lady had made clear her contribution to the play would be set design. She was merely waiting for her roommate to be finished so they could join their study group at the library. Now Lily was pulling the poor girl to the center of the stage and thrusting a script in her hands.

"Read this passage, dear; I think you would be a perfect Iago," Mrs. Isley cooed.

A bewildered Miss Carver gave Concordia a pleading look. "M-m-miss…."

"Mrs. Isley," Concordia said sharply. "This senior is already assigned. Pick one of the young ladies who has auditioned for the part, if you please."

Lily Isley pouted and waved a dismissive hand. Concordia held out her clipboard, but Lily ignored it. "You," she said, pointing to a short, dark-browed girl in the back, "read this passage aloud."

When the young lady complied, Concordia was astonished. How had she missed this girl? "I don't recall you signing up to audition for Iago."

"No miss," came the soft answer, "I saw how many girls wanted the part, so I wasn't going to try for it."

Not exactly a go-getter in life, Concordia thought, which was ironic for this particular character, but the student certainly had something that carried from the stage. Once it was coaxed out of her.

Mrs. Isley beamed. "Congratulations...Miss Stephens, is it? You are our new Iago." A chorus of disappointed sighs followed this pronouncement.

"Not to worry, lambs!" Lily called to the other girls. "We need everyone's contribution to make the play a success. Miss Wells here will find a meaningful job for each of you."

Miss Wells will find a job for each of you? Splendid. So much for a lighter work load.

Concordia rummaged among the scripts. She passed one to Miss Stephens. "It's a significant part to learn," she warned. "You should get started on it right away." The girl nodded delightedly and left, clutching the script.

Lily wrapped herself in her fox fur and picked up her reticule. "I must go; I have an appointment. Oh! I almost forgot. I'm giving a dinner party in two weeks' time. It's a small affair; no more than forty guests. It's in honor of Mr. Sanders— he's the Republican candidate for the state senate seat, you know. I was hoping you could come, my dear. And bring that young man of yours...Mr. Bradley, isn't it?"

Concordia nodded stiffly. *That young man of yours,* indeed. She was hardly a debutante, but rather a staid older woman of twenty-nine. Practically on the shelf, as they say. Sometimes being "on the shelf" suited her just fine.

"I cannot speak for Mr. Bradley, but I'll ask him, if you'd like," Concordia said. A *small* dinner party of forty people? *Mercy.*

"Wonderful!" Lily beamed. "I'll have the invitations sent 'round to you."

After Mrs. Isley left, Concordia made short work of the remaining senior assignments, tidied the auditorium, and locked the door behind her. The early March skyline had long since faded to black, the cold making itself felt through her wool coat. She shivered as the wind picked up around the quadrangle. No one was out on the grounds at this hour. She'd better hurry; there wasn't much time before lights out. She pulled her coat closer and started at a brisk pace for Willow Cottage, her boot heels ringing upon the cold stones.

She was just about to step onto the shrubbery-lined path to the cottages when she saw something move in the distance. She turned. The bracketed lights of the Memorial Chapel doors illuminated the outline of a slim man. Her breath caught in her throat. It was the same youth she had seen last month on Rook's Hill.

Could one of the girls be involved with the young man, setting up trysts after hours?

Concordia's lips thinned in a stern line. Not if she had anything to say about it. She hastened toward the chapel, but by the time she reached it the man was gone.

Concordia gritted her teeth in frustration and turned toward the gatekeeper's cottage. At least she could inform Clyde of their unauthorized visitor.

Chapter 14

The next afternoon, Concordia stared in dismay at the pile of mail taking over her desk. How long had it been there—a week? She'd neglected it terribly.

Her thoughts returned to Eli as she worked to clear her desk. Would they be able to find him and learn the truth about Florence's murder? She trusted Capshaw's ability, but each passing day without progress increased her worry.

Concordia sifted through the pile of envelopes, throwing away the advertising circulars (*"Our 57-cent Princess Hair Tonic Restorer!"*), opening the department store bill (she was nearly finished paying for those winter boots), and finally reaching the bottom of the stack.

She picked up a plain white envelope. The hand was unfamiliar, with no return direction upon it. Concordia slit it open and glanced at the signature. *Florence Tooey.* Her heart beat faster. Also within the envelope was a tiny, locket-sized picture of what Concordia assumed to be the woman in her younger days. As small as it was, she could make out Eli's features in the large, luminous eyes of the mother.

Settling herself in the chair, Concordia started back at the beginning.

> *Dear Miss Wells,*
>
> *I hope you'll pardon the presumption of my engaging in a personal correspondence. I know that you care about Eli, so I'm using this as an excuse for imposing upon you. I hope I have been able to persuade you by this point that I really am his*

mother, although I could see you didn't believe the tissue of lies I thought I was so clever in creating. I will share some of the real story with you now, in hopes that you will do something for me.

The child's birth was under less than ideal circumstances. I was very young, and unmarried. I come from a respected family. My parents acted in the best way they knew to protect me from ruin, sending me away to have the baby and arranging to have him cared for by a former servant. For a goodly sum, the woman and her mother were willing to raise him and keep his parentage a secret.

I do not offer any excuse for letting him go, except that I was young and frightened. Other life events have intervened in the past eleven years, and I have tired of the facade. I've secured enough money to leave the area and live comfortably abroad.

As you know, I intended to take Eli with me. But you made a persuasive argument for leaving him here, where he can be raised by a loving family. I was appalled when Miss Newcombe told me of what he had been through. His foster mother must have been subjected to desperate circumstances. I never knew.

There is another reason why I've changed my mind about taking the boy. Certain unscrupulous people with whom I've had dealings are tracking my movements. I may expose Eli to danger if he accompanies me. I've already had one near miss, in an alley near the settlement house. If a good stranger had not come along, I would have been attacked. Thank heaven I wasn't followed to my lodging.

But before I leave for good, I am resolved to spend a bit more time with the child. I think he is coming to like me, but when I tell him goodbye, I know he'll be relieved to stay. I hope it won't be too much of a risk to remain for one more day, so we can spend it together. They haven't found me yet.

If you could do something for me: when you judge the boy old enough, please tell him my story. Perhaps he won't look upon his mother too unkindly. I have enclosed a photograph of myself that I hope he would like to keep someday.

*Please assure Eli's new parents that I will not trouble them
in the future.*
Regards,
Florence Tooey
*P.S.— If something should happen to me, ask Eli to show you
the gift I gave him. —F.T.*

Concordia sat back in her chair, took off her spectacles, and
rubbed the bridge of her nose. Obviously "one more day" had
been too long, and the men from the alley had caught up with
her. But what had happened to Eli? Had he been with her when
she was killed? Concordia shuddered.

What had Florence been involved in, that she had made
enemies such as these?

She glanced again at the postscript. *Ask Eli to show you the gift
I gave him.* However, both Eli and the gift—no doubt the pocket
watch Florence had given him at the settlement house—were
gone.

Capshaw needed to see this. It could be the break in the
case he needed. Besides, if Concordia were honest with herself,
she hoped to learn what progress Capshaw had made.

But it was nearly dinnertime. She would be expected to
accompany the students in her charge to the dining hall and eat
at the faculty table. Surely the lady principal would understand if
she didn't attend this time, although Dean Maynard might not.

She would have to risk it.

Chapter 15

Week 5, Instructor Calendar
March 1898

Sadie led Concordia to the Capshaws' parlor, where she found Sophia pacing, as she was wont to do when upset. Capshaw stood beside a wing chair, imploring her to sit down. They both stopped when Concordia entered.

"Aaron's been taken off the case," Sophia said.

"When? Why?" Concordia turned to Capshaw. "They weren't satisfied with your progress?" She had difficulty believing the lieutenant would fail. "It's only been a week, after all."

Capshaw made a low growling sound in the back of this throat. "I *was* making progress. That's what I don't understand. Chief Stiles called me to his office this morning and notified me that I was being reassigned."

"Why?" Concordia repeated.

Capshaw made a face. "He said I was going too far afield in my investigation, spending too many man hours on wild goose chases, looking into the background of Florence Willoughby."

Concordia started. "Willoughby? Not Tooey?"

He nodded, pulling out his sheaf of wadded notes. "Florence Cassandra Willoughby, thirty years old, never married. Of the Providence Willoughbys. You may have heard of them. "

Concordia nodded. "I think so. Is that the family who supplies half of the dry goods' retailers in New England, and holds the summer cotillion every year in their Newport mansion?"

"The same."

"Speaking of her background," Concordia said, fishing in her reticule, "Florence sent me this. It's dated the day before she died." She passed Capshaw the letter.

Capshaw raised an eyebrow. "She wrote to *you?*" He shook his head in disbelief. "Your talent for becoming entangled in murder investigations never ceases to amaze me."

Concordia suppressed a smile as Capshaw read through the letter, Sophia looking over his shoulder.

"I wish I'd seen this *before* I was off the case," Capshaw said, glaring at Concordia. "I would have been able to investigate the *unscrupulous people* she mentions here, and that aborted attack in the alley."

"I'm sorry," Concordia said. "I brought it over as soon as I found it."

Sophia gave her husband a sharp eye before turning back to Concordia. "Don't mind Aaron. He's upset about Eli."

Capshaw grimaced in apology.

"Isn't an investigation into Florence's background a reasonable step, Lieutenant?" Concordia asked. "Why would your chief object to that?"

Capshaw shook his head. "I don't know."

"Perhaps the family has complained about your inquiries," Sophia offered.

"If so, they care more for their privacy than catching their daughter's killer," Capshaw retorted.

Sophia stopped pacing and sat down. "And what about Eli?"

"I asked the chief about that," Capshaw said. "He said the boy is clearly an unstable street arab, and has probably moved on. The chief sees no connection to Florence's murder, even though she was the boy's mother, and his disappearance coincided with her death. Apparently," he added bitterly, "sentiment is clouding my judgment in the matter."

"But Eli's cat was found in the room, with the body," Concordia said.

"Yes, I reminded him of that. It's absurd to believe that Eli is *not* involved," Capshaw said.

"Has Chief Stiles ever interfered with an investigation of yours before?" Sophia asked.

Capshaw shook his head. "This bothers me in many ways. He has replaced me with an officer who is new and relatively inexperienced, and put me in charge of a minor case—over at your school, in fact," he added, looking at Concordia.

Concordia started. "My school?"

"It seems there have been reports of a strange man slipping past the gatekeeper and onto the college grounds at odd hours. He hasn't been caught yet; no one knows who he is or what his purpose might be."

That was fast, Concordia thought. She'd only spoken with Clyde last night. Unless they were talking about.... "Which one?" she asked.

Capshaw raised an eyebrow. "There are more than one?"

Concordia nodded. "A youth, and an older man." She started with the youth, describing the times she had seen him on the school grounds, including last night.

"But I was too far away for a good look," she said.

Capshaw scribbled in his oft-folded wad of notes. "That doesn't sound like the man I was instructed to investigate, but I'll check on him. What about the other one?"

"He was a large, burly man, quite disagreeable. Unfortunately, I had closer contact with him."

Capshaw pursed his lips thoughtfully. "The burly one sounds like the stranger the school has complained about. He's been seen on two occasions."

Concordia shifted uneasily. "I didn't realize he'd returned. I only met him once."

"But you spoke to this man?" Capshaw asked. "What did he say?"

"He was obviously intoxicated. He asked for Ruby, who wasn't there. He held a newspaper clipping and said he wanted to see *the famous Mrs. Hitchcock*. I had him escorted off the grounds."

Capshaw looked up with interest. "He asked specifically for Ruby?"

Concordia nodded. "I spoke with her later about it; she doesn't have a clue who he might be. We think the newspaper article is to blame. But surely, this is a simple security matter that a less experienced policeman can handle?"

"That's exactly my point!" Capshaw exploded. "I cannot help but think the chief is under orders to take me off the case."

"Orders from whom... and why?" Sophia asked.

"Perhaps you're getting close to learning something that someone else doesn't want known," Concordia mused aloud. "The Willoughbys?"

"It's possible." Capshaw picked up Florence's letter. "They may have been trying to keep their daughter's secret, which is a moot point now. One would think that catching the killer would take precedence."

"Are they so influential that the police chief would accede to their wishes?" Sophia asked.

"I don't know."

"Can you investigate on your own time, without Stiles finding out?" Concordia asked.

"I'm afraid that's impossible." Capshaw said. "He warned me about attempting that very thing. My activities will be closely monitored."

Concordia bit back her disappointment. The boy's continued absence was twisting her stomach with worry. Sophia and Capshaw must feel it even more deeply. Where could he be? She hadn't realized until now that all of her hope was resting upon Capshaw's detective abilities.

He was the only detective she knew, and now….

She sat up a little straighter. Capshaw was *not* the only detective she knew. There was someone else.

The ever-perceptive Capshaw gave her a sharp glance. "You've thought of something."

"I'm not sure you're going to like this. I think we need to call in an old friend to help us."

Sophia eyed them in confusion. "Who?"

Capshaw tapped his pencil thoughtfully. "Ah. You mean…."

"Yes," Concordia said, "Penelope Hamilton."

Sophia narrowed her eyes, puzzled. "Miss Hamilton... wasn't she the lady principal at the college a few years ago? When you first started teaching there. How could she possibly help us?"

Concordia gave her a wide grin. "Not many people know this, Sophie, but Miss Hamilton is a *Pinkerton*. If anyone can help us, she can."

Chapter 16

You have been hotly call'd for.

***Othello**, I.ii*

Week 5, Instructor Calendar
March 1898

It was well past dark when Concordia reached the gate of Hartford Women's College. Clyde scowled in disapproval as he passed her a slip of paper.

"Miss Pomeroy left this for ya," he said.

With a murmur of thanks, Concordia opened it.

Concordia, please come to my office when you get this. We need to have a chat.

Yours, Gertrude Pomeroy.

Concordia's heart sank. While the tone of the note was cordial enough, she knew she was in trouble.

Only a few lamps glowed in the windows of Founder's Hall as Concordia crossed the quadrangle. No one lingered outside on this chill March evening. She thought back to her conversation with Capshaw, about the stranger—two of them—who had been slipping onto campus at odd hours. For what purpose? She shivered, and glanced over her shoulder one last time as she pulled open the door of the Hall.

The lady principal's light was on. Concordia rapped lightly on the partly open door.

"Come in!"

"I received your note, Miss Pomeroy," Concordia began hesitantly.

"Yes, yes," Gertrude Pomeroy said, pushing her spectacles back up her nose as she turned away from her work. "Do sit down."

Once again, that posed a problem, as every surface was littered with papers and books.

"Here," Miss Pomeroy said, shifting one pile aside and plunking it on top of another. "I've been meaning to straighten things," she added vaguely.

"Now, Concordia," the lady principal said, when they both were seated, "I don't want you to take this the wrong way, my dear. You are an excellent teacher, and your work is exemplary, but there is an issue...." Her voice trailed off, and she hesitated.

Concordia sighed, knowing that discipline was not Miss Pomeroy's strong suit. "Miss Pomeroy, I understand what you're trying to say."

Miss Pomeroy leaned forward in surprise. "You do?"

"You're unhappy with my frequent absences from campus lately. I'm quite sorry for that. I've had some personal...issues come up."

She didn't want to have to explain about Florence's murder, Eli's disappearance, or the setback in the investigation. Miss Pomeroy didn't know these people, except for Eli, whom she probably hadn't paid much attention to.

Gertrude Pomeroy nodded. "I see. Unfortunately, your absences have been noted by others—"

"Indeed they have," a deep voice interrupted, and Randolph Maynard walked in. Concordia wondered how long the dean had been listening at the door.

"If your personal troubles are causing you to shirk your duties, Miss Wells," he continued, glowering at her under those thick black brows, "you are free to give notice and attend to them at your leisure. Here at the college, we expect our staff to give the needs of the students their highest priority."

Concordia bit back a retort about how the *male* staff were permitted to have private lives, without being accused of compromising the care of their students.

"That won't be necessary," she merely said, through gritted teeth. Blast the man.

"And *you*, Miss Pomeroy," Maynard said, turning to the lady principal, "the female teachers and students are your responsibility. Are you going to permit your teaching staff to simply leave whenever they wish, without a care for their duties? What sort of example does this set for the students? You are flirting with anarchy here."

Concordia rolled her eyes. Quite a leap in logic from a single teacher with a personal emergency to a student revolt.

Miss Pomeroy flushed a mottled red, but otherwise remained composed. "Mr. Maynard, the students of Miss Wells' cottage were well cared-for and properly chaperoned by the cottage matron in the meanwhile. I'm confident Miss Wells ensured that before she left."

Concordia stayed silent, realizing that she had not in fact done so. Thank heaven for the ever-patient and understanding Ruby.

"Be that as it may," Maynard said, "Miss Wells' reputation precedes her. When I first got here, I learned enough about this young woman to know I'd have to keep my eye on her. The *lady sleuth*. Climbing out of windows. Finding dead bodies. Trapping an embezzler. Confronting a murderer, alone, in the dark. Getting herself nearly strangled while confronting yet *another* murderer." He waggled a finger in Concordia's direction. "You, young lady, invite trouble."

Concordia listened to the diatribe in stunned silence. She had assumed the gossip about her had died out long ago. Of course, he'd overheard the newspaperman's comment at the reception, so it was naïve of her to assume he would let it go. The way Maynard characterized it, her conduct seemed most unsavory. Certainly not decorous behavior from one's teaching staff.

But Maynard couldn't know the urgency that guided her actions at the time, the necessity of protecting her students, her family, and herself. She knew she would do it all over again.

"And now," Maynard continued, when no one said anything, "you are no doubt involved in another unseemly undertaking, and playing detective again."

Although this was uncomfortably close to the truth, Concordia folded her hands and looked Maynard square in the eye. "Indeed?" was all she trusted herself to say.

Inwardly, she felt less than composed. Having the dean closely monitor her activities would pose a problem, should she and Capshaw persuade Miss Hamilton to come and resume the search for Eli. Concordia planned to ask Miss Pomeroy's permission for Miss Hamilton to stay at DeLacey House, where the women administrators and senior teachers lived. Perhaps that would be too close for comfort. It would not do for Maynard to discover that Miss Hamilton was a Pinkerton detective.

Maynard pounded his fist on the desk, making both women jump in their chairs. "You aren't paying me any attention, Miss Wells."

Miss Pomeroy stood, her expression grim. Concordia stared, open-mouthed, as the lady principal stalked over to Maynard and leaned close. Maynard shrank back, despite the fact that he was a foot taller and at least eighty pounds heavier than the diminutive old lady.

"I will deal with my staff as I see fit, Mr. Maynard," the lady principal said sharply, "and I shall not allow you to harass anyone in my charge. Are we clear?" Her clear blue eyes held him in a glare.

Maynard flushed an angry red and backed toward the door. "I—I only m—meant…." His voice trailed off.

"Are we clear?" Miss Pomeroy repeated.

Maynard cleared his throat. "Yes, Miss Pomeroy. If you'll excuse me," he said, and made as dignified an exit as he could muster.

Concordia saw a fleeting smile cross Miss Pomeroy's lips before she turned aside and sat back down.

Both were quiet for a few moments. Miss Pomeroy tucked a stray frizzy brown lock of hair back into her bun and adjusted her spectacles.

"Miss Wells," she said at last, "I have given you a certain amount of latitude in the past. I would ask that you not take advantage of it, but take particular care to fulfill *all* of your duties, including those of a domestic nature, most meticulously in the future."

"Yes, ma'am," Concordia said meekly.

"And further," Miss Pomeroy said, "I want you to obtain my permission first before you leave campus in the future. Agreed?"

Concordia nodded.

"If you could hand me those papers," Gertrude Pomeroy said with a sigh, "I believe I'll do a little translating to clear my mind."

Concordia handed her the stack and left her to it.

Chapter 17

*'tis in ourselves that we are thus
or thus.*

Othello, I.iii

Week 6, Instructor Calendar
March 1898

The day dawned crisp and clear, with not as much chill as last week. The trees had begun to plump with buds and the grass was changing over from its winter brown to a tender green. A perfect day for a bicycle ride. Perhaps it would be a welcome respite from the endless worry about Eli. Certainly the fresh air would do her good.

Concordia was the faculty sponsor for the college's bicycling club, but it had been months since she and her fellow club members had enjoyed weather temperate enough for an excursion. She sent notes around to the girls, telling them to meet her at the quadrangle at one o'clock. That should afford them ample time for their excursion as well as dressing for dinner. She didn't want to incur Maynard's wrath again, or to get Miss Pomeroy in further trouble.

In the meantime, she sat down to re-read *Othello*. Despite her preoccupation, she was soon caught up in the story: a betrayed father, a cunning villain, a jealous new husband, an innocent young wife, unaware of the slaughter to which she was being led. The spectator could see it all, the net slowly closing around the principals of the piece, helpless to do anything except watch....

Concordia tossed it aside before she finished. The smothering of Desdemona called to mind the all-too-recent image of Florence Willoughby, flung across the bed like a discarded rag doll, the mark from a garrote wire around her neck.

Oh, *where* was Eli? Had he seen something? Had the murderer kidnapped him, or worse, killed him and hidden his body? But that made no sense; why hide a second killing? Concordia clung to that bit of logic, hoping Eli was still alive. She also hoped that Miss Hamilton would reply to her letter soon, and take on the investigation. It had been nearly a week since Concordia had sent it, with no word yet.

The mantel clock struck the three-quarter-hour.

Mercy! She'd better hurry. Concordia pulled out her bicycling outfit and gave it a good shake. She should have given it time yesterday to air out. It smelled strongly of mothballs. Planning ahead was not her strong suit.

She felt the familiar rush of anticipation as she put it on—the leggings, shortened over-skirt, blouse and vest. She glanced in the mirror as she tucked her hair under the matching cap. It did show a bit more leg than people were accustomed to seeing.

She wrangled her machine from the shed—never an easy task, as the bicycle was quite heavy—and set out for the quadrangle.

Four girls waited impatiently as Concordia braked in front of the fountain.

"Isn't this a beautiful day, Miss Wells?" Maisie Lovelace said eagerly.

Concordia smiled. "Indeed it is."

"Shall we take the path over to the old railroad line?" Miss Lovelace asked.

Concordia shook her head. "That might be too arduous for our first ride in months. After a few more excursions we could try it. We'll stay on the sheep tracks down to there—" she pointed to the stream, below Rook's Hill "—and circle back, behind the pond. That should be an hour's ride, more than enough for today. Miss Lovelace, will you lead us?"

The girl grinned broadly.

It felt wonderful to be riding again. Concordia delighted in the sensation of the breeze on her face, the smell of damp earth and new growth, and the hush that settles upon a group engaged in a physical task. For a long while, there was just the huffing of breath and the whirring of gears.

Concordia felt her mind drift as she pedaled in rhythm with the girls. They were about to crest the hill. This was the part she loved, where one could feel the tug of gravity in the spine, pulling one down faster, faster, before touching the brakes.

As pleasant as the ride was, her thoughts drifted back to her letter to Miss Hamilton. Why hadn't she heard anything? Concordia had a sinking feeling—more than the rush of her machine down the slope—that Miss Hamilton was not in Chicago, but away on a case. If so, what would they do?

"Watch out," Miss Lovelace called out, as they got to the bottom. "This part's quite boggy."

As they successfully maneuvered around the obstacle, Concordia felt the gear slip under her pedal. "Oh, dear." She jumped off the bicycle as the others braked to a stop.

"What is it?" Miss Lovelace asked.

Concordia struggled with the slippery, muddy chain. "I'm having trouble getting the chain to engage with the gear teeth."

Heedless of her skirts in the damp grass, the girl knelt down for a better look. "Ah. I have just the thing." She ran off to grab a pouch from her basket.

"What's that?" Concordia asked, as the other girls crowded around.

"My tool kit," Miss Lovelace said nonchalantly. "My uncle owns a clock-maker's shop. He had some spare tools he was willing to lend me. I thought they would come in handy on long rides."

"How resourceful," Concordia murmured, watching the young lady wield the pliers with ease. "What is it you're doing?"

"A link...is...bent. It must have happened as the chain slipped off." The young lady grunted with the exertion, not looking up from her work. "It's close to coming apart. Beth, would you mind?" She gestured to the pouch. "The spool of wire, if you please."

Another girl rummaged around and passed the wire over.

"I've bent it back in place, Miss Wells, and the wire should hold it together for the return trip," Miss Lovelace explained, standing up and pulling out a rag from her kit to clean her hands. "I'm afraid you'll need a machine shop repair, though."

Concordia was impressed. "Thank you, dear. Did you learn this from your uncle?"

The girl nodded, gesturing to two other girls. "His shop is where we made the sled, too. We love making and fixing mechanical things. In fact, there are several of us here at the school who want to study engineering. But it isn't offered here, or at *any* women's colleges. We want President Langdon to start one."

"Really?" Concordia said in surprise. "You understand that such a move requires approval by the board of trustees, and a faculty sponsor?" Not a light-hearted undertaking. Of course, these young ladies had certainly demonstrated a knack for such pursuits. The sled must have been difficult to make.

"Professor Merriwether agreed to be our sponsor," Miss Lovelace said. "He's already spoken to the president, twice. But Mr. Langdon says such a course of study isn't suitable for young ladies." The other girls gave glum nods.

"Mr. Isley is dead set against it, too," someone else chimed in. "In fact, we think he's the one who convinced the president to reject our petition. Professor Merriwether had been sure he could get President Langdon to agree."

Concordia suspected the bursar's motive was more about finances than propriety. No doubt instituting such a program would be costly. "I suppose the dean was against the plan as well?"

The girls shrugged. Apparently, Maynard had not made known his opinions on the subject. Concordia found that surprising, as he didn't hold back his views in other matters. She winced, remembering the meeting in Miss Pomeroy's office.

"I'm sorry. I suppose there's nothing more to do about it this year," Concordia said.

Miss Lovelace thrust out a stubborn chin. "We'll think of something."

The group headed back around the pond, keeping to a slower pace so as to not risk breaking Concordia's chain.

They had just rounded the bend and were approaching the benches when Concordia braked to a sudden stop, her knees weak with relief.

There, just under the willow that overhung the pond, Penelope Hamilton stood, watching their approach. Everything about the lady spoke of elegance, directness of purpose, and action: the sleek blond hair, coiled in a braided coronet under a jaunty carmine hat that matched her suit; the upright posture; the strong jaw-line; the no-nonsense piercing gray eyes that missed little.

During much of Miss Hamilton's time as lady principal at Hartford Women's College, Concordia had found her remote and intimidating. Now, having come to know her better, she found her decisiveness reassuring.

Concordia had never been so happy to see anyone in her life.

"That's all for today," Concordia called to the girls, as she rushed to embrace her friend.

"Penelope!" Concordia cried. "I'm ever so glad to see you. Surprised, too. When I didn't receive a reply, I worried I'd missed you."

Miss Hamilton smiled. "It's good to be back here again, even if the circumstances are distressing." She looked closely at Concordia. "Quite distressing."

Conocordia swallowed. "Yes, we're worried about Eli."

Miss Hamilton took Concordia's arm. "Why don't we have a cup of tea and talk about it? I've already spoken with Miss Pomeroy. She's given me guest quarters at DeLacey House."

Concordia stopped. *Drat,* she'd forgotten to ask Miss Pomeroy's permission to invite a guest. "Does she know that I asked you to come?"

Miss Hamilton smiled. "You must know I would be more circumspect than *that*. I am merely visiting a niece who has just had a baby, but it turns out they don't have enough room for me. There didn't seem to be a problem with me staying here." She glanced at Concordia. "What is it that worries you?"

"Dean Maynard has been—difficult," Concordia said, wincing. "All of this business with Florence and Eli, and Sophia's wedding before that, has taken me away from campus a few too many times for his liking. He's been pressuring Miss Pomeroy to enforce strict rules for the staff. Especially me. But that isn't the worst of it."

She told Miss Hamilton about the gossip Maynard had heard regarding her "lady sleuthing."

Miss Hamilton snorted. "It's fortunate that he never learned about the time you prowled Founder's Hall at one o'clock in the morning in your night dress."

Concordia blushed.

"So Maynard suspects you are once again engaged in detecting?" Miss Hamilton asked.

Concordia nodded. "That's why it's imperative he not know who you really are and why you're here."

They had reached the door of DeLacey House, set along a deep, flagstone porch that later in the spring would sport well-worn rocking chairs and planters of bright geraniums. Miss Hamilton reached for her guest key, but hesitated.

"Concordia," she said softly, "you *are* involved in this, you know. I'm going to need your help if we are to succeed. And yes, it requires detecting. The choice is ultimately yours to make."

Concordia met her steady gaze. She hadn't wanted to admit that she was involved, yet again. When a lady engaged in such inquiries, it was deemed *unseemly* or, as Lieutenant Capshaw termed it, *meddling*. Yet forces beyond her control seemed to carry her repeatedly to this juncture.

As Miss Hamilton was making plain, she *did* have a choice: bystander, or participant?

Concordia gave a small smile. "Count me in."

The guest rooms weren't as large as those Miss Hamilton occupied in the days when she was lady principal, of course, but they were nonetheless quite comfortable. Two cozy upholstered chairs flanked a hearth, where a fire had already been lit, more to dispel the damp than for warmth. Soon they were ensconced in front of a tray laden with fragrant tea and muffins.

Concordia felt herself relax in a way that she had not in the past few weeks. Miss Hamilton would solve the mystery and dispel the cloud that seemed to hang over them all. Concordia had every confidence of that. After all, the lady had once discovered an embezzler in their midst and solved multiple murders that had plagued the school, had she not? Concordia hoped that Capshaw was coming around to Miss Hamilton's involvement in the case.

As if reading her mind, Penelope said, "I've already sent word to the lieutenant. He and Sophia will be joining us soon. In the meantime, I want you to catch me up on what you know."

Concordia fished in her pocket for Florence's letter, which she'd taken to carrying around and re-reading for a clue she might have missed. "I found this in my stack of mail last week. I've already shown it to the lieutenant. She wrote it the day before she died."

Miss Hamilton read it through with great interest. "So, there had been an attempt on her life before. And she knew who was behind it. How exasperating that she didn't name them here."

"She was a very cautious woman. I doubt she trusted me with that information. However, her postscript points to some sort of clue in what she gave Eli," Concordia said. "It was a pocket watch, as I remember."

"Did you get a good look at it?"

Concordia shook her head. "I didn't pay much attention. It seemed to be an ordinary watch. Not unusual at all."

"And I assume the watch is with Eli? It wasn't found in his belongings at the settlement house?"

"You'll have to ask Sophia. She planned to search his belongings herself," Concordia said.

"You said in your letter that the Capshaws wish to adopt the boy, correct?" Miss Hamilton asked.

"Yes, they were waiting until they returned from their honeymoon."

"But it was at the wedding that Florence turned up?"

Concordia nodded. "Although she didn't come forward and claim she was Eli's mother until after they'd left on their trip."

"I see." Miss Hamilton tapped a lip thoughtfully. "What were your impressions of the woman?" She sat back and took a sip of her tea.

"Deeply suspicious, unwilling to volunteer any more information than necessary," Concordia began, thinking back to her only encounter. "Awkward with Eli, but that's understandable given the circumstances. She seemed under great tension. Well-spoken, though plainly dressed. That part was a surprise to me, until I read her letter. Based on Eli's own account of his childhood, I assumed the mother was a servant who'd gotten herself in trouble."

"Women of all stations can get into trouble," Penelope Hamilton pointed out.

Concordia nodded ruefully. "Yes, I can see that."

"In your letter," Miss Hamilton said, "you recounted finding Florence dead in her room at the boarding house."

Concordia took a deep breath. "She'd been...strangled. The Capshaws and I went over there to try talking Florence out of taking Eli."

"And you said the boy's cat bolted out of the room when you opened the door?"

"That's what has me worried. Eli adores the animal. He rarely goes anywhere without it. I cannot imagine him willingly leaving it behind."

"And no one has seen anything of the boy since?" Miss Hamilton asked.

Concordia shook her head mutely.

Miss Hamilton gave her a keen glance. "You are very fond of this child."

Concordia sipped her tea to fight down the lump in her throat. "It's so absurd, I know. Children usually scare the tar out of me. I simply don't understand them. But Eli and I...well, you know what we had been through together, last year. I'd written to you about all that."

Miss Hamilton nodded. "That's a powerful bonding experience. He sounds like an extraordinary child."

"He is."

Concordia kept her gaze at her lap, trying not to cry. She'd tolerate a litter of raggedy cats just to see Eli again.

"Setting aside the presence of the cat, is there any chance that Eli could have left voluntarily?" Miss Hamilton asked.

Concordia thought about that. "Perhaps," she conceded, "but to be gone this long, without any word...I'm just so worried that he's—"

There was a knock at the door, and Sophia and Capshaw came in. Once additional chairs were brought in and more tea sent for, the four of them sat facing each other.

"So, Lieutenant, it's nice to see you again," Miss Hamilton commented. "Allow me to express my best wishes on the occasion of your marriage."

She got wan smiles in return.

"Tell me how I can help," Miss Hamilton went on. "I am at your disposal, and not due back for some time."

Capshaw's face contorted into what passed for a grateful look, although Concordia knew he struggled with a bit of wounded pride. Years ago when they first worked together on a case, Capshaw had been the official arm of the police force, with Miss Hamilton dependent upon what he decided to share with her. Now the power balance had shifted, with Penelope doing the favors.

"Tell me more about your investigation, before the chief took you off the case," Miss Hamilton said. "Perhaps there is some information you had uncovered which was making someone nervous."

Capshaw cleared his throat. "After examining the scene, talking with the coroner, and interviewing witnesses, we had very little to go on. Miss Willoughby had no visitors that day except Eli. But then he left around one o'clock—the maid saw him on his way out. No one saw Eli return."

"And how long had Florence Willoughby been dead before you found her—at three in the afternoon, I believe?" Miss Hamilton asked.

Capshaw nodded. "Close to that time." He explained the locked door, the repeated knocks, the maid who was sure Florence hadn't gone out. The discovery of Rose.

"I see. Did you establish who in the household had last seen Florence alive, and when?"

"It was mid-morning. The maid said Florence came to the kitchen for a headache powder, and said she was going to lie down," Capshaw said.

"And Eli was her only visitor?" Miss Hamilton asked.

"As far as anyone knows, but I had been looking into the possibility of a stranger slipping in unnoticed. It's possible—the back kitchen door isn't locked during the day. But there are so many people bustling around the kitchen that it doesn't seem feasible."

Miss Hamilton tapped her chin thoughtfully. "I know what you mean: butcher's boy, vegetable seller, milk man, cook, servants...not to mention the boarders who might stop in to make special requests. But, no matter how difficult to accomplish, we know that she had to have been killed between one o'clock and, say, a quarter to three."

"Exactly. There's a fire escape in back of the building, but that would be a bold move in broad daylight. None of the neighbors saw anyone on it."

"And we're assuming that Eli's disappearance is connected to his mother's death?"

Capshaw shrugged. "It's the only explanation that makes sense."

"I understand from Concordia that the boy has gone off on his own before," Miss Hamilton said.

"That was early on," Sophia said, "when he first came to us. He wasn't accustomed to anything but the vagrant life. But then he began to follow the routine, and seemed happy here. We spoke to Eli about adopting him after our marriage, and he was most eager for that. There would have been no reason for him to simply vanish like this."

"And certainly not without his cat," Concordia pointed out.

Miss Hamilton was quiet for a few minutes, twirling her pencil in her hand, notepad in her lap. "Suppose he left voluntarily, but because he was afraid," she said.

"Afraid because he witnessed the murder? Or because his mother was dead?" Capshaw shook his head. "He would have come to us for help, not run away."

"But he's just a child," Concordia said. "Children don't always think things through very clearly."

"The murderer could have taken him," Sophia said, her voice barely above a hoarse whisper.

Miss Hamilton frowned. "For what purpose? Because he was a witness? If so, why not just kill him, too? I doubt a man who murders a defenseless woman would scruple to kill a child."

Sophia blanched. Concordia reached over and patted her hand reassuringly as she shot Miss Hamilton a warning look. The woman had a habit of blunt speaking that could be disconcerting, to say the least.

"I'm sorry," Miss Hamilton said with a shrug. "Our best chance of finding the boy is to face facts squarely."

"The killer might have taken Eli for some other purpose. Information, perhaps," Capshaw said. "The murderer could have been after something Florence knew or possessed. He may not have known that Eli's acquaintance with her was recent."

"I'd like to see what you've uncovered, if you would, before you were taken off the case," Miss Hamilton said. "Especially what you've learned about the victim."

"Of course. I've made you a copy of my notes." Capshaw passed her a sheaf of papers.

Everyone was quiet as Miss Hamilton skimmed the pages. She raised an eyebrow. "I had no idea the Willoughby family was so prominent. Interesting," she murmured. "Is it fair to say that you believe the family pressured your superior to take you off the case?"

"It's a theory," Capshaw said.

"I've read Florence's letter to Concordia," Miss Hamilton said. "Perhaps they feared a scandal."

"But to interfere in the murder investigation of their own daughter," Concordia protested, "that seems horribly cold-hearted."

"Indeed," Miss Hamilton said.

"But it is possible that Eli was kidnapped," Sophia said, hands clenched.

"While not *im*possible," Miss Hamilton said, "it seems highly unlikely that Florence's murderer could have carried a robust eleven-year-old boy down several flights of stairs and out the door without being noticed."

"Unless he'd been knocked unconscious," Capshaw said. "But there's still the issue of the locked door. Only a key can lock it from the outside; the landlady had the key, of course, and Florence's key was in the room."

"That leaves the fire escape," Sophia said.

Concordia imagined the difficulty of someone climbing down with Eli in his arms.

"If Eli left voluntarily, without anyone seeing him," Concordia said, "where would he be now? In hiding somewhere?"

"That's my conjecture, although we can't answer the *why* of it," Miss Hamilton said.

"Where do we start?" Sophia asked anxiously.

"First, I'll work on picking up Eli's trail. I'll need to learn more about him—favorite haunts, friends or family elsewhere, and so on."

"I can tell you some of Eli's background," Sophia said, "but the person you should really talk to is Martha Newcombe, who's in charge of the settlement house. She and her staff interviewed him thoroughly when they first made arrangements for him, and have been living with him and working with him daily. I'll send a note around, telling her to expect you."

Miss Hamilton nodded, then was silent for a long moment. "What is it?" Capshaw asked.

"There's one question I have to ask," she said hesitantly, "and I don't want to offend your sensibilities—"

Sophia leaned forward. "If it can bring him back to us, by all means, ask."

"Very well. You say that Florence was planning to take Eli with her, forcing him to leave a place and people that he had grown attached to. Could the *boy* have killed her?"

Her question was met with a stunned silence. Miss Hamilton waited, hands calmly folded in her lap.

Concordia's mind was reeling. Eli, though thin, was tall for his age. Florence had been a petite woman. If she'd been caught off guard, it was physically possible. She felt a little queasy.

After a moment, Capshaw broke the quiet. "No," he said firmly. "Had Florence been hit over the head, or smothered in her sleep, then I'd have to concede the possibility. But the woman was quickly—and expertly—garroted. Whoever did this has murdered before."

Concordia breathed a sigh of relief, even as a chill prickled the base of her neck.

"Ah." Miss Hamilton gave Capshaw a quick look. "Did you inquire about other garroting deaths in the area over the past few years?"

Capshaw nodded. "I'd only gone back five years when I was taken off the case, but there were no incidents that I could find."

"Eli has been missing for nearly two weeks now," Concordia said. "Surely the trail has grown cold?"

Miss Hamilton smiled. "I'll manage."

"You'll have to be careful not to alert the police to your investigation," Capshaw warned.

"I'm more than familiar with that precaution, believe me." She stood, along with the rest of them. "This will suffice, for now. I'll look over your report more thoroughly this evening, Lieutenant. Please inform Miss Newcombe that I'll see her at her earliest convenience in the morning. Try not to worry," she added, looking at the white-faced Sophia. "I'll find him."

As they were leaving DeLacey House, Capshaw came up to Concordia and murmured, "Do you have a moment?"

"Of course," Concordia answered, checking her watch, "but I have to dress for dinner." She looked ruefully at her bicycling outfit.

"Don't worry, I won't keep you long," Capshaw assured her. He glanced over at his wife.

Sophia took the hint. "I wanted to say hello to Hannah Jenkins, anyway. Do you know where she'd be?"

Concordia thought for a moment. "This time of day? I'd try the gymnasium, cleaning up the equipment."

With a wave, Sophia headed down the path.

"What is it, Lieutenant?" Concordia asked, as they walked to the cottage.

"I'd like you to accompany me while I question Ruby about this mystery man who asked for her," he said. "I stopped by a few days ago, but she was too busy to talk. Policemen make some people nervous. Perhaps your presence would reassure her."

"She'll likely be rounding up the girls to get them ready for dinner, but she should have a few minutes free."

Once inside Willow Cottage, Concordia removed her jacket and gloves. "Why don't you take a seat in the parlor. I'll let her know you're here."

A senior walked past. "Hello, Miss Wells. Oh, Lieutenant Capshaw, hello!" she exclaimed, no doubt recognizing him from his visits last year. "What are you doing here?"

"Never mind," Concordia scolded. Really, these girls had barnyard manners. "Have you seen Ruby?"

The girl nodded. "Does he want to see her?" she breathed excitedly. "Ooh, I'll get her." She strode down the hall, calling: "Ruby! A policeman to see you!"

Concordia rolled her eyes at the flagrant lapse in decorum. Ruby would no doubt give the young lady a talking-to that would make her ears burn. She sat across from Capshaw to wait.

The girl returned after a few minutes. "I could have sworn she was in the kitchen, right before you came in," she said. "But I can't find her anywhere. She must have stepped out."

Capshaw stood with a sigh. "I'll come back tomorrow."

Concordia nodded. "Right after breakfast is the best time. Nine o'clock?"

Capshaw nodded and left.

Concordia checked the mantel clock. *Drat!* She would have to hurry now.

After she was dressed and had hustled the girls out the door, they found Ruby, alone, heading back from the dining hall.

"Ruby! We'd wondered where you'd gotten to," Concordia said.

Ruby made a face and juggled a cloth-wrapped bowl in her hands. "I was gettin' some broth for Miss Portnoy, who's feeling poorly. We were all out."

Concordia frowned. "You should have sent one of the students to fetch it."

Ruby shrugged.

"Oh, before I forget, you missed Lieutenant Capshaw just now."

"You don't say?" Ruby exclaimed. She turned to look at the girls milling around, listening. "Well, I'd better let you get 'em to their suppers. I'll be there in a little while."

Chapter 18

'twas strange, 'twas passing strange,
'Twas pitiful, 'twas wondrous pitiful.

Othello, I.iii

Week 7, Instructor Calendar
March 1898

Concordia's thoughts were most definitely elsewhere when she nearly bumped into the bursar on the path to Founder's Hall. "Oh! I beg your pardon, Mr. Isley."

The man smiled and tipped his hat. "No harm done."

They fell into step together, or at least as much as Concordia could manage. The bursar, though shorter than most men, walked with a brisk, powerful stride. She struggled to keep up with him.

"It was most kind of Mrs. Isley to invite me to your dinner function this week," Concordia said politely, huffing a little to catch her breath.

Isley gave her an apologetic glance and slowed his pace. "We are happy to have you, dear. Lily tells me that your young man will be joining us as well?"

Your young man. Concordia suppressed a grimace. "Yes."

"Excellent. Be sure to tell him that our guest of honor will be Mr. Sanders, the Republican candidate for the state senate seat. The conversations are sure to be stimulating."

Concordia wasn't so sure that *stimulating* was quite the word she would have used, but she kept that opinion to herself. "I understand your wife is just as involved in the campaign as you are," Concordia said. "Quite commendable." *And unusual,* she added silently.

Isley nodded. "Alas, with no children to keep her occupied in the home, Lily involves herself in several charitable projects. But her involvement in politics came about when I made an early bid for the Republican seat—the ticket that Mr. Sanders is now running on. She was indispensable. In fact, Lily was most disappointed when I withdrew my name."

"Why did you withdraw?" Concordia asked.

"Both Langdon and Maynard made direct appeals to me to step in as bursar, given the school's financial straits at the time."

"We are certainly grateful that you did," Concordia said.

Isley inclined his head in acknowledgment. "Now that the school's situation has vastly improved, I may consider a run in the next election." He sighed.

Concordia heard a tinge of regret in that sigh. It would be two more years before the next campaign, and who knew what could happen in the meanwhile? If Sanders won the seat this time and had a successful term of office, Isley would not have much of a chance against him later.

"But you decided to throw in your support for Mr. Sanders?" she asked politely.

"Well, we certainly were not going to support the *Democrats*." Isley snorted in derision. "Sanders is far better than that scapegrace, Samuel Quint, who looks to win the Democratic primary next month. A pro-Silver man. It's as plain as the nose on one's face that bi-metallism caused the run on gold in the Panic of '93, along with an assortment of ills. We've barely climbed out of that hole."

"Ah," was all Concordia could trust herself to say. The current economic issues held little appeal for her. If she were to pay attention to politics at all, it would be those of her favorite authors, many of them dead for more than a hundred years.

They parted ways in the hall. Concordia was about to turn toward the stairwell to continue up to her third-floor office when she noticed the bursar hesitating at his door.

"Something wrong, Mr. Isley?" She walked over to see. Isley was fingering his key ring and wearing a puzzled look. He glanced at the floor.

"My key isn't on the ring."

Concordia surveyed the floor, but didn't see a dropped key. "Perhaps you should have Mr. Drew let you in for the time being." She gestured to the custodian, rummaging in the broom closet nearby.

Soon Mr. Drew had the key turned in the lock, and Isley impatiently flung open the door.

He, Concordia, and the custodian stared, their mouths hanging open.

"Saints preserve us!" the custodian whispered, eyes wide.

President Langdon's buggy took up the entirety of Isley's office.

Concordia rubbed her eyes and looked again, certain that it was some mad vision that would go away in a moment of clarity.

But no—the buggy was here to stay. The other furniture in Isley's room had been pushed against the walls, and the president's shiny new buggy—his hard-won pride and joy—stood in the middle of the bursar's office. Completely intact.

"How? Wh-what? Why?" Isley sputtered.

All good questions, in Concordia's mind. There was no elevator in the building, and the doorway of Isley's office was much too narrow to accommodate the conveyance. As they squeezed into the room for a better look, she ran a hand over the door and bent down to look underneath. Not a bolt or a screw loose.

From its roof to its wheels and everything in between, the buggy had to have been disassembled in the coach house, its parts carried up the stairs and into the bursar's office—after swiping Isley's key, no doubt—and reassembled in his office. Quite a feat, and all done without getting caught.

"Who would do this?" Isley demanded of no one in particular. He turned to the custodian. "Get President Langdon—quickly." Mr. Drew scurried off.

A laugh threatened to bubble out of Concordia as she grasped the absurdity of the situation. The vehicle was perfectly intact and undamaged, but someone now had to *get it out of here*, a problem dumped neatly into Isley's lap by the pranksters.

And Concordia knew exactly who they were.

"You needn't look so amused, Miss Wells," Isley snapped.

Concordia tried to keep a straight face. She turned as President Langdon hurried down the hall, accompanied by Dean Maynard. Both stopped dead in their tracks. "When Mr. Drew told me, I couldn't believe it," Langdon said slowly. The president passed a large hand over his graying beard, as he was wont to do when lost in thought.

Behind them, a crowd had gathered outside the bursar's door. Students in various states of awe and amusement were taking in the sight of the president's buggy occupying all of Bursar Isley's office.

Miss Pomeroy came along next, shooing students from the door. She stopped and stared. "Oh. Oh, *my.*"

"Who would do this?" Isley repeated, voice high-pitched with indignation.

Langdon scratched at his beard again. "How do we get it out of here?"

Concordia wondered how long it would take someone to ask that question.

Dean Maynard, standing beside Concordia, gave her an angry glance. "Did *you* have anything to do with this?" he demanded.

Before Concordia could offer a retort, Miss Pomeroy spoke up. "What nonsense, dean! You don't see Mr. Isley and President Langdon, who have every reason to be upset, making such outlandish accusations. Miss Wells is a respected faculty member, who would never stoop to such shenanigans."

Concordia, remembering a time last year when "shenanigans" were called for—unavoidable, even—remained silent.

Langdon was inspecting the buggy. "It looks perfectly unharmed. A stunt like this requires a great deal of mechanical skill," he mused aloud. "Could some of the Trinity boys have broken in and pulled this?"

Concordia shook her head. Langdon was missing the point. The female students who had petitioned for a mechanical engineering certificate program at the college—a petition which had been rejected—had obviously pulled the prank to prove that they were as capable of such work as men, and wanted the chance to develop that talent. The fact that Langdon wasn't able to conceive of the girls being the culprits demonstrated why the petition had failed. She remembered the words of Miss Lovelace.

We will find a way.

But she said nothing. The men would catch on, eventually. Perhaps after a few days of trying to maneuver around a full-size buggy. That should do the trick.

She didn't bother to suppress a grin this time.

Chapter 19

C oncordia was nearly ready for the Isley dinner.
       She watched as Penelope tugged with the
buttonhook, giving a little grunt of exertion. The new shoes
were a bit stiff, but perfectly matched Concordia's green silk
dinner dress, so she wasn't about to change them for her old
broken-in black pumps. If only her corset weren't so tight, she
would be able to lean over and button them herself.

Concordia noted the glints of silver in Penelope's braided
coronet as the woman bent over the shoe. Since Miss Hamilton
moved with the grace and ease of a much younger woman,
these little reminders of the lady's actual age were a continual
surprise.

"There!" Miss Hamilton said in satisfaction, handing back
the hook.

"Have you made any progress in your search for Eli?"
Concordia asked, her voice tinged with hope.

"Some," Miss Hamilton said. "One of the newsies who
works the corner of Pearl and Asylum, in front of the druggist's,
thought it was Eli he saw that afternoon. He was running as if
he were chasing something, the boy said."

Concordia leaned forward in excitement. "If true, then Eli
left the boarding house under his own power, rather than being
kidnapped, or—" She couldn't complete the sentence, not
wanting to think about the *or*.

Miss Hamilton nodded. "It negates my original idea that Eli
ran away in fright. As wild as it may seem, he could have been

chasing the killer. But if that's the case, why not simply call the police?"

"Eli tries to avoid policemen as much as possible," Concordia said. "Before he lived at the settlement house, he had a number of sad experiences with them, when he was caught stealing food and sleeping in abandoned houses. Capshaw is the only policeman he's ever trusted. But I wonder why Eli didn't go to Capshaw with anything he might have known."

Miss Hamilton shook her head. "Having never had children of my own, I cannot pretend to understand them. But I'm pursuing the lead further. I've also learned more about the Willoughbys. That's why I wanted to intercept you on your way to the Isleys' dinner. There's something I want you to do for me."

Concordia gestured to a chair. "We don't have much time. David will be picking me up soon. How can I help?"

"Let me tell you first what I found out. Did you know that the Willoughbys are closely associated with Mr. and Mrs. Isley?"

Concordia shook her head. "I know very little about any of them. Is it important?"

"I'll let you decide for yourself. First of all, they share the same solicitor, a man named Flynn—"

"*Robert* Flynn? The Irishman?" Concordia interrupted.

"You know him?"

"He and my mother have been spending a lot of time together lately."

"Indeed?" Miss Hamilton raised an eyebrow. "That may be useful later."

"Perhaps." Concordia certainly didn't want her mother involved in the case.

Miss Hamilton dug out her notepad and glanced at it briefly. "They have a financial connection as well. Barton Isley acted as consultant to the Willoughbys before his retirement from investment banking. He may yet serve them in that capacity, at least informally. Both families are invested in copper mines in Rhodesia."

"What does this have to do with tonight's dinner?" Concordia asked.

"I'm getting to that. There's also a political connection between the families. The Isleys are quite involved in Republican politics at the state level—"

Concordia nodded, remembering her conversation with Mr. Isley.

"—and the Willoughbys and Isleys support the same local senate candidate—"

"Mr. Sanders," Concordia supplied.

"Correct. He's the guest of honor at tonight's dinner party," Miss Hamilton continued. "I read in the society section that several Willoughbys are expected to be in attendance tonight."

Concordia smiled briefly at the thought of Penelope Hamilton scouring the society pages.

"There's one more thing, and it's the most interesting item of all," Miss Hamilton went on. "I've learned from a trusted source that several of the Willoughby men belong to a secret society."

Concordia's mouth dropped open. "You mean, Freemasons or something of the sort? That seems somewhat...medieval, doesn't it?"

"Rather cloak-and-dagger, yes," Miss Hamilton said. "I haven't been able to learn as much as I'd like. I do know that it's called the Fraternal Order of the Black Scroll."

"I've never heard of it," Concordia said.

"Nor would you be likely to. It was formed ten years ago as an organization of secret philanthropy; its membership is that of men in the legal, financial, and law enforcement professions. But I don't know anything about the membership size, who besides the Willoughbys belong to it, what its mission and code of conduct currently are, or the breadth of its influence. Given your bursar's close affiliation with the Willoughbys, however, it's likely that Isley is a member."

"But how would Florence be involved?" Concordia objected. "As a woman, she couldn't possibly belong to such an organization. Isn't it rather far-fetched to assume the group has anything to do with her death? You said it was philanthropic."

Miss Hamilton shook her head. "I said it *started* as philanthropic. I need to learn more about its current agenda. And although Florence did not belong to the organization, she lived in a household with family members who did. She also could have had acquaintances, friends, even a paramour associated with the Black Scroll. With that degree of familiarity, people don't always keep secrets they are expected to."

Concordia eyes widened as something occurred to her. "If the Black Scroll membership includes men in law enforcement, could it be behind the removal of Capshaw from Florence's murder investigation?"

Miss Hamilton grimaced. "A disturbing thought, is it not? We must learn more. Some of the most socially and politically influential people will be together at the Isleys tonight. It is a unique opportunity for you to listen in on conversations."

"You want me to *spy* on the dinner guests?" Concordia asked incredulously. "That seems to be more along your line."

"I was not invited to the party, you were." Miss Hamilton hesitated. "But for heaven's sake, be careful."

Chapter 20

Let's teach ourselves that honourable stop,
Not to outsport discretion.

Othello, II.*iii*

Week 7, Instructor Calendar
March 1898

Concordia alighted from the carriage, David at her elbow to steady her. The Isleys' residence was an elegant structure, with deep-set gables and grand white columns set at intervals along the porch. Concordia admired the freshly-painted, crisp-white gingerbread molding that adorned the wraparound porch and railings and tall urns of clipped topiary flanking the granite steps. The décor had been enhanced with festive Chinese lanterns strung between the balusters and be-ribboned vases of red tulips. Music from a string quartet drifted through the windows.

This was only a dinner? Concordia wondered how Lily managed to get her parsimonious husband to go along with such an expense.

She and David exchanged glances. "Impressive," he said, his dimples widening in a boyish grin. "Perhaps the college's young ladies had a hand in decorating the bursar's house."

Concordia smiled. The students did indeed have a flair for ostentation when it came to social occasions. From what she had seen of Lily Isley, they had that in common.

She took a deep breath as they approached the front door. How could she best gather information for Miss Hamilton? She had little skill in subterfuge. Her knees felt a little wobbly and she tightened her hand on David's arm.

David glanced at her in concern. "Are you all right? You look pale."

"Yes, yes, I'm fine." Concordia said, with a weak laugh. "I suppose I'm a bit intimidated by the grandeur."

"Don't worry," David murmured, "I've seen you at this sort of thing before. You can hold your own with any of them."

Concordia doubted if he would be as encouraging if he knew what she was *really* here for. But it wouldn't do to tell him. Not at all. He had grown quite protective, and she knew her past involvements had worried him greatly. It was touching...and inconvenient.

A maid greeted them and took Concordia's wrap and David's hat. "The missus is receiving in the Molière Room." In response to their blank stares, she smiled. "That 'ud be the conservatory. At the end of the hall, on your left. Mrs. Isley likes ta name the rooms after famous playwrights, you see."

"Charming," Concordia murmured, as they made their way through the throng. They passed the drawing room—she wondered briefly what Lily had named it—where the musicians played. Some guests had gathered there to listen. One of the taller gentlemen seemed familiar from the back. As he turned in profile, Concordia recognized Randolph Maynard. What was *he* doing here? Isley and Maynard didn't strike her as particularly chummy. She hurried on before he saw her, although she knew it would be impossible to avoid him all evening. No doubt she would be on the receiving end of a scowl and perhaps a barbed remark about neglecting her school duties while frittering her time at a party.

"Ah, there you are, my dear Concordia!" Mrs. Isley cried, as they entered the Molière Room. She was dressed in a satin gown of pale blue, the bodice low-cut, tightly corseted, and liberally trimmed in spangled jet beads that glinted in the light. The effect was striking, but Concordia wondered how the woman was able to breathe.

"And you must be Mr. Bradley. I've heard a great deal about *you*," Lily continued, winking at Concordia.

David raised a questioning eyebrow as he bowed over Mrs. Isley's gloved hand. "The pleasure is mine, Mrs. Isley."

"Dinner will be served shortly, but please, help yourselves to *hors d'oeuvres.*" Lily gestured to a heavily-laden buffet table in front of the tall conservatory windows, then turned to greet more newcomers.

This could be dinner in itself, Concordia thought, looking over the lavish offerings of *foie gras,* fried oyster sandwiches, marinated *champignons,* and deviled eggs. And she couldn't see the rest of the table. As Concordia's corset was already too tight for her liking, she declined the food. She wasn't sure she would make it through dinner. She did, however, accept the lemonade David offered. The room was getting warm.

Concordia stepped back to make room at the buffet for other guests, when she heard an *oomph* behind her and felt a painful step on her ankle. She swayed and gripped her sloshing cup.

"Oh, I beg your pardon!" She heard a familiar male voice say. It was Barton Isley, who reached out a hand to steady her. "So nice to see you, Miss Wells, though we *do* keep bumping into one another. You are unharmed, I hope?"

Concordia nodded.

Isley's eyes lit up when he saw David. "Ah, you must be Mr. Bradley. So good of you to come, sir."

They shook hands and exchanged pleasantries.

"Barton." A man Concordia didn't recognize came up beside them and touched Mr. Isley on the arm. "Can I speak with you a moment?"

"Of course. But first, may I present Miss Concordia Wells and Mr. David Bradley, two of our instructors at the college? Miss Wells, Mr. Bradley, this is a very good friend of mine, Sir Anthony Dunwick."

The man bowed. Though of advanced years, he had a trim, dapper figure, and twinkling eyes. "My pleasure." Then, in an aside to Isley, he said, "the others are waiting in the Cowper Room."

Isley's forehead creased briefly. He turned back to Concordia. "If you will excuse me?"

David and Concordia watched them turn down the hall. "That seemed terribly urgent for a relaxed dinner party," Concordia said thoughtfully. She wondered about what might be going on in the Cowper Room.

David shrugged. "I noticed the arrival of Mr. Sanders, the guest of honor. Everything is urgent to politicians." He smiled at her in a way that brought a flush to her cheeks.

But she had to keep her mind on the task at hand, and now was the time. "Can you excuse me? I believe I spilled some of the lemonade on my dress. I'd like to tend to it before the dinner bell."

She turned toward the hall, waiting until she was out of sight of the conservatory before going in search of the Cowper Room, where this urgent meeting was being held. Could Sanders be part of it, too? Perhaps she could linger nearby, and catch some of what was being said—and who was doing the talking—without being noticed.

After a murmured inquiry to one of the staff, she learned that the Cowper Room was in fact the library, which thankfully was tucked into a quiet side corridor away from the festivities. Before putting her ear to the keyhole, she made sure the hall was empty. Anyone who happened along would find it bizarre to see her in such an undignified position.

Concordia hunched over and put her ear to the keyhole.

Drat. The voices were muffled.

She straightened. There had to be another way.

On such a temperate evening, the library window was sure to be open. The side porch just beneath would make an ideal place to listen. But how to get outside? The front door wasn't feasible. She would encounter any number of guests by that route.

Footsteps alerted her to someone approaching. She shouldn't be caught here. She slipped farther down the hallway to another paneled door. Taking a breath for courage, she turned the knob and slipped inside.

The room was mercifully empty. In the dim light of a single desk lamp, she recognized it as Barton Isley's study. The brown leather chairs, dark wood paneling, and faint odor of cigars made this unmistakably a gentleman's domain.

Concordia's heart sank when she realized that the only other means of egress was a small window. *Mercy.* She'd thought her window-clambering days were over.

There was no help for it. She had to hear what was going on.

Having successfully climbed through the study window with only a small tear in her hem—easily accounted for if it were noticed—she stepped into the gloom of the side porch. The glow through the partly-drawn drapes of the library window helped guide her as she quietly groped along. She couldn't see inside, but at least now she could hear. She crouched below the window on the slatted wood floor, taking care not to creak the boards.

"...don't see why you are hesitant, Sir Anthony. Joining our little group would be a significant step in your career." It was Barton Isley's voice, quite close to the window. Concordia huddled further into the shadows.

"I am flattered, but how does the Inner Circle differ from the general membership I have in the brotherhood? And why must it remain secret from our fellows?" she heard Sir Anthony say.

Concordia's eyes widened. *The Inner Circle.* What was that?

"The brotherhood is an admirable group, but it has become quite large and cumbersome," said another man. Concordia didn't recognize the voice. "It is difficult to get things done in an expeditious manner. Far too many disagreements, debates, counter-proposals, votes, and re-votes. We few are men of action, and decided to band together for special projects."

"But why the secrecy?" Sir Anthony persisted.

"You know how touchy some of these fellows are," Isley said. "Many of them are used to getting their own way, and enjoy a certain amount of status in their particular sphere. Being excluded from our group would feel like a snub."

"What would you want from me, should I join?" Sir Anthony asked.

Holding her breath, Concordia waited for the answer.

Unfortunately, the reply came from the far side of the room. All she heard was a low murmur.

A bell broke through the background noise. Concordia nearly fell over. *Land sakes,* why did those frightful things have to be so loud? She'd better not be caught lingering on the porch, where she had no reason to be. She dearly wanted a look at who was in that meeting. Sanders, perhaps?

If she stood just along the end of the hall at the entrance to the dining room, she'd have a good view when the room cleared. And it would look as if she had been there all the while. She wanted to at least have a few names to give Miss Hamilton, regarding this "Inner Circle."

She slipped back into the house and lingered in the main hall, trying to blend in with the line of people heading for the Shakespeare Room, otherwise known as the dining room. She glanced back at the corridor that led to the library. The occupants should be coming out at any moment.

David saw her and made his way over. "Concordia, at last. I've been waiting for you so we can find our seats."

Of course, he was too well-mannered to ask "what took you so long?" but his expression spoke volumes. And now he was blocking her view. *Drat.* Concordia resisted the impulse to stand on tiptoe and peek over his shoulder. She had no conceivable explanation for such conduct. She merely gritted her teeth and took note of the guests ahead of her. At least she could eliminate those who had *not* been in the meeting. The problem was, she didn't know half of these people. How would she remember them later?

"You seem preoccupied," David said, helping her into her chair.

"I'm just hungry," Concordia lied, looking around.

As her luck would have it, her seat faced away from the entrance. She couldn't take note of anyone who was seated late without swiveling her head like an owl. With the jumble of serving staff and guests thronging around, Concordia had to give it up as hopeless.

As the dishes were served, she thought back to what she had overheard. Miss Hamilton hadn't mentioned an Inner Circle. The group didn't seem nefarious, but a secret within another secret was enough to warrant caution. Who else besides Isley and Sir Anthony were involved? She'd heard two other voices, but there could have been more.

She glanced across the dining room at the man she now knew to be Mr. Sanders, seated at the main table. He spoke with great animation to a man she didn't recognize. From this distance, his voice didn't sound like anyone she'd heard in the library.

David interrupted her thoughts. "More asparagus?" She shook her head. He lowered his voice. "You've been unusually quiet tonight. Is something wrong?"

Concordia smiled. "I'm a bit overwhelmed by talk of politics. I've never paid much attention to the subject, I'm afraid. I know so little of who these men are, how they are associated, and why they are here."

David blotted his lips on a napkin. "I've actually been following recent developments with Sanders, his supporters, and his key opponent. I can explain some of it if you like."

As much as Concordia would prefer to have a splinter removed than listen to political talk, she knew the best way to fulfill Miss Hamilton's commission was to be more conversant about the principals involved.

Concordia inclined her head toward Sanders. "Who's he talking to?"

David followed her glance. "That's Dayton. A banker. From what I've heard, he's involved in Sanders' campaign because he wants to make sure the gold standard isn't tinkered with. Those Silver Democrats make him nervous." He nodded at the pudgy man seated beside Lily Isley. "That's Merritt, the city's head prosecutor and one of the Republican party's staunchest supporters. He likes to back a winner. And Republicans are a safe bet these days. We've had Republican governors for the past six terms—if you don't count Luzon Morris, who interrupted the streak—and the general assembly has sent only Republican delegations to the United States Congress for the last eighteen years."

"Is that Merritt's only motivation?" Concordia asked.

"Oh, he's interested in getting generous funds for the city, and currying favor for a big political appointment later. That's the case with many of the people here tonight, unfortunately." He gave a bitter laugh. "Their reasons are more self-serving than altruistic. Frankly, I'm glad that women don't have the vote. Politics can be a sordid business."

Concordia bit back a retort. While she couldn't argue with David's assessment of the political sphere, she thought the arena would be far less sordid if women were an equal part of it. But that was a discussion for another time. For now, her thoughts were preoccupied with wondering how the Black Scroll was connected here. Had the organization strayed from what Miss Hamilton described as its philanthropic beginnings and become a political machine? Was it responsible for removing Lieutenant Capshaw from the investigation into Florence's death? If the Black Scroll was powerful enough to change the course of a murder inquiry—although the *why* of it was still unanswered—she didn't like to conjecture what else the organization was capable of. She shivered.

"Are you chilled?" David asked.

"No, no, I'm fine. What do you know about the Isleys?" Concordia asked, dropping her voice as one of the wait staff removed her barely-touched plate. "Mr. Isley told me that he and his wife support Sanders because it was essential to defeat the Democrats. But based on what you say, the Democrats are not really a threat. So are the Isleys involved in Sander's senate bid because of the campaign issues, or from the desire to cultivate a powerful connection?"

David took a sip from his water goblet before answering. Concordia waited.

"I don't want to be unfair," he said at last. "This is only based upon impressions, and things I've heard...." He hesitated.

"Go on."

"Mrs. Isley is very passionately involved, more than one merely cultivating an advantageous connection. Surprisingly engaged for a woman, in fact. I don't know enough about her, though, to tell you what issue is close to her heart."

Concordia nodded. "What about our bursar? Is he merely humoring his wife?"

"Even if that's the case, such connections work to Mr. Isley's advantage. Although to truly broaden his influence, he'll want to cultivate friends beyond the state level. He'll require federal connections. Leverage in the national legislative sphere would give him considerable power."

"Is Barton Isley really that ambitious?" Concordia asked.

"I cannot say, but he has some international interests that would benefit from having friends in the government. From what I understand—keep in mind that this is from the rumor mill," David cautioned, "most of the Isley wealth is tied up in mining interests abroad. I've heard something about mines in the southern part of Africa. No doubt he'll have a splendid return on his investment eventually, especially if he can pull off a tariff exemption."

Concordia remembered Miss Hamilton mentioning copper mines. "How could Sanders help Isley with that?" she asked.

"Connecticut's general assembly is responsible for appointments to the United States Congress. There's talk of changing that system eventually—state-wide elections being the fairest method—but that's how it works at the moment."

Concordia thought about that as plates came and went. She would have made room for some of the *creme brulee*, if she had noticed it in front of her before it was whisked away.

She observed the others as David chatted with an elderly lady on his other side. Across the room, Sanders was conversing heatedly with another gentleman. "…Cooke is playing his cards too close to the vest…re-election to another term? Unheard of. Violates gubernatorial tradition. Time for him to cede the field to another."

The other man set aside his napkin. "I disagree. Surely it is better the devil you know—"

"Gentlemen!" Barton Isley interrupted good-naturedly, "Shall we leave such subjects to the after-dinner conversation in the library? I'm sure the ladies don't appreciate such a boring topic."

Concordia couldn't agree more.

"Speak for yourself, Barton," Lily Isley shot back.

Isley laughed indulgently. "Yes, dear."

The murmur of conversations resumed.

Concordia turned back to David. "I was wondering, did you know Florence Willoughby at all?"

He knitted his brow in concentration. "I've heard of the Willoughby family, of course. They dominate the Register in New York, Boston, and Providence. I've never met Florence. Why do you ask?"

Concordia hesitated. "I met her, but she was killed a few weeks ago."

David leaned in to speak more quietly. "You're not getting involved in another murder investigation, are you? I understood it was personal for you when Sophia was accused of murdering her father—who could stand idly by and do nothing when one's best friend is in trouble? But surely, Florence Willoughby's death can't possibly concern you."

"No, no, it's not like that," Concordia protested in a low voice. It was Eli's disappearance that was getting her involved this time, but she couldn't explain that right now. There were too many people close by to overhear.

"Just trust me, David," Concordia said. "Do you see any Willoughbys here?"

He sighed in resignation and surveyed the room. The final plates were being removed from the tables as guests got up from their chairs.

"I see none of the Willoughbys here tonight," David said, "but those two over there—" he discreetly motioned to the left, where two men had stood to help their female companions out of their chairs "—are connected to the family. That fellow is old man Willoughby's banker, and the other is the family's minister."

Miss Hamilton had said the Willoughbys would be attending, but perhaps they had declined at the last minute because of Florence's death. That would be the decorous thing to do. Concordia casually turned her head to look at the men associated with the family. She'd never seen them before. Could one or both of them have attended the meeting in the library? She would need to hear their voices at close range to be able to tell.

But that would have to wait until they were all together again. Now was time for the ladies to enjoy after-dinner coffee in the parlor—the *Marlowe Room*, Concordia amended—and the men to talk in the library over brandy and cigars.

The doorbell rang and a maid hurried to answer it. Concordia lingered in the hallway, curious about the latecomer. To her immense surprise, in the open doorway stood her mother, on the arm of Robert Flynn. The maid took the gentleman's hat.

"Concordia!" Mrs. Wells said delightedly. She embraced her. "How lovely to see you, dear. Have you seen Sophia since she's returned from her honeymoon trip? Yes? Oh, do tell me all about it."

Robert Flynn bowed. "'Tis a pleasure, Miss Wells." He touched Mrs. Wells' elbow. "I'll see myself to the library to join the gentlemen."

Concordia watched him walk away before turning back to her mother.

"I'm so surprised that you're here!" Concordia exclaimed. "What—"

Concordia broke off as Lily Isley rushed up to greet her mother. "Letitia, dear, so happy you could come! I know you are only just returning from the Cartwright benefit; how unfortunate that it coincided with my dinner party."

Mrs. Wells made a face. "I *am* sorry I couldn't get away sooner, Lily, but you understand I was already committed to it.

We came over as soon as we could decently get away. I do hope I'm not inconveniencing you?"

"No, no, not at all," Lily assured her. "Let me get you some coffee and introduce you. We have the most fascinating ladies in our group tonight." She turned mischievously to Concordia. "And of course, you know your own charming daughter. It is so lovely to work with her on the seniors' play this year," she purred.

Mrs. Wells gave Concordia a look, and Concordia stifled a laugh into a hiccup. Obviously, her mother was familiar with Lily Isley's effusive ways and found them amusing. Even though Concordia and her mother approached the world differently— her mother as a well-bred society widow and Concordia as an unconventional lady professor—they'd come to realize they shared the same sense of humor and perceptions about people. She looked forward to regaling her mother with stories of Lily Isley and the senior play preparations. Later, of course.

Concordia followed them into the parlor.

"Ah, Lady Dunwick, may I present Mrs. Wells?" Lily Isley said. "She unfortunately could not join us for dinner, but has graciously taken the time from her charity benefit to pay us a visit over coffee."

"Charmed, Mrs. Wells." Lady Dunwick extended an age-mottled, bony hand that clinked with multiple bracelets. Though by all appearance a petite, thin-boned old lady, she examined everything beneath hooded eyelids, missing little.

"And this is her daughter, Miss Concordia Wells," Mrs. Isley added.

Lady Dunwick peered at Concordia with close interest. "Oh, I have heard of you, my dear."

Concordia was startled. "Me?"

"Oh my, yes," continued Lady Dunwick. "My niece is Charlotte Crandall, who graduated from your college. Nearly two years ago, I believe."

"Charlotte! Why, of course I remember her," Concordia said, smiling. "She was Head Senior and did amazingly well. Quite a composed and studious young lady." Except for that one incident in the garden with a young man, but the less said about that the better. "How is she?"

"Actually, rather at loose ends at the moment," Lady Dunwick answered. "Her school has been shut down and its staff dismissed after a scandal last month. It seems the headmaster eloped with one of the students. The society matrons are all in a dither over *that*. Not Charlotte's fault, of course, nor any of the other instructors. She has a glowing reference but nowhere to go, since it's mid-term at all the schools."

Mrs. Wells sat down and smoothed her skirt. "What a shame."

Concordia joined her mother on the settee. "Let me talk with our lady principal," she said to Lady Dunwick. "We're short-handed at the moment. Perhaps we can use her."

Lady Dunwick clapped her hands together, making the bracelets clink once more. "Wonderful! Charlotte has just come to town for a visit. I know she would be delighted to see you and hear all the news."

"Don't say anything to her yet," Concordia urged. "I wouldn't want to raise her hopes until I'm sure. But I would love to see her again."

"Oh, my dear, come visit us, any time you wish." Lady Dunwick took out one of her cards, and scribbled on the back. "We even have one of those new-fangled telephone contraptions, so I'm writing the number on here. However," she added darkly, "I don't think much of them—one can barely hear the party at the other end. Sounds like there's cannon-fire going off in the background." She shuddered. "So much for modern improvements."

Concordia smiled. She remembered calling Capshaw at the police station once, and it was just like that.

The parlor door opened, and the gentlemen came in. Several rejoined their companions while others headed for the card tables, including Sanders and Sir Anthony.

Maynard, Isley, Flynn and David Bradley were clustered together in earnest debate. Maynard glanced across the room, noticing Concordia for the first time that evening. As she had predicted, the dean scowled in her direction. She resisted the urge to scowl right back.

Lily walked over and tucked her arm in her husband's. "Barton, darling, come join us." She beckoned to the other men in the group. "We'll have a cozy chat over coffee."

Robert Flynn and a smiling David Bradley complied readily. Maynard gave Concordia another black look and reluctantly pulled over a chair.

Concordia looked away. Why did the dean hate her so?

"Barton, this is Letitia Wells, the lady I met at the Atheneum last month. She's a friend of Mr. Flynn."

My pleasure, Mrs. Wells," Isley said, bending over her gloved hand.

A servant came over with the tray of coffee and sweets. "Delightful, thank you," Lily said. "Shall I pour?"

"Please," Concordia said. While she was more of a tea-drinker, the coffee smelled heavenly, and perhaps might serve to sharpen her wits, which felt dulled by the late hour. It was well past her ten o'clock bedtime.

"How is the play coming along?" Barton asked, looking at his wife and Concordia.

Lily smiled and set down her delicate cup to free her hands. Concordia noticed she was fond of gesturing as she spoke. "Wonderfully, dear. Don't you think so, Concordia? For someone with little experience on the stage, this young lady professor has quite a knack for drawing out the best in the girls. And we have discovered a gem of a senior for our Iago. We only have to get her a teensy bit out of her shell, and she will be perfect."

Both Maynard and Flynn reached for their cups in a half-hearted attempt to conceal their disinterest in a mere student play.

"You are doing *Othello*?" Isley asked, eyebrows raised. "Isn't that a bit...dark? I would think a lighter comedy of the bard's would suit better."

Concordia smiled. "The seniors get to choose. Over the past two years, they seem drawn to the 'darker' plays. Last year was *Hamlet;* the year before that was *Macbeth.* This one is no worse than those, really."

"Egad," Flynn chimed in, "'tis rather indelicate to play-act at a woman being...strangled...onstage." His face flushed in his agitation.

Irishmen went red quite easily, Concordia noticed. Mr. Flynn seemed rather stuffy, even for Mother.

Concordia and Lily exchanged a glance, and Lily spoke with some spirit. "Smothered, actually," Lily said blithely. "*I* will be playing Desdemona, Mr. Flynn. I have dramatized more dire roles than this, I can assure you."

Now Barton Isley turned red. "You are *in* the play? You didn't tell me that. I was under the impression you were solely helping to direct."

"It was...recent," Lily lied glibly.

"And we're so fortunate to have such talent at our disposal," Concordia interjected quickly. Her mother's mouth was twitching, either in amusement or disapproval; she couldn't tell which.

But it was Lady Dunwick who smoothed the waters. "Wonderful! I look forward to your performance. I'm sure the addition of such a celebrity will sell a great many tickets, too, Barton." She winked.

At last, Lady Dunwick had found an appeal close to Bursar Isley's heart. "Yes, of course," he said gruffly.

Concordia hid a smile behind her coffee cup.

In a pointed change of subject, Lady Dunwick turned toward David, seated beside Concordia. "Mr. Bradley, I've heard wonderful things about you as well. You teach Chemistry at both Hartford Women's College and Trinity, do you not?"

"Yes, ma'am," David said.

"And I hear that the young ladies are showing an avid interest in the subject." Lady Dunwick waved her fan coquettishly in his direction. "I wonder why that would be?"

David flushed pink. "I cannot say, Lady Dunwick."

She laughed, "My dear boy, don't play coy with me. I would have given my eye-teeth to have a tutor as handsome as you!"

David cleared his throat. "We have several students who have shown quite an interest—and ability—in the mechanical sciences, actually," he said. "A number of them have petitioned our president to seek board approval for a mechanical engineering program at the college."

"Mechanical engineering?" Mrs. Wells interjected. "That doesn't seem a suitable employment for a young lady. Can you imagine these girls wearing *overalls* and tramping down mine-shafts?"

"Mother," Concordia said. She didn't want to open this Pandora's box.

David turned to Mrs. Wells. "It would only be a certification program, not a major course of study. I wouldn't be teaching it, naturally. Professor Merriwether has agreed to be the program's faculty sponsor, and I know of professors at neighboring colleges who would be willing to work with the young ladies on an independent study basis. They would need access to equipment—but the local thread mill would do, to start."

"I've already told Langdon that I'm against it," Barton Isley interjected, puffing out his chest in self-importance. "Besides the cost and the unfeasibility of the enterprise, these young ladies, while hard-working and eager, need to understand boundaries— what's suitable and what's not."

"Exactly," said Mrs. Wells, nodding.

"With all due respect, Bursar Isley, it's not your decision to make," David said firmly.

"Perhaps not, but I have convinced the president to heed my advice, and to not even bring this nonsense before the board," Barton Isley said with a smug look.

Concordia resisted the impulse to ask Isley if the president's buggy had been removed from his office yet. It had been nearly a week. The last she had heard, they had not found anyone skilled enough to safely disassemble the vehicle and remove it. No one had come forward to confess, either.

Better not, she decided. But if things weren't sorted out soon, she would have a word with Miss Lovelace.

Lily Isley interrupted the awkward silence. "Concordia, you and David make a lovely couple."

Having taken this inopportune moment to sip from her cup, Concordia choked and started coughing. Her mother dispassionately patted her on the back, smiling broadly. David shifted in his seat.

"Er, umm," Concordia sputtered, "we are good friends, Mrs. Isley." She turned to David for help.

David took her hand in his. That was certainly *not* helping, Concordia thought frantically. "Thank you, Mrs. Isley," he said solemnly.

Barton Isley chimed in. "Ah, yes, it was only a matter of time, wasn't it? We'll be sorry to lose you, Miss Wells."

Concordia slipped her hand out of David's. "I beg your pardon? I have no intention of leaving the school, Mr. Isley."

Dean Maynard gave a snort. "Should you and Mr. Bradley marry, it would be ludicrous to believe you can maintain a career apart from the home. Hartford Women's College cannot possibly hire a married woman. But perhaps marriage would have a—*settling* effect on you, Miss Wells."

Isley nodded his agreement. "Besides, my dear, it is the duty of every young woman to marry and have children. *That* is your true vocation."

"I have a true vocation already," Concordia said through clenched teeth. Really, what were these men thinking? And they were administrators at a *women's college*?

Maynard had tired of the conversation and was sipping his coffee in silence, a small smile tugging at his mouth. But Barton Isley was not about to let the subject drop. "It's all very well for a young lady to teach and make her little independent way in the world, for a time. In fact, it's quite good for one's character to do so. But when the time comes...." His voice trailed off as the maid approached.

"Excuse me, sir? There is someone at the door, and he insists upon speaking with you." She handed him a card.

One quick glance at it, with Lily looking over his shoulder, and Isley rose. "Put him in the Sophocles Room. Tell him I'll be with him shortly." He turned to the company. "I beg your pardon. Some business has come up that I must attend to."

"What is it, Barton?" Lily asked with alarm. "Is it news of our Africa holdings?"

Barton pressed his lips together. "Later, Lily. Later."

Concordia watched the interchange with fascination. Barton Isley had gone pale at the sight of the name on the card, and was willing to abandon his guests to see to the problem. Could it have something to do with the Inner Circle? But his wife seemed familiar with the name, too, and the Inner Circle would not include women. Then she remembered that both Miss Hamilton and David had mentioned mining investments in ...was it Rhodesia?

Very interesting. Perhaps this was something Miss Hamilton could use, although the connection to Florence's murder and Eli's disappearance seemed difficult to conceive.

Chapter 21

I do perceive here a divided duty.

Othello, *I.iii*

Week 7, Instructor Calendar
March 1898

A short while after Barton left the group, the party broke up. David and Concordia were among the first to leave, while her mother and Robert Flynn remained behind. "Lily and I have some matters to discuss, dear," Mrs. Wells said, with an airy kiss to Concordia's cheek. "But I'll be seeing you soon...your spring recess is next week, is it not?"

Concordia nodded. "We'll make plans for an excursion. Maybe some shopping, or the Atheneum? Splendid. 'Bye, Mother."

The late-March evening air penetrated Concordia's shawl and dress with chill fingers. She shivered as they waited for their cab to pull up.

"Here," David said, taking off his jacket and putting it around her. She nodded her thanks, breathing in the warmth and the scent of sandalwood that clung to it. He helped her up the step.

They rode along in silence for a while. David cleared his throat. "Nice party."

"Yes." Concordia said. "It was a shame that business matters interrupted Mr. Isley's evening."

David was looking out the window, lost in thought. They rode in silence for a while.

In the passing light of street lamps, Concordia stole surreptitious glances at him, noting the heavily-lashed brown eyes, luminous in the light; the broad jawline, with a hint of days-end stubble; the dark hair that curled along his ears and the nape of his neck. Familiar details of someone she felt she knew comfortably well, and yet at the same time she had the sensation of seeing someone new. How well did she know this man? Over the years, they'd chatted about their day-to-day lives—the frustrations, the absurdities. But had she ever asked David about his hopes, his dreams, or even his fears? Suddenly, she wanted to know. Everything. She realized with a shock that she loved him.

As if aware of her glance, David turned toward her. He opened his mouth to say something, then hesitated.

In a flash of understanding she realized that what he wanted to say had been an unspoken barrier between them for a long time.

"What is it, David?" she asked gently.

He took her gloved hand in his, and Concordia let it rest there.

"I've been thinking about this for quite a while," he said. "I love you, Concordia. I want you to marry me."

Concordia's hand trembled in his, and he held it tightly.

"I would make you a good husband," he continued. "I want you to have a place that you can call your own, where you can be mistress of your own house, where we could be partners, sharing our life together."

Concordia looked up at him, searching his eyes for something—what, she didn't know. "What about my teaching?" she asked in a shaky voice.

He kissed a spot on her inner wrist, just below her glove, which made her breath catch in her throat. "You're a wonderful teacher, my dear. I know it will be difficult to give that up. But your talents won't go to waste, I can assure you. When children come along...what a wonderful mother they will have."

Mercy! Children.... Concordia felt as if she'd been pulled into a whirlwind. She had never particularly cared for children, whom she found loud, runny-nosed, and generally annoying. Except for Eli. Her expression softened. The boy had slipped into her heart and found a place there. Surely, that would happen with her own children.

"You can see how impractical it would be for you to continue at the college after we're married," David went on. "That is the sphere for single ladies. But when they marry, they start a new life. A wonderful new life."

Concordia's chest constricted. "I do love you," she said.

"Oh, my dear," he gathered her into his arms and she put her head on his shoulder.

Eventually, he pulled away to look into her eyes. "So, will you make me the happiest man alive? *Will* you marry me?"

Concordia hesitated.

"Trust me," he said, holding both of her hands firmly. "Your happiness will be my goal, for the rest of our lives together."

He waited patiently through the silence.

"Yes," she said, after a long moment. "Yes, David, I will marry you."

He pulled her close and kissed her, for a long time. Concordia felt her worries dissolve away, replaced by something else, a longing she'd only half-suspected she possessed.

He chuckled deep in his throat when he finally let her go. "I have been wanting to do that for a very long time."

"When did you know?" she asked.

"It may have been as early as the first time we met—when you ran me down with your bicycle."

She laughed. "*Almost* ran you down," she corrected.

The cab lurched to a halt outside the college gate. Concordia could see the gatekeeper waiting.

"We have so much to take care of—" David began.

Concordia held up a hand. "Will you do one thing for me?"

"Of course."

"I want to keep this just between us for the time being, until the end of the semester."

David frowned. "Why?"

"I don't want the work I'm doing now to be—changed—by everyone anticipating my departure. You heard how Mr. Isley talked tonight, even though you hadn't even made a declaration. During this spring term—my last—I don't want to feel that people are treating me as if I'm already gone. Can you understand that?"

David hesitated, then nodded. "I think I do. I suppose we can wait to tell everyone, although that won't be easy for me. I want to stand on top of this cab and tell the world. But what about the school? They'll need to replace you."

"The college will have plenty of time during the summer to find someone. We can announce it near the end of term."

David grinned and, when the gatekeeper wasn't looking, snuck another kiss on her wrist that made her shiver. He helped her out of the carriage.

"I'll be fine walking back from here," Concordia said. "Good night, David."

"Good night, Concordia. Pleasant dreams."

Chapter 22

March 1898
Week 7, Instructor Calendar

Between the coffee and the proposal, Concordia barely slept at all. She smothered yawns throughout her morning classes.

She returned to Willow Cottage to find Miss Hamilton waiting in the parlor. She stopped short. "Weren't we supposed to meet this evening?"

"I was anxious to learn how last night went," Miss Hamilton said. "Do you have a few minutes now?"

Concordia glanced at the mantel clock and nodded.

After glancing down the empty hallway, Miss Hamilton closed the parlor door. "Did you learn anything?"

"Did I ever." It had been quite an evening of discovery, in fact, but Concordia pushed David firmly out of her mind. She wasn't ready to talk to Penelope Hamilton, or anyone, about her engagement yet. *Engagement. Mercy.*

She recounted what she had overheard beneath the Isley library window.

Miss Hamilton tapped her chin thoughtfully. "So an 'Inner Circle'—whatever that may be—exists within the Black Scroll. Interesting. But we only know the identities of two men in the group: your bursar and Sir Anthony Dunwick."

"Based upon voices alone," Concordia said, "I know there were at least two other men in the room. I didn't recognize those. There may have been others who weren't contributing to the conversation."

"Did any of the Willoughbys attend the party?" Miss Hamilton asked.

"No direct family members, but Mr. Bradley indicated a couple of guests with Willoughby family connections – a banker and a minister. They left before I had a chance to strike up a conversation and hear their voices."

"So this meeting happened before dinner?" Miss Hamilton asked.

"Yes, shortly after the Republican candidate, Mr. Sanders, arrived," Concordia said. "Perhaps that is not a coincidence."

Miss Hamilton considered this in silence.

"How is this connected to Florence's death?" Concordia asked. "You told me she had family connections to the Black Scroll. But are they Inner Circle members?"

"That's what troubles me," Miss Hamilton answered. "The existence of this Inner Circle can only mean that some men from the Brotherhood have their own agenda: one so secret—perhaps illegal—that they would not care to share it with the rest of the members. Instead, they've formed their own enclave. It could be very powerful indeed."

"Mr. Isley characterized the Inner Circle's existence as necessary to more efficiently carry out special projects," Concordia said. "It didn't sound particularly nefarious."

"Did you hear any discussion as to what these 'projects' might be?" Miss Hamilton asked.

"No, but our bursar doesn't strike me as a man craving power for himself. Dropping out of the state senate race to help with the finances of a women's college doesn't seem terribly ambitious."

"We know that Isley is wealthy in his own right, besides being well-connected," Miss Hamilton said. "I doubt the man has abandoned his political aspirations. He could have other reasons for withdrawing his candidacy, and may simply be biding his time."

"Perhaps," Concordia said. "That reminds me. Mr. Bradley told me there's a rumor that the Isley wealth is 'tied up' in mining investments—I'm assuming these are the Rhodesian copper mines you were telling me about—and the Isleys haven't seen much return on it yet. And near the end of the gathering, someone came to see Barton Isley. His wife asked him if it was in reference to their 'Africa investments.' She seemed quite anxious."

Miss Hamilton perked up. "Did she? I'll look into that. Perhaps that's why Isley was in such a black mood when I encountered him on the path this morning."

Concordia smiled. "That probably has more to do with President Langdon's buggy making his office unusable this past week."

Miss Hamilton chuckled. "I heard about that. But tell me more about Lily Isley. How involved is she in her husband's affairs? One would think that a wife would be bored to tears with politics."

Concordia shook her head. "Not so with Lily. She's an unusually talented woman, quick-witted and charming. She certainly held her own when political topics crept into general conversation last night. Yet I find it surprising that she is so warmly accepted into that sphere."

"Glamour and money can go a long way in bringing a candidate's name to the front of people's minds," Miss Hamilton said with a smile.

"So, even though she is a woman in a man's realm, Mrs. Isley's involvement has been accepted because associating with a celebrated, flamboyant former stage actress will draw more attention?"

Miss Hamilton nodded. "Exactly." She fished among the papers littering the coffee table—when would those heedless girls learn to clean up after themselves, Concordia wondered—and pulled out a sheet of newsprint. "I read an account of the dinner party this morning. It lists everyone in attendance. Perhaps you can put names to the faces you saw in the corridor during the dinner bell."

Concordia glanced at the title: *Former Celebrated Stage Actress Lily Isley and Husband Host a Charming Evening for Republican Candidate Sanders*. She glanced over the list, shaking her head as she handed it back. "I recognize a few. It was too crowded for me to see anyone coming directly out of the library as we were being seated. I only know we can eliminate David, Lily, and Lady Dunwick, but the women wouldn't be suspect, anyway. Oh, and my mother and Mr. Flynn, who didn't arrive at the party until after dinner."

"What about—" Miss Hamilton glanced at the clipping "—Dean Maynard? Could he have been among the group in the library?"

Concordia grimaced. "I'd hate to think so, but it's possible. I didn't notice him until we were all seated in the dining room. He was on the far side." Which suited her just fine, given his sour disposition. "I take it you believe the Inner Circle is in some way connected to Florence's death?"

"That is what my instincts are telling me," Miss Hamilton said.

"Instincts? That doesn't sound very reliable," Concordia said with a smile.

"Sometimes, instincts are all one has to go on. Associations, rumors, coincidences. My job involves following all of these leads, and pulling on each thread until it either leads me to something more, or stops cold."

Following rumors and associations was a sordid business, as Concordia herself remembered from earlier experiences with Miss Hamilton's investigation. But she knew it had to be done.

Then she thought of something. "There may be someone who can help us," Concordia said. "I'll be right back."

Miss Hamilton raised a quizzical brow as Concordia hurried across the hall to her rooms.

She soon returned, holding Ben Rosen's business card. "He's a newspaper reporter," Concordia explained, passing it over. "He helped during the investigation into Colonel Adams' murder last year. I saw him again a few weeks ago, when he was at the college doing a story on Ruby and her award. He gave me his card and offered any future help I might need."

"Indeed?" Miss Hamilton said, lips quirked in a wry smile. "And why would a newspaper reporter imagine a lady professor having need of his services?"

Concordia, not inclined to repeat Rosen's *lady sleuth* comment, merely shrugged.

Miss Hamilton turned the card over thoughtfully. "I'll contact Mr. Rosen, and ask him to meet us at his earliest convenience."

"What about Eli? Have you made any progress?" Concordia asked.

"I've made inquiries at the train station. I'm convinced that's where Eli was headed after the newsie saw him chasing a cab."

"Really? Why?" Concordia asked.

"It's not far-fetched to believe the cab was headed toward the depot. Asylum Avenue runs right through there. Since Eli couldn't possibly maintain a foot pursuit with a moving carriage, what did he do next? He hypothesized that this person was taking the train. Thus, Eli could hitch a ride aboard, say, an expressman's wagon heading for the station. The difficulty lay in finding the killer again along the right platform. But we can assume that Eli was successful, since he didn't return here to notify the Capshaws. He was hot on the trail."

"Did anyone see him there?"

"No one noticed an unattended boy on the platform—but you know how crowded that place can be. I've interviewed all of the porters, and nearly all of the conductors, save one. A family emergency called him out of town. The company has promised to contact me when he returns."

"What can *I* do?" Concordia asked. "I feel so helpless, waiting here doing nothing."

"We know Bursar Isley is a member of the Inner Circle," Miss Hamilton said. "Learn everything you can about him."

"But how can I do that?" Concordia objected. Then she had an idea. "Perhaps by getting closer to *Mrs.* Isley?"

"Splendid," Miss Hamilton said.

Chapter 23

Week 8, Instructor Calendar
March/April 1898

The students were restless in the Shakespeare class, anxious to start their spring recess.

"I have a surprise for you," Concordia said, handing back graded papers. "Mrs. Isley will be speaking with us today about the modern dramatization of Shakespeare. As you may know, she was a stage actress years ago, before her marriage to our bursar."

The students leaned forward in interest.

"Now, I expect you all to give her your undivided—"

She was interrupted by a brisk knock.

Concordia motioned to a girl to open the door while she cleared off the podium for her guest.

"Hello, my dears!" Lily Isley exclaimed, beaming at the class. She was accompanied by a boy carrying a box. "Just set it down over there, young man. Excellent."

"We are so looking forward to your talk, Mrs. Isley," Concordia said. She glanced at the box as she seated herself among the students. She hoped they weren't in for any monkeyshines.

As Concordia watched Lily Isley dig through her box, she wondered what the woman might know about her husband's Inner Circle activities. It was doubtful she knew anything at all, and more doubtful that Concordia could tactfully lead a conversation along such lines. Still, she resolved to try.

At least Miss Hamilton had arranged for Mr. Rosen to meet with them later today. That was bound to be more productive.

The students sat in rapt attention as Lily began her presentation, using props from her box. She employed simple items—hats, wigs, cloaks—along with mannerisms, voice, and posture to expertly convey the sense that they were seeing a queen, an old woman, a spritely nymph. The effect was mesmerizing.

"Amazing," Concordia murmured at one point in the presentation. The woman had more ability than she'd thought.

Just as class was drawing to a close, a scuttling sound came from the back of the room. A mechanical object moved toward Lily Isley at a rapid pace.

"*Eek!*" Lily shrieked, jumping onto the instructor's platform. There were a few smothered laughs, but most of the students merely stared, open-mouthed. The mechanism wound down as it bumped against the step.

"Mrs. Isley, I apologize!" Concordia said, horrified. " Are you all right?"

Lily, hand on her chest, gave a shaky laugh. "I'm fine, dear. My, my! I've had many a strange thing happen on the stage, but never...this." She gestured toward the object.

"Who did this?" Concordia demanded, glaring at the students. A tentative hand was raised. It was Miss Lovelace, soon followed by two more girls raising their hands.

The bell rang.

"What a—*lively* bunch of young ladies," Mrs. Isley murmured. Before Concordia could say anything more, or offer to take her to the faculty lounge for a restorative cup of tea, the lady turned on her heel and hurried out of the room, giving the mechanism on the floor a wide berth.

Concordia hesitated, wondering if she should follow Mrs. Isley and apologize again. But she had the miscreants to deal with. "You three, remain behind," she said in a stern voice. "Class dismissed. Remember your assignments over the spring recess." She gingerly picked up the contraption and held it with two fingers as the class filed out.

When the room was cleared of all but Concordia and the three pranksters, Concordia sat down and motioned to them to do the same. "What exactly *is* this...thing?"

Miss Lovelace spoke up. "It's our first attempt at a wind-up toy. The three of us have been working on it, off and on, for several weeks. Uncle Warren—remember I told you about him?—let us borrow more of his tools, and gave us spare gears and other parts." She gestured to the object. "I know it looks rather strange, but we're starting with something four-legged because it's more stable."

Concordia examined it more closely. It had a clock-work body and sharp-toothed external gears. "The key-winding mechanism appears to be stuck," she said, turning it over. Although crude in appearance, it was astonishing what these girls had been able to do on their own.

One of the girls nodded. "That's been giving us trouble. We've taken apart several old clocks, but we don't have soldering tools to really make the parts fit together the way we want. We're planning to keep working on it at my house during the recess." She paused. "If you don't confiscate it, that is."

"We'll see. Whatever possessed you to set it off in class? You know I cannot tolerate that sort of disruption. And in front of Mrs. Isley, too."

"It was an accident, Miss Wells," Maisie Lovelace said sheepishly. "I pulled it out of my satchel to make room for a book, and the gear had some life left in it. We'll write a note of apology to Mrs. Isley," she added.

"That's not the only apology you have to make," Concordia said sternly. Noting the partly-open classroom door, she closed it before continuing. "How long are you going to allow Mr. Langdon's buggy to reside in Bursar Isley's office? It has been over a week now."

She waited through the silence. The girls shifted from foot to foot, looking at Miss Lovelace.

"We were going to say something right away, honestly," Miss Lovelace said. "We thought for sure they would figure out it was us, and we could put in another plea for our program. But

Mr. Langdon started looking into whether the Trinity boys could have done it, and then it got into the newspapers...."

"You mustn't let fear guide your actions," Concordia said. "*Courage is resistance to fear, mastery of fear—not absence of fear.*"

Miss Lovelace gave her a quizzical look. "*Macbeth?*"

"*Pudd'nhead Wilson,*" Concordia said.

Maisie Lovelace gave a weak smile.

"I will make the decision easy for you," Concordia said. "Either go to President Langdon today and confess, or by supper-time I will tell him."

They heard a polite tap on the classroom door.

"Come in!" Concordia called.

David Bradley walked in. He hesitated, taking in the sight of glum-looking students and a tight-lipped Concordia.

"Pardon me, ladies. I hope I'm not interrupting?"

"Not at all," Concordia said. "Come in, Mr. Bradley. We're finished here." She handed back the students' wind-up device. "Best to take care of your...task, right away."

The girls glanced at Mr. Bradley as they shuffled past, nudging and whispering to each other, giving Concordia a meaningful look as they walked out.

Land sakes.

"What was that about?" David asked.

Concordia shook her head. "Just something between me and my girls." She smiled, then checked her watch. "Were we supposed to meet?"

David leaned against the desk and regarded her warmly. "It feels like ages since I saw you, even though it's only been a few days." He came closer. "You look lovely."

As Concordia was wearing only her second-best pleated shirtwaist and a plain navy wool skirt at the moment, she very much doubted she appeared at her best advantage. Still, she blushed at the compliment, self-consciously groping for the pencil that inevitably found its way into her topknot and smoothing straggling wisps of hair back into their pins. "You are too kind." She turned away and grabbed her satchel case.

"Regrettably, I'm late for DeLacey House. Later this evening, perhaps?"

David's smile dimmed. "I have a lecture. I'd hoped we could have tea in the faculty lounge, since you're finished with classes for the day. I haven't seen you in a while."

Concordia saw the disappointment in his eyes. "I'm sorry, David. I have an appointment."

David held the door for her. "I see. The lady principal wants you?"

Concordia hesitated. She couldn't tell David that she and Miss Hamilton were meeting with the newspaper reporter. Heaven only knew how he'd react to *that*.

She tried to be as honest as she could. "Miss Hamilton, actually."

David's expression brightened as they walked up the path to DeLacey House. "I recall seeing her on campus these past two weeks. Her niece just had a baby, is that right?"

Concordia nodded wordlessly, loathing all of the lies she was telling the man she had just promised to marry. *Oh, what a tangled web we weave…When first we practice to deceive!*

"Perhaps I can join you two," David offered. "I'm sure Miss Hamilton wouldn't mind."

Now would be the time to tell him about Eli's disappearance, to explain that they were meeting Ben Rosen in order to find answers that might bring them closer to finding the boy.

And yet, she stayed silent, unsure how to even begin.

As they approached the door of DeLacey House, Concordia's heart sank as she saw Mr. Rosen ringing the bell. He tipped his bowler politely in their direction. "G'afternoon, miss. Glad I'm not late." He gave David Bradley a puzzled look before his brow cleared. "Ah yes, I remember you. Mr. Bradley, isn't it? The Masquerade Ball last year." Rosen extended a hand. "Ben Rosen, from the *Courant*."

David perfunctorily shook his hand and turned to Concordia. "What is going on? You're here to meet *this man*?" His voice was stiff with anger.

The front door opened and the maid looked at them curiously when no one responded. "Miss Wells? Miss Hamilton is expecting you and the gentleman in the parlor."

Concordia put a conciliatory hand on David's arm as Rosen raised an eyebrow. "I can explain later."

David shook off her hand and walked away.

Chapter 24

You shall more command with years
Than with your weapons.

Othello, I.*ii*

The parlor fire at DeLacey House burned brightly in the grate, but it could do nothing for the chill Concordia felt after watching David stalk off without a word. She should have told him everything when she'd had the chance.

But she didn't have the luxury of dwelling on that now. Mr. Rosen stood waiting for Concordia to take her seat.

"Tea, Mr. Rosen?" Miss Hamilton offered, gesturing to the tray.

"Got any coffee, miss?"

"I'm afraid not," Miss Hamilton said.

"Then no, thanks. I cannot abide tea. Only fit for the sickroom." Rosen sat and put his hat on a nearby chair. "Ladies, what can I do for you?"

Concordia glanced at Miss Hamilton. How much should they reveal?

Miss Hamilton carefully plucked a sugar cube with delicate tongs, stirred, and sipped before answering. "We require information about an organization called the Fraternal Order of the Black Scroll: its members, its mission, and what its current activities might be."

Rosen rubbed a hand through his grizzled beard. He chuckled. "That's all? Anything else? How 'bout a private audience wi' the queen?"

"I know it's asking a great deal," Miss Hamilton said, unruffled, "but were the information easily acquired, we would have done it ourselves."

Rosen grunted. "I'll bet you would have." He pointed a thumb toward Penelope Hamilton and asked Concordia, "Is she a lady sleuth too?"

Concordia stiffened. "Certainly not."

Mercy, she'd told a number of lies today. What would her minister say?

"Then why d'you want to know about the Black Scroll?" Rosen asked.

"Let us just say we're concerned about a...relative...who is a member. We want to know more about what he may be involved in," Miss Hamilton said.

"Ah, you think something illegal's going on?" Rosen's eyes brightened. "Say, that sounds promising."

"We don't know for sure, you understand," Concordia broke in quickly. "That's why we need you to look into it. Will you help us?" She gestured to the purse beside Miss Hamilton. "We can pay you."

"Well, I don't think you're bein' quite honest with me," Rosen said warily, "but I never turned away a greenback in my life. I've heard of the Black Scroll, the name at least. I should be able to find out something. All right, miss, you have a deal. But I want the exclusive on this, if it turns out to be a story worth printing."

"When the time is right," Miss Hamilton answered. "For now, it must be a *discreet* inquiry."

"Of course."

Miss Hamilton passed him half the bills, which he stuffed in his jacket pocket. He picked up his hat and stood. "I'll contact you by the end of the week. Is there anything else I should know?"

Concordia and Penelope Hamilton exchanged a long look. *Should we tell him about the Inner Circle?* was the unspoken question between them. Concordia wondered if they were sending Mr. Rosen on a dangerous errand, and groping blind. Shouldn't he know about Florence's murder and Eli's disappearance? Rosen would then be in a better position to help. But could they trust him?

Rosen eyed them quizzically as the silence lengthened.

"We should tell him," Concordia finally said aloud.

Miss Hamilton sighed. "You're right." She gestured to Rosen. "You'd better sit back down. My apologies for not being as forthcoming as we should." She gave Concordia a quick glance. "Let us hope you're inclined to take on this job after you learn the whole story."

After Rosen left—still willing to help, thankfully—Concordia asked, "What do we do next?"

"I have an appointment tomorrow with the Hartford station train conductor who has been away," Miss Hamilton said. "He may have some of the answers we need."

Chapter 25

Week 8, Instructor Calendar
March/April 1898

Concordia returned to Willow Cottage, where a flurry of packing was underway.

"Don't take too much," Concordia warned, as she caught sight of one girl lugging two suitcases from the storeroom, "it's only a week, after all."

"Ooh, but Miss Wells," she said excitedly, "I've been invited to Miss Smedley's country house! I'll need my best dresses, and Mabel has promised to lend me her riding outfit, and—"

"Have a wonderful time," Concordia said, cutting across what promised to be a lengthy description of the young lady's wardrobe necessities. "Have you seen Ruby?"

"In her room, packing."

"Packing?" Ruby never left for the spring recess.

Concordia went down the hall to the bedroom behind the kitchen and knocked.

"Ruby?"

"Come on in, miss," Ruby called. "I'm jes' finishing up."

Concordia pushed open the door. "Where are you going?"

"To my sister's, in New Haven," Ruby said, struggling with a suitcase buckle. "Well, you needn't look so surprised," she added tartly, noting Concordia's raised eyebrow. "I got family, and like to take a vacation as much as the rest o' you."

"Of course," Concordia said hastily, "I'm only surprised. You didn't say anything about it before."

"I didn't know I needed your 'pproval," Ruby muttered under her breath.

Concordia took a step back, confused. She'd known Ruby for several years now, and thought she'd seen all of her moods. But this sulky defensiveness had never been one of them. What was going on?

Judging from the set of the woman's jaw, pressing her now wasn't going to get an answer.

"Well, I'll leave you to it, then. Have a good visit," Concordia said hesitantly, and closed the door behind her.

Concordia clambered around several luggage-laden students in the hallway—why did the girls feel compelled to pack all of their worldly belongings for an eight-day visit home? Her own rooms were probably the safest place away from the hubbub. She dearly needed a cup of tea, and time alone to think.

She stopped short when she saw Maisie Lovelace walk through the front door. One glance at the girl's tear-streaked face told Concordia that the interview with President Langdon had not gone well. She went over to her, putting her arm around the girl's shoulders. "Let's go to my rooms where we can talk."

Miss Lovelace sagged into a chair and put her face in her hands as Concordia closed the door. "We've been ex-expelled," she moaned.

Concordia had feared as much. President Langdon, though not generally a strict disciplinarian, was understandably distressed about his brand-new buggy being stuck in Bursar Isley's office for the last ten days. Then there was the newspaper publicity, too.

"I take it he was quite angry," Concordia said.

Miss Lovelace nodded. "The dean and bursar came in when they heard Mr. Langdon shouting, and that just made things worse. It was Dean Maynard and Bursar Isley who insisted that we be expelled. We are to remove the buggy during spring recess, and then leave. For...for good."

It was unfortunate, Concordia thought, that the other two administrators had intervened. Langdon might not have taken such strict action if he'd had the solitude to consider his own penalty. Even a suspension for the rest of the semester would have been preferable.

She passed the girl her handkerchief. "Take a moment to compose yourself, then we'll talk about what we can do."

Concordia took a deep breath and knocked on Langdon's door.

"Enter!"

She poked her head in. "May I speak with you?"

"Of course." Langdon stood and gestured to the chair beside his desk.

Concordia took a deep breath for courage. She'd known President Langdon since she had started teaching at Hartford Women's College, back when he was dean. She'd always found him to be fair-minded. Although the man harbored many of the old ideas about women and what their role in society should be, he was dedicated to the college's mission to provide the young ladies with the best education possible.

Concordia got right to the point. "Mr. Langdon, I want to speak with you about Miss Lovelace and her friends, who are on the verge of being expelled."

Langdon's brow furrowed, and his usually amiable expression took on a scowl. "Are you here to plead on their behalf? You're wasting your time."

Concordia held up a hand. "What they did was certainly disruptive and ill-considered, but can you hear me out?"

President Langdon gave Concordia a long, silent look. Finally, he sighed in resignation and sat back in his chair. "If it were anyone but you, Concordia, I would not. But I do respect your opinion, and I know you're not easily influenced by sentimentality. Perhaps you can help me at least understand why in blazes they decided to do such a thing."

She nodded. "That is the very issue. This wasn't some high-spirited prank, done in malice or to show off to their peers. They had an earnest motive behind it."

Langdon waved a dismissive hand. "You mean the engineering program? The girls have already explained their reasons. It makes no sense to me, and I certainly cannot condone such behavior. If anything, these young ladies have already acted in a distinctly unwomanly fashion. A course of study like engineering, suited to *men,* would exacerbate the problem, not solve it."

Concordia clenched her teeth. She needed all of the patience she could muster. It certainly would not do to fly off the handle when faced with this all-too-common misconception about a woman's "nature."

"Sir," Concordia began, "the act that you call *unwomanly* is merely the attempt on the part of these girls to prove that they are capable of the mechanical complexity called for in an engineering program. Granted, the demonstration was flamboyant, designed to draw attention to the issue, but you said yourself that not even the local mechanic wants to attempt dismantling and reassembling the vehicle because of the risk of damage to it. Doesn't that speak to extraordinary skill, that these young ladies were able to do so?"

Langdon regarded her with a skeptical eye.

"Do you deny that they have exceptional ability?" Concordia persisted. She knew Edward Langdon would not allow bias to interfere with the evidence of his own eyes.

Langdon's expression softened. "Just between us, I was astounded when each girl described her role in the process; what tools they knew to borrow and use, how they had taught themselves to do certain things. Yes, Concordia, they certainly have skill; talent, even. However—"

Concordia jumped in. "God-given talent?"

Langdon hesitated. "Yes, I suppose it is."

"So, let us suppose, in the hypothetical," Concordia went on, "that a different talent bestowed by Providence was at issue. Suppose one of these girls had an extraordinary singing voice. What would you do—redirect her into another area of study for which she was ill-suited, forever muting her beautiful voice? Would you forbid her to use and develop her talent because of her sex?"

Langdon was quiet.

"The President Langdon whom I have come to know," Concordia said softly, "would want her to take singing lessons with the best teacher available, and he would attend her performances as her most avid supporter. The Edward Langdon I know believes deeply in the education of young women, and wants them to reach their full potential." Concordia let out a deep breath, and sat back in her chair, gloved hands folded in her lap.

Langdon rubbed a hand across his beard, lost in thought. Concordia waited.

"At least we know where you belong, my dear," Langdon said. "Right here, teaching and supporting these girls. They are lucky to have you."

Concordia blushed and smoothed her skirts.

"Although I cannot refute your logic, I see two issues," he went on. "There's the disciplinary action for a prank of this kind—although I cannot say there has ever been a prank *quite* of this kind before—and then, there's the original problem that the girls were reacting to: the lack of an engineering program."

Concordia's eyes lit up. "So you're not going to expel them?"

Langdon threw up his hands in surrender. "Why waste such ability? But we need to direct these young ladies along more productive pursuits. We certainly cannot have them disassembling and reassembling other school machinery when they are disgruntled."

Concordia suppressed a shudder. Heaven knows what the girls would have resorted to next.

"You never brought the certificate program before the board of trustees?" she asked.

"No, I did not," Langdon said. "Bursar Isley was vehemently opposed to the expense. You know how, umm...frugal...our bursar can be. Without the support of the entire administration, it was doomed to fail. Besides, there is a great deal of skepticism regarding such a program to begin with. It's never been done at a women's college before, you see."

Concordia did indeed see. "I have an idea. Perhaps we can take care of both issues in a single stroke."

Langdon propped his elbows on the desk. "I'm listening."

"Obviously, the first step is to have the young ladies disassemble your buggy, remove it from Mr. Isley's office, and restore it, correct?"

Langdon nodded.

"Well, then, why not make an event out of it?" Concordia continued. "The incident has already been made public, anyway. Call in that newspaper reporter—" Langdon winced "—and the engineering students from the local colleges, and have the girls show everyone how they worked the process. It would have to be after we're back from spring recess, of course, so you'd have to wait a bit longer for use of your vehicle. But the publicity may make others more aware of what talent we have here, and sow the seeds for the engineering program, which you can present to the board next year."

"But that doesn't seem sufficient punishment for the young ladies involved," Langdon objected. "They cannot just seize upon valuable property that doesn't belong to them, and use it for their own purposes."

"Ah, but that isn't all," Concordia said. "And I think the next part will please Mr. Isley in particular." *Bless his penny-pinching heart,* she added silently. "You can place the girls on restriction for the rest of the semester, where in their free time they are put to work fixing various mechanical problems that have arisen at the school. Door latches, sticking windows, broken pulleys on window-blinds, things like that. We never want for those sorts of annoyances. Of course, you'll want someone knowledgeable in such things to supervise them and help if there are any difficulties. Perhaps the custodian?"

Langdon's smile was growing wider by the minute. "I'm beginning to see the appeal of your plan." He tapped his chin thoughtfully. "And by putting these girls to work on such projects, we can see if they are truly dedicated and suited for such tasks."

"No doubt they will learn a great deal, too," Concordia pointed out. "It's certainly not the certificate program that they wanted, but they'll be getting a lot of hands-on practice."

"It may even prove to be useful if we go to the board next year about the program," Langdon mused.

"So you'll do it?" Concordia asked.

He nodded. "I suppose I can wait another week to have my buggy back. At least Isley won't be in need of his office during the recess." He stood, as did Concordia. "Tell the young ladies to be prepared for a great deal of work when they return."

Concordia grinned, and hurried back to share the good news with the girls.

By the end of the following day, the campus was nearly deserted. The students and most of the teachers had gone. Even Miss Hamilton was nowhere to be found. Concordia wondered if she had learned anything at the train station yesterday.

The cottage was strangely quiet as she finished grading examinations. She knew she would have no time to work once she visited her mother tomorrow. The rest of the week was sure to be a whirlwind of outings, shopping, and social calls. But the visit would be as good a time as any to share the news of her engagement.

Concordia puckered her brow, wondering how to tell her mother that the engagement was to be kept secret for now. Would Mother accede to that request? Or would she haul Concordia around town, shopping for a trousseau?

That would not do. She would have to be very firm.

A knock at the door roused her.

"This is a surprise!" Concordia exclaimed, opening the door to Lieutenant Capshaw.

"Hello, miss." Although the shadows of sleepless nights smudged his eyes—worry about Eli's long absence was surely taking its toll—Capshaw greeted her with a half-smile.

She led him to the parlor. "Please, sit down. You have news?"

Capshaw crouched gingerly upon a low rocking chair, his long legs bent nearly double. "Indeed, yes. I just received a telegram from Miss Hamilton. She was writing in haste, and asked me to inform you as well. Her interview with the conductor has given her the lead she needed. She's picked up Eli's trail."

"Wonderful!" Concordia exclaimed.

"But you're not going to like the rest of it," Capshaw said, in his usual melancholy tone. "Eli spent time in the Cranston town jail for sneaking aboard the train bound for Hartford."

Concordia clenched her hands together. "They put a *child* in jail?"

"It was the day after Florence's murder," Capshaw explained, his jaw rigid. "He was released three days later, into the care of a reformatory school matron, but he slipped away from her. Miss Hamilton is trying to trace his whereabouts since then."

"Wait," Concordia said. "How did Eli come to be boarding a train *to* Hartford? From where? And why Cranston, Rhode Island?"

"The train originated in Providence. The boy was caught between there and Cranston."

"And Miss Hamilton thinks he's been following Florence Willoughby's killer," Concordia said. Her stomach twisted in worry. Where was Eli now? It would have been several weeks since the boy's release from jail. Why hadn't he returned?

Capshaw ran a hand through his hair. "I am sorely tempted to join Miss Hamilton in the hunt, and risk losing my position," he said. "Why didn't Eli send word?"

The pained look on Capshaw's face spoke volumes about the agony of a parent who cannot do anything but sit back and wait.

"I assume Miss Hamilton is checking with the doctors in the town, in case the boy was injured?" Concordia asked.

Capshaw nodded. "I have to say, my respect for Miss Hamilton has grown considerably. She's a very thorough investigator."

Indeed she was. Concordia smiled.

"But that's not the only reason for my visit," Capshaw said. "I need to speak to Ruby."

Concordia raised an eyebrow. "You haven't talked with her yet?" It had been weeks since Capshaw had begun his investigation of the mysterious man on campus.

Capshaw frowned. "I've rescheduled our meeting twice, after she sent me messages with some excuse or other as to why it was inconvenient. It seemed prudent to simply show up to talk with her."

Concordia shook her head. Something was wrong here. Why was Ruby acting so strangely? "Ruby left for vacation yesterday. She won't be back until the end of the week."

Capshaw's frown deepened into a scowl. "She's deliberately avoiding me."

Concordia nodded. "Reluctantly, I'd have to agree. But why?"

"I can think of only one explanation, miss. Ruby knows this man. And she's protecting him."

Chapter 26

Why do you speak so faintly?
Are you not well?

Othello, *III.iii*

Spring Recess
April 1898

Concordia rang the bell of her mother's house in the Frog Hollow section of Hartford.

The housekeeper opened the door wide. "Miss Concordia! So glad you've come for a visit." She reached for Concordia's valise. "Here, let me take that. Come in!"

"It's nice to be home," Concordia said. "How are you, Mrs. Houston?"

The housekeeper bobbed her head. "Doin' just fine, dear, but you look a bit thinner than when I saw you last, if you don't mind me sayin' so. You've been working too hard, I expect."

Concordia smiled at the housekeeper's maternal ways. Some things never change. "Where's Mother?"

"She's resting," Mrs. Houston said, "but she'll be getting up any minute now. Why don't you go into the parlor? There's a nice fire going, and I'll bring you a cup of tea."

"That would be lovely."

The parlor was much the way Concordia remembered. Her mother's love of order was evident in the matching armchairs with their ornately turned legs, the regimental arrangement of portraits along the far wall, and the evenly spaced set of candlesticks on the mantel. However, the décor seemed to have softened over time; the heavy drapes had been replaced with lighter sheers to let the light and the breezes in; several large crystal bowls of cut flowers topped the tables.

She settled into the burgundy velvet armchair that had been a favorite of her father's while he was alive. Was it her imagination, or did she catch a faint scent of his pipe tobacco, nearly thirteen years after his death? Impossible, she decided.

Concordia was pouring out tea for herself when her mother walked in, dressed in a simple dove gray sateen wrapper, her silvering blonde hair piled in soft waves atop her head. Concordia was struck by how happy Mother looked these days, and much younger than her fifty-six years.

Mrs. Wells came over and gave her an airy kiss on the cheek. "Concordia dear, I've been looking forward to your spring recess for weeks. We'll have such fun. The first order of business, of course, is shopping."

"It is?" Concordia repeated blankly. *Oh, no.* Had Mother already heard about her engagement? Were they going shopping for bridal clothes?

"Yes, of course...oh! I forgot to tell you. I'll be accompanying Robert and his family on a steamer tour of Ireland in the summer. I need traveling clothes."

Concordia blinked. "Excuse me?" Her mother, traveling with a man? And Mr. Flynn at that. The relationship seemed to be progressing faster than Concordia realized.

"I'm sorry," Mrs. Wells said, flustered. "I got so busy that I forgot to write you about it."

"Not at all," Concordia reassured her. "I'm usually the one who forgets to tell *you* things." That brought a smile. "Why don't I pour you some tea and you can tell me about this trip." She picked up the antique silver teapot.

"It's a group of us, really," her mother explained. "Several ladies from the Irish Aid Society, Mr. Flynn, his mother and sister. It's all very proper," she added hastily. "I'll be sharing accommodations with two other ladies, and we'll be visiting the orphanages that we have been raising funds for. We'll also visit the Flynn family's birthplace. Robert is most eager to have me see it."

"That sounds quite exciting," Concordia said politely. "You are serious about Mr. Flynn, then? Does he return the feeling?"

Her mother flushed and kept her eyes upon her cup. "We don't have a spoken understanding, but we spend quite a bit of time together, and he's a most agreeable gentleman. I esteem him greatly."

"I'm happy for you, Mother, truly I am. Be careful not to give your heart away before you're sure of him." How odd to be cautioning her mother, instead of the other way around.

Mrs. Wells nodded as she met Concordia's eyes once again. "I know. I think I've learned a thing or two about that. But let's talk about you. How are your classes this term? Have you been seeing much of Mr. Bradley?"

At least her mother asked about her work first, before asking about David. That showed improvement.

Now was the time to tell her. Concordia took a sip of tea before answering. "Actually, I have good news to share with you," she said. Why was she having trouble putting a smile on her face? Perhaps any kind of change had its disquieting aspects, even happy occasions. "David and I are going to be married."

"Oh!" Her mother clasped her hands together. "Oh, my dear, I am so happy for you!" She reached over and hugged her daughter enthusiastically, as Concordia scrambled to keep her cup upright in her lap.

"But," Concordia held up a hand, once her mother had sat down again, "it needs to be a secret, until the school term is over."

Mrs. Wells' face fell. Concordia imagined her taking a quick inventory of all the neighborhood matrons she wanted to tell. "I can't tell anyone? Whyever not?"

"I fear it would pose a distraction for my students. Once they are finished with end-of-term examinations, I'll notify Lady Principal Pomeroy, and share the news with everyone."

Letitia Wells was quiet for a long moment, looking at her daughter with anxious eyes.

"Concordia, I cannot believe I'm saying this, but—are you *sure* you want to marry David? You don't seem terribly delighted about it."

Concordia set her cup aside with trembling hands. "I'd be less than honest if I said I had no…reservations. It's a big change in my life. I'm not sure I'm ready for it. But David is a wonderful man. I do love him."

"So why not wait?" Mrs. Wells said gently.

Concordia, open-mouthed in astonishment at her mother's question, was at a loss for words. This was the woman who had taken to her bed for a week when her daughter left home for a college education and a career. Now she was advocating that Concordia postpone her engagement?

Mrs. Wells chuckled at the look on Concordia's face. "Yes, really. You know that the day you marry and the day I hold your first child in my arms will be the happiest of my life. But *your* happiness comes first. So I'm asking you, why not wait?"

Emotion flooded Concordia. She choked back a sob and put her head in her hands. "I'll lose him."

Mrs. Wells moved to the settee beside her daughter and embraced her. The strain that had been there too long gave way at last. Concordia buried her face in her mother's arms and cried.

After a few minutes, Letitia passed her a handkerchief. "Better?"

Concordia sniffed and nodded.

"Let me tell you something about men."

Concordia looked skeptical.

Letitia smiled. "This is what mothers are for, dear. You can't learn it in school. Don't worry about taking the time you need with David. Waiting is good for a man. It builds character. Heaven knows men could use more character-building, if our politicians are any indication of the general population."

Concordia smiled through the last of her tears. "Does that mean you're in favor of women's suffrage, Mother?"

Mrs. Wells grimaced. "Don't be impertinent," she said mildly. "If David is half the man I believe him to be, he'll wait—and count himself lucky to do so. You won't lose him."

Concordia sat up straighter. "You really think so?"

"I'm sure of it. I'm surprised he didn't come to me first, since your father has passed away, before proposing. David strikes me as old-fashioned that way. But if he had, I would had told him the same thing."

Concordia felt the tightness in her chest ease. She laughed. "I thought I was too old to need a mother. Thank you."

Mrs. Wells patted her hand. "A daughter is never too old to need her mother."

Chapter 27

Spring Recess
April 1898

Concordia spent the rest of the college recess at her mother's house. She helped Mother shop for her upcoming trip, browsing through the latest dinner dresses suitable for a steamer voyage. In addition, they toured the current exhibit at the Atheneum and enjoyed a quartet performing in Keney Park.

Alas, not all of their activities were congenial. Several women of Mrs. Wells' social circle, learning Concordia was here for a visit, stopped by for tea.

Most were well-meaning elderly ladies, indulging idle curiosity about their friend's spinster daughter who *worked* for a living. A lady professor was a novelty.

The cattier among Mother's acquaintances, however, were less well-intentioned, having come to pry and jibe, preening the feathers of their self-importance in the process.

Mrs. Griffiths was one of these. The triple-chinned matron was both firmly corseted and firmly fixed in her opinions of this woeful world.

"So, my dear, you are still teaching at that...girls' school?" Mrs. Griffiths inquired politely. Her eyes glittered with barely-disguised disapproval as she finished off her scone.

"It's a women's college, and yes, I am," Concordia answered.

"How disappointing for you, Letitia," the woman said, looking to Mrs. Wells, her voice dripping in false sympathy. "No doubt you expected your daughter to have married and produced grandchildren to console you in your old age." She made a clucking noise, which unsuccessfully masked the alarming *creaking* sound of her corset's elastic-and-coraline boning as she leaned forward to pluck the last cucumber sandwich from the tray. The woman hadn't popped a seam yet, but Concordia was waiting for the day.

"Not much chance of that, now—she's not getting any younger," Mrs. Griffiths continued. "A pity, too. We need a larger population of our *own* kind, lest we be overrun by the foreigners in our city. They are breeding with abandon!" She fixed both women with a glare.

Mrs. Griffiths was in fine form today, Concordia observed. The woman's remarks had the effect of buckshot, hitting the widest possible radius wherever it was pointed. She had belittled Concordia's profession, relegated her to empty-wombed spinsterhood, placed Mrs. Wells firmly in her dotage, and had disparaged the entire immigrant population of Hartford, all within five minutes. It was enough to make one want to jump into the Connecticut River, pockets bulging with rocks.

Judging from the pained look on her mother's face, Concordia knew she was dying to tell Mrs. Griffiths more about the current state of her daughter's love life.

"Well, Agatha, actually—" Mrs. Wells began.

"Mother, would you mind ringing for more of Mrs. Houston's excellent cucumber sandwiches?" Concordia interrupted, passing her the empty plate and giving her a warning look.

Mrs. Wells gave her a sheepish smile and rang the bell.

After Mrs. Griffiths left and they were recovering from the experience, Concordia asked her mother about the lady. "That woman has gotten more churlish with age. Why do you put up with her harpy ways?"

Mrs. Wells made a face. "I *had* been letting the acquaintance lapse, but she's a fixture among Robert's social set, so there's really no avoiding her. Ever since my involvement with this charity project, I've been obliged to humor the woman."

"You mean she has donated money for Irish orphans?" Concordia asked incredulously.

"I pointed out that they needn't emigrate *here* if they weren't starving over *there*." Her mother smiled.

"Ah, nicely done," Concordia murmured.

"Speaking of the Irish Aid Society," Mrs. Wells added, "we are holding a charity luncheon tomorrow. I was hoping you could join us. You already know several of the attendees: the Dunwicks, the Isleys, Mr. Maynard, and Miss Pomeroy."

"I didn't realize the plight of Irish orphans was such a popular cause," Concordia said. But it did sound promising; many of the same people who had attended the Isley dinner party would be at the luncheon. Perhaps she could learn something more to tell Miss Hamilton when she returned. Concordia sent up a silent prayer, hoping Miss Hamilton was close to finding Eli. There had been no word from her yet.

Letitia Wells smiled. "Ever since the announcement that Candidate Sanders will be our guest speaker, we have doubled our ticket sales for the event. So you'll come?"

"I wouldn't miss it for the world," Concordia said.

The benefit luncheon had been moved to the Yacht Club to accommodate the larger crowd, and they rode there in Mr. Flynn's carriage.

"*Begor*, you look absolutely lovely, Letitia," Flynn said with a smile. "I'll have a time of it, with other fellows trying to get a look-in." He turned to Concordia. "And how nice 'tis to see your charming daughter. You two could be sisters, you both look so young."

Concordia's stifled snort came out as a cough. They didn't look anything alike, and neither of them were what one would call "young" any more. What was the word used to refer to an Irishman's false flattery—*blarney*? Most definitely.

As they pulled up to the building, Concordia stared at the structure, appreciating the grandeur of the marble pillars—adorned with banners of the club's colors—flanking the wide steps and reaching to the vaulted windows of the building's mezzanine level. "Impressive," she murmured to her mother, as Mr. Flynn helped each of them out of the vehicle.

"The interior is equally remarkable," Mrs. Wells said. "We were fortunate to get this venue at the last minute. Thank heaven the regatta season has not yet started."

The dining hall was tastefully decked out for the event. Concordia had expected a nautical theme—seashells, rope nets, semaphore flags and the like—but was pleased to see crisp white linens, swathes of pale green tulle, and generous vases of bright spring blooms adorning each table. Not a seashell or barnacle in sight.

Mrs. Wells had arranged for Concordia to be seated with Miss Pomeroy and Randolph Maynard, although the rest of her table companions were unfamiliar to her. She attempted a cordial exchange with Dean Maynard, but he merely grunted and turned to the man on his left.

"Excuse me, miss—you dropped this," said a familiar voice.

Startled, Concordia turned to see Ben Rosen at her elbow, holding out a slip of paper. Yes, of course: he must be here to do a story on the event. The newspaperman gave her a quick wink and left it on her saucer. She watched him walk over to Mr. Sanders and Mr. Flynn, pulling out his notebook and pencil stub from the rim of his bowler.

Miss Pomeroy looked at her curiously. "I didn't notice you drop anything."

Concordia glanced quickly at the scrap before putting it in her purse. "I'm always dropping something," she said with a sheepish laugh.

Gertrude Pomeroy nodded sympathetically as she pushed her spectacles back into place. "So am I, dear."

But all through the salad and entree courses, as Concordia made small talk with the lady principal, she kept thinking about Rosen's note.

Have urgent information. Can't reach Miss H. Watch for my signal and meet me at the gardener's shed.

Perhaps he'd learned something about the Inner Circle? She chafed at the wait.

The luncheon drew a varied gathering: society ladies, the usual philanthropic well-to-do families…and politicians. Always politicians. Even Mr. Sanders' opponent, Mr. Quint, attended the function, though he was a bit late. Concordia saw both Flynn and Isley glare at the man when he came in. Quint hesitated, glancing uncertainly their way before being seated. The plight of Irish orphans must be close to the man's heart for him to risk straying into Sanders' territory, Concordia thought.

After the main course came the speeches: from her mother, thanking the volunteers and attendees, from Mr. Sanders, speaking of the privilege of service to others, and from Mr. Flynn, talking about the desperate plight of orphaned children back in his homeland. Listening to Flynn, in his lilting Irish brogue, she felt as if she were really there, breathing in the smoky peat fires, feeling the sharp hunger pangs of the children. She was embarrassed to find that her eyes prickled with tears.

Concordia sniffed into her handkerchief and observed the Isleys, who sat next to her mother at the head table. Both were absorbed in the speech: Lily, mouth parted in a half-smile, hand stroking her water glass; Barton leaning forward, chin resting thoughtfully on his palm. If Flynn could coax money out of Isley, his charm knew no bounds.

After a round of enthusiastic applause, it was time for a break before the dessert course, giving guests the opportunity to mingle and perhaps put money in the ribbon-wrapped pails distributed throughout the room. Flynn got up to circulate among the crowd.

Concordia made her way over to congratulate her mother. "You spoke beautifully."

"Indeed." Lady Dunwick was at her elbow. She extended a gloved hand. "Letitia, such a lovely function. It looks to be a rousing success."

Mrs. Wells blushed.

Lady Dunwick turned to Concordia. "I want to thank you for recommending my niece to your lady principal. Charlotte starts at the college next week."

"It was my pleasure," Concordia said. It would be nice to see Charlotte Crandall again.

Lady Dunwick patted her on the arm. "If you should ever need anything, please don't hesitate to call upon me."

"Thank you." Concordia said, catching sight of Rosen across the room. The man raised his bowler hat in her direction before stepping outside.

"If you'll excuse me," she said to her mother, "I think I'll get a little fresh air before the dessert course."

Mother, engrossed now in conversation with Sir Anthony, gave barely a nod as Concordia headed for the exit.

But fresh air was not easily come by, as the press of people made navigating the room exceedingly difficult. She found herself dodging tables, chairs, waiters clearing plates, and elderly patrons who moved at a snail's pace. As she tried to squeeze past one lady in an enormous floral hat, Concordia's parasol caught on a table skirt. The tea service came along with it and crashed to the floor.

Mercy, why was she carrying this blasted thing anyway?

"I-I am s-so sorry," Concordia stammered. A waiter hurried to clear the mess with a resigned sigh.

By the time Concordia reached an exit, it had been several minutes since she'd seen Mr. Rosen. She hoped they would have time to talk before she was missed.

Now to find the shed. She followed the gravel path to the arbor, looking around. On such a temperate day, many others were out as well, strolling along the paths or seated on benches, admiring the sweep of tulip beds.

Where was the shed?

Stepping off the path, Concordia found it a few minutes later, tucked behind a lattice fence. She glanced quickly behind her before going through the gate. It would not do to be seen alone in such a secluded spot, as if she were keeping a lovers' tryst.

"Mr. Rosen?" she murmured into the gloom. Silence.

The shed door was already open, and she pulled it wider. She smothered a yelp as she stumbled over a shovel in the dim light. Then she noticed something dark at her feet. Mr. Rosen's bowler.

She picked up the hat and brushed it off. She had a bad feeling about this. "Mr. Rosen?" she called a little louder, trying to keep the quaver out of her voice. She raised her parasol handle, ready to swing it if need be.

Then she saw him, slumped over a wheelbarrow. "Mr. Rosen!"

The man was unconscious, the back of his head encrusted with dirt and blood. Concordia tentatively leaned closer. He was still breathing, but barely.

"Stay calm," Concordia said, even though she knew he couldn't hear her. "I'm going for help."

She turned toward the door just as a very tall shadow crossed through it. She squeaked in fright.

"What in blazes is going on here?" demanded a voice.

Concordia's knees went weak with relief as she recognized it. "Mr. Maynard, thank goodness. It's Mr. Rosen. It looks as if he's been attacked."

Maynard crossed into the light of the shed's window. He gave a snort. "Come now, Miss Wells, let us not be overly dramatic." He went over to Rosen and felt his pulse. "He's still alive. It was most likely an accident, but just in case—we cannot put our young lady professors in danger from marauders—I'll stay with him while you go get help. Doctor Ruggers is at table six; bring him back with you. But for heaven's sake, be discreet about it. There are nearly two hundred guests. We don't need a panic—or a scandal." His jaw clenched. "Later, you can tell me what one of our respectable teachers was doing in a secluded shed with a newspaper reporter. Go!"

Concordia ran.

By the time Concordia returned with the doctor, Maynard had shifted Rosen to a prone position on the dirt floor, carefully supporting the man's head with his rolled-up jacket. The doctor set his bag down and crouched as best as he could within the cramped confines of the shed.

He looked up at Concordia. "When did this happen?"

She shook her head. "I don't know. I saw him walking this way not more than half an hour ago."

"Should we summon an ambulance?" Maynard asked.

After a careful examination, the doctor shook his head and put his instruments back in the bag. "His skull is fractured. There was nothing more we could have done."

"*Was?*" Concordia repeated.

"The man is dead." The doctor stood and brushed off the dirt from his knees. "Have you called the police? This was no accident."

Maynard gave Concordia a startled glance. Concordia nodded, though the sight of the dead newspaperman chilled her. The gardener would never leave a shovel lying upon the ground to be tripped over, and it was too much of a coincidence that Rosen had been anxious to pass along information to her but now could not.

Rosen, who had winked at her just an hour before. She swallowed.

It was the Inner Circle. She was sure of it.

In the gloom of the shed, she gripped the door and took a slow breath to steady her knees.

The perceptive doctor was quick to support her elbow. "Here, miss," he said kindly, leading her over to a stone bench beyond the gate. "You rest here. We'll take care of everything, although I suppose the police will want to ask you a question or two. Try not to worry."

Concordia made no protest, but sank onto the bench. The cool stone felt like the only solid thing she had to cling to.

The next hour was a flurry of people coming and going; the gardener and building custodian, to watch over the body until the police arrived; Maynard and the doctor, bringing Flynn back with them; uniformed policemen, talking with the men and giving Concordia an occasional curious glance; stretcher-bearers, to remove the now-shrouded form. Concordia watched it all with a sense of detachment, as if a play-acting scene were going on. How odd, this sensation of feeling nothing.

Concordia had hoped that Lieutenant Capshaw would come, but a different policeman arrived. He was a short, thin man, with a youth's complexion and a hesitant manner, dressed in a uniform that seemed two sizes too large for him.

He approached her.

"You are Miss Wells?" he asked, his Adams' apple bobbing along his throat.

Concordia nodded.

"Sergeant O'Neil, miss. I need to ask you a few questions." He paused. "Can I get you some water? You look pale."

She shook her head.

"How did you know Mr. Rosen?"

"He was a newspaper reporter, and frequently came to our school functions to cover events for the *Courant.*"

"Your *school*, miss?" the man asked in confusion.

"Hartford Women's College. I teach there."

"I see." He scribbled a note and then observed her more carefully. "I never met a college lady before."

As there didn't seem any good answer to that, Concordia stayed silent. The man was obviously young. Why hadn't they sent someone with more experience to investigate a murder?

"And what brought you to the shed, Miss Wells?"

Concordia had been dreading the question ever since she saw O'Neil. If it had been Capshaw in charge, she would be eager to share everything she knew. But she remembered her conversation with Miss Hamilton:

If the Black Scroll membership includes men in law enforcement, could it be behind the removal of Capshaw from Florence's murder investigation?

A disturbing thought, is it not?

Most disturbing.

Concordia folded her hands primly in her lap. "The luncheon was crowded, and the air stifling, so I decided to take a walk on the grounds before the dessert course."

O'Neil made a note on his pad. He gestured to the main gravel path up the slope behind them. "But as you can see, the shed is out of the way. What brought you *here?*"

"I was standing at the end of the path," Concordia said, pointing behind her. She hated the lie, but had better do a good job of it. Safer not to trust this man, at least until she could speak with Capshaw. "I thought I heard something. Like a moan," she added, for dramatic effect.

This earned her a sharp look from the doctor, who was standing within earshot. Concordia flushed. She wondered if Mr. Rosen had been in no condition to moan. Perhaps embellishment wasn't a good idea.

"So you know of no reason why Mr. Rosen would have been in the gardener's shed?" Sergeant O'Neil persisted.

Concordia shook her head and leaned heavily on her parasol, a perfect vision of feminine distress. "I have no idea. Will that be all, sergeant? I'm feeling light-headed. I think I need to lie down."

There was one thing to be said for having an attack of the vapors: everyone left you alone to recover from it. Of course, the smelling salts that Mrs. Houston insisted upon waving under Concordia's nose when they first returned to the house weren't all that pleasant, but at least now Concordia had the solitude to think about her next step.

She paced the confines of her childhood bedroom. What had Rosen wanted to tell her? It was obviously connected to the Black Scroll; that's what she and Miss Hamilton had asked him to look into. Presumably that was why he was murdered.

Then she had a chilling thought. If Rosen was killed to ensure his silence, that meant the killer knew of Concordia's involvement. And perhaps Miss Hamilton's as well.

She must talk to Capshaw, right away. He might know where to locate Miss Hamilton so they could warn her. And perhaps he would know what they should do next.

She glanced at the little clock on the desk. Almost dinner. Concordia changed quickly and went downstairs.

Concordia's mother and Robert Flynn, who was joining them for the evening, were waiting in the parlor for Mrs. Houston to announce dinner.

"How are you feeling, dear?" Mrs. Wells asked anxiously. Flynn had stood politely as Concordia entered the room, but she waved him back to his chair and sat down herself.

"Much better." Concordia looked over at Flynn, ever elegant in his stiff white shirt and black worsted evening tails. "I know I was originally planning to accompany you to the musical entertainment at Mrs. Griffiths' this evening, but would you mind going without me?"

"Never fear, we'll make your excuses to the lady," Robert Flynn assured her. "'Tis a dreadful experience you've had."

Mrs. Wells shuddered. "I cannot believe this has happened. Who would want to kill this...newspaperman? And at our luncheon, too."

Flynn patted her hand. "I'll allow 'tis a dreadful thing, but thank the stars we managed to keep the guests out of it. Except for the doctor, and he's as discreet a fellow as ever stood in shoe leather. It's unlikely to be a prominent story when the guests learn of it later, I imagine."

Concordia suppressed a sigh. The newspaperman would have been quite upset to know that his own murder wasn't considered a "prominent story."

"I imagine a quiet evening at home is just what you need," Mrs. Wells said to Concordia.

"Actually, I had hoped to visit Sophia," Concordia said. "Would you mind dropping me off there on your way to the Griffiths' function?"

Mrs. Wells' face brightened. "Sophia? I haven't seen her since the wedding. Oh, I would love to visit with her, even if it's only for a little while." She turned to Flynn. "Would you mind if we left a little early, and stopped briefly at the Capshaws? I'm sure we could be at Agatha's in time for the quartet."

"It's equal to me," Flynn said with a shrug. "A policeman's house, eh?" He pursed his lips thoughtfully. "Should be interesting."

Mrs. Wells turned to Concordia. "But how will you get home? We'll be out quite late."

"I'm sure I can stay the night. Then I can walk back or take the trolley tomorrow morning. It's not that far," Concordia said. "I'll send a note 'round to her, just to make sure."

The evening ride from the Wells' home in Frog Hollow to the Capshaws in the Clay Hill neighborhood was mercifully free of traffic, and they made quick time. Flynn told the driver to wait nearby. "Look lively, lad, and don't go far. We'll be no more'n thirty minutes."

Sadie opened the door and took their wraps. "The missus is in the parlor," she said, leading the way.

Robert Flynn's eyebrow quirked as his eyes swept over the cracks in the plaster walls and the scuffs in the wood floor. Concordia gritted her teeth when she caught Flynn giving her mother an amused smile, to which Mrs. Wells paid no attention.

"Sophia!" Mrs. Wells exclaimed, when they entered the parlor. She clasped the young woman's hands warmly. "You look wonderful. I knew marriage would agree with you."

Indeed, Concordia noted in surprise, Sophia seemed lighter and happier today, as she smiled and exchanged greetings with Concordia's mother and Mr. Flynn.

"Aaron will be back in a few minutes. Please, be comfortable," Sophia said. She turned back to Mrs. Wells and Mr. Flynn. "Would you excuse us for a moment?" Without waiting for a response, Sophia grabbed Concordia by the elbow and nearly dragged her from the room.

"What is it?" Concordia whispered, when they were in the hall and Sophia had closed the parlor door behind them.

Sophia was hopping up and down in her excitement. "Eli has been found! He's coming home."

Concordia put a hand to her mouth. *Thank heaven.* "How is he? Did Miss Hamilton tell you what happened?"

Sophia shook her head. "It was a short telegram. She merely said that he's recovering from injuries, but he'll be fine."

Injuries.

Concordia felt a little sick. Had the boy been in a strange hospital all this time? It was agonizing that Miss Hamilton hadn't revealed more. No doubt it was all she could do to send them word.

Sophia must have read Concordia's expression, because she reached out and squeezed her hand. "She said he'll be fine," she reminded her.

"When are they coming?" Concordia asked.

"I'm not sure. She said she would find the fastest conveyance possible. Now we wait."

"Once mother and Mr. Flynn leave, there's something urgent I need to talk with you and Cap—Aaron about," Concordia said.

Sophia raised an inquisitive eyebrow, but stopped short when the front door opened. Capshaw walked in, followed by…David Bradley?

"Fortunately, Mrs. Gilley's shop was open late," Capshaw said, holding out a string-wrapped box. He grinned. "I got your favorite, Concordia—lemon tarts." He gestured to David. "Look who I met on the walk back. I've just caught him up on our news."

David nodded. "I was returning from a lecture, and realized I've been remiss in visiting you two since your marriage. And now, we have a great deal to celebrate, don't we?" He eyed Concordia warmly. "Plenty of good news to go around."

Capshaw gave her a quizzical look, but Concordia pretended not to notice.

At least David had recovered his good humor. There was no trace of his pique from last week's encounter with Mr. Rosen in front of DeLacey House. But *land sakes*, how was she going to tell David about Rosen's murder? How would he react when he learned that she'd been the one to find the dying man?

"We'd better go in to our guests," Sophia said.

"Yes, let's," Concordia said, putting on a smile. "They cannot stay long."

The group settled in over dessert. The talk turned to police work, in which Flynn took a great interest. Capshaw regaled them with outlandish stories of foolhardy criminals.

"The devil, you say!" Flynn exclaimed, at one point in Capshaw's narrative. "The thief cooked a steak for himself and ate it, *before* taking the jewels? Egad, the cheek of the man!"

Capshaw grinned.

"More coffee?" Sophia offered, holding up the pot.

A rueful smile tugged at Flynn's mouth as he pulled out his watch. "A pity it is to break up such a gathering, but we will be late if we don't leave soon."

"Oh my, yes!" Mrs. Wells exclaimed.

The doorbell rang at that moment, and Concordia caught a glimpse of Sadie hurrying to get it.

When Concordia saw who was at the door, she unabashedly stood up and craned her neck for a better look.

Miss Hamilton.

The next few minutes were an awkward jumble: the Capshaws rushing to the hall, heedless of their guests, with Concordia close at their heels. David, Letitia Wells, and Robert Flynn made polite, awkward talk as they waited.

And wondered.

Soon Concordia returned to the parlor, her expression a mixture of apology and pure happiness.

"Sophia asked me to extend her regrets for the disruption," she said, "but her husband has police business he must attend to. Sophia and I are needed as well."

David stood beside Concordia. "I'd be happy to stay and wait for you." He dropped his voice. "I behaved quite foolishly last week. I wanted to apologize."

Concordia smiled. "Yes, please stay. Perhaps we can talk more when you take me home later." Now was not the time or place to discuss postponing their engagement. She didn't know how she was going to broach *that* subject.

Sadie came down the hallway. "Mr. Flynn's carriage is waiting."

Flynn got to his feet and helped Mrs. Wells out of her chair. "'Tis past time we were leaving."

Letitia Wells gave Concordia a worried glance. "Are the Capshaws all right?"

Concordia smiled. "Actually, it's good news. I'll explain tomorrow."

Mrs. Wells nodded in relief and followed Flynn into the hallway, where he retrieved his hat and walking stick from the coat rack. Concordia heard him mutter "'Twould be a shame if we've missed the contralto," to her mother, as he draped her shawl over her shoulders. He glanced through the open door of the study and paused, taking in the sight of the group seated by the fire: Miss Hamilton, Capshaw, and Sophia, with a very grimy Eli fast asleep in her lap.

"Robert? What's wrong?" Mrs. Wells asked, following his frozen stare.

He flushed an angry red, gesturing toward the group in the study. "*This* is the *police business* for which we were kept waiting?" His voice was a low growl. "Who the devil are *they?*"

Mrs. Wells, mouth set in a grim line Concordia knew all too well from childhood, stalked out the front door to the waiting carriage without a backward look at her rude companion. Robert Flynn hurried to catch up with her as quickly as his dignity would allow.

Concordia didn't envy Flynn the talking-to her mother would no doubt give him. And it was exactly what he deserved. Apparently the man wasn't *all* charm; he obviously had a temper, along with an exaggerated sense of his own importance.

Concordia shook her head and joined the others in the study, where Sadie had set out some more tea and pastries for the guests.

Penelope Hamilton looked up. Concordia could see the exhaustion evident in the lady's puffy, shadowed eyes, her creased brow and pale lips. "I regret our arrival made things awkward. Eli couldn't bear to be away a minute longer. I hired a driver to bring us directly here, rather than travel by tomorrow's train."

Concordia regarded the sleeping boy in Sophia's lap, a strand of dark curly hair obscuring part of his pale cheek. She would have done the same.

"I read the evening paper on the way here," Miss Hamilton went on, with a sharp glance at Concordia. "I understand you dealt with a disturbing event today."

Concordia sat down beside Sophia with a sigh. "Most disturbing."

"I haven't seen this evening's paper. What's happened?" David asked.

"Mother's charity luncheon at the Yacht Club took a nasty turn." Concordia turned to Capshaw. "That's why I came to see you tonight, but we haven't had a chance to talk. Mr. Rosen...is dead."

"Rosen. The reporter from the *Courant?*" Capshaw asked. "How are you involved?" He gave her that look Concordia knew so well: *You college ladies... always finding trouble.*

Concordia clenched her hands together. "I found him in the gardener's shed. He'd been hit over the head with a shovel."

David drew in a sharp breath and looked in her direction, but Concordia wouldn't return his glance. He no doubt wondered if the newspaperman's murder was connected to their meeting at DeLacey House. She didn't want to argue with him now about the perils of getting involved in a murder investigation. Although there was no avoiding that discussion later, she was sure.

"I'd heard there was a disturbance at the Yacht Club," Capshaw said, "but I was on my way out of the station and had no time to learn the details." He shook his head. "Had you gone searching for him? It's a wonder you weren't killed, too."

Concordia bristled and started to speak, but Miss Hamilton interrupted. "Rosen was looking into the Black Scroll, specifically the Inner Circle. You remember the conversation I told you Concordia had overheard at the Isley party? Since we weren't able to learn more about the group, we asked the reporter to make discreet inquiries. Certainly, we didn't anticipate *this.*"

Sophia sucked in a quick breath as she glanced at Capshaw. "That was the group you told me about? The one who might be involved in you being taken off the case."

Capshaw nodded, tight-lipped.

Miss Hamilton turned to Concordia. "Tell us what happened. From the beginning."

Concordia dug into her skirt pocket and pulled out Rosen's note. "He gave me this as the luncheon guests were being seated."

Capshaw gave it a quick glance before passing it to Miss Hamilton. "And you have no idea what he was going to tell you?"

Concordia shook her head. "There were too many people likely to overhear. He didn't dare say anything at the time." She proceeded to describe Rosen's signal, her delay in being able to get out of the room, finding Rosen in the shed, barely alive, then Maynard coming upon them.

"Wait a moment," Capshaw said. "How did Randolph Maynard come to be on the scene? You said the gardener's shed was off the path. What was he doing there?"

Concordia sat back in surprise. "I don't know," she said slowly. "I didn't think of that before. I was simply grateful for the assistance. I didn't want to leave Mr. Rosen alone in order to fetch help, and the dean offered to stay with him. He made him more comfortable while I ran to get one of the guests—a doctor."

Capshaw and Miss Hamilton exchanged a glance.

"What is it?" Concordia asked.

"It seems suspicious," Capshaw said.

"You mean, Maynard could be the murderer?" Concordia asked. "But why return to the shed? Wouldn't he want to be as far from there as possible, for that very reason?"

Miss Hamilton leaned forward. "If Maynard is the murderer, he might have returned to make sure that Rosen was truly dead—" Concordia winced "—or perhaps he feared he had dropped something incriminating at the scene and had gone back to retrieve it."

"And going with that assumption for a moment," Capshaw added, "you leaving him alone with his victim would give him ample opportunity to scour the area."

Concordia hesitated. "The dean *was* sitting right next to me when Mr. Rosen slipped me the note," she said reluctantly.

"If Maynard were a Black Scroll member and realized the reporter knew something damaging, he could have decided to silence him," Miss Hamilton said. "Perhaps Rosen wasn't quite so cautious in his inquiries."

"But our *dean?*" Concordia said incredulously. As disagreeable as Maynard was, could he really be a cold-blooded killer? He had seemed more concerned with the propriety of Concordia meeting a man alone in a remote shed.

"Now what do we do?" Concordia asked.

"Who's assigned the case?" Capshaw asked her.

"A man named O'Neil."

Capshaw grimaced. "The sergeant is diligent enough, though inexperienced. Did you tell O'Neil about the note, and the reason why you had gone looking for Rosen?"

Concordia shifted in her seat and glanced at Miss Hamilton. "I thought it was better to leave out that part."

Capshaw rolled his eyes. "You're playing a dangerous game," he said grimly. "If someone killed Rosen to keep him from telling you what he knew, then you—and possibly Miss Hamilton—are known to be involved. Do you think whoever it is will scruple to kill another woman? We've discussed this before, miss. Leave the detecting to the professionals."

"You must concede, Lieutenant," Miss Hamilton said, coming to Concordia's defense, "that we don't know whom to trust in your department. Your removal from the Willoughby murder investigation does not inspire confidence in that regard. I believe Concordia's caution was warranted. We don't know anything about this man O'Neil, or what his superiors may request of him." She gave Capshaw a stern look. "When this case is done, your department will have some unpleasant housekeeping to do."

Capshaw scowled. "If our chief did indeed allow a group such as the Black Scroll to obstruct an investigation, he would have much to answer for."

"Has your replacement made any progress in Florence Willoughby's murder?" Concordia asked.

Capshaw's jaw tightened. "Not what I would call 'progress.' The attack on the woman has been ascribed to the actions of an unstable individual. With no additional garroted victims since then, it is thought that the killer left the area and the danger to the public has passed. I don't believe that for a moment, of course, but my opinion was not considered," he added bitterly.

"So the case is still open, but inactive?" Miss Hamilton asked.

"Yes."

"Mr. Rosen was not garroted," Concordia said. "How do we know his death is connected to Florence Willoughby's murder?"

"We don't," Miss Hamilton said reluctantly. "We must learn what Rosen wanted to tell you. It wouldn't hurt to look into Maynard's activities as well."

Eli murmured in his sleep, and all eyes turned to the boy.

"At least Eli is safe," Concordia said. It was the best news she'd had all day. "What happened?" She pointed to the crutch propped next to the divan.

"The boy was grievously injured after his release from jail," Miss Hamilton said. She turned to Sophia. "You'll want your doctor to give him a good going-over tomorrow. Do you mind if I start back at the beginning, for Concordia's and Mr. Bradley's benefit?"

Capshaw nodded and pulled out his wad of paper, folded and unfolded so many times Concordia could see the smudge of its creasing from where she sat. "Hearing it again may clarify a few things."

"I know little about any of it," David volunteered, with a swift glance at Concordia, "but I'll try to follow along."

Miss Hamilton folded her hands in her lap and began.

"When I learned from Eli's friend—the boy who sells newspapers near the Pearl Street trolley stop—that he saw Eli running after a cab on the afternoon of Florence's murder, I came to two conclusions: one, that the boy was chasing someone—no doubt the person he was convinced had murdered his mother; and two, that the cab was headed toward the train station. He found another means to get to the station in order to stay on the trail."

Capshaw made an irritated gesture. "What could he have been thinking, to take such a danger upon himself? Why not come to me?"

Miss Hamilton opened her mouth to speak, but Sophia interrupted. "I think I understand it." She smiled at her husband. "Although Eli had a mother—a surplus of mothers, it seems—he's never had a father. A boy his age needs that. He's become quite attached to you, dear. It's clear he admires you. He's stated more than once that he wants to grow up to become a police detective."

"So when the opportunity arose to catch his mother's killer, he acted on it," Concordia added. "He wants to earn your approval."

Capshaw's expression could have been embarrassment, pride, or vexation; it was difficult to tell.

"In the heat of the chase, I doubt there was time to reach you, anyway," Miss Hamilton said.

"So what did you do next, Miss Hamilton?" David prompted.

"No one saw Eli take a train out of Union Station that day. However, once I was able to talk with the conductor who had been on leave, I learned that a boy matching Eli's description had been arrested and jailed for sneaking aboard a train the next day. He was traveling *back* to Hartford from Providence. He couldn't pay for his passage. They've had trouble with scofflaws lately, and have tightened their rules."

"Three days in jail seems extraordinarily harsh for such an infraction. And a child at that," Concordia said.

Miss Hamilton nodded. "Indeed. "The conductor worried that the man who'd pointed out the boy was a spotter. The conductor didn't want to risk being reported for not following the company policy. Eli was only supposed to remain in police custody until his family came to get him."

"Why didn't Eli contact the Capshaws?" Concordia asked.

"The boy insists that when he was put in jail he did ask that Sophia be contacted. He was told that a telegram was sent, but there was no response." Miss Hamilton shrugged. "I don't know what went wrong, but in his eyes, he was convinced that you'd rejected him."

"The poor child," Sophia murmured, smoothing the hair from the boy's forehead.

"Prison officials then referred Eli to a reformatory school, and the school matron came to collect him," Miss Hamilton said.

Concordia shook her head. "He would have hated that."

"Exactly," Miss Hamilton said. "He managed to slip away from her in the street, shortly after they left the jail. It was just after that when Eli was run over by the hansom," she added.

Concordia and David both started out of their chairs. "'Run over!'" Concordia exclaimed.

"I was explaining that when you joined us," Miss Hamilton said with perfect composure, as if boys got run over by hansoms every day.

David leaned forward, brow creased in concern. "Was it an accident, or deliberate?"

"I feel certain it was deliberate," Miss Hamilton said. "It happened about three blocks from the jail. Witnesses told me the driver had been lingering at the corner, and suddenly whipped up the horse at great speed. He didn't stop after Eli was knocked to the ground. Only the fact that the horse shied at the last minute saved the boy from worse injury."

Concordia shuddered. What sort of man would callously run over a child?

"What happened after that?" Capshaw asked, scribbling in his pad. "Someone has obviously been taking care of him."

"Yes," Miss Hamilton said, "the bystanders who witnessed the incident carried Eli to a nearby house of a woman who's a midwife. I've spoken with her. The boy was unconscious, and no one knew who he was. She set his leg and dressed his other wounds. Soon after, he developed a fever, and was not lucid for some time. She didn't like the idea of a vulnerable young boy staying at the local hospital for the poor and indigent, given the sanitary conditions of that particular place, so she simply took care of him herself."

Sophia exhaled in relief. "How extraordinarily kind. Can we pay her for the expense?"

Miss Hamilton smiled. "It's already done."

"What happened next?" Capshaw asked.

"Eli regained consciousness a couple of days ago. He wouldn't tell her anything about himself—remember, he thought you had washed your hands of him—and she was at a loss. Fortunately, that's when I found them."

"Are you mad at me?" a quavering voice whispered.

Eli, now awake, looked up anxiously at Sophia.

Sophia stroked his hair. "No one is angry with you. We never got the telegram. I'm sorry about that."

Eli smiled at her, then wiped his eyes on his sleeve. "Miss 'amilton tole me. You still want to 'dopt me?"

"Of course," Sophia said. "But one rule: no more running off. If you have a problem, or something bad happens, you come to us, right away. You aren't alone anymore."

Eli nodded and struggled to sit up. "I'm real sorry about not tellin' you where I was, but I didn' have a chance."

Capshaw squatted next to the boy. "I know you gave Miss Hamilton an account of what happened, but I'd like to hear it straight from you. Do you feel well enough to talk?"

"Let's get him more comfortable first," Sophia said, reaching for cushions.

Once Eli was settled between Concordia and Sophia on the divan, his leg propped up on a pillow and a mug of tea in his hands, Capshaw got down to business.

"Start with when you last saw Florence alive."

Eli took a deep breath. "It was after lunch. She sent me 'round the corner with some money, to get a paper, and she said I could get myself a stick candy with the extra, if I wanted." His eyes softened. "She was real thoughtful. I was starting to like her. She tole me that day that she decided she shouldn' take me away, that she knew I was happier here. Cat seemed to take to her, and stayed in the room while I was gone."

"How long did it take you to get the paper?" Concordia interrupted, which earned her a look from Capshaw. She could almost hear the thought in his head. *Hmph. Meddling females.*

"Dunno, it was a while. I was talkin' with Whitey on the way," Eli said. "Then I figured I was late an' she was waiting, so I hurried back."

"What happened then?" Capshaw asked quietly.

Eli kept his eyes on his clenched-together hands. "I found her on the bed. At first, I thought she was sleepin' but when I got closer her eyes were open, jes' starin'…and she looked…." He drew a ragged breath. "She was dead."

Concordia patted his back. "Go on," she gently urged.

"I heard someone on the fire escape, so I hid under the bed. Cat was there with me." Eli's eyes held worry and regret. "Is he okay?"

Capshaw nodded. "He's fine, son. Martha has him back at the settlement house."

Eli wiped away more tears of relief, and blew his nose noisily in the handkerchief Capshaw passed over.

"Back to the person on the fire escape," Capshaw said. "Did you see who it was?"

Eli shook his head. "It was a man, but I couldn' peek through the bedskirts without giving myself away. I heard him mutterin' to himself."

"What did he say? What was his voice like?" Capshaw asked.

"It was real snarly," Eli said. "And he said: 'Takin' a big chance comin' back. I gave 'im ev'ry scrap o' paper in the stinkin' place—there weren't no more. I better get paid good fer this one.'"

"Did you hear anything else?" Capshaw asked.

"No. He pulled out a lot o' drawers, but quiet-like. I was real scared he'd look under the bed next."

"What happened then?"

"It sounded like he was fiddlin' with the door knob at first, and then I heard him at the window, climbin' out. I did peek under the edge of the bed, then."

"Did you get a look at him?"

Eli shook his head. "Not a good one. He was too quick. All I saw was a big hand, with hairy knuckles, as he was pulling down the window."

"So you decided to follow the man," Capshaw prompted the boy, "leaving the cat behind."

Eli nodded. "I was real sorry to do that, but I thought Cat would slow me down. I figured someone would find him soon and let him out, when they found...." He shuddered, then whispered, "Her."

"How did you avoid being seen?" Concordia asked, breaking the silence.

"I waited until he was out of the alley and across the street. When he weren't looking, I went down the fire escape as quiet as I could. It can make an awful clatter if you're not careful. He couldn't see me by then, 'cause the buildings are so close together. I followed him for a few blocks, and that's when he met the man in fancy dress."

Concordia gave Eli a sharp look. "*Fancy dress*? Do you mean like formal wear?"

Eli shrugged. "He was wearing a black jacket, striped pants, white shirt and collar. Looked fancy to me."

"Then what?" Capshaw asked.

"They talked for a couple o' minutes, and the fancy man handed a bundle of somethin' to the other man. I think it was money. Then they split up." He gave Capshaw a curious glance. "How do you decide which one to follow, when you're on a case?"

Capshaw tousled the boy's hair. "We'll talk about that later. The more important question at the moment is, how did *you* decide?"

Eli pursed his lips. "I figured the fancy man paid the other man to—you know." His voice faltered briefly. "I thought I'd follow the fancy man."

Capshaw nodded in approval. "Good choice. And then?"

"After a few blocks, he took a cab an' I couldn't keep up. But," he added, "I heard him say 'station,' so I hitched a ride on a couple of street cars and then a fella's veg'table dray."

"Were you able to catch up with him at the station?" Concordia asked, completely absorbed in the narrative.

Eli made a face. "It was hard, 'cause there were a lot more fellas with the same kind o' clothes on. And then when I did find him, I had to sneak on board, 'cause I didn' have any money." He looked at them apologetically. "I figured it was for a good reason."

"We'll get back to that later," Capshaw said. "You were able to get aboard without being, uh, detected?"

"Yessir, but I had to hide in the water closet whenever the conductor came around. I was real worried I'd miss the fancy man's stop. But I didn't dare get close enough for him to notice me."

"Were you able to determine where he got off?"

"I got off at the stop for Providence jes' in time. Then he got into another hansom cab." The boy hesitated.

"What is it?" Capshaw prompted.

Eli sighed. "I'm sure he saw me then. The window curtain twitched, and suddenly the cabbie whipped up the horse, and took off."

"Did you see the man's face when he moved the curtain?" Capshaw asked, his voice hopeful.

"No sir. All I saw was his hand and wrist."

"Describe them," Capshaw said.

"The hand was pale, with long, slender fingers. The cuff looked nice and white—not wrinkled or dirty at all. And there was a big gold button with a black design on it."

"You mean a cufflink?" Capshaw walked over to the desk, pulled out paper and pencil, and handed them to the boy. "Can you draw the design?"

Eli bent over the paper, teeth pulling on his lower lip as he worked. After several erasures and corrections, he finally finished. "Here."

After passing it to Capshaw, he eyed the dessert plate hungrily. Concordia brought it over with a smile.

Capshaw examined the rough drawing of what looked to be a tube that was slightly pinched in the middle, with a spiral at one end. "A cylinder of some kind. I don't recognize it," he muttered, handing it to Miss Hamilton, who puzzled over the sketch. Concordia got up and looked over her shoulder. Something about the drawing looked familiar.

"If I were on the case I would show this around, and make inquiries," Capshaw said, jaw clenched.

"Just tell me whom to ask," Miss Hamilton said.

Capshaw pulled out his notebook and scribbled down names and street addresses. "These four jewelers specialize in custom pieces," he said, tearing out the sheet and passing it to her. "We'll need to know who commissioned the cuff links, when, and if more than one pair was—"

Capshaw stopped short as Concordia rushed out of the room. They heard her rummaging in the coat closet.

She returned a moment later, holding up a pin, which she passed to Miss Hamilton. "I thought that sketch looked familiar. What do you think? Is it the same design?"

Miss Hamilton examined it against Eli's drawing. "They are very like." She turned to Eli, who was already working on his second pastry. "Did the cufflink look similar to this?" she asked, showing him the pin.

The boy nodded, mouth full.

Capshaw came over to look at the pin. "Where did you find this?" he asked Concordia.

"Remember the stranger I told you about? The youth I only saw from a distance? He dropped it."

Capshaw started. "This is the first *I've* heard of it."

"I stuck it in my jacket at the time, and forgot all about it." Concordia grimaced. "I'm terrible about emptying my pockets. It's been there ever since."

"Could Eli's *fancy man* and the school's mysterious youth be the same person?" Capshaw mused aloud.

David shifted uneasily in his seat. "I don't like the idea of *any* stranger strolling the college grounds at will, much less the one responsible for Miss Willoughby's death."

Concordia didn't like it, either, but the man hadn't been seen on campus in weeks.

Miss Hamilton got back to the business at hand. "Our first course is to trace the source of this pin. Between that and the sketch, we should be able to find the jeweler."

Concordia, looking once again at Eli's drawing, sucked in a sharp breath.

"What?" Capshaw asked.

"It's not a cylinder; it's a...*scroll*."

In the silence that followed, Capshaw glanced anxiously at Eli, who was reaching for a third pastry. He got up and moved to the far end of the room away from the boy, gesturing to the rest of them to do the same.

Once they were out of earshot, Miss Hamilton said, "No doubt the man is a member of the Black Scroll."

Sophia clenched her trembling hands together. "What do we know about this group?"

"Precious little," Miss Hamilton admitted.

"So this man—from the Black Scroll—is responsible for the attempt on Eli's life? Could he try again?" Sophia's voice was strained, but quiet.

Capshaw looked uneasy. "I don't know."

"Well," Sophia said, "we're not taking any chances. Eli's staying with us—permanently."

Capshaw smiled. "Whatever you say, dear." He walked back over to Eli. "How would you like to live here from now on, son...yes? Good. I'll send word to Martha to collect your things."

Sophia gave Capshaw a grateful look. She sat down beside Eli and held him close.

Concordia smiled. "Don't forget the cat."

"Okay, so we know about the day of the murder," Capshaw said to Eli, after he'd finished eating. "Miss Hamilton says you were arrested the next day. Tell us about that."

Eli brushed off the last of the crumbs and sat up straighter. "After the fancy man got away, I went back to the station. But I missed the last train. I slept near the station and got on the first train to come back here in the morning. I figured, since I couldn' follow him no more, I'd come back real quick and tell you, so you could take over. But at the first stop, the conductor grabbed me. They took me to a policeman, who locked me up." Eli shrugged. "I'm not so good at sneakin' as I used to be, I guess."

Capshaw laughed out loud.

Concordia smothered a grin. Apparently, reforming a child's criminal behavior had its disadvantages.

Sophia gave them both a sharp look. "But you told them to contact us?" she asked.

Eli plucked at the cushion next to him. "When they said that you gave no answer, I thought you didn' want me no more."

Sophia held him close. "Of course we want you. There must have been some mistake along the way."

Miss Hamilton, who had been listening to Eli's narrative in silence, looked over at the boy. "You may not be as poor at concealing yourself as you think." She glanced back at Capshaw. "Remember the spotter the conductor told me about? Perhaps he was neither a spotter nor a disinterested passenger."

Capshaw's eyes lit up with interest. "Ah, yes, that's a possibility."

Eli shrugged. "Well, it don't matter. Someone noticed me."

"I think Miss Hamilton's point is that the man who tipped off the conductor may be the one you were following," Capshaw said.

Concordia leaned forward excitedly. "Do you mean that, when the man noticed Eli was on his trail, he eluded him long enough to then turn around and follow the boy himself?"

Miss Hamilton nodded. "Quite clever, I must say."

"And bold," Capshaw added.

"So then, the man in fancy dress got me put in jail on purpose?" Eli asked. "Why?"

Capshaw tapped his pencil against his chin thoughtfully. "Perhaps to allow him time to learn more about you, and whether you were actually a threat to him."

Miss Hamilton nodded grimly. "It cannot be a coincidence that the boy was run down in the street, just when he was released from jail."

Eli paled. "He's tryin' to kill me, too?"

Concordia winced at Miss Hamilton's habit of plain speaking.

Capshaw placed a reassuring hand on the boy's shoulder. "You're safe now. We won't let anyone hurt you. But tells us the rest of it. What else do you remember, after you were released from jail?"

Eli grimaced. "I got away from that school mistress, and was tryin' to figure out what to do next. Then I heard a loud clattering, and saw the cab, coming real fast. I tripped when I tried to get out of the way. The last thing I remember was the horse bein' on top of me." He shuddered. "When I woke up, my leg and head hurt a lot." He pointed at Miss Hamilton. "She found me at Mrs. Jardin's house."

"The midwife," Miss Hamilton clarified.

The boy nodded. "She took real good care of me, even though I don't remember a lot of it." He smothered a yawn.

"The poor child's tuckered out," Sophia said, stroking his hair. "What time is it?"

That reminded Concordia of Florence Willoughby's letter. *If something should happen to me, ask Eli to show you the gift I gave him.* "Eli, do you still have the pocket watch from Florence?" After all he'd been through, chances were slim.

To Concordia's surprise, the boy reached for his cap, set aside on the table. "I hid it in here." He pulled it out of the lining and passed it over to Concordia.

"Is this the only thing she gave you?" she asked, turning it over in her hands.

Eli nodded.

It didn't look remarkable, just a plain watch of brushed gold with a hinged cover. Judging by the nicks and scratches it was obviously old, perhaps passed down from a previous generation. She passed it along to David.

"How is this significant?" he asked, turning it over in his hands.

"Florence's letter talked about the present she had given Eli." Concordia tapped the watch. "She hinted that something was hidden in it."

David pulled out his pocketknife. "I'll take a look under the casing," he said, walking over to the desk lamp.

Capshaw picked up his pencil once again. "Okay, one more thing, and then you can sleep," he said to Eli. "Describe the men in as much detail as you can."

When he was done, Eli curled up on the divan and promptly slept. Sophia covered him with a throw, and they all shifted to the other side of the room to talk.

"I wish he'd gotten a closer look at them, but this is a start." Consulting his notebook, he read: "Two men. First—short, stout, gray hair, reddened neck, thick grayish whiskers, scruffy bowler hat, dressed in workmen's clothes. Second—tall, slim, black morning coat, light striped trousers, top hat, dark hair heavily streaked with gray, and a graying, neatly-trimmed beard."

Concordia shook her head. Those descriptions could apply to any number of men. How were they to find a killer only seen from the back, and at a distance, by a young boy?

But wait, the conductor saw the man, too—if they were going on the assumption that it was the same person. "Did the train conductor give you a description of the man who alerted him to Eli?" Concordia asked.

Miss Hamilton nodded. "It matches Eli's. A middle-aged gentleman, with dark graying hair and close-trimmed beard. The man was seated, so the conductor isn't sure how tall he was."

"Any distinguishing facial features? What about the voice?" Capshaw asked.

She shook her head. "The conductor noticed nothing striking in his appearance. And the man merely slipped him a note and pointed to the washroom, where the boy was hidden. The conductor was under the impression the man had some throat ailment. And the conductor has long since tossed away the note. I asked."

David Bradley rejoined the group, eyes alight with excitement.

"You've found something, Mr. Bradley?" Miss Hamilton asked.

David grinned. "I'll say. Look at this." He held out a small piece of what looked to be a brown paper wrapper, dirty and worn. "It was wedged beneath the back plate."

Concordia watched over David's shoulder as he smoothed it out. The print was barely visible: an image of what looked to be a muscular figure in a helmet, and the letters HERC on one line and DANGE below that.

David passed it to Miss Hamilton. "Do you know what it is?"

Miss Hamilton's lips thinned in a somber line. "I recognize it." She passed it to Capshaw. "It's a fragment of an explosives wrapper. Dynamite."

Chapter 28

He that filches from me my good name
Robs me of that which not enriches him
And makes me poor indeed.

Othello, III.*iii*

Week 9, Instructor Calendar
April 1898

Concordia was happy to return to the college after what had been a most disturbing week. The soothing chatter of high-spirited girls, catching up with one another about their adventures, was a welcome relief from recent events. She was looking forward to the familiar routine of classes, chapel, teas, and bicycle rides. Even play rehearsals didn't seem so disagreeable.

Another bright spot came in the form of the newly-hired Charlotte Crandall, who would be living with them at Willow Cottage for the rest of the spring semester.

"I hope you don't mind staying in student quarters," Concordia said, as she helped Charlotte carry her suitcase up the steps. "We're short on space everywhere."

Charlotte surveyed the room. "It certainly brings back memories of when I was a freshie. I don't mind. My instructor quarters at the boarding school weren't much bigger, anyway." She gave Concordia a hug. "It's good to be back."

Concordia smiled. She'd always admired the young lady, who had made many friends during her time at Hartford Women's College with her charm, quick wit, and warm-hearted ways. Although she came from the wealthy Crandall family, Charlotte had been determined to make her own way.

Concordia hoped the young lady would be offered a permanent position at the school. For the time being, it was wonderful to have the extra help at the cottage. Perhaps even Miss Smedley would come around under Miss Crandall's influence.

Charlotte regarded Concordia closely. "Was your break not as restful as you'd hoped? You look a bit...tired, if you don't mind me saying so."

Concordia shook her head. The less said about her spring recess, the better. "I suppose even a vacation can be exhausting." She checked her watch. "Do you have everything you need? I have to be somewhere."

"I'm fine," Charlotte assured her.

Concordia hurried across the quadrangle toward her office, her thoughts returning to the alarming find inside Eli's pocket watch. Florence had obviously hidden it there to keep it out of the hands of her pursuers. No doubt the explosives wrapper was the "scrap of paper" the killer had been sent back to recover when Eli was hiding under the bed. The *why* of Florence's murder was becoming clearer, even if the *who* of it was not. Florence had associated with unscrupulous men and had possessed dangerous knowledge. A disastrous combination.

The idea of the Black Scroll in possession of explosives made Concordia shudder. If the group was indeed responsible for the deaths of Florence Willoughby and Ben Rosen, along with the attempt on Eli's life, then nothing good could come of them having weapons with broader destructive power.

Lieutenant Capshaw and Miss Hamilton had acted quickly upon that possibility, with Miss Hamilton leaving town the very next day for what Capshaw termed a "short trip." Concordia hoped it would bring them answers soon.

"Is there a problem?" a peremptory voice called.

Concordia glanced up to see Randolph Maynard standing on the path, wearing an amused smile. "One more step and you would find yourself in the fountain, Miss Wells."

She was, indeed, standing beside the fountain, having no idea how she got there.

Maynard glanced at his watch. "Are you attending the farce being perpetrated in Bursar Isley's office? It's almost two o'clock now."

Concordia nodded.

"This should be amusing," Maynard said derisively. "I have my doubts about the ability of these young ladies to dismantle the president's buggy and restore it whole. They must have had help in pulling the prank. They won't be getting any help today."

Concordia straightened and met Maynard's eye. "I wouldn't miss it for anything." She hoped to see Maynard eat crow for dinner later.

Maisie Lovelace and her cohorts, clad in leather aprons to protect their shirtwaists and skirts from grease, were already crouched beside the vehicle, a litter of tools at their feet. At Mr.Isley's office door,Concordia and Maynard joined the growing crowd of teachers who had come to watch, including Barton Isley, President Langdon, and Lady Principal Pomeroy. A newspaper reporter invited from the *Courant* peppered the girls with questions as they worked.

Concordia's chest felt heavy at the sight of a different newspaperman. She would never again see Ben Rosen here, tipping back his bowler when introducing himself, scribbling notes with the tiny pencil that seemed swallowed up in his grip, or giving an impertinent wink when he had privileged information to share.

The girls conducted themselves with lady-like self-assurance, describing the intricacies of taking apart the vehicle as they worked. With such cramped quarters, the other students on campus had been restricted from coming in to watch, but Concordia could hear a chorus of shouts each time one of the girls brought a piece of machinery outside and laid it on the lawn.

Concordia stayed long enough to watch the smirks on the faces of Isley and Maynard fade, replaced first by incredulity, and then with a grudging respect. But it was time to get back to Willow Cottage. She had promised Lieutenant Capshaw a favor.

She touched President Langdon on the arm before leaving. "Thank you again," she murmured.

He grinned. "It's supposed to be beautiful weather this week. I'm looking forward to a nice, long drive." He patted the vest pocket over his pear-shaped belly. "And the custodian has given me a list of items throughout the campus in need of mending. *That* should keep these young ladies busy through June."

Back at Willow Cottage, Concordia tidied the parlor for Lieutenant Capshaw's arrival, then went looking for Ruby. She had a plan to keep the housekeeper from slipping away from Capshaw this time. She grabbed the sewing basket on her way to the kitchen.

"Ruby?" Concordia called out.

"You need somethin', miss?" Ruby asked, drying her hands on her apron.

Concordia smiled apologetically and gestured to the basket. "We have some mending that the girls don't have quite the needle-skills to manage. Would you mind?"

The matron squinted over a puffed-sleeved shirtwaist Concordia extracted from the basket. With a sigh, Ruby retrieved her magnifying spectacles and perched them on her nose as she examined the tear. "Wot do they teach these girls at home? Ah well, I should have enough time b'fore dinner to take care o' it." She sat down at the kitchen table and pulled out a spool of thread.

"Thank you," Concordia said. Sewing was the one task she could count on to keep Ruby occupied and sitting still.

On her way down the hall to wait for Capshaw, she heard the faint *snuffle* of a girl crying. She followed the sound, climbing the stairs and stopping at Charlotte Crandall's room. She hesitantly tapped on the door.

There was a brief silence. "Come in," Charlotte called.

Concordia stopped in her tracks at the sight of a red-eyed Alison Smedley, kerchief to her nose, sitting across from Charlotte. *That was fast,* Concordia thought.

"Am I intruding?" Concordia asked from the doorway.

"Not at all," Charlotte said. "I found Miss Smedley alone in her room, and we decided to have a cozy chat here. I was just about to make us some tea." She passed the girl another handkerchief. "Things have not been going well for Alison lately."

"Indeed?" Concordia sat on a stool. "What seems to be the problem?"

The girl gave her a skeptical look and sniffed. "I know *you* don't care," she said. "You like those other girls better. That scapegrace Maisie Lovelace and her crowd. The clever ones. But not me."

"That's not true," Concordia said. "But I don't approve of your behavior toward them, or your lack of effort in your own studies."

"Ooh, those girls are infuriating. I cannot stand it!" Miss Smedley exclaimed. "They do something outrageously stupid, like putting the president's buggy in the bursar's office of all things, and now the whole campus is cheering them on, and they get their names in the *newspaper.*" She put her face in her handkerchief and sobbed again.

Concordia sat next to the girl, putting an arm around her shoulders. "There's much more to it than it seems," she said, her voice gentle, "but it's pointless to compare yourself to others. Why worry about them? What do *you* want from your life? And how are you going to make that happen?"

"Alison, may I tell Miss Wells what you told me?" Charlotte asked.

The girl shrugged and wiped her eyes.

Charlotte turned to Concordia. "Alison is beginning to have doubts about the sort of life her parents have in mind for her, but she fears trying to do anything else. She thinks she would not be capable, or that her father would forbid it."

Alison nodded miserably.

"Alison and I come from a similar upbringing," Charlotte continued, with a half smile in the girl's direction. "In fact, our families know each other. Our parents want us to become leaders within our social sphere, to be a help-meet for the man we will eventually marry, and further his career—in the parlors of genteel society, at least. I'm not saying that isn't a laudable ambition, but it isn't suited to every girl. To our families, the purpose of a women's college is to make advantageous connections and to enhance our pedigree. No one back home expects us to apply ourselves to the mental rigor of college work–I doubt they imagine we are required to do rigorous work. They certainly don't expect us to pursue a career after college."

Concordia sat back and considered this in silence. That explained a great deal: the scorn, the aborted efforts, the desperate need for an attentive following.

"Miss Smedley," Concordia said finally, "I know you are capable. I have seen glimpses of it. Why not explore your abilities? We can help, *if* you are willing to try." She gestured to Charlotte. "I suggest you ask Miss Crandall how she came to be here now, as a *teacher*, a woman making her own way in the world. I think you'll find it inspiring."

She got up and left them to it.

Concordia was just in time to meet Capshaw as he stepped onto the porch. She quietly ushered him into the parlor and went to get Ruby.

"Would you mind coming out to the parlor for a moment?" Concordia asked, sticking her head in the kitchen. She turned and walked back down the hall before Ruby could ask why. With a puzzled crease of her brow, the matron put aside her work and followed.

Lieutenant Capshaw stood as they entered. "Mrs. Hitchcock."

Concordia saw the raw panic flit across Ruby's features before she suppressed it. Her shoulders slumped. "Lieuten'nt."

"Would you sit, please?" Capshaw gestured to the settee.

Concordia closed the door and sat beside the trembling housekeeper. "It's all right, Ruby," she said. "Lieutenant Capshaw just wants to ask you a few questions."

"I know what questions he has," Ruby said, eyes blazing, "but I don't have any answers for him." She faced him squarely. "Don't know why you're pokin' your nose here, anyhow."

Capshaw raised an eyebrow. "An unsavory stranger wanders the grounds, and you don't think that's a problem? Aren't you charged with the safety of your girls?"

Ruby kept her eyes on her shoes. "It's been a while since then. Nobody's been hurt," she added defensively.

"Ruby," Concordia said, "it's clear you're trying to protect this man. You know him, don't you?"

Ruby shuddered and buried her face in her apron, sobbing.

Capshaw looked as if a live snake had slithered into the room. He cleared his throat and gave Concordia a beseeching look.

For the second time that day, Concordia found herself consoling a weeping female. "We want to help. Just tell us. Who is he?"

Ruby lifted a tear-streaked face. "My husband."

Concordia's mouth hung open. *Husband?*

Capshaw calmly pulled out his notepad and started to write. "I thought you were widowed, ma'am," he said politely.

Ruby gritted her teeth and dabbed a handkerchief to her eyes. "*So did I.* For the past thirty-four years, no less! I got a widow's war pension, pitiful as it was. That cowardly, no-good excuse for a man let them think he was dead, along wi' the dozens scattered on the battlefield. He switched the contents of his pockets and papers with another man who..." her voice faltered, "didn' have much of a face left."

"Why?" Concordia asked.

Ruby shrugged. "He didn' want to fight anymore. He told me he left the country for a long time, working as a logger in Canada, and picking up odd jobs in the off season."

"And you haven't been in communication with him all this time? How did he find you?" Capshaw asked.

The matron scowled. "He's living in Hartford for a time, he says, and he found *me* because of that blasted newspaper article, when I got the staff award. Says when he read it he figured I was doing well for myself. Wanted money. He threatened to tell President Langdon he was my husband."

"Did you give him any?" the lieutenant asked.

Ruby nodded, and turned to Concordia with pleading eyes. "Wot could I do? If the school knew I was married, I'd lose my position for sure. And I'll certainly never live with that shady, no-account Johnny Hitchcock while I still have breath in me!"

"So he's going by Johnny Hitchcock these days?" Capshaw asked, scribbling rapidly.

"Guess he in't scared of being caught by the War Office anymore." Ruby shrugged.

"Any other names he's gone by? What's he doing in Hartford?"

Don't know why he's back in these parts, but he's up to no good, I'm sure," Ruby said. "I have no idea wot names he's used in the past."

"What do we do now?" Concordia asked Capshaw.

The policeman rubbed his mustache as he thought. "Where have you met this man, to give him money?"

"At first, he came to the kitchen door. I was kinda scared that's what he was goin' to do, after you told me he'd come looking for me, miss," Ruby said, glancing at Concordia. "But I told him he was attracting too much attention being on a girls' campus, and he could get me in trouble. So he sent me a message with the name of a saloon. I'd go, and have a messenger boy step inside to ask for him while I waited outside. Then he'd come out, I'd give him the money, and leave."

"The name of the establishment?"

"The Brass Spittoon."

Concordia's lips quirked. The name said it all.

Capshaw stood. "Mrs. Hitchcock, this is what you're going to do: first, stop communicating with him. Completely. And don't give him any more money. If he comes to campus, call me."

Ruby blanched. "But he'll tell Mr. Langdon!"

Concordia interrupted. "Mr. Langdon will already know, because *you* are going to tell him. Today. I'll go with you."

Capshaw nodded. "That's right, ma'am. It's the only way to remove this man's hold over you. In the meantime, I'll locate the...gentleman, and make him see the error of his ways. We have plenty of blackmailers in prison, you know. I'll remind him of that fact. He should leave you alone after that."

Ruby put a trembling hand on Concordia's arm. "But I'm still—married to him," she whispered.

"We'll talk with Mr. Langdon about that, too," Concordia said. "I'm sure there is something that can be done, when a man has been declared dead all these years. Don't worry," she added, "we'll get this straightened out."

Chapter 29

Concordia had just finished grading themes in her office when David Bradley tapped on her door. "Am I interrupting?" He hovered uncertainly in the doorway, which meant that his compact, muscular build took up most of it.

Concordia smiled. "Not at all. Come in."

He pulled a chair from the corner of the room and put it in front of her desk. "You said you wanted to talk, and we never got the chance after Miss Hamilton returned with Eli," he said. "I'll be busy with laboratory exams all week. Can we talk now?"

Although his posture appeared casual and relaxed, she could see the tension in his jaw. His usual dimpled smile was fleeting.

Concordia hesitated. She had been postponing this long enough. Best to get it over with.

"What did you want to talk to me about?" he prompted.

Concordia took the plunge. "Our engagement."

David leaned forward anxiously. "You've changed your mind. I know we've been arguing more lately, Concordia, and I'm sorry about Rosen—"

"No, no, it's not that," Concordia interrupted hastily. "But I do want to talk about the engagement. I was hoping you would be willing to...postpone it for a while." She tried to take courage in her mother's words. *If David is half the man I believe him to be, he'll wait—and count himself lucky to do so.* Concordia hoped she was right.

David frowned. "Postpone it? For how long?"

"I-I'm not sure." Concordia bit her lip. "I do love you, David. I'm just not…ready. I think the fact that we've been arguing more often points to us needing more time."

"When *will* you be ready?" he asked carefully.

"I don't know. I'm sorry," she added, her voice catching. "I know it's terribly selfish of me to ask you to wait. But it's a big step for me. It doesn't feel right to take it yet."

David reached over and clasped her hand. "But you're not retracting your promise?"

She shook her head, tears welling in her eyes, her throat burning with words she couldn't say.

He gave her a tentative smile. "I was worried," he said quietly. He got up and turned toward the window. Concordia watched him struggle to maintain his composure.

After a moment, he turned back to face her. "I can wait."

Concordia let out a breath she didn't realize she was holding. "Thank you."

David glanced at her desk clock. "I'd better be going." He gestured at the bowl on her desk, brimming with pansies. "They're lovely."

Concordia smiled. "A breath of spring in a dusty office. Though I don't know how they got here. There's no note. Perhaps President Langdon had an abundance in his garden. I was going to ask him later." All the staff knew that Langdon spent as much time in his garden in the spring than in his office. Many an impromptu staff meeting took place among the hydrangeas and rhododendrons in front of Sycamore House.

David looked closely at the bowl, turning it. "Ah, *here's* a note." He pulled a slip of paper embedded in the leaves and handed it to her.

Concordia opened the plain white scrap of folded paper, titled CONCORDIA. Her chest felt tight as she read:

YOU HAVE BEEN SPARED, THIS TIME.
ABANDON YOUR INQUIRIES OR PREPARE
TO JOIN ROSEN.

"Concordia, what is it?" David picked up the paper where she'd dropped it. He sucked in a breath as he read. "We should call the police."

"No."

"What do you mean, *no*? Someone slips into your office without your knowledge and leaves this note, threatening to kill you, and you will do nothing?"

His voice had risen in his agitation, and Concordia made a *shushing* gesture. She got up and closed the door. "Of course I'll 'do something'," she answered tartly. "But we don't know who in the police department we can trust. You were there when Miss Hamilton returned with Eli; you know how powerful the Black Scroll is. I'll inquire if anyone observed a man lingering near my office this morning."

Maynard's and Isley's offices were just down the corridor. How easy it would be for either of them to place the flowers and note on her desk. She felt a chill at the base of her spine. "I'll also show this to Capshaw—and Miss Hamilton, when she returns," she continued. "They may figure out something."

David shook his head. "I don't want you part of this any more. The risk is too great."

"I can't pull out now. There is still a danger to Eli." If she were honest with herself, she knew a big part of her reluctance to walk away was that she could not abide being bullied. It stung her pride.

"The Capshaws and Miss Hamilton can protect the boy. They don't need you for that," David said.

But Concordia wasn't listening. Why was she getting this note *now*? She hadn't been an active part of the investigation since she and Miss Hamilton had hired Mr. Rosen to inquire about the Inner Circle. Rosen had been killed a week later, during the spring recess. Wouldn't they be satisfied now that their secret was safe?

Ah. Capshaw had come to Willow Cottage yesterday. Although his visit didn't have anything to do with the Inner Circle, perhaps someone thought otherwise. A person who was a regular on campus. Isley? Maynard?

David paused. "You're not attending to me, at all."

"Oh! I'm sorry, David. What were you saying?"

David took her hand in his. "Concordia, if you care anything for me, you will cease to play a part in this investigation. First the dynamite wrapper, and now this. It's too dangerous. I'm telling you to stop."

David's dark brown eyes, usually so open and warm, were narrowed in anger. She pulled her hand away. "I will not," she said firmly. "I'm sorry." She turned away.

"Then you will do it alone. I will no longer be a party to it." David stalked to the door, flinging it open.

Chapter 30

Week 10, Instructor Calendar
April 1898

"*No, I will speak as liberal as the north: Let heaven and men and devils, let them all, All, all, cry shame against me, yet I'll speak.*"

Miss Roth, otherwise known as Emilia, wife of the villain Iago, delivered her lines with all the energy of a long-deceived woman who has finally seen the truth. Concordia nodded in approval from her seat in the audience. Mrs. Isley had done a splendid job with them. For all the woman's frivolous ways, she certainly knew her stagecraft.

All in all, the dress rehearsal was going well, especially with Charlotte Crandall out behind the stage, helping students into their costumes and out upon the set on cue. There had been a few snags, of course. Several minor players forgot where they were supposed to stand, upstaging other characters. Iago tripped over her too-long cloak. And although Lily Isley executed her lines beautifully as the much-maligned Desdemona, she seemed to have trouble lying still once she was supposed to be dead.

But all of that would be worked out by next week. She hoped.

Concordia was roused by the smattering of applause as the dress rehearsal came to a close.

Now she was free to run her errand.

In case her movements on campus were being noted, Concordia had decided the best way to talk to Capshaw about the note was to visit him and Sophia at their residence. She had obtained permission from Miss Pomeroy to miss dinner after the dress rehearsal. She wouldn't want to incur Maynard's wrath again.

Sophia answered the door herself, her apron on. "Concordia! What a pleasant surprise. Eli will be thrilled to see you. Would you like to join us for supper? It's almost ready."

Concordia nodded. "Can I talk to your husband first?" She didn't want to bring up the note in dinner conversation, especially in front of Eli.

Sophia gestured to the parlor as a kitchen timer *dinged.* "He's reading the paper. If you'll excuse me, I have to rescue the shepherd's pie."

Capshaw stood as Concordia walked into the room. He regarded her closely and cleared a litter of newspapers from a wing chair. "Sit. What has happened?"

Concordia held out the slip of paper.

Capshaw scowled over the note. "Where was this?"

Concordia explained David finding the note among the flowers. "I thought at first the flowers had come from President Langdon. Sometimes, when he's trimming back his garden, he'll donate blooms to the staff or the dining hall. But he certainly didn't write this."

"I assume you talked to Mr. Langdon?" Capshaw asked.

Concordia nodded. "I asked everyone with offices in that corridor; no one claimed to have put flowers on my desk or to have seen anyone near my office. Of course, I didn't mention the note."

Capshaw gave her one of his melancholy looks. "It looks as if the Inner Circle has become more active on campus. Very disturbing. Do you mind if I keep this?" At Concordia's nod, he tucked it into his pocket. "I would take the warning seriously, miss. It's time to leave this to the professionals. Miss Hamilton is making progress, and I am helping her behind the scenes. We should have the case resolved soon."

Concordia leaned forward in interest. "What has she learned? When will she return?"

Capshaw rolled his eyes. "You college ladies suffer from incorrigible curiosity. She sent a short telegram to say she's solved the mystery of the cuff links, and has a lead on the wrapper. Of course, she couldn't go into particulars, but she's due back in a few days. No doubt she will fill you in on the details soon after that, but I insist on having the *first* conversation with her."

Sophia poked her head in the doorway. "Supper is ready."

Capshaw put a hand to Concordia's arm as she got up. "Remember, stay out of it."

All through the dinner conversation—which centered around Eli's progress in his studies, his healing leg, and his new interest in whittling—Concordia kept thinking about what David—and now Capshaw—had said. *Stay out of it. The risk is too great. I'm telling you to stop.*

Perhaps they were right, although she didn't like it. Not at all. The thought of someone malevolent, either the killer himself or someone who knew and condoned such behavior, walking into her office, touching her things, leaving the note—bizarrely accompanied by flowers—made her shudder. Who was this man? The sooner they had answers, the better.

Chapter 31

Week 11, Instructor Calendar
May 1898

At last, Capshaw sent word that Miss Hamilton had returned to Hartford. Soon afterward she heard from the lady herself, arranging to meet at Mrs. Gilly's Tea Shop.

Concordia saw her before she was even halfway down Canton Street. The tall woman of flawless posture, her graying-blonde hair smoothly tucked under a stylish hat of melon green, the elegant tilt of her head…Miss Hamilton was unmistakable in a crowd. Just the sight of her felt reassuring. Heaven only knew where they would be without her aid in this affair.

They sat at one of the outdoor tables under the striped awning, taking in the sight of passersby as they sipped their tea and shared a lemon tart.

Concordia felt some of the tension drain away as she sat. As eager as she was for Miss Hamilton's news, she took a moment to let the world pass in front of her. Worries about her students, her classes, and her fiancé faded as she fixed upon the dappled sunshine on the sidewalk, the babies pushed in their carriages, and the profusion of ladies carrying brightly-frilled parasols.

Penelope Hamilton, however, was ill-disposed to sit idle. She cleared her throat. "Capshaw showed me the note from your office."

Concordia nodded, pulling herself back into the game of detection once again. "I haven't been able to determine who left it."

"I agree with Capshaw that the Inner Circle is a strong presence on campus now," Miss Hamilton said. "When I returned to my guest quarters at DeLacey House, I found that my belongings had been thoroughly searched."

Concordia started. "You think it was Isley or Maynard?" she whispered.

Miss Hamilton shrugged. "Probably. That's why I wanted to meet you here. I've already moved my things to a hotel. One cannot be too careful."

Concordia suppressed her disappointment. Miss Hamilton had been the only other person on campus who knew what was going on. She would miss her being right nearby. But of course, the precaution was a necessary one.

"What did you learn about the Black Scroll during your trip?" Concordia asked.

The lady leaned in and dropped her voice. "I've investigated secret societies before, but the Noble Order of the Black Scroll is a particularly close-mouthed group. On the surface, it seems to be a charitable organization, justifying its secret nature as the necessity of anonymous philanthropy. Indeed, recipients such as Hartford Settlement House have benefited lately from a number of anonymous donors. I've learned that the Black Scroll was behind that."

"While secrecy for the 'greater good' is not so terrible, the explosives wrapper we found certainly points to something..." Concordia searched for the word "...evil."

Miss Hamilton plucked absent-mindedly at the gaily-checkered napkin in her lap. "Secrecy is a double-edged sword, hiding villainous deeds as well as benevolent ones. And then there's the issue of *who* determines the 'greater good'—one man's good could be another man's bane."

"Yes, of course," Concordia agreed. "Even when men are convinced that their motives are pure, many barbarous things have been done in the name of justice, or Providence. The Crusades and the Inquisition are examples of that."

"Exactly," Miss Hamilton said.

"What else did you learn?" Concordia asked.

"I've discovered the three binding principles of the Brotherhood that every member must unconditionally agree to upon joining: to do charitable works; to never reveal that he is a member—or that anyone he knows is a member; and to help a brother in need, no matter what the circumstances."

"The last two tenets do seem worrisome," Concordia said.

Miss Hamilton nodded. "And really, it isn't the general membership of the Brotherhood that troubles me. It's this rogue organization within the heart of the Black Scroll. My source couldn't find any indication that the general membership is aware of its existence."

"Lieutenant Capshaw's police chief must be a Brother," Concordia said. "Was the Brotherhood's obedience rule used to compel him to remove Capshaw from the case?"

Miss Hamilton swatted at a stray fly. "I expect so. No doubt the Circle felt that Capshaw was getting too close to learning about them."

"Then members of the Inner Circle—" Concordia began.

"—need only invoke the rules of the brotherhood to get the cooperation of others, with no one the wiser. Those not in the Circle would believe the motives and actions to be as benevolent as their own, when that may be far from the case."

"Do we at least know the members of the Black Scroll?" Concordia asked.

Miss Hamilton smiled. "Thanks to the conversation you overheard at Barton Isley's dinner party, I had a start, but it has been slow-going. I've acquired a partial list of members, any of whom could also belong to the Inner Circle. You know some of these." She ticked off a list on her gloved fingers. "Barton Isley, Sir Anthony Dunwick, Republican Candidate Sanders, Robert Flynn, Randolph Maynard, Police Chief Stiles, and several Willoughbys, Florence's father and each of her three brothers. We know for sure that Isley is associated with the Inner Circle, and that Sir Anthony had been approached to join them. Based upon the jeweler's information, we're guessing that the Inner Circle is a very small group, consisting of six members, with a seventh on the way."

Concordia should not have been surprised by the list, but the idea of Robert Flynn being a Black Scroll member made her uneasy. Should she say something to her mother? Yet he struck her as an outsider, the Irishman with his quaint turns of phrase.

Then she realized Miss Hamilton had skipped over something. "What do you mean, 'jeweler's information'?" Concordia asked.

"Ah, yes, I forgot that part," Miss Hamilton said. "I tracked down the jeweler's shop where the cufflinks had been made. Five sets of cufflinks had been commissioned, along with the pin you'd found. Oh, and an additional cufflink set has just been ordered," she added.

"Sir Anthony," Concordia said. So he had decided to join the Inner Circle, after all. She wondered what his niece, Charlotte Crandall, would think of that if she knew.

"That seems a safe assumption, as is the notion that these were intended for Inner Circle members," Miss Hamilton said.

"But *who* ordered the jewelry? Barton Isley?" That didn't seem consistent with the man's frugal nature.

Miss Hamilton shook her head. "Not Isley. Randolph Maynard."

"*Our dean* placed the order?" Concordia exclaimed, inadvertently raising her voice.

Miss Hamilton made a *shushing* gesture. "The same."

Concordia felt a chill settle in her spine. With both Isley and Maynard as Inner Circle members, the school was sure to face yet another scandal. "Have you learned anything of the Circle's current plans?" she asked.

"Not yet, but it usually comes down to power and money. And now that they have explosives?" Miss Hamilton shuddered. "They are all the more dangerous."

"But how much did Florence know? How did she come by the dynamite wrapper?" Concordia asked. "One doesn't leave that sort of thing lying around. It *is* dynamite, as you surmised?"

"Yes indeed," Miss Hamilton said. She pulled out a small notepad. "It's the 'Hercules' brand of powder explosive, from the California Powder Company. As to how she got the wrapper, I've learned she was on intimate terms with someone in the Black Scroll, no doubt an Inner Circle member. She probably stumbled upon it by accident."

"'Intimate terms'?" Concordia asked.

"To put it bluntly, she had a lover. I haven't learned his identity, but I know he's a family friend of the Willoughbys. I wonder, though, if Rosen had learned who he was. Such a discovery might be what killed him. My source tells me Rosen was asking a lot of questions of the Willoughbys, with some trumped-up story about a feature article in the business pages of the *Courant*. I wish he'd been able to talk with you before he died."

Concordia couldn't count how many times she'd wished that herself, but she stayed on topic. "Why did Florence take the wrapper? Was she going to the police with it?"

Miss Hamilton shook her head. "She had ample opportunity to go to the authorities, but did not. Based on that and her letter to you, I suspect she was engaged in a dangerous little blackmail scheme."

Concordia remembered that part of Florence's letter: *I've secured enough money to leave the area and live comfortably abroad.* She leaned forward. "But how would she know the significance of the explosives wrapper? Have *you* discovered what they plan to do with such a device?"

Miss Hamilton's eyes brightened in excitement. "I've researched recent cases involving the use of dynamite. One looks particularly promising. There was an explosion in Boston harbor several months ago, aboard the *Gascogne*, arrived from Le Havre. It was carrying high-priced Valenciennes lace and other valuable commodities. The case was never solved—even though the insurance company investigated. The company considered the policy owners possible suspects. They were eventually cleared, however. The cargo turned out to be much more valuable than the insured price for it. The incident was eventually attributed to anarchists, and quietly dropped."

Concordia raised an eyebrow. "Anarchists? Here?" She'd heard of isolated anarchist incidents, the most famous being the

Haymarket riots in Chicago more than a decade ago, but it seemed more of a European phenomenon.

Miss Hamilton shrugged. "I suppose it's possible, but I don't believe it either. They make a convenient scapegoat group. Anyone can write a dithering note and shift the blame upon anarchists."

"What do you think really happened?" Concordia asked.

"The owners sustaining the loss are in the dry goods business, just like the Willoughbys. They are, in fact, the family's biggest competition. The financial loss wasn't substantial, especially since it was insured, but can you imagine the time involved to replace the goods? Who, then, would have the advantage of inventory?"

"The Willoughbys," Concordia answered.

"Exactly. And there's something else," Miss Hamilton added quietly. "The harbor watchman who died in the blast? The explosion didn't kill him. He'd been garroted."

Concordia shivered. "The same as Florence."

Miss Hamilton gave a slight nod. "It's no coincidence. We're looking for the same killer."

"But didn't Lieutenant Capshaw investigate garroting murders in the area over the past several years and find nothing?"

"True, but that's not Capshaw's fault," Miss Hamilton said. "Initial reports merely said the guard died in the fire. The coroner's corrected notation as to the manner of death was easy to miss. I've been looking specifically for incidents involving explosives—something we didn't know about before now."

"So you think Florence connected the ship-board explosion and the wrapper she later found—among her paramour's possessions, perhaps?—and on that evidence alone, she decided to blackmail her lover and his group?" Concordia couldn't keep the skepticism from her voice.

"A paper scrap is hardly damning evidence, I grant you," Miss Hamilton acknowledged. "However, the Inner Circle member she blackmailed may not have been sure what proof she actually had. Or perhaps that scrap was all she managed to conceal before her death, and other physical evidence she'd possessed was taken away by her killer."

"So the Inner Circle paid her, at least for a while, until they could figure out if she had told anyone else, what evidence she had, and where she'd hidden it." Concordia shivered.

Miss Hamilton nodded in agreement. "And no doubt planning to silence her, at a place and time that wouldn't disrupt their own operations."

"But Florence must have suspected them," Concordia said. "So she went into hiding."

"Stopping only to visit Eli," Miss Hamilton added. "That delay to see the boy gave them the chance to find her."

To hide the tears that blurred her vision, Concordia took a sip of her tea, now gone cold. Her stomach clenched at the dangerous game the woman had gambled at, and lost—one that had nearly cost Eli his life, too.

Miss Hamilton checked her watch. "I have to go. I'm interviewing the conductor at the train station again. I want to show him the cufflink design."

Concordia checked her own timepiece. "Oh! I have to be back in time to help with final preparations for tomorrow's performance of *Othello*. We're going in opposite directions, but at least we can keep each other company at the same corner." She looked up at the sky, where gray clouds had swept in, blotting out the spring sunshine. "I hope the sky doesn't open up in the meantime."

Waiting at the crowded stop, Concordia asked Miss Hamilton, "After interviewing the conductor, what's your next step?"

Since people hovered quite close to them—Miss Hamilton would have quite a time getting a seat on the downtown car with this crush—the lady leaned in to whisper in her ear. "I have an appointment tomorrow to speak to the chief of police, to inquire as to why he took Capshaw off the case."

Concordia's eyes widened. "He won't tell you anything," she murmured back. "If he's a Brother, he can't."

"I know." Miss Hamilton's gray eyes took on a determined look. "But I have to try."

"Won't that get the lieutenant in trouble?" Concordia protested.

"He's given me his blessing," Miss Hamilton said. "He wants to get to the bottom of it as badly as the rest of us. But it's most certainly a risk."

Concordia nodded, feeling miserable. Here was Capshaw, newly married and adopting Eli, and he could very well be dismissed—or worse—if the Inner Circle was alerted.

"The chief's the only link we have," Miss Hamilton said, her jaw set in determination.

The trolley for the downtown line was approaching, and people began to jostle one another for a front position. Concordia and Miss Hamilton hung back.

"Hey! Outta my way, you," growled one rough-and-tumble man to another, and swung a hairy elbow. Concordia caught a glimpse of a seaman's anchor tattoo as the man caught another tough full in the face and bloodied his nose.

Pandemonium erupted. Before they could move out of the way, Concordia and Penelope Hamilton were caught in a sea of knuckles and elbows. They held up their hands to protect their heads from the cross-blows as they tried to retreat to a safe distance. A woman screamed. People stumbled in their panic to get away. Concordia found herself separated from Miss Hamilton, who was swept into the thick of the chaos.

The trolley continued to glide smoothly toward the corner, its driver ignorant of what was happening.

"Stop it! Stop!" Concordia yelled, fending off stray blows as she struggled to close the gap and reach her friend.

To her horror, just as the trolley was bearing down upon the corner, a shove—she couldn't tell from whom, there were so many bodies—sent Miss Hamilton flying. The lady landed in the street, directly in the path of the trolley car, its driver now frantically applying the brake.

Miss Hamilton lay motionless.

"No!" Concordia screamed. Several women put their gloved hands to their mouths in terror. The men seemed oblivious to everyone except whomever they were pummeling.

Concordia made a final push toward Miss Hamilton's still figure in the street. She launched herself in one leaping tumble, snatching at the woman's waist as her momentum rolled them into the middle of the dusty street. Concordia felt a painful *snap* of her shoulder as she landed on her side.

The last thing Concordia remembered seeing before she blacked out was the grimy underside of the streetcar bumper, stopped at last, inches from her ear.

Chapter 32

This accident is not unlike my dream:
Belief of it oppresses me already.

Othello, I.i

Week 11, Instructor Calendar
May 1898

Concordia awoke to the sound of rain pattering against unfamiliar windows. Why wasn't she in her bed at Willow Cottage?

Then she remembered. Miss Hamilton lying motionless in the street. The oncoming streetcar.

"Miss Hamilton?" she called out, struggling to push herself into a sitting position, wincing. *Drat.* Her left arm and shoulder were immobilized in a sling and throbbed like the devil.

She surveyed her surroundings, taking in the sight of two rows of iron-rail beds containing women in various stages of wakefulness. At the foot of each bed, clean, shiny pails were positioned on the linoleum flooring.

Mercy. She was in a...hospital. She craned her neck to get a look at the other women in nearby beds. None of them was Miss Hamilton.

"Concordia! Oh, thank heaven." Mrs. Wells hurried over to her bedside. She was followed by a short, rotund man whom Concordia took to be the doctor.

"Mother," Concordia said, taking her hand and blinking back tears, "Where's Penelope Hamilton?"

"Who?" Mrs. Wells asked.

The gentleman interrupted. "Do you mean your companion, the other lady who was injured?"

Concordia nodded, wincing as her head ached.

"I'm not in charge of her case," the doctor said, "but I understand that her condition is considerably more serious. She's on a different ward."

"More serious? Will she be all right?" Concordia asked anxiously.

The doctor hesitated. "I'm sorry, miss, but I don't have the particulars to be able to say."

"Can I see her?" Concordia persisted, struggling to swing her legs to the floor.

Mrs. Wells made a gesture of protest, and the doctor put out a gentle restraining hand. "The lady is being well cared-for, and there's nothing you can do at the moment. I must insist that you stay in bed. You have significant injuries yourself: a blow to the head, a dislocated shoulder that has been set into place, and a good many scrapes and bruises."

Concordia's mother paled and she gave him an anxious glance. "Will she be all right? When can I take her home?"

The man shook his head. "I need to conduct my examination now. Mrs. Wells, why don't you have a seat over there?"

The doctor motioned to the nurse nearby. With the nurse's help, the doctor poked, prodded, and listened. Finally, he straightened up as the nurse smoothed the covers and settled Concordia, pale and trembling, more comfortably.

"I expect you'll recover completely, miss," the doctor said, putting his stethoscope back in his bag, "but you need to be off your feet for at least a week. You should be able to go home in a few days."

Concordia's mother started. "A few days? Why not now?" she asked anxiously.

The doctor smiled. "No doubt you share the widespread perception of hospitals as places for the poor, rife with infection, and to be avoided at all costs. Let me put your mind at rest, Mrs. Wells. Hartford Hospital employs a wide array of modern antiseptic procedures. Unlike many of the older hospitals, we are an institution already looking toward the twentieth century. We have the latest medical equipment and the best in professional staff. You need not fear leaving your daughter in our care."

Mrs. Wells gave the man a long look before giving a resigned nod.

"Doctor," Concordia asked, "could you find out about Miss Hamilton's condition? She has no family in the area. I'm very worried about her."

The doctor frowned. "You are a most persistent young woman. Very well. I will inquire about the lady and be back shortly."

Concordia nodded her thanks and closed her eyes.

She must have been asleep for a while, because the rain had stopped and the light from the windows was ebbing to dusk when she awoke. Her mother smiled.

"I'm glad you got some rest, dear. Would you like a sip of water?" She held the glass for her as she drank. "Sophia stopped by while you were sleeping, but we didn't want to wake you."

"Did I miss the doctor?" Concordia asked. *Drat.*

"I have someone better." Her mother gestured toward the corridor.

Concordia smiled when she caught sight of the tall, thin figure of Lieutenant Capshaw, sporting his usual full head of wavy red hair and mustache to match. "Lieutenant!"

Capshaw bowed.

The nurse pulled over another chair for the policeman. "You can't stay long, mind," she warned. "Miss Wells needs her rest."

Mrs. Wells pulled out her embroidery basket, making it clear she wasn't going anywhere. Capshaw looked over at the lady uncertainly.

Concordia knew there would be no budging her. "Mother, will you give me your word that you won't repeat what we discuss?"

Mrs. Wells pursed her lips in disapproval. "What are you involved in, Concordia? I understood your...entanglement... in the matter of the missing boy, but he's been found now. What more is there for you to meddle in?"

"Unfortunately, that wasn't the end of it," Concordia said. She had explained to her mother the basics of Eli's disappearance, but nothing regarding the murders of Florence and Rosen, or the Black Scroll. "Stay if you must, but I can't explain until later. Matters are too urgent now."

Mrs. Wells shook her head and resumed her needlework.

Concordia turned to the policeman. "Have you seen Miss Hamilton yet?"

Capshaw looked grim. "I wasn't permitted to, in her current condition. She's still unconscious, with a head injury, a fractured wrist, and several broken ribs. Even if she awakes, the doctors fear pneumonia."

Concordia felt her stomach clench. *If she awakes.* What would she do if Miss Hamilton didn't pull through?

She must not think of that.

"Does she have any family?" Capshaw's question broke into her thoughts.

"The only family I know of is a sister in Chicago. I'll give you her address," Concordia said.

Capshaw nodded. "Good. I'll send her a telegram."

"Lieutenant..." Concordia began, with an anxious look over at her mother, placidly working at her linen, "I'm not sure it was an accident."

Mrs. Wells lifted her head and stared, mouth open.

"I was wondering that myself," Capshaw said. He pulled out his well-worn pencil nub and wad of paper, waiting expectantly.

Concordia went through it all, starting with the crowded stop. She described the jostling for position when the streetcar approached, then the chaos of the fist fight. "Miss Hamilton was pushed into the street as the car was pulling up. The conductor tried to stop. I pushed past some people, and sort of...rolled us out of the way," she said, wincing and glancing ruefully at her sling. There had been no time for anything more graceful or lady-like.

Mrs. Wells made an involuntary *tsk*ing sound, and Capshaw gave a mighty sigh that Concordia understood all too well. *You college ladies are so...impetuous.* She could almost hear him saying it.

"Did you see who actually pushed her?" Capshaw asked.

Concordia shook her head.

"Can you describe the brawlers? Any distinguishing marks?" Capshaw asked.

"There were about a dozen men, but a range of ages. A few youths, but most were in their twenties, I'd say. There was even an older man. I thought he might have been a sailor once—oh!" she stopped. "I remember now—he had a tattoo. An anchor with a snake curled around it."

Capshaw was scribbling furious notes. "Anything else?"

Concordia sank back against the pillow. "No. I'm sorry."

Mrs. Wells patted her arm. "Perhaps, when you are less fatigued, more details will come back to you."

"What makes you think it was intentional?" Capshaw asked.

"Well," Concordia said, thinking back, "no one else was knocked down, and Miss Hamilton was shoved hard enough to land in the street, rather than crumple to the ground where she stood."

Capshaw stroked his mustache absent-mindedly. "Hmm. If deliberate, there are two possibilities: either someone had been following you both and, on impulse, took advantage of the chaos, or—" Capshaw hesitated.

"Or what?" Concordia prompted, leaning forward. By this point, Mrs. Wells had dropped her embroidery in her lap and leaned forward, too.

"—this was all planned ahead of time, and the brawl itself could have been staged to provide the opportunity to injure Miss Hamilton," Capshaw continued.

Concordia shuddered. If so, the power of the Inner Circle was formidable. And this was a group that didn't leave anything to chance. She met Capshaw's eye. "Miss Hamilton had an appointment to see your Chief of Police today," she said quietly.

Capshaw nodded. "Someone didn't want that interview to take place."

Mrs. Wells shifted restlessly in her seat. "I'm getting a bad feeling about this. Who's behind it all?" She fixed her eye upon Capshaw. "And how is your chief involved?"

Concordia and Capshaw exchanged glances. Concordia sighed. "You may as well tell her."

Capshaw eyed the row of beds. The two immediately adjacent to Concordia's were empty. Satisfied that no one was close enough to overhear, he gave Mrs. Wells a quick, low-voiced account of what they suspected to be the Inner Circle's involvement in Florence Willoughby's death.

Concordia could tell that her mother, despite herself, was listening with increased fascination. Perhaps Concordia wasn't the only member of the family who was drawn to unraveling a mystery.

"What did you say the organization was called?" Mrs. Wells asked.

"The Noble Order of the Black Scroll," Capshaw said.

Mrs. Wells tapped a finger thoughtfully against her chin. "I've heard of the Black Scroll...let me see...oh, yes, Agatha Griffiths mentioned it."

Concordia's mouth hung open. "Mrs. *Griffiths* knows about the Black Scroll?"

Mrs. Wells nodded. "Except she was referring to the *Daughters* of the Black Scroll. It's a ladies' charitable club. Agatha's a member, and she seemed pleased as punch to have recently convinced Lady Dunwick to join. She's asked me to join, too, but I haven't yet decided."

Concordia was silent, thinking of the possibilities. The Daughters of the Black Scroll sounded like a sister organization. How closely connected were the two? Had Charlotte Crandall's aunt joined it because her husband, Sir Anthony, was a Black Scroll member? Perhaps she and Charlotte could pay Lady Dunwick a visit.

Once she was out of the hospital, drat it.

Capshaw stood to leave. "I'll get started on these leads right away."

"So, you are embroiled in yet another police case," her mother said, when they were alone. She shook her head. "It makes your teaching profession appear—dare I say it—remarkably lady-like by comparison. Can't you just stick to teaching, dear? Why get involved in such unseemliness?"

Concordia didn't bother to answer, nor did her mother seem to expect her to. But it reminded her of something else. "Does the school know what happened?"

Mrs. Wells smiled. "The hospital has one of those telephone contraptions, so I called your school and spoke with your lady principal...Miss Pomeroy? Yes, that's the one. Lady Dunwick was right about telephone communication. All those crackles, pops, and assorted noises on the line are very disorienting. Certainly not an elegant way of conducting a conversation, but a great time-saver. It was all I could do to convince the woman to hold back your students, though. They were all set to cancel their play and tramp over here to visit you."

"I'm glad they are going ahead with the play, but I'll be sorry to miss it," Concordia said.

"Miss Pomeroy said to tell you that Mrs. Isley and Miss Crandall have everything well in hand, and that the production will go splendidly."

At that moment, they heard the rattle of dinner trays. The nurse came over with Concordia's tray. "I'm sorry, but visiting hours are over."

Mrs. Wells reluctantly disentangled herself and her belongings from the chair.

Concordia gave her mother a grateful look. "Thank you. For everything."

Concordia passed a restless night. If the sounds of strangers moaning, staff moving about, and the occasional electric light switched on in the hallway weren't enough to keep her awake, the discomfort of her injuries and her worry about Miss Hamilton were sufficient. She was relieved when she saw dawn tinting the windows.

That morning, another nurse changed her bandages, remade her wrinkled bed, and helped her wash her face and comb her hair. Concordia's arm and shoulder were feeling much better, and she hoped to soon dispense with the sling entirely. Her head didn't throb nearly as much, and her hip soreness had subsided enough that she could hobble across the room with only minor support. At her first opportunity—no matter what the hospital staff had to say about it—she would find Miss Hamilton and see for herself how the lady was doing.

Soon people streamed into the ward for visiting hours. Concordia's mother was the first to arrive. She was soon followed by college infirmarian Hannah Jenkins, along with Charlotte Crandall, Ruby, and several students from Willow Cottage.

"Ooh, Miss Wells, you're a hero!" one of the girls exclaimed, as Miss Jenkins checked Concordia's bandages with a critical eye.

The infirmarian gave a satisfied grunt. "Everything should heal nicely." She pointed to the sling. "I'd imagine you'll only need that for another day."

"I hope so," Concordia said, "it's quite a bother."

"How are you feeling?" Charlotte Crandall asked. She placed a satchel at the foot of the bed. "Ruby and I packed some of your personal items, along with a couple of books from your bedside table."

Concordia smiled her thanks at them both. "Did Miss Pomeroy assign you my classes?" she asked Charlotte.

The young lady nodded.

"Excellent," Concordia said. "I cannot think of a better substitute." Charlotte flushed.

"We missed you at the play, Miss Wells," a senior said.

"How did it go?" Concordia asked.

"Splendidly, although Miss Stephens tripped over her cloak again."

"You should have seen how crowded the theater was," another girl added. "There were people standing at the back and sides!"

Concordia could imagine. A former stage-actress, playing the lead in a college production? Perhaps missing that spectacle was a blessing in disguise.

"When are you coming back?" Ruby asked.

"Soon," Concordia said. "Believe me, I don't want to be away any longer than necessary."

"Even when you return, you must recuperate," Miss Jenkins warned. "You won't be able to jump right into your normal routine, you know."

"Don't you worry, I'll make sure she rests," Ruby said firmly, giving Concordia a wink. Concordia was relieved to see the matron looking more like herself these days. She hoped they had seen the last of Johnny Hitchcock. Thankfully, President Langdon had insisted that Ruby remain in her position as cottage matron, and let the police deal with her long-lost husband.

The nurse soon came in to shoo them all out. Concordia touched Miss Jenkins' elbow. "Do you think you could visit Miss Hamilton while you're here? I can't find anyone to tell me how she is today."

Hannah Jenkins grinned. "I already have. I stopped by on our way in; I know the attendant on duty. Miss Hamilton's condition is quite serious, so she's in a private room. She's not conscious yet. She seems to be breathing with ease, and no fever, thank goodness. I understand that is an improvement. They are hopeful that the danger of pneumonia has passed."

Concordia expelled a breath. "Do you think you can convince the nurse to allow *me* to visit her?"

Miss Jenkins patted her arm. "I'll see what I can do."

Just as the nurse was growing apoplectic in her effort to clear out Concordia's visitors, David Bradley walked in. Everyone crowded around Concordia's bed as the nurse's voice became more strident.

"Out, everyone! This is not a concert hall, if you please!" The nurse pointed to Concordia's mother. "*You* may stay, but everyone else needs to go." She turned to David Bradley. "You, too, young man."

"But I just got here," David pointed out.

"Besides," Mrs. Wells cut through the hubbub, addressing the nurse, "he's Miss Wells' fiancé."

All conversations stopped.

The students gaped at Concordia, who resisted the urge to pull the covers over her head.

Miss Jenkins stepped in. "All right, young ladies, you heard the nurse. It's time to go." She hustled them out the door before anyone had a chance to say another word. Miss Jenkins did, however, throw a puzzled look in Concordia's direction as she left.

Concordia groaned and buried her face in the pillow. Even though David had privately agreed to a delay, there was no point to it now. Word would spread like wildfire throughout campus by the end of the day. Everyone would consider her as good as gone.

Mrs. Wells, hand to her mouth as if she could hold back the words, sank into a chair. "Oh, dear, I am so sorry."

David waved a dismissive hand, and smiled briefly. "It was bound to come out sooner or later." He pulled up another chair and took Concordia's hand, his expression more somber. "I was alarmed to learn about your accident...or *was* it an accident? Is it connected to the note we found?"

"I don't know," Concordia said wearily.

"What note?" Mrs. Wells asked.

David cleared his throat and shifted uneasily as Concordia glared at him.

"Well?" Letitia Wells demanded.

When Concordia said nothing, David explained. "A note of warning was anonymously left in Concordia's office. It told her to stop her inquiries...or end up like Rosen."

Mrs. Wells gripped the arm of the chair, her knuckles white.

"David, get her a glass of water," Concordia said. "Quickly. It's all right, Mother. No one tried to hurt *me*."

In a few moments, Mrs. Wells had regained her composure. "Perhaps no one actively tried to harm you, but an attempt was certainly made on Miss Hamilton's life."

David's brow creased. "But how did you get hurt?"

Concordia related the bare bones of the incident in an attempt to make it sound less dangerous than it was. She didn't want to upset David any further.

But it was too late for that. "You threw yourself directly into the path of the streetcar?" David asked incredulously. "You're lucky you weren't both killed. I know you greatly esteem Miss Hamilton, dear, but was that quite the prudent thing to do?"

Concordia's eyes narrowed. "Would you have me wringing my hands at the curb, helplessly watching Penelope die?"

David scowled. Mrs. Wells interrupted in an attempt to smooth the waters. "I'm sure he meant nothing of the sort. David is merely concerned for your welfare."

"I'm very tired." Concordia closed her eyes. She didn't open them again until after they left.

Although she truly was exhausted, the second night in her hospital bed was no better than the first. She knew what the problem was: she hadn't yet been able to see Miss Hamilton.

Giving up on sleep, she decided to at least try for a quick peek into Miss Hamilton's room to see the lady's condition for herself. Penelope Hamilton's sister would no doubt arrive tomorrow, but no one was with her now.

Slowly and quietly, Concordia swung her legs over the bed and felt around for her slippers. She hesitated, then slipped her arm out of the sling, experimentally flexing her arm and shoulder. Just a little stiff, but otherwise fine.

Staying close to the shadowy side of the corridor, Concordia quietly shuffled past the nurse rummaging in the supply closet, and at last found Miss Hamilton's room along the far wing. She stepped inside.

Miss Hamilton looked so very still and fragile, head wrapped in an enormous bandage, the side of her face bruised, arm in a splint. Concordia's heart constricted in her chest. In the dim light of the room, she could see Miss Hamilton's gray-blond hair, tousled and loose around her shoulders. But she was breathing easily, her face relaxed. Concordia limped to the head of the bed. "Miss Hamilton," she whispered.

The lady's eyes fluttered but didn't open. And yet, that seemed to be a good sign. Had Miss Hamilton recognized her voice?

Concordia heard footsteps approaching.

She knew she shouldn't be here, so she retreated to the corner shadows. If the nurse didn't come in, she could slip out after the woman passed by. If she did come in, well, Concordia would apologize and go back to bed with as much dignity as she could muster.

Drat. The figure was coming in.

Her heart leapt in her chest. *It wasn't the nurse.*

The silhouette was much too wide, more like a barrel-chested man. Surely, the doctors didn't attend to patients so late?

Concordia froze in place, hardly daring to breathe. She had a sick feeling in the pit of her stomach. Something was amiss.

She waited.

As the figure came into the dim light of the bedside lamp, she recognized the scarred, balding head, the unkempt beard, and the missing ear lobe.

Johnny Hitchcock.

She sucked in a soft breath and groped toward the door. She must get help.

The man hesitated, turning toward the sound. Light glinted along the metal wire in his hand.

Concordia screamed.

The man growled and shoved her, hard, as he ran out.

Chapter 33

After a flurry of attendants rushed in to find a shaken Concordia struggling to get off the floor, she was taken to a private room and ordered to stay in bed until the police arrived.

Capshaw came quickly, hair mussed, shirt mis-buttoned, hat askew on his head. Concordia waited impatiently as she heard him go into Miss Hamilton's room first.

Capshaw came to see her next, shaking his head in disbelief.

"How you manage to find trouble—even while recovering in a hospital—is beyond me, miss." He regarded her pale face. "Are you well enough to give me an account? The sooner the better, if we have any hope of catching him."

Concordia nodded. "It was Ruby's husband, Lieutenant. Johnny Hitchcock." She shuddered. "I'm sure of it."

Capshaw muttered something under his breath, ran to the door, and spoke to the sergeant standing outside. After a moment, Concordia saw the man give a quick nod and leave.

"We'll telegraph Hitchcock's description to all the precinct night watches," Capshaw said, coming back to stand beside her bed. "I'll need to speak with Mrs. Hitchcock again. She may know other places he frequents. When I went looking for him last week, he hadn't been seen at the Brass Spittoon in a while. But first, recount to me exactly what happened."

Concordia told Capshaw about her worry for Miss Hamilton, and slipping into the lady's room; then, the shadow in the hall, and Hitchcock at the bed holding the wire.

Capshaw nodded. "So Hitchcock murdered Florence Willoughby, and was attempting to use the same method on Miss Hamilton. Come to think of it, the man's burly figure, grizzled beard, and rough manner of speech match the description Eli gave of the man returning to Florence's room after the murder."

"Hired by the Inner Circle," Concordia said.

"That seems a safe assumption. And I've learned a few interesting things about Hitchcock in the meantime—" he broke off as Concordia shivered again. Capshaw gently tucked the blanket around her. "You've had quite a shock. Why don't you rest now? We'll talk again in the morning."

Concordia swallowed. "What if he comes back...to try again?"

"Then we'll have him, for sure," Capshaw said grimly. "I have a patrolman posted at Miss Hamilton's door. Oh, and you'll be happy to learn the lady has opened her eyes."

Concordia sat bolt upright in excitement. "She's awake?"

"Indeed. The commotion roused her. While the doctor said he wouldn't recommend screaming as a means of waking an unconscious person, it seems extraordinarily effective in this case."

Concordia smiled weakly.

"I've been told we can speak with her tomorrow, if she continues to improve," Capshaw said.

Concordia breathed a sigh. Miss Hamilton was going to recover.

If they could keep her away from garrote-wielding murderers.

Eventually Concordia fell asleep, her dreams punctuated by shadowy figures stalking dark corridors, clutching deadly wires.

Chapter 34

Farewell the tranquil mind! Farewell content!
Othello, *III.iii*

Week 11, Instructor Calendar
May 1898

Miss Hamilton seemed enormously improved since last night. True, the lady still sported a large bandage around her head and a splint on her wrist, but her complexion had a tint of pink under the bruises, and her eyes were bright and clear as she gave Concordia an equally frank perusal.

Concordia knew she looked poorly, with dark, sleep-deprived circles under her eyes, a purpling bruise on her forehead, and her arm back in its sling. After last night's fall, the doctor had ordered her to wear it a few days longer.

Concordia sat down on the chair beside the bed. "It's good to see you awake. We were all so worried."

Miss Hamilton nodded, wincing. "The nurse told me what happened at the trolley stop. I remember nothing after I fell. Thank you, my dear. Your courage and quick-thinking saved me."

Concordia, blushing, waved off the praise. "Were you also told about last night?"

Miss Hamilton's eyes flicked to the patrolman by the door. "They were reluctant to, but I insisted. After all, it's not every day that a strange man in uniform stands outside a lady's door in the wee hours of the morning. I understand I have you to thank for that as well."

Concordia gave a fleeting smile. "At least now we know who is responsible. The police are searching for Hitchcock."

"Indeed," Miss Hamilton acknowledged, "and we can assume the Inner Circle is behind this. But if so, what are they planning next?"

They were interrupted by a polite knock, and Capshaw came in.

"Any word on Hitchcock?" Miss Hamilton asked the policeman.

Capshaw shook his head and glanced over at Concordia. "I just spoke to Ruby. She remembers another place he frequents, so my men are checking there now. I'm sorry to say that I inadvertently distressed her, calling at such an early hour, and incurred the displeasure of your lady principal in the process."

Concordia smiled. As the past few weeks had shown, Miss Pomeroy possessed an unexpected steely side.

Miss Hamilton frowned. "Then he's fled the area."

Capshaw shook his head. "More likely, he's in hiding. I think the Inner Circle is still in need of his services. But I'll explain that later. First," he pulled out his notepad, "if you're feeling up to it, Miss Hamilton, I want to get your account of what happened at the trolley stop." At Miss Hamilton's nod, he pulled out his pencil and gave an absent-minded scribble on his cuff to test its point.

Miss Hamilton succinctly described what she could remember of the incident. It closely matched Concordia's account, including the same sailor with the anchor tattoo.

Capshaw flipped through his notes. "The tattoo sounded familiar when Concordia first described it. I did some checking and identified the man. Sam Blackstone. He was in the Navy, but got kicked out for thieving. Has had a few run-ins with the law since then. He works at the docks these days. Hasn't been seen this week, though."

"Are we assuming this man—and the others in the crowd—were hired by the Inner Circle?" Concordia asked.

"That's the most promising line of inquiry, especially after last night," Capshaw said. "Their first attempt at getting rid of you failed, so they sent in Hitchcock."

Concordia glanced anxiously at Miss Hamilton. "Lieutenant, you said the Inner Circle still needs Johnny Hitchcock. Why?"

"In looking over his army records," Capshaw said, "he joined the Nutmeg Regiment shortly after he and Ruby married in 1863. According to the story he told Ruby, he faked his death during the second battle of Petersburg the following year and fled to Canada. We haven't been able to confirm his whereabouts during those decades, but we learned that he'd been employed in a factory in New Jersey for the past five years." Capshaw looked up from his notes. "An explosives factory."

Concordia sucked in a breath. As if Hitchcock's nefarious talent for strangling women was not enough to recommend him in criminal circles.

"So that's what the Inner Circle wants," Miss Hamilton said with perfect calm, as if one dealt with garrote-wielding explosives experts every day. "Someone to acquire devices for them."

"Or make them," Capshaw added.

"What do we do if we can't find Hitchcock?" Concordia asked. "Will you go after the Inner Circle? Question Barton Isley, or Sir Anthony Dunwick? We're sure of their involvement, at least. And Miss Hamilton told me Randolph Maynard had ordered the cufflinks. He must be part of it, too."

Mercy, Hartford Women's College would lose half of its administrators at this rate.

"One cannot simply drag upstanding citizens to police headquarters," Capshaw said. "We only have your account of a conversation heard through a window, and a man's personal mercantile dealings."

"I agree," Miss Hamilton said. "Besides, such a public inquiry would cause the Inner Circle to shut down its activities, and we would be none the wiser about what those might be."

"That would at least stop them," Concordia said.

"Only for a little while," Miss Hamilton said. "Once the investigation was suspended, the Circle would resume business as usual."

Capshaw scowled. "The hand of the Black Scroll—or more properly, the Inner Circle—has been well concealed." He stood resolutely. "Except for one man, whom I *know how* to find."

Miss Hamilton nodded knowingly.

"My police chief." Capshaw squared his shoulders. "I pray I don't lose my job over this, but I'm going to have a talk with him whether he fires me or not. This morning." He looked at Miss Hamilton. "I may have to reveal your role in this in order to make my point."

Miss Hamilton nodded. "I trust your judgment in the matter. Good luck, Lieutenant."

Once Capshaw was gone, Miss Hamilton turned to Concordia.

"He cannot do this alone. In fact, once he confronts his superior, even if he is not fired outright, his movements will be watched. He could be kept busy chasing false trails deliberately put in his path."

Concordia gestured ruefully toward Miss Hamilton's collection of bandages. "What can be done? You're certainly in no condition to investigate."

Miss Hamilton met her eyes squarely. "But you are."

Concordia swallowed. Miss Hamilton was right. She was nearly recovered from her injuries, and would be leaving the hospital tomorrow. She was better able to help Capshaw. A chill ran through her as she remembered the warning note.

"We must identify the rest of the Inner Circle, and ascertain their plans," Miss Hamilton continued.

"But how?" Concordia asked. "We have no way into—" She stopped.

"Yes?" Miss Hamilton prompted.

Concordia leaned forward eagerly. "Yesterday, my mother mentioned that there exists a *Daughters* of the Black Scroll, and that Lady Dunwick is a member. She's Charlotte Crandall's aunt. And she owes me a favor."

Miss Hamilton raised an inquiring eyebrow.

"I helped Charlotte find a job at the school," Concordia explained. "It was nothing, really, but Lady Dunwick was particularly grateful for it."

Miss Hamilton eyes gleamed in interest. "That sounds promising. Sir Anthony may have confided in his wife, or she might have heard something of the Inner Circle from the Daughters' organization. Or other wives. Try to see her as soon as possible."

"It may help if I take Charlotte with me," Concordia said.

The nurse came in. "Miss Hamilton, your sister is here. Shall I send her in?"

Concordia stood. "I was just leaving."

"Oh, and Concordia," Miss Hamilton called out. "Be careful. Your usual blunt approach may not be best in this circumstance."

Chapter 35

Capshaw decided to walk the ten blocks to the Kinsley Street Station, rather than take a streetcar. The sight of two women injured at the hands of criminals who should have been caught long ago made him want to throttle someone, and he needed the calming effect of physical activity. It would not do to barge in shouting at the Chief of Police and flinging very serious accusations. He would be summarily escorted out and stripped of his position, and have nothing to show for his sacrifice.

Capshaw was sure that a sacrifice was coming. His stomach tightened at the thought of telling Sophia and Eli that he no longer had a job. What could he do for a living? He was sure to be blacklisted from any police force in the area: New Haven, Boston, New York. Word would circulate that Aaron Capshaw was a loose cannon who suborned authority, a troublemaker who saw conspiracies where there were none.

But this *was* a conspiracy. And conspiracies only worked effectively in secret. The solution was exposure. If he had to go to the newspapers, he would.

Even so, Chief Stiles deserved a chance to explain himself first. Before this incident, Capshaw respected Stiles' integrity and sharp mind. He was a good leader and let his men follow their judgment, only stepping in when needed. Until recently, that is.

As his anger cooled and his steps slowed, he developed a plan to get the chief to see the danger of the Black Scroll's influence. The chief may have only reluctantly adhered to the Black Scroll pledge to help another brother without question, without any knowledge of the Inner Circle. If Capshaw could make the chief understand that the Circle was actually the force behind the request....

Such assumptions were not without risk, of course. If the chief was in fact part of the Inner Circle, Capshaw would be showing his hand, revealing everything he knew. They would all be in danger: he, his family, Concordia, and Penelope Hamilton.

Inside the station, the sergeant at the front desk looked up in surprise. "Why, Lieutenant! We don't see much o' ye here at K Street, sir. How can I help ye?"

"I'd like to see the chief, if he's free."

The man waggled a thumb toward the chief's office. "You're in luck, sir. He's jus' finished wi' the night watch reports, but hasn't gone over to the jail yet."

"Thank you." He walked down the corridor to the paneled door, the chief's name emblazoned across the inset of frosted glass. Giving one last tug of his tunic, he took a deep breath and knocked.

"Enter!"

"Ah, Capshaw, come in," Chief Stiles said. He gestured toward a chair.

"I've read your report about the identity of the stranger lurking on the grounds of the ladies' college," Stiles continued, when Capshaw was seated. "Good work. Any leads on locating the man?"

"Actually, he was seen again last night," Capshaw said. "At Hartford Hospital."

Stiles frowned. "The log mentioned some sort of a disturbance there. You were called in, correct?"

"Yes, sir. I haven't yet written out a report of last night's incident, but I wanted to inform you of the connection to the college's intruder. It's the same man."

"Indeed. You're sure the man was—" the chief hesitated, glancing down at his papers.

"Hitchcock," Capshaw supplied. "We have an eye-witness, someone from the women's college. The lady has been a hospital patient for the past few days."

Stiles sat back, steepling his fingers against his mustache, lost in thought. Finally he asked, "Your earlier report said the man was married to the cottage matron. Is she the eyewitness you're speaking of?"

Capshaw shook his head. "This young lady is a teacher at the college. Miss Concordia Wells."

"Wells…Wells," the chief muttered. "The name sounds familiar." He paused and gave Capshaw a sharp look. "Is this the same woman who was involved in the Durand affair last year?"

The chief had an excellent memory. Capshaw nodded. "Yes."

The chief rolled his eyes. "Lord save me from meddlesome ladies." He leaned forward. "Is Hitchcock targeting Miss Wells?"

"No," Capshaw said. "Her friend, Miss Hamilton, was the target. Miss Wells happened to be in the lady's hospital room when Hitchcock slipped in."

"Any injuries?" the chief asked.

"No sir. Miss Wells screamed, and Hitchcock fled."

"But this took place in the middle of the night," Stiles said. "How did Miss Wells come to be in Miss Hamilton's room at such an hour?"

Capshaw explained Concordia's concern for Miss Hamilton's welfare, her sleeplessness that night, her decision to visit her room. He left out the trolley incident, not being certain of the connection until he investigated further.

The chief muttered something yet again about "meddlesome females." Capshaw suppressed a smile.

"How do we know Hitchcock intended harm to Miss Hamilton?" the chief went on. "There was nothing in your earlier report about the college sightings that mentioned him being a physical threat to the women there."

Capshaw took the plunge, knowing there was no going back now. "Because the man was holding a garroting wire." He watched the chief carefully, waiting for him to make the connection.

"A wire?" The chief paled. "You mean...just like...." He stopped.

"Yes. Just like Florence Willoughby," Capshaw said. "The case you took away from me," he added pointedly.

The chief propped his face in his hands and sat, silent. Capshaw waited. If the chief was part of the Inner Circle, no more questions would be asked. Stiles would dismiss the hospital incident as unrelated, and the garroting wire as a mistake on the part of the witness. He would order the report filed and do no more with it.

Capshaw prayed the chief was the man of integrity he thought him to be.

The chief leaned forward. "You've taken steps to track down Hitchcock since last night, I presume?"

Capshaw stifled a relieved sigh and nodded. "A full description of the man has been sent to all the precinct watches."

"Good." The chief peered at him closely. "What's Miss Hamilton's connection to the case? Why was Hitchcock trying to kill her? There's more to this than you've told me so far. I want the whole story."

"You're not going to like it," Capshaw warned, thinking of the investigation they had undertaken behind the chief's back. He could still lose his job.

The chief, grim-faced, pressed his lips together. "I know."

"I told you to *get out*! You are finished here, Capshaw!"

The sergeant at the front desk stood up, startled, as Lieutenant Capshaw forcefully threw open the door. The glass in the frame rattled so violently the sergeant feared it might shatter.

Without a word or backward glance, the red-faced lieutenant whipped past him and out the front door.

The sergeant tentatively poked his head in the chief's office. "Anything I can do for ye, sir? The lieutenant left in quite a hurry."

The chief, also flushed, looked up. "He is no longer a *lieutenant*," he said, through gritted teeth. "I've fired him for incompetence and suborning authority."

"I see," the sergeant answered, confused. *Lordy, what was going on?* Capshaw, incompetent? Insubordinate? The man was one of the best they had.

The chief waved him out. "Close the door. I have reports to write. I don't want to be interrupted for the rest of the morning."

After the brief surge of adrenalin wore off, Capshaw's footsteps were heavy and slow as he turned toward the settlement house. He wanted to see Sophia and break the news to her before she heard it from someone else.

His chest tightened at the thought of telling her that he had been fired from the only job he loved, a livelihood that they depended upon.

But what tugged at him the most was the lie. Sophia was so forthright, and trusted him to be the same. And he had been. If the matter was confidential and he couldn't share it with her, he would say so, and she respected that.

Now, he had to convey the devastating news that he had lost his job, when he hadn't been fired at all. What would it do to her? How could he maintain the pretense?

And yet, their lives—including the chief's, now—depended upon keeping secret the plan the chief had proposed.

"It's crucial that everyone be convinced I've fired you," Chief Stiles had said, after Capshaw told him all he knew about the Inner Circle and how the group was connected to the deaths of Florence Willoughby and Ben Rosen, to the attack on Eli, to the trolley incident that had sent Concordia and Miss Hamilton to the hospital, and to the aborted assassination at the hospital. "Except for Isley and Dunwick, we have no idea who belongs to the Inner Circle, correct? We need to learn more, without anyone catching on. Otherwise, we could all be in danger. Both your investigation and mine must be very quietly done. I'll use my contacts in the Black Scroll to find out what I can about the Inner Circle. You must find Hitchcock."

Capshaw had agreed. What choice did he have? Yet, he felt a prickle of doubt. What if this was, in fact, a very cunning strategy on the part of the chief, inventing this scheme to make Capshaw believe that something was being done? What if the chief was a member of the Inner Circle after all?

There was one precaution he could take. He ran up the steps of the settlement house and sent a girl to fetch Sophia. He waited impatiently in the hall, going over what he would say to her.

"Aaron!" Sophia exclaimed, coming toward him. Her cheeks were flushed and strands of hair had slipped from their pins. Capshaw's heart twisted.

She laughed and reached back to tidy her hair. "What a lovely surprise. I'm a bit mussed after playing hoops with the children." When he said nothing, she gave him a penetrating look. "Something's wrong."

Capshaw pulled her to the far corner of the hallway. "There is. I want you and Eli to pack your things."

Chapter 36

Concordia was happy to return to Willow Cottage, although when David brought her back from the hospital, Miss Jenkins summarily put her to bed. Concordia was too exhausted from the events of the past three days to put up much of a protest. It had taken all of her energy to insist to Mother that she would be perfectly fine recuperating at her college residence.

Before she retired, however, she couldn't help but notice the special attention the girls paid to David.

"Oh, Mr. Bradley!" one girl exclaimed. "Don't leave us so soon. Ruby has made tea, and her scones are divine. Won't you stay?"

With a sideways grin at Concordia, David had agreed. Concordia, of course, knew the young ladies would pump him for information about the engagement and future wedding plans.

Miraculously, word of her engagement had not spread. She learned after the fact that Ruby had sat the girls down and sternly sworn them to secrecy until such time that Miss Wells decided to give them leave to talk about it. Concordia was touched by the respect for her privacy. So far the girls had been true to their word, not even speaking of it to the rest of their cottage-mates. Which was a marvel in itself.

So she didn't begrudge them a bit of wedding talk with David. He'd have little to tell, anyway, since they hadn't yet discussed the matter in any depth. Concordia skipped the tea party and went to bed, falling asleep almost as soon as her head touched the pillow.

After a day of bed rest, Concordia was ready to resume her classes.

Miss Jenkins, however, was having none of it. "You are recuperating rapidly, I grant you. But I'd like to see you rest a bit longer. Miss Crandall is doing a splendid job with your classes. Why not let her finish out the week, and then you can return?"

There was some sense to that. Concordia nodded. "Would you mind asking her to stop by today, after the Shakespeare class? I'd like to go over some things." Including how to approach her aunt, Lady Dunwick.

"Of course. But one more thing," Miss Jenkins added sternly. "No bicycle riding for another week."

Concordia sighed as she glanced through the window at the sparkling May morning. "It never entered my mind."

When Charlotte arrived, Concordia brought her straight into her study and closed the door. Charlotte raised an eyebrow at Concordia's somber look but said nothing.

"I don't know what I would have done without you," Concordia began. "I cannot think of a better substitute teacher for my classes."

Charlotte turned a pretty pink. "I've been happy to, Miss Wells. I've missed teaching."

Concordia was silent for a moment, then decided to dive right in. "I have another favor to ask."

Charlotte leaned forward. "Yes?"

"Could you arrange for us to pay a call on your aunt in the next few days?"

"Of course," Charlotte said. "Aunt Susan likes you. I'm sure she would enjoy a visit." She gave Concordia a sharp look. "But this is not a social call, is it? There's more going on."

Concordia hesitated. She had confidence in Charlotte's discretion, but she was reluctant to involve the girl too deeply. The danger was real.

"You can trust me," Charlotte prompted. "I'd be better able to help if I know what I'm dealing with."

"You're right, of course," Concordia said. "But there's some risk to involving you." She touched the small bandage at her temple. "This was not an accident."

Charlotte's eyes widened, but she otherwise sat, quite composed. "You may have noticed that you've already involved me," she pointed out.

Drat. The girl's logic was impeccable.

"You must promise you won't share what I'm about to tell you. With anyone," Concordia warned.

Charlotte nodded.

Concordia described the discovery of a secret society that called itself the Noble Order of the Black Scroll, along with the existence of the dangerous "Inner Circle" within it, succinctly recounting what had happened thus far. Concordia left out the names of Randolph Maynard and Barton Isley, as well as Charlotte's uncle. She wasn't sure Charlotte could act normally around these men if she knew.

Charlotte listened with rapt attention. "So you think that visiting my aunt will help you learn more about this Inner Circle, because she's a member of the Daughters of the Black Scroll?"

Concordia gave a start. "You *know* about your aunt's involvement with the group?"

"Of course. I understood it to be a charitable club—a sister group to the men's organization. I've been invited to join as well."

Perfect. This could be the opening they needed.

"I had no idea the men's group was engaged in something sordid," Charlotte went on. "I'm not so sure I wish to join."

"It's the secret splinter group within the brotherhood that's dangerous," Concordia said. "However, some tenets of the Black Scroll—notably, the oaths of secrecy and helping a fellow brother *without question*—have been twisted to suit the purposes of the Inner Circle. Miss Hamilton is convinced that the general membership is unaware of its existence."

Charlotte narrowed her eyes, puzzled. "How is Miss Hamilton involved? Why was she targeted at the trolley stop?"

Concordia had forgotten that Charlotte didn't know about Miss Hamilton's line of work. There was no way to delicately explain it. "She's a Pinkerton," she said simply.

Charlotte raised an eyebrow in disbelief. "She's a...*what?* You mean a detective?"

Concordia nodded.

"Amazing," Charlotte murmured. "I didn't know there was such a thing as a lady detective."

"Miss Hamilton is...one of a kind," Concordia said.

"So she's been investigating," Charlotte asked. "Did she learn why they killed Florence Willoughby?"

"We're fairly certain that Florence had been blackmailing the group, and was a threat to their plans."

"Do you know what those plans are?" Charlotte asked.

Concordia explained about the scrap from the dynamite wrapper.

Charlotte's mouth formed a silent *o*. "I can see the urgency," she said, after a pause. "How about Monday? Aunt Susan and I have already arranged to lunch together. I'm sure she won't mind a third to our party. I can send a note 'round to her."

"Excellent," Concordia said. "In the meanwhile, let's figure out what we tell her."

The two settled in and made their plans.

Chapter 37

Where is that viper? bring the villain forth.

Othello, *V.ii*

Week 12, Instructor Calendar
May 1898

It was with a heavy heart that Capshaw put his wife and Eli on the train south to Washington, where Sophia had a friend they could stay with for a while. He had work to do, and now his mind was clearer, knowing they were safe.

He felt the eyes upon him as he made his way back from the station to his house. He recognized the slim youth, casually leaning against the street lamp at the far end of the block as he smoked a tiny stub of a cigarette. No change of cap and jacket could hide the fact that he'd been at the same post the previous evening.

But Capshaw had been at the game too long not to have a few tricks of his own.

Once inside his home, he drew the blinds and made sure all of the windows and doors were locked. Sadie and the cleaning woman had been given the next two weeks off. He was alone in the house. He turned out all the lights, except for the lantern he carried into his windowless dressing closet.

In the dim light he shaved off his mustache and clumsily trimmed his flaming-red hair as short as he could, until it was easily concealed under a tweed cap. His startled reflection in the shaving mirror above the washstand assured him that the spies would have a hard time recognizing him now.

Capshaw pulled out a rucksack. He wouldn't need to bring much. Money, a change of personal linen, a pocketknife, his notes on the case, a pencil. He dressed in older clothes, frayed at the cuffs and knees, and pulled on broken-in boots with worn heels. It was the nondescript attire of a man a bit down on his luck but otherwise hard-working.

He snuffed the lantern and groped his way down to the kitchen. He stopped to wrap a couple of bread slices and a slab of ham in a kerchief, stuffing it in his bag for later. In the dark, he carefully opened the back door a crack.

The Inner Circle was thorough. Beyond the rows of neighboring clotheslines, Capshaw could see the faint glow of a cigarette ash as a second man stood watch. Fortunately, the observer had no choice but take a position farther away. The Capshaws' rear yard adjoined their neighbors at both the back and sides, save for a short alleyway blocked for the night by the local vegetable seller's wagon.

Capshaw hunched over and slipped outside, crouching behind a rubbish bin. He waited, then cautiously peeked around the bin. He could see the pinprick of light from the watcher's cigarette, unchanged in position.

Capshaw scooted close to the fence line, crossed into the alley, and squeezed past the wagon. He settled the rucksack more comfortably for the long walk to Widow Murtry's, a boarding house well out of his precinct. It was a place where Capshaw could be reasonably sure no one would recognize him. He'd learned that Mrs. Murtry cooked a decent meal, took cash, and asked no questions.

But first, he would pay a visit to Miss Hamilton. He needed her help if his plan was to succeed.

It was an easy matter to slip in through a hospital side door and climb the employee stairs without being discovered. Just before entering the corridor that led to Miss Hamilton's room, Capshaw hesitated in the shadows. He'd forgotten about the patrolman guarding the lady's door. Now he wished he hadn't disguised himself before coming here.

He could see the back of the man, hands clasped behind him, nodding politely as an orderly passed him by. Capshaw couldn't see enough for recognition. No doubt whoever it was had been told about his dismissal. Should Capshaw risk taking the man into his confidence? Would he be believed?

The man turned his head toward the stairwell. Capshaw felt weak with relief. Sergeant Maloney.

Capshaw and Maloney had joined the force at roughly the same time, and worked together on many cases over the years. They shared a mutual trust and respect. Chance had just turned in Capshaw's favor.

The next time Maloney turned his head, Capshaw moved, ever so slightly. The perceptive sergeant, hand to his club, strode over to him.

"What is your business here?" he said sharply, then sucked in a breath. "*Lieutenant?*" he said in disbelief. He dropped his voice. "What are you doing here, sir? And why are you—" his gaze swept over Capshaw's altered appearance "—looking like *that?*"

Capshaw drew Maloney into the corner of the stairwell. "I can't explain. But it's important I speak to Miss Hamilton."

Maloney frowned.

"I need you to trust me," Capshaw urged.

Maloney looked at him for a long moment, chewing his lip. "I knew there was something wrong wi' the chief firing you," he said.

Capshaw nodded. "I'm not at liberty to tell you about it right now. I promise I shall when this is all done. Agreed?"

Maloney smiled. "Now that's a story worth waitin' for, I'm sure. Okay, I'll check with the lady first and then let you in, but you daren't risk more than a few minutes. Wait here."

Capshaw watched Maloney return to Miss Hamilton's door, tap quietly upon it, and stick his head in her room. After a moment, he motioned to Capshaw.

Capshaw crossed the corridor quickly and gave Maloney a grateful look as he closed the door behind him.

"Sit down, Lieutenant," came a quiet voice. In the dim light Capshaw could see Miss Hamilton sitting up in bed, looking alert and much better than a few days before. She gestured toward the chair beside her.

"I might not have recognized you if the sergeant hadn't told me in advance," Miss Hamilton went on. Her gaze swept approvingly over his clean-shaven face, threadbare clothes and worn shoes. "An excellent disguise."

Capshaw quickly filled her in on the conversation with Chief Stiles, and his decision to go undercover.

"You're taking a big chance in trusting the man," Miss Hamilton warned.

Capshaw nodded. "It's a necessary risk. He plans to use his connections in the Black Scroll to learn more about who might be in the Inner Circle..."

"...while you find Hitchcock," Miss Hamilton finished. "Yes, I see. So how do you proceed now? What do you need from me?"

"Information," Capshaw said. "Who in the area could supply Hitchcock with the necessary materials he would need to make a bomb?"

Miss Hamilton raised an inquiring eyebrow.

"Our best chance of catching Hitchcock is to learn where he's getting his materials and tools. That man could lead us to him," Capshaw explained. "And, if Hitchcock has already completed any of the devices, we're going to need someone who knows how to deactivate them."

Miss Hamilton's expression turned thoughtful. "Hmm. Yes, that might work."

"I know you were looking into the subject after we found the scrap of dynamite wrapper," Capshaw said.

Miss Hamilton sat up straighter, her face tense with excitement. "Indeed. Pull out your pad, Lieutenant. I have two names for you."

Chapter 38

Week 13, Instructor Calendar
May 1898

Charlotte tapped on the door. "Ready?"
"Just a moment!" Concordia called. She glanced once more at the note she'd received by messenger.

My dear Concordia,
By the time you get this, Eli and I will be gone—to visit with a friend down south for an indefinite period. Aaron is worried for our safety. He has already lost his position, and says more trouble is to come.
If it had just been me, I would have stayed to fight. But I have to think of Eli now.
I wish I could have said good-bye to you in person.
I know you are recovering from your injuries, but please help him if you can, Concordia. You have made a difference in past cases of his. He doesn't like to admit it, of course.
But be careful. Our mail may be monitored, so don't send anything sensitive by that route. I'm taking the precaution of having this hand delivered to you.
I hope this will be resolved soon.
~Sophia

Concordia continued to stare at the slip of paper, as if it would speak up and account for itself further. So Capshaw had been fired, just as he had anticipated. Didn't he have recourse to someone higher up in authority?

But then again, who knew what other men on the force belonged to the Inner Circle?

Obviously, his movements were being watched, and as Sophia said, perhaps his communications as well.

Concordia shivered. She would have to figure out how to send him word of what she might learn from Lady Dunwick today. If she learned anything.

The Dunwick home was situated in the Asylum Hill neighborhood, only blocks from where Sophia Adams—Sophia *Capshaw*, Concordia amended silently—grew up. In addition to some of the wealthiest families in town, this section of the city was an enclave for artists, writers, and the social philosophers of a generation.

The house was situated on a quieter side street a block away from the bustle of Farmington Avenue. Like many houses in the neighborhood, it was constructed in the Queen Anne style, typified by its spindle work, overhanging eaves, and Dutch gables.

The maid answered the door promptly and bobbed a curtsy. "Miss Charlotte, so nice to see you again." She glanced at Concordia and said: "Lady Dunwick will be down shortly. She asked if you would kindly wait in the parlor?"

Concordia and Charlotte followed her down the hall. The Dunwick parlor was a pleasant room, quite unlike the current fashion of parlors as a showcase for as much expensive furniture and curios as could be crammed in. The French doors had been opened to catch the light spring breeze that fluttered the curtains. Hydrangeas spilled over in vases atop tables of deep cherry, polished to a shine. Charlotte and Concordia settled themselves in opposite settees and waited.

"Nice house," Concordia commented.

Charlotte nodded. "It was my grandmother's. She left it to Aunt Susan. Each daughter was given a house, actually." She ticked off the list on her fingers. "Aunt Lydia got the brownstone in New York City, Aunt Charlotte—that's who I'm named after—got the villa in Provence, and Mother got the cottage on Cape Cod."

"Oh," was all Concordia could trust herself to say. She was aware of the Crandall family wealth, but apparently the mother's side were no paupers, either. With such a background, it must have been quite difficult for Charlotte to convince her family that she wanted to work for her living.

Lady Dunwick walked in at that moment. "Ah, Charlotte." She leaned down to bestow a kiss upon her niece's cheeks, Charlotte steadying the frail woman.

Lady Dunwick turned to Concordia, who had stood during the interchange, waving her back to her seat. "Oh, do sit down, dear. We aren't quite so stuffy around here. Be comfortable. I am so glad Charlotte decided to bring you along."

Lady Dunwick gave Concordia a closer glance, noting the scrapes and bruises on her face. She leaned in, her brow creased in concern. "It appears that you've had a difficult time lately. Can I bring you a stool, to put up your feet? An extra cushion?"

Concordia flushed and shook her head. She had removed the last bandage—the one which had covered her temple—this morning, but there was no hiding the lingering marks. "No, thank you; I'm fine, really."

Although Concordia could tell that Lady Dunwick's curiosity was aroused, the lady was too well-bred to ask personal questions. Concordia didn't offer an explanation. It would have required a carefully-annotated account, and she frankly found the prospect exhausting. She glanced at Charlotte, who wasn't volunteering any information, either. Good.

"We'll be ready to go into the dining room shortly," Lady Dunwick said, checking the mantel clock. "We're waiting for Anthony and Mr. Isley, who have been delayed."

Concordia's stomach lurched. She and Charlotte exchanged a worried glance.

"I didn't realize there were more than just the three of us," Charlotte said.

Lady Dunwick smoothed the folds of her silk skirt. "Anthony finished a case earlier than planned, so his afternoon is free. I believe he and Mr. Isley have business matters to discuss. It made sense to have him join us for lunch first." She turned to Concordia. "You don't mind, I hope?"

"Of course not," Concordia said, hiding her dismay. This was going to complicate things. She looked again at Charlotte, who was no doubt thinking the same thing. *Now or never.*

"Aunt Susan," Charlotte began, shifting in her seat a little to face Lady Dunwick, "I've been considering your offer of membership in the Daughters of the Black Scroll. It sounds like a most worthy charity."

If Lady Dunwick was surprised at such a bald mention of a secret organization in front of an outsider, she was too self-controlled to show it. "My dear, perhaps we should discuss this another time...Miss Wells could not possibly be interested in such a topic."

Concordia jumped in. "Black Scroll? My mother mentioned something about that to me. She said the ladies have raised crucial funds for worthwhile causes." It seemed as good a guess as any.

Lady Dunwick smiled in relief. "Ah, your mother? Yes, I do believe she has been offered membership—her commendable work with the Irish orphans, you know—although I don't think she's informed us yet of her decision."

"Lately she's been...busy," Concordia said. Visiting a daughter in the hospital can be a substantial drain upon one's social calendar.

"Anyway," Charlotte Crandall went on, "I'd be interested in learning more. Are meetings involved? Social events?"

Lady Dunwick must have determined that confidentiality wasn't needed in front of Concordia (bless her mother for that piece of information), because the lady now sat back, perfectly at ease. "We meet once per month. Each member speaks briefly about her current project, and solicits help where needed. As far as less serious pursuits, we do have a masquerade ball coming up. It is considered the highlight of the year, in fact."

Lady Dunwick paused, looking around as if to assure herself that no one was nearby to eavesdrop—a purely involuntary reflex, as the door was closed and they were seated quite far from it. Nonetheless, the lady leaned in and dropped her voice. "And the ball is one of the few times that members of the

Brotherhood join us. After all, what good is a ball without *men?* This will be my first one—I joined recently, you see—and I am looking forward to it."

Concordia's heart beat a little faster. The ball sounded like a perfect opportunity to identify members of the Black Scroll, and possibly the Inner Circle. She might even overhear information of value. *If she could get in.* "It sounds lovely, Lady Dunwick." Concordia raised an eyebrow at Charlotte.

That young lady caught the hint. "Would I be permitted to attend, Aunt Susan? I'm most interested in joining your group."

Lady Dunwick tapped her chin thoughtfully. "I imagine that would be all right. Technically, it's supposed to be only for the members. The invitations were sent out weeks ago. But I heard that Sadie Walker brought her daughter last year, and no one batted an eyelash." She sniffed. "No doubt trying to find an eligible bachelor—at a masquerade ball, of all places! But the woman *is* desperate." She shook her head. "The girl is as plain as a bowl of milk, with a personality to match, I'm afraid."

Charlotte smiled. "Where is it being held?"

"At Randolph Maynard's country house, in Cottage Grove. We can ride together. It's an hour's drive, but quite scenic. Beautiful orchards, quaint old dairy farms…many families have built summer homes there."

Concordia's heart thumped faster. So Maynard was opening his home to the biggest Black Scroll social function of the year. Maynard had ordered the Inner Circle cuff links. Maynard had been at the shed, nearly as soon as Concordia had found poor Mr. Rosen. Was he the murderer?

"…however," Lady Dunwick was saying, "the affair is this Saturday. Have you any gowns with you, Charlotte?"

Concordia stifled a snort. She doubted Charlotte would have packed a ball gown to come teach at a women's college.

Charlotte gave a small smile as she shook her head. "But I can send for one. I have that lovely midnight taffeta you gave me, remember? Can you get me a suitable mask? Excellent."

Concordia cleared her throat. "I assume, since my mother hasn't yet accepted membership, she wasn't invited to the affair? She hadn't mentioned it."

Mother rarely shared her social doings with Concordia, but Lady Dunwick didn't know that.

"Oh!" Lady Dunwick shifted uncomfortably, appalled at what could be construed as a breach of manners. "I'm so sorry. How careless of me to mention it at all."

"No, no, it's fine," Concordia soothed, hoping this was leading where she thought it would. "Perhaps Charlotte can tell my mother about it, later. I'm sure Mother would find such a social and charitable group quite appealing, once she knows it better."

Lady Dunwick looked at Concordia thoughtfully. Concordia waited in mock innocence, hands placidly folded in her lap, hoping her gambit of offering her mother as the prize would work.

"Would *you* be interested in attending the ball, Miss Wells? You are such a good friend to Charlotte, and we are grateful for your help in securing her a position at your college. I'm sure it would be all right. I can tell them that you are a prospective member. You two girls would have a great deal of fun."

Concordia pretended to consider it.

"I know it's appallingly short notice," Lady Dunwick added apologetically. Charlotte made a decent show of sending Concordia a beseeching look, as if to convince her.

"I would love to, Lady Dunwick," Concordia said, smiling. "Thank you very much."

They heard men's voices in the hallway.

"Let's discuss the details later, shall we?" Charlotte proposed, casting an anxious eye at the parlor door. "I'm sure Uncle Anthony and Bursar Isley have little interest in the mundane details of a masquerade ball."

"Agreed," Lady Dunwick said.

Concordia breathed a sigh. Perhaps they could make this work, after all.

The parlor door opened, and Sir Anthony crossed the room in long-legged strides. "Susan, dear," he said, "there's been a slight change in plans."

Behind him, Concordia saw Barton Isley.

And Isley's wife, Lily.

Lady Dunwick gave her husband a startled glance.

Mr. Isley cleared his throat. "We are sorry to impose upon your luncheon," he said stiffly, looking over at his wife.

Lily Isley fluttered a handkerchief. "Oh, Lady Dunwick! It was entirely my fault. I was with Barton when he met Sir Anthony, and I realized it had been ages since we had seen each other last. I simply had to come! I hope you don't mind?"

Lady Dunwick, with perfect composure, crossed the room and clasped Lily's hand. "Nonsense, Mrs. Isley, it's so *kind* of you to join us. What a festive group we will have now! Please, be comfortable," she added, gesturing to the plump-cushioned settee where Concordia sat. Concordia obligingly moved over.

They seemed to be collecting guests as avidly as the Pied Piper collected rats, Concordia thought. Their quiet lunch of three had now doubled to six. Concordia wondered how the Dunwick kitchen staff would react. Mother's cook would have been in no end of a dither.

At least she had accomplished the object of her visit. The ball seemed a promising opportunity to learn more about the Black Scroll.

And here was an opportunity as well. Concordia was in the same room with the only two men whom she knew for sure were part of the Inner Circle. Perhaps she could learn something. If Lily Isley didn't dominate the conversation, of course.

Lady Dunwick pulled the bell. "Marie," she said, when the maid answered the summons, "there are six of us for luncheon now. Please set a place for Mrs. Isley." The girl nodded and left.

"We should be ready momentarily," Lady Dunwick said, taking a seat.

Meanwhile, Concordia shifted uneasily under Lily Isley's frank scrutiny.

"Oh, my dear Concordia!" Lily exclaimed, "I heard about the incident at the Canton Street stop last week. The students cannot stop talking about it. How horrible for you! How do you feel?"

Concordia, mouth open in surprise at the woman's directness, clenched her hands together. Perhaps Lily had done her a favor. If Isley or Sir Anthony, as part of the Inner Circle, played a role in arranging Miss Hamilton's "accident," this could be a chance to watch their reactions.

She cleared her throat. "Your concern is most kind. I feel much better, but sadly, Miss Hamilton is still in the hospital."

Was it her imagination, or did Isley give a start at the mention of Miss Hamilton? He covered it with shifting in his seat and crossing his legs, but she felt sure he knew something. Sir Anthony, on the other hand, merely listened attentively, polite concern tugging at his brow. Lady Dunwick, curiosity satisfied at last, was nodding and leaning forward sympathetically.

Time to test the theory further. Concordia remembered that Miss Hamilton had warned against taking the "direct approach," but no one had anticipated the current circumstances.

"In fact, the entire matter is most distressing," Concordia continued, keeping her gaze upon Lily but watching Barton Isley out of the corner of her eye. It would not do for him to realize he was under scrutiny. "The police now think that the ruffian who pushed Miss Hamilton into the path of the streetcar did so deliberately."

Concordia sat back with a sigh of mock distress, so she could get a good look at Isley and Sir Anthony.

Lily patted Concordia's hand. "Surely not!" she said. "Whyever would they think that?"

Concordia explained about the abortive attack upon Miss Hamilton in her hospital room later, leaving out her own presence in the hospital room.

Lady Dunwick's eyes widened. "How dreadful! Do they know who it was?"

Concordia shook her head. "Sadly, no," she lied.

"I'm not familiar with the lady, but why would anyone want to harm her?" Sir Anthony asked. He seemed perfectly at his ease, which made Concordia doubt her conviction that he'd been party to the scheme to get Miss Hamilton out of the way. Or was he merely skilled at masking his feelings?

Isley, on the other hand, had paled. Concordia saw Lily cast a concerned glance in his direction.

"Yes, who is this Miss Hamilton? Is she a friend of yours?" Lady Dunwick asked.

Concordia nodded. "She used to be lady principal at the school two years ago. She's visiting a niece in town, who just had a baby." She turned to Sir Anthony. "We cannot imagine who would want to harm Miss Hamilton. It's all a perplexing mystery."

"And obviously distressing," Sir Anthony said, with a warning tone to his voice. He looked meaningfully at his wife.

Lady Dunwick took the hint. "Indeed, yes," she said briskly, "do let's talk of other things."

Talk passed to more innocuous topics. The maid stepped in a few minutes later to announce lunch.

"Ah, at last," Sir Anthony said, standing and offering an arm to his wife. "I'm famished."

The meal was as good as Concordia would have expected in such a household, with oyster soup, duck *a l'orange*, and baby carrots in a ginger cream sauce, followed by a lemon ice. Concordia could have easily eaten more, but it wouldn't do for a lady to display a voracious appetite. Unless that lady was a college student. Those girls ate anything that wasn't nailed down.

"So, Sir Anthony, I understand you recently resolved a legal matter," Concordia said, wanting to learn more about the man. "What sort of case was it?"

Sir Anthony blotted his lips on his napkin before speaking. "I work in the field of patent law. It was a difficult case, though most interesting. I won't reveal any names, but an inventor, holding a patent for what promises to be a very lucrative device, was accused by another fellow of having stolen the invention.

The preliminary evidence this challenger offered appeared damning, and I despaired of being able to establish that my client had sole right to the invention. They had been colleagues early on, you see."

Concordia nodded. Isley shifted forward in his chair, eyes on Sir Anthony.

"However, it turned out the plaintiff was all bluff and bluster," Sir Anthony went on. "We went to court this morning, with as much documentation as my client could provide. I feared a lengthy, drawn-out process. Instead, my client's accuser arrives in court, hair mussed, collar disarranged, claiming he was attacked on the way to court, and that his blueprints and other documents were stolen. Can you imagine? He put on quite a show. He could not produce a single witness to corroborate his account. The judge dismissed the case, and we were finished in thirty minutes."

"How unusual," Charlotte said politely.

"It sounds as if the man could have benefitted from acting lessons, wouldn't you say, dear?" Barton Isley asked his wife.

Lily smiled, and the conversation shifted to lighter topics. Lily kept them all laughing with anecdotes of her days on the stage, and the superstitious rituals the cast employed before performances.

"So what are your plans for this afternoon?" Lady Dunwick asked Lily. "Shopping?"

"Oh my, no, nothing as frivolous as that," Lily said. She smiled at her husband. "Barton and I are meeting with Mr. Sanders in an hour to discuss the upcoming debate. He wants us to help him with practice questions." Her eyes were alight with excitement.

Concordia saw Lady Dunwick grimace behind her lunch napkin. No doubt the lady found the idea of a woman actively engaged in politics somewhat distasteful.

"Has the venue for the debate been settled upon?" Sir Anthony asked.

Barton Isley pushed his plate away and sat back. "We've decided upon the Long Brothers' Palace Restaurant and Hotel."

Sir Anthony gave an approving nod. "At City Hall Square. Excellent location."

"Indeed," Lily said. "The restaurant holds up to five hundred people, so the Ladies Civic Committee will have ample room for the candidates' breakfast that precedes the debate."

"We are hoping for good weather," Isley added, "so that the debate itself can be held outside on the square."

Charlotte checked her watch. "Oh! I should be getting back, if I'm to make my three o'clock lesson."

"I'll walk with you," Concordia said. She turned to their hostess. "Lady Dunwick, this has been delightful. Thank you for your hospitality."

Lady Dunwick smiled. "Come back anytime, dear. It was a pleasure to have you."

Barton Isley leaned over to his wife and murmured, "Sir Anthony and I have a matter to discuss. It shouldn't take us long."

Lily nodded as the men headed for the study. Charlotte and Concordia collected their things from the maid and left.

They stood outside the house, pulling on their gloves and straightening their hats.

"Which way?" Charlotte asked. She pointed to the left, toward Sigourney Street. "We could take the trolley right at that corner, but the route winds through the downtown district…"

"…or we could walk a few blocks to Garden Street, and take the line that circumvents the traffic, and has fewer stops," Concordia finished. "Yes, I think the latter prospect is the better choice."

Turning in that direction, they passed the Dunwick's open study window. Concordia slowed her steps, and put her hand on Charlotte's arm as she heard the clear ringing voice of Barton Isley.

"…you could have more successes like this one, with our help. Think of the future cases! You would be unstoppable."

Charlotte Crandall's eyes widened, as she, too, recognized the bursar's voice.

"What are you saying?" Sir Anthony answered angrily. His voice was getting closer to the window. Concordia stooped as if she'd dropped something. Charlotte walked hastily down the sidewalk to avoid being seen. Sir Anthony closed the leaded window with a thud, effectively making the rest of the conversation inaudible.

"I don't like the sound of *that*," Charlotte murmured, as they continued on. "What has Uncle Anthony gotten involved in?"

"It sounds as if the Inner Circle is going to great lengths to persuade your uncle to join." Concordia was relieved. It was apparent that Sir Anthony had not yet committed himself. But the Circle had not given up. Their "aid" in his latest case, with a plaintiff attacked and evidence stolen, was meant to persuade. And perhaps serve as a threat,too? Now Concordia was sure that Sir Anthony had nothing to do with the attacks on Miss Hamilton and Eli, or the murders of Florence Willoughby and Ben Rosen.

Charlotte turned accusing eyes to Concordia. "You knew Bursar Isley to be an Inner Circle member, but didn't tell me?"

Concordia flushed. "I'm sorry. I was worried that you might not be able to act normally around him on campus."

Charlotte tossed her head defiantly. "I am more capable than you think. But you have to trust me."

"You're right." Concordia said. "I apologize." She must start thinking of Charlotte Crandall as a younger colleague, not a former student to be shielded. She would also have to tell her about Maynard, but out here on a public sidewalk was not the time.

Charlotte gave her a long look. Satisfied, she continued walking.

"Do you think your uncle will join the Inner Circle, under these circumstances?" Concordia asked, after a few minutes' silence.

Charlotte shook her head vehemently. "Absolutely not."

"I don't think the Inner Circle will be content with performing a favor for your uncle and not getting something in return," Concordia said carefully.

Charlotte looked at her with widened eyes. "So when he refuses their offer of membership, what will they do?"

"I wish I knew," Concordia said.

Chapter 39

The first man on Miss Hamilton's list, Alan Goff, only took Capshaw a few days to find. It was a simple matter of learning the fellow's favorite watering hole and keeping watch. Capshaw supposed that a businessman such as Goff would want it to be easy for customers to seek him out. If he had supplied Hitchcock with bomb-making materials, then a little bribery might loosen his tongue.

Capshaw's hopes were dashed, however, when he walked into the saloon on the fourth day and Goff was pointed out to him.

Alan Goff's blank stare and shuffling gait belied the reputation of a man who was supposedly an explosives dealer in the criminal underworld.

"*That's* Goff?" Capshaw asked in disbelief.

The bartender nodded. "Sad now, in't it? Right as rain a month ago, then has a few too many, falls down drunk, hits his head. Hasn't been the same since. He just come back after weeks a'bed." He glanced at the clock on the shelf. "It's gettin' late. I expect his missus will come for 'im soon."

Capshaw walked back to Mrs. Murtry's boardinghouse. He was accustomed to dead ends in an investigation, but the stakes here were as high as they had ever been. If Goff had been the supplier, the link to Hitchcock was lost.

There was yet a chance: Artie Lindquist, the other supplier on Miss Hamilton's list. She had thought him less likely, however.

"He has a smaller operation going," she had said. "He was trained in munitions during the war, so his knowledge is extensive, but everyone knows Goff has the better prices. Goff has more contacts than Lindquist."

"How do you know so much about him?" Capshaw had asked.

Miss Hamilton smiled to herself. "When my husband was alive, he and Artie were friends. Of sorts."

Capshaw prayed the second man hadn't had an accident, too.

It took Capshaw the rest of the week to find Lindquist, a cautious fellow of reclusive habits. That certainly seemed the case when Capshaw set up a meeting with him.

The location was an abandoned storage shed along the docks. Capshaw, arriving alone for his midnight appointment as instructed, prayed he wasn't walking into a trap. At least Lindquist had no way of knowing Capshaw was a policeman. Otherwise, his life wouldn't be worth a nickel. As far as Lindquist knew, Capshaw was the agent of a prospective customer.

Nevertheless, Capshaw looked over his shoulder as he approached the shed, nervously fingering the weighted pocketknife in his jacket. Mercifully, no one waited in the shadows.

Capshaw knocked quietly on the rough door and opened it at the sound of a voice.

Artie Lindquist was seated deep in the shadows, behind a long counter once used to clean fish. Even after years of disuse, the smell lingered. As far as Capshaw could see, the man was alone. Another stool had been provided. An oil lamp was positioned behind Lindquist, glaring in Capshaw's eyes and obscuring the man's face. All that Capshaw could make out was a grimy peacoat and a dark scarf muffling him up to his chin, even though the night was temperate.

"You have something for me," Lindquist said, once Capshaw was seated. His voice held the wheezy strain of damaged lungs.

Capshaw passed over a slim, paper-wrapped packet. Lindquist opened it and counted the money. Capshaw suppressed a gasp of surprise at the sight of the man's right hand. Gloved though it was, he could see thick burn scars, puckered and twisted, extending past the wrist. So Lindquist's choice to remain in shadow was not just a desire for anonymity.

The man noticed Capshaw's glance. He gave a hoarse laugh as he pulled down his sleeve and pocketed the bills. "Let us just say that I no longer deal in nitroglycerin. You'll have to look elsewhere if that's what you want. But a little friendly advice: don't make your own at home." He tucked his hand back under the table.

"I don't intend to."

Lindquist sat back. "So now that I have your down payment, let us talk about what you want me to get. Timers, blasting caps? Iron casings? Phosphorous?"

Capshaw shook his head. "Information. I need to locate a certain person who may have been a customer of yours."

Lindquist was silent for a long moment, looking at Capshaw carefully. "You are police, then." He stood and pointed to the door. "If you leave now, I will let you live."

"No, wait!" Capshaw exclaimed, standing up and leaning over the counter. "I'm not trying to interfere with your...operations. I'm only here because Penelope Hamilton told me you could help. We must stop a ruthless group of men, before they cause more harm."

Lindquist hesitated. "Did you say 'Penelope Hamilton'?"

Capshaw nodded.

Lindquist sighed and sat back down. "I haven't heard that name in years." He regarded Capshaw with penetrating eyes. "Did she tell you anything about us?"

"Merely that you and her husband had been friends."

"That is true. It was more of a friendly rivalry, he and I. The private detective and the criminal. A strange alliance, is it not?" Lindquist shook his head over the memory. "And Pen. So smart. And brave. She worked a few cases with her husband back then. She even saved my life. I wouldn't have survived this—" he touched his face in shadow "—if she hadn't pulled me from the fire in my workshop, years ago. I owe her a great deal."

"You can repay that debt," Capshaw said. "Miss Hamilton was grievously harmed by the same people I'm looking for."

Lindquist started. "How bad are her injuries? Will she survive?"

Capshaw could hear the anxiety in the man's voice. "She will, if she isn't harmed further. But a man tried to attack her in her hospital bed the other night, and he's the one I'm after. Have you ever had dealings with someone named Hitchcock? Johnny Hitchcock."

Lindquist hesitated, then pulled out a small leather notebook.

Capshaw waited. The only sound in the room was the turning of pages.

Lindquist marked an entry with his finger, then looked up at Capshaw. "Before I tell you, I want your assurance that no one will know I gave you this information. I will lose my other customers. And if you capture this man, you must promise that the police will not then come after *me*."

As dearly as Capshaw wanted to put a stop to Lindquist and the dangerous materials he peddled, he knew it was a battle that would have to wait for another day.

"I can promise you this," Capshaw said. "I will never speak your name in connection with this case to any police or court official. If I do capture Hitchcock, no one else but Miss Hamilton will know that it happened through your help. But—I cannot promise anything about your involvement in *future* cases."

Lindquist hesitated, then shrugged. "It seems I have made yet another uneasy alliance with law enforcement. Just like the old days. Very well." He scribbled something on a scrap of paper and closed the book. "I met with Hitchcock on two occasions. He needed better fuses than the cheap stuff Goff foists on his customers. Half of them don't hold a burn and fizzle out partway through." His lips twisted in a distorted smile. "You get what you pay for."

"When was this?"

"Our last meeting was a week ago," Lindquist said. He passed the paper over. "This is where I had them delivered. He said he couldn't show his face in public to pick them up."

Capshaw imagined not, since that was just after the aborted attack at the hospital, and the entire Hartford police force was searching for the man. "When were the fuses delivered?"

"Yesterday." Lindquist stood. "If that is all, I must be going."

Capshaw held up a hand. "There's one more thing." He took another envelope of money out of his pocket and handed it to Lindquist, who raised a puzzled eyebrow.

"What's this for?" Lindquist asked. He thumbed through it and started counting. "It's quite a sum."

"I need to learn how to defuse a bomb, should I encounter one."

"You want me to *teach* you?" Lindquist asked incredulously.

"Who better?" Capshaw asked.

Lindquist was quiet for a moment. He counted the bills again. "You are an intriguing man. And a brave one. All right, I'll teach you. Just the basics, mind. I assume it's Hitchcock's bombs you want to know about? Well, it just might work."

After arranging to meet the next night for his first "lesson," Capshaw left. He took a cab directly to Maloney's lodgings.

A grumpy, disheveled Maloney answered the door. His brow cleared at the sight of Capshaw. "Lieutenant!" he cried. "What on earth are you doin' here at this time o' night?" He opened the door wider and let him in.

"I'm sorry for the late hour, but I know where you can find Hitchcock," Capshaw said. He handed him the paper Lindquist had given him. "Since I'm off the force, you'll have to make the arrest."

Maloney grinned. "It'll be a pleasure. I'll have to come up with a story about how I found him, though." He peered closely at Capshaw. "I assume I shouldn't ask how you got this."

Capshaw shook his head. "I promised my source he would remain anonymous. Good luck, sergeant." He pulled open the door to let himself out. "I'm staying at Widow Murtry's. Send me word when you have him, will you?"

Maloney was already dashing up the stairs as Capshaw closed the door behind him.

Chapter 40

This is the night
That either makes me or fordoes me quite.

Othello, *V.i*

Week 14, Instructor Calendar
May 1898

"Nonsense, you look wonderful," Charlotte insisted, pinning the last stray tendrils of Concordia's hair under the silver netted hair covering. "I knew the gown would fit you once we hemmed it."

"Once *Ruby* hemmed it," Concordia said, thinking about how hard the house matron had worked on such short notice. "That woman's a treasure."

The gown Charlotte had lent her was certainly lovely, with its crossed bodice of black velvet accenting the shimmering fabric of pearl-gray satin. The cap sleeves were trimmed with more narrow bands of velvet, and the deeply-pleated sides of the skirt caused the skirt to drape in graceful folds and enabled greater freedom of movement. It was a bit tight, of course. Charlotte was slimmer than she, but the corset was doing its job. Concordia had given up trying to take deep breaths.

Concordia made a face at her reflection. The gown showed a more ample expanse of pale bosom than she was accustomed to. Still, the color suited her, deepening her green eyes and softening her freckled complexion. Not that it would matter much once her mask was in place.

She stepped back to inspect Charlotte's gown, a high-necked creation of midnight blue, trimmed at waist and hem with sheer ivory scarves, shirred several rows deep. "What a lovely gown."

Charlotte flushed. "It was a graduation gift from Aunt Susan. I'm sure she'll be pleased to see me in it."

"Do you have our masks?" Concordia asked anxiously. The thought of this being a masquerade ball was both worrisome and reassuring. She was comforted by the thought that her eye expressions would be difficult to read, but it would be equally difficult to establish the identities and temperaments of the men in the room.

Charlotte nodded, fished in her reticule, and passed her a domino mask of black silk, ornamented at the temples with tiny pearls. She checked the mantel clock. "Aunt Susan's carriage will be at the gate soon."

Concordia collected her wrap and reticule. "Ready."

Charlotte paused, listening. "It sounds like everyone is settling down for the night. How strange to be going out at this hour."

"Don't worry. I made sure Miss Pomeroy approved our outing," Concordia said. She put a hand on Charlotte's arm. "Thank you," she added quietly. "For all of your help. This has been a trying time. It feels good to have an ally."

Charlotte smiled. "Whatever you need, miss."

They collected their wraps and walked to the front gate.

The drive to Dean Maynard's country home in Cottage Grove was a pleasant one.

They passed a number of stately houses, refurbished from modest farmhouse structures. Nearly all of them were closed up until the summer season.

At last they pulled up to the Maynard house. The surrounding property had retained some of its dairy farm origins, with a silo, barn, and split-rail fencing, but the house itself had been rebuilt in a grander style, with a deep, white columned porch and asymmetrically-proportioned high-peaked gables of Windsor blue.

Festive Chinese lanterns were strung along the portico, and every window glowed. Band music drifted faintly through the open door as they alighted from the carriage. Concordia and Charlotte exchanged glances as they straightened their trains and settled their wraps over their shoulders.

Lady Dunwick caught the glance. "No need for worry," she said cheerfully, "I'm sure there will be no problem." The diminutive lady took Sir Anthony's extended arm and led the way.

They were among the last to arrive, which proved fortuitous. The maid gave the Dunwick invitation barely a glance as she greeted them and took the ladies' wraps. Concordia settled the mask more firmly across her eyes and cheekbones, tying it securely behind her head. She had to avoid Isley and Maynard. There would be no explaining her presence. Her conspicuous red hair was covered by the silver netting of her hairpiece so that she could better blend in with the crush of people, but Maynard in particular had a sharp eye. But the worst that could happen, she reminded herself, was that she would be shown the door.

As the Dunwicks toured the room and made polite introductions, Concordia recognized a number of men, including a law professor from Trinity, the mayor, the state's prosecutor, and several friends of her mother's.

Conversation within the groups was kept to light topics and generalities, and it was easy to disconnect from the talk of one group and engage in another. None of the men had elected to attend in costume; the dinner jacket, pleated shirt, and dress trousers seemed the standard uniform of the evening, though each gentleman sported the same black velvet mask across his eyes. On some, the mask looked quite dashing; on others, absurd. One man fussed with it as it crept up his forehead.

Concordia tried to memorize the names and details of the men unfamiliar to her: hair, hands, figure, build, voice. She hoped it would be enough for Capshaw and Miss Hamilton to learn more about these men, and determine who belonged to the Inner Circle. She had hoped there might be a conversation she could eavesdrop upon regarding the Inner Circle, but perhaps such a large gathering made that unlikely.

The one man she dreaded seeing was Randolph Maynard, but there was no sign of him. Strange. The man was hosting a party in his own house, but wasn't in attendance? The Isleys were instead acting as hosts, circulating among the groups and making sure guests were well-provisioned with punch and lemonade. She had avoided them so far, but she found such maneuvering an exhausting exercise, on top of making endless small talk about the weather or the rising cost of silk.

Once, across the room, Concordia spotted Barton Isley standing beside his wife. Lily was animatedly recounting a story that, by the looks of it, had their group in stitches. The lady was dressed in an Arabian costume of turquoise and tangerine, her flowing skirts affixed to a low-hipped sequined belt, and gauze veil crowned with a simple gold circlet. She must be Scheherazade, Concordia guessed, the Persian queen who seduced a king with her tales. How appropriate. Concordia made sure Lady Dunwick steered clear of that group.

As they circulated among the crowd, Concordia wasn't so sure that she and Charlotte were as readily accepted as Lady Dunwick had claimed. The female attendees seemed to take the extra guests in stride, perhaps concluding that Lady Dunwick was trying to find a marriage prospect for Charlotte. However, Concordia noticed a few of the men, behind their masks, raise an eyebrow when they were introduced. All had been polite, but she felt uneasy when she caught sight of several men beside the terrace murmuring and glancing their way.

"Excuse us," Concordia said to Lady Dunwick, and maneuvered Charlotte over to a quiet corner beside a potted plant.

"What's wrong?" Charlotte asked, fiddling with her fan.

"I don't think we're as welcome as your aunt assumed," Concordia said, pointing discreetly with her own fan toward the terrace. "We may have to leave sooner than anticipated."

"But you haven't seen everyone yet," Charlotte protested. "There are a number of men in the billiard room. We should wait until supper, at least. Then we'll all be in the same place."

"You're right, of course. But it's nerve-wracking, this worry about being recognized by the Isleys," Concordia said.

"Your hair is wonderfully obscured by your head covering," Charlotte said. "It should be all right. And what's the worst that could happen, in the middle of a crowded hall? We'd be asked to leave."

Concordia reluctantly followed Charlotte back to the Dunwicks, trying to shake off this feeling of unease.

Later, she wished she had listened to her instincts.

Concordia surreptitiously checked her watch again. When would they go in to dinner? Could she risk staying that long? It was only a matter of time before she encountered the Isleys. She doubted if she could convince them that she was a prospective member of the Daughters of the Black Scroll.

At last, the supper bell rang. *Thank goodness.* If she could get one final look at the entire assemblage to check for anyone she had missed, then she and Charlotte could make their excuses and leave. She was anxious to write everything down before she forgot something.

Concordia and Charlotte were following Sir Anthony and Lady Dunwick to the supper room when one of the maids approached them.

"Excuse me, sir?" she said. She bobbed a small curtsy to Sir Anthony. "Mr. Isley asked you and your party to join him in the study. Would you please step this way?"

Concordia's heart sank. She and Charlotte exchanged a glance.

Barton Isley was waiting for them in the study. There was no sign of Lily. "Please be seated." He waved a hand toward the maid. "Close the door behind you as you leave."

"Something wrong, Barton?" asked a puzzled Sir Anthony.

Isley lowered himself into a chair. "Most certainly there is. Do you understand the need for confidentiality among our order? Why have you brought these two ladies—" his gesture included Concordia and Charlotte "—to such a gathering?"

Sir Anthony looked at his wife. "I thought you had secured permission for Charlotte and Miss Wells to attend."

Lady Dunwick maintained her dignified air. She addressed both men. "No, I did not. Since this was to be a purely social occasion, such a formality seemed unnecessary."

Barton's face grew red. "You foolish woman. A basic tenet of the order is that the membership remain unknown to outsiders."

Lady Dunwick had gone pale. Sir Anthony leaned over and patted her arm before looking back at Isley. "Now then, Isley, there's no need to address my wife in such a rude manner."

"This *is* a social event, is it not?" Lady Dunwick retorted, her voice quavering with barely-concealed anger. "These ladies are hardly 'outsiders'. Charlotte is my niece, and is considering membership in the Daughters of the Black Scroll. Miss Wells is a good friend of hers. Her mother, Mrs. Wells, has also been offered membership, based upon her exceptional charitable works. It is quite natural that Miss Wells would be interested in attending this function."

Isley gave a bark of laughter. "This young woman—" he pointed to Concordia "—has proved herself, time and again, to be exceptionally *nosy*, prying into the affairs of others, no doubt out of some prurient curiosity known only to her sex. She is the worst possible outsider you could have brought here tonight."

"And why is that, Mr. Isley?" Concordia asked, giving the man a hard look, even as she clenched her gloved hands together to keep them from trembling. "What do you fear I would learn?"

Sir Anthony gave Concordia a sharp glance of understanding.

Barton Isley glared at Concordia. "Nothing," he said, through gritted teeth.

Concordia stood, heart pounding. Perhaps retreat was the prudent course. "I apologize for distressing you so. It would be better if we were to leave."

There was a light rap on the study door, and Lily Isley walked in.

"Barton, shouldn't you be joining the party?" She stopped, taking in the sight of her red-faced husband and the subdued Dunwicks, rising from their chairs and collecting their belongings. Then she noticed Concordia. "Well, this is a surprise! I hardly recognized you. Whatever are you doing here?" She turned to her husband. "Barton?"

Isley spoke through clenched teeth. "The Dunwicks took it upon themselves to invite Miss Wells and Miss Crandall to our gathering."

"Oh." Lily regarded her husband uneasily. "I'm sure it was a misunderstanding, dear."

"Indeed," Lady Dunwick interjected apologetically, "I didn't realize…."

"Of course not," Lily said sympathetically. "And no doubt my Barton has over-reacted," she added. "These people are our friends, dear, and certainly do not mean us any ill-will."

Barton Isley shifted uncomfortably. "Perhaps so," he said gruffly. "I apologize."

"Now, that's better, isn't it?" Lily said. "And since you are already here, why not rejoin our little gathering?"

Isley glowered at his wife.

"You are most kind, but I believe we've had enough revelry for one evening," Lady Dunwick said smoothly, looking only at Lily and turning a stiff back to Barton Isley.

"I'll have your carriage brought around," Lily offered, pulling on the bell, "but I was wondering…Concordia, could you possibly stay? Only for a little while. I know it's terribly late. You didn't have the benefit of seeing the production, but there is a most promising senior I want to talk with you about. I'm thinking of taking her under my wing."

"Unfortunately, I came with the Dunwicks," Concordia said, glancing uneasily at Barton Isley.

Lily waved a dismissive hand. "Oh, don't worry about that. I'll send you back to the college in my coach as soon as we're done, I promise."

Concordia was torn. She was tired and felt the instinct to retreat, but on the other hand, her plans had been interrupted. Perhaps she could learn more in a confidential tête-à-tête with Lily Isley, if the discussion could be turned to the Black Scroll. Concordia turned to Lady Dunwick. "I'll stay here for a little while longer. Thank you for your kindness. I regret the trouble it caused."

Lady Dunwick squeezed her hand as she turned to leave. "No matter, my dear." She dropped her voice. "Actually, it has given Sir Anthony and myself a great deal to consider, regarding this group."

Charlotte said goodbye to Concordia next, her forehead puckered in concern. "You're sure you want to be alone with them?" she whispered.

Concordia nodded. "The house is full of people. I'll be fine."

Charlotte reluctantly followed the Dunwicks out.

"Oh, Barton," Lily said, "the judge was asking for you. Perhaps you should return to our guests?"

Not bothering to suppress a scowl in Concordia's direction, Isley gave a curt bow and left them.

"Well, then!" Lily said brightly, "let's leave this awful manly space—Randolph Maynard likes to surround himself with a great many riding trophies, doesn't he? Quite the horseman. There's a cozy little sitting room upstairs that's much more pleasant."

Lily led the way, down a walnut-paneled hall on which half a dozen portraits hung. No doubt Maynard's ancestors, Concordia guessed. Several appeared as heavy-browed and curmudgeonly as Maynard himself.

"Why wasn't the dean in attendance tonight?" Concordia asked as they walked.

"Oh, he was here early on, but was called away, most likely before you arrived." Lily shrugged. "Some urgent school business. We assured him that we would take over his host duties."

Concordia wondered what might be going on at the college that would require Maynard to drop everything and leave a major social function. Everything had seemed fine when she'd left.

Lily stopped one of the maids along the corridor. "Bring us some tea in the sitting room, will you?"

The room was quite luxurious, in fact, with floor-to-ceiling drapes of burgundy velvet, deep leather club chairs, and the most cushiony carpet that Concordia had ever sunk her heels into. Mr. Maynard certainly enjoyed his creature comforts.

Concordia smothered a yawn as she tried to sit upright in her corseted gown. The sooner she could be out of this contraption, the better. "What student were you referring to?" she asked. "Miss Stephens, perhaps?"

"Oh," Lily said vaguely, gesturing to the maid to set the tea tray on the table beside the window, "Give me a moment to get this tea steeping. It's a special herbal blend I like to keep around. More like a medicinal tisane, really. The steeping time is the key: too long and it's rather bitter, and too little, and it's less effective. But it's good for soothing the nerves. The extra effort is worthwhile, I think."

She went over to the table as the maid left. Concordia saw her fussing with a tin and strainers, but with Lily's back to her, she couldn't see much else.

"What makes you think my nerves are strained?" Concordia asked bluntly.

Lily hesitated. "That's part of the reason I wanted to speak with you in private, dear. I wanted to apologize for my husband's behavior." Her brow puckered. "Barton's been under a great deal of pressure lately."

"There's no need to apologize," Concordia said politely.

Lily brought over the cups, passing one to Concordia, and went back to retrieve a plate of appetizers the maid had brought from the dining room. She set it down between them. "I realize you never had supper; you must be famished."

Concordia took a sip of her tea first, suppressing a shudder. Despite Lily's care, it was rather bitter. She plucked two cubes from the sugar bowl.

"What sort of strain has Mr. Isley been subjected to? I'm not aware of any problems going on at the school," Concordia said.

Of course, President Langdon's hansom had monopolized Isley's office for a fortnight, but she couldn't imagine the bursar still sulking over that.

Lily fluttered a hand dismissively. "He can be a bit...highly strung, especially when it comes to finances. There have been several investments which have been preoccupying him lately." She observed Concordia closely. "How do you like the tea?"

Obligingly, Concordia took another sip. It was marginally better with sugar. "It's...unusual," she said, politely drinking the rest of the dreadful stuff.

Lily nodded. "I've found it to be an acquired taste."

"So," Concordia said, trying to return to the topic at hand, "what did you want to discuss regarding...." She hesitated.

What were they talking about? Why couldn't she remember? She glanced over at Lily in confusion. "Um, regarding...."

Lily was looking at her in concern. "Are you all right, Concordia?"

Concordia tried to answer, but no words came. She was also having trouble moving her fingers, and could do nothing but watch as the teacup slid from her grasp. She felt a dizzy, plummeting sensation, as her mind tried to form her next thought.

"Let me help you, dear," she heard Lily say anxiously.

dear...dear...dear echoed in her head as she slid to the floor, sinking into the blackness.

Chapter 41

Dean Maynard had reached the end of his patience with student pranks. At his former school, the lady principal had kept her young ladies under strict control. Here, the girls ran amuck. Miss Pomeroy was sadly lacking as a disciplinarian. And many of the faculty were no better.

Especially Miss Wells. It was no surprise that she was a literature teacher. Through sad experience, Maynard had concluded that scholars in those arts weren't possessed of the orderly mind one found among those dedicated to the sciences and mathematics. Add to that the lady professor's unbridled curiosity and tendency to meddle where she had no business, and it made for a vexing combination. He remembered the unease he felt when he saw the newspaper reporter hand a piece of paper to Miss Wells at the luncheon, and that lady later leaving the room. He'd felt an obligation to see what she was up to. And what did he find? The lady crouched over a nearly-dead Rosen in the gardener's shed.

Maynard shook his head. Nothing but trouble, that one.

At least Miss Wells wasn't the problem this time. Maynard scowled as he re-read the slip of paper.

There is an emergency at the college. You are needed at once. ~Gertrude Pomeroy

He had just begun greeting his guests at the Masquerade Ball that evening when it was delivered. He'd made his apologies and hurriedly left, reaching campus at breakneck speed.

Only to find that there was no emergency. It was well past the students' ten o'clock bedtime and everyone had settled down for the night. All was quiet.

Just to be sure, Maynard went to his office. Nothing was amiss there, either; no note, no one waiting for him.

The only other soul in the building was President Langdon, working late in his office. Maynard tapped on his door.

"Something wrong, Randolph?" Langdon asked.

"There certainly is," Maynard retorted. He tossed the note on Langdon's desk. "Take a look."

Langdon frowned as he read.

"Where is Miss Pomeroy now?" Maynard asked.

"She mentioned retiring early," Langdon said. He stood. "I hate to disturb the lady, but we should get to the bottom of this." He glanced at Maynard's formal attire. "How unfortunate that you were called away from a special event." His brow arched in polite inquiry, but Maynard, who took his Brotherhood oath seriously, said nothing.

DeLacey House had a single porch light burning, and it was with great reluctance that Langdon rang the bell. Langdon and Maynard waited for several minutes before the housekeeper, a dressing gown hastily tied around her waist and hair in a fraying braid over her shoulder, opened the door.

"Mr. Langdon! Mr. Maynard! Why, what's wrong?"

Maynard stepped forward. "We must see Miss Pomeroy," he said brusquely.

President Langdon glared at Maynard before turning back to the housekeeper. "I apologize for the late hour, but it's urgent we speak with her. Can we wait in the parlor while you get her?"

"O' course, sir," the woman said. "Right away." She closed the door behind them and hustled up the stairs.

Miss Pomeroy, graying-brown hair twisted sloppily atop her head and glasses askew, walked into the parlor a few minutes later.

"Whatever's wrong?"

Maynard passed her the note.

Miss Pomeroy's eyes widened as she glanced at it. "I never sent such a thing. There's no emergency here. Why, I wouldn't have known where to reach you even if I'd wanted to."

Maynard sat back in surprise. The lady principal raised a point he hadn't considered. Who would have known where he was?

President Langdon stood apologetically. "Of course. We'll let you get back to bed. My apologies again for disturbing you."

Miss Pomeroy waved a hand dismissively. "No matter. Rest assured, I'll do my best to get to the bottom of this in the morning."

"Thank you Miss Pomeroy," Maynard said, also standing. "Good night."

Randolph Maynard had two choices: return to the ball—but that was an hour's drive—or simply walk back to his on-campus quarters and go to bed. As it was nearly midnight, the latter option was looking better. The surge of worry had long since ebbed. He felt drained.

And yet, the riddle troubled him as he carefully hung up his jacket and trousers. Someone from the Brotherhood had sent him the false message. Only the Black Scroll members knew he would be hosting the event at his country house. He'd been very careful about that. But the bigger question was—why?

Sleep, when it came, felt snatched in bits and pieces. His dreams were fitful, disturbing. Men, elegantly attired and wearing masks, came up to talk to him. He didn't know them. He felt himself itching to snatch the mask off each face, to learn who they were. In his dream, he finally succumbed to the impulse. There was another mask beneath the first. He pulled off the next mask, and then the next, and felt himself swallowed up in an endless line of masks....

CHAPTER 42

The blackness faded. Concordia lifted her head from the bed. She cautiously propped herself on her elbows and waited for a dizzying wave of nausea to pass. She was alone in what appeared to be a man's bedroom, with framed paintings of horses on the walls.

Where was she? It was an enormous effort to concentrate. Then she remembered. The masquerade ball. Randolph Maynard's country house. She must be in Maynard's bedroom. She didn't like the thought of that.

What happened?

Concordia tentatively shifted her legs over the side, and fingered the silk of her ball gown, trying to remember.

The bedroom door opened, and Lily Isley walked in with a tray.

"Oh, my dear! Thank goodness you're awake. I've been so worried." Lily set down the tray and felt Concordia's forehead. "An illness, perhaps?"

Concordia shook her head, trying to clear the cobwebs. This sudden collapse had felt nothing like a gradual illness.

"Perhaps your corset was too tight," Lily went on. "I loosened it a bit for you, while you were sleeping. I hope you don't mind."

Concordia minded very much, actually. She was starting to remember. The bitter-tasting tea. Her glance fell upon the tray Lily had brought. "What's this?"

"Oh, just a cup of beef broth and some toast," Lily said soothingly.

"Thank you, but I should go," Concordia said, clutching the bedpost in an attempt to stand. The room teetered and she closed her eyes.

"Nonsense, you can't travel in this condition," Lily said firmly. "Why don't you lay down for a bit longer? Then we can take you home. Here, have some broth." She held out the cup.

Concordia took it, although she had no intention of consuming another thing in this household. She glanced suddenly at the window, which was open a crack for air. "Did you see that?"

"What?" Lily went to the window, and Concordia, with an unspoken apology to the dean for ruining his carpet, dumped half the broth over the far side of the bed. When Lily turned around, Concordia had the rim of the cup to her lips.

"I don't see anything."

Concordia gave her a sheepish look. "I thought I saw a lantern in the orchard. A trick of the light, I suppose." She passed the cup back to Lily and lay back against the pillows with a sigh. "That was very good. Thank you."

Lily glanced into the cup before setting it aside. "Of course, dear. Now, you just rest here for a bit. I'll leave you the toast." She closed the door quietly behind her on her way out.

Was it Concordia's imagination, or was there the faint *click* of a key being turned in the lock?

She sat up again, taking deep breaths to fight through the dizziness. After a little while, the floor no longer loomed up at her. She groped her way to the door, and quietly tested it. It was locked, as she had suspected.

She knew better than to bang on the door and demand to be let out. Lily had no intention of letting her go.

Concordia crossed over to the window, opening it as far as it would go. The cool night air soothed her throbbing head.

She was about twelve feet from the ground, without so much as a vine or tree branch to aid any climb down. She wasn't sure she could have managed a climb, anyway; she wasn't quite steady yet.

Then she noticed a figure in the darkness, moving stealthily toward the side of the house.

What on earth?

Concordia breathed a sigh of relief when she recognized Charlotte Crandall. How did the girl manage to return undetected? Bless the resourceful young lady for realizing there was trouble.

"*Psst!* Charlotte!" Concordia called in a hushed voice.

The figure looked up. "Miss Wells," she whispered. "Thank heavens. I'll be right back; I saw a ladder in the shed." Charlotte slipped into the shadows around the corner, re-emerging in moments with a long ladder. After a few attempts, she managed to softly prop it against the wall. "I'll hold it while you climb down."

Concordia shook her head, but she couldn't explain. The more she talked while leaning out the window, the more likely someone would hear them.

Charlotte's expression was unreadable in the darkness, but after a pause the girl got on the ladder and climbed up.

Concordia helped in the bedraggled girl. "Am I glad to see you."

"What happened? Why didn't you climb down?" Charlotte Crandall asked.

"Lily put something in my tea to knock me out. I feel a little wobbly. Oh, and the door's locked from the outside." Concordia sank back into a chair.

Charlotte sucked in a breath. "So she's part of this, too. These are desperate people."

Concordia nodded, gingerly. "What made you come back?"

"When you hadn't returned to Willow Cottage by one o'clock this morning," Charlotte said, collapsing into a chair and re-pinning her straggling bun, "I grew worried. That last conversation we had with Bursar Isley...something wasn't right. I didn't know what to think. I wanted to see if you were here."

"But *how* did you get here?"

"I borrowed a horse," Charlotte said matter-of-factly.

Concordia shuddered. She didn't especially like horses, and they didn't seem over-fond of her, either.

"When I was out on the grounds, I overheard Mr. Isley through a downstairs window, talking with another man,"

Charlotte continued. She gave Concordia an anxious look. "Are you feeling any better? We have to get out of here."

Concordia stood and crossed to the window. The dizziness had ebbed. "I can do it now." She hesitated and turned back to Charlotte. "Isley was talking with another man? What did they say?" She was willing to bet it was Inner Circle business.

"Apparently there's to be a meeting at three this morning. They're waiting for whoever's in charge to come, to finalize plans for something."

Concordia started. "You mean Isley's not the one in charge of the Inner Circle?"

"Not the way I heard it, no." Charlotte glanced uneasily at the bedside clock. "It's past that time now. Shouldn't we leave? All of the other guests are long gone. We'd have no one to turn to for help if someone comes in."

Concordia shook her head. She was very curious about this man in charge, who wasn't Isley. Could it be Maynard? Where had he been all evening, if not in his own house? "Did Isley say anything else?"

"Not really," Charlotte said. "They stopped talking when the maid came down the hallway. Isley told her to get the fire stoked in the billiard room, and lay out port and cigars."

"Where's the billiard room?" Concordia asked.

"My guess is the top story," Charlotte said. "I saw the maids turning up the lights and opening the windows in the room just above this one." She regarded Concordia anxiously. "You're not considering what I think you are...."

"We have to learn their plans," Concordia said. "This may be our only opportunity."

"Setting aside for the moment how *dangerous* that is," Charlotte said, "how are you going to get up there?"

Concordia went to the window where the ladder was propped and looked up. Even though it extended past her window, it didn't quite reach the balcony above.

However, just to the right of the balcony was the deep ledge of a gabled window.

She pointed it out. "I can reach that window sill. On a mild night like this, they are bound to leave the windows and balcony doors open. I'll be able to hear everything."

"Unless one of them steps out on the balcony and sees you first," Charlotte protested.

Concordia regarded Charlotte, nervously glancing out the window. "Charlotte, there's no sense in both of us risking capture. Why don't you go back down the ladder, and wait for me…where did you tether the horse?"

"In the orchard, but out of sight of the house," Charlotte said.

"Then wait for me there, and if I don't join you in thirty minutes, leave and get help."

Charlotte shook her head stubbornly. "You'll need someone to keep the ladder steady. At that height, it would be sure to tip. I can stay here and support it from the window. No one would see me with the lights in the room turned out."

Concordia hesitated, then smiled. "Thank you."

Charlotte looked over Concordia's ball gown with a skeptical eye. "But how are you going to climb a ladder and stand on a window ledge wearing *that*?"

Concordia regarded her gown in dismay. "You're right." She went over to the armoire and pulled it open, scanning the contents for something suitable. All men's clothing, of course; even if he were not a bachelor, Randolph Maynard certainly wouldn't keep women's attire in his own wardrobe.

Charlotte stifled a laugh. "You're not going to wear the dean's clothes, are you?"

Concordia held a pair of trousers against her waist, trying to get a sense of their size. Fortunately, Randolph Maynard was a lean man, and the waist didn't seem too large. Of course, he was much taller than she.

"Why not?" Concordia asked with false bravado, trying not to think about how ridiculous she was going to look. "I can roll up the cuffs so they don't catch…and these suspenders will hold up the trousers. Help me, will you?"

Charlotte helped her out of the gown and corset. Concordia left her chemise on, tucking it awkwardly into the trousers. Lumpy but effective, she decided. She added a cotton shirt, rolled at the sleeves to free her hands, with a dark jacket over top, so the white wouldn't catch the light. As her dress pumps were impractical for climbing and none of Maynard's shoes fit, she went in her stockinged feet.

"I am a sight, I must say." Concordia turned away from the mirror. "Okay, ready."

With Charlotte holding onto the ladder from inside the room, Concordia grasped a rung and tentatively pulled herself up. She paused briefly, looking at Charlotte. "If you hear someone at the bedroom door, climb down and get help."

"But that will leave you stranded," Charlotte protested.

"I can reach the balcony from that gable window, if I have to," Concordia said. "By that point, I'd be discovered, anyway. No sense in us both being caught. And if you get away, you can bring back help."

Charlotte nodded miserably, and Concordia started to climb.

There was a refreshing freedom in wearing men's clothing, and Concordia climbed up quickly.

When she was nearly at the top, the ladder began to wobble. Concordia froze and looked down. She could see Charlotte's hands, firmly curled around the sides. Thank heaven the girl had insisted upon staying. The sill was to her left, and she could see the balcony beyond that, bright light spilling onto it from the open French doors of the billiard room.

She reached for the top frame of the gable with her left hand, then shifted her right hand to the top ladder rung. Taking a deep breath, she stepped onto the window ledge—left foot, then right foot, not daring to look down. The balcony was less than an arm's length away, with a wide balustrade blocking some of the view. She flattened herself against the building as best she could and tipped her head to listen.

Chapter 43

Maynard woke with a pounding heart. He glanced over at the clock: three in the morning.

What did the dream mean? He must be more troubled about the note than he'd thought. He trusted the men in the brotherhood—men who believed in philanthropy without the egregious self-congratulatory posturing that accompanied most charitable works. But he couldn't shake the idea that someone from the Black Scroll didn't want him at the ball tonight. Didn't want him in his own summer house.

Early as it was, he gave up on sleep and dressed. Perhaps a visit to the college's stable would settle his disquiet. He'd always found the company of horses soothing. Ever since he was a boy, the summers spent on his uncle's farm were more pleasurable than anywhere else. He could read a horse's mood, and understood its temperament.

As Maynard made his way to the stable, he thought more about the Black Scroll. Some things had been odd about the Brotherhood lately: Isley's request that he place an order with his brother-in-law, a jeweler, for cufflinks and a pin emblazoned with the symbol of the organization. Too few to be given to each member, certainly, and Maynard hadn't seen them distributed to anyone. Then there was the request that he open his summer house early, to host the Masquerade Ball.

But it wasn't the Brotherhood as a whole that was odd, he realized. During membership meetings, the same few men—Isley among them—broke away afterward to talk among themselves. Were they responsible for the bogus message? But why lure him away from his own home? What in blazes was going on?

There was only one solution: Maynard had to see for himself. Surely, President Langdon wouldn't mind if he borrowed his new buggy, even at this hour.

At the stable, Maynard was greeted with a sleepy whinny from Ransom, a sturdy black Frisian. Maynard rubbed the velvety nose that was thrust his way and glanced into Chestnut's stall.

Chestnut was gone.

Chapter 44

Gentlemen, let's look to our business.

Othello, *II.iii*

Concordia held onto the window frame and strained to listen.

"—Lily has assured me that she'll sleep until dawn, at least." The voice was Barton Isley's.

"That lady professor's a nosy one. Makes me uncomfortable, with our plans so close to fruition. I'll be glad when it's over tomorrow," another man answered.

"That's why I took it upon myself to act, when I spotted her," Isley continued, his voice touched with pride and self-importance. "I wanted to make sure we could keep her contained. She knows nothing of our arrangements," he added hastily, "but she was scrutinizing the guests quite carefully."

Concordia let out a small sigh. So much for her attempt at subtlety during the ball. Miss Hamilton would have carried it off easily.

"'Twas a wise precaution, to be sure," said another voice. Concordia gripped the ledge, her knuckles white. The voice had a familiar Irish lilt to it.

Robert Flynn.

Her breath grew shallow as she strained to hear every word.

"We'll let her go after she wakes, won't we?" Isley asked.

"Do you think me a bounder? Of course we'll let her go," Flynn said. "I see no harm in it. Lily led her to believe she was suffering from an indisposition, isn't that so? Miss Wells knows only that those in attendance at the ball tonight are members of the Black Scroll. She knows nothing of our Circle."

Concordia knew Flynn was lying. He hadn't spared Florence or Ben Rosen. He'd tried to kill Eli and Miss Hamilton. Why would he let Concordia go? He didn't dare.

Other pieces were falling into place now. Eli's man in "fancy dress" fit Flynn: the tall, slim frame, salt-and-pepper hair, and the neatly trimmed beard. Flynn had been the first to notice Florence, after the Capshaws' wedding. That sharp glance across the street had been one of startled recognition, she realized now. Flynn was the man who had turned in Eli as a stowaway on the train, feinting laryngitis so that his distinctive Irish accent would not be noted. He later ran down Eli in the street and left him to die.

It must have been quite a shock when Flynn had caught a glimpse of Eli, alive, through the partly-open study door while at the Capshaw house. He had concealed his reaction well, turning his initial shock into exaggerated anger.

Why hadn't she thought of him before?

What a simpleton she'd been. He hadn't been at the Isley's dinner party during the Inner Circle meeting in the library, so she had eliminated him from consideration. Isley had obviously acted in his stead, working to recruit Sir Anthony. Then Flynn and her mother had arrived at the Isleys' house later.

Her mother. Concordia felt a chill at the back of her neck. How would her mother handle the news that the man she had begun to feel affection for was a ruthless criminal?

She couldn't think about that now. She had to know more of their plans. Careful of her footing, she leaned closer toward the balcony.

"It will be only the one device, correct?" Isley asked.

Device? Concordia felt cold all over.

"Johnny has made two more, in case one fails," Flynn answered.

"We're setting *three* devices? That's reckless. You said no one would be seriously hurt," Isley protested, anxiety in his voice.

"Oh, for heaven's sake, Barton," someone interrupted impatiently, "we are trying to get you elected. Don't turn missish on us now."

"Now, now," Flynn said. "I applaud Barton's caution. 'Be first in a wood and last in a bog,' as we say. Don't worry; Johnny's very adept at his work. He'll place them at the debate where they will produce the most dramatic destruction of property, but they won't be lethal. Perhaps some will suffer cuts and bruises, but that cannot be helped."

"I want to see where these devices are being placed," Isley insisted.

"Hardly practical," Flynn said. "You must be as far from the scene as possible."

"But Sanders is expecting me there," Isley said.

"You will be indisposed and send your regrets," Flynn said firmly. "I would advise the rest of you to be elsewhere tomorrow, going about your usual morning routines."

"What if Johnny's caught planting the bombs?" Isley asked. "Three are more difficult than one."

"Johnny will be working with someone who's very adept at slipping in and out without being noticed," another voice chimed in.

"Who?" Barton asked.

"Oh, someone local, let's just leave it at that," Flynn said smoothly. "Why don't you pour us some of Maynard's excellent brandy? I think we all need a break."

Concordia's hands were cramping in their grip on the sill. As she shifted position, one of the metal suspender buttons scraped against the stone. She froze.

"Did you hear something?" someone asked. Concordia pressed herself into the shadows of the deep gable. She held her breath.

In the small gap between the balustrade and wall, Concordia saw Flynn step out onto the balcony. He gazed out into the darkness and lit a cigar. Another man whom Concordia recognized from the ball joined him, and the two were puffing away, contemplating the shadows of the orchard trees in the moonlight.

Flynn leaned in toward the man and dropped his voice, although the night air carried it to Concordia's ear. "I want you to get a message to Johnny. But keep it quiet. He's needed for another job."

The man rubbed the back of his neck and glanced back toward the room. "You mean—?"

Flynn nodded. "A pity it is – she's a fair *cailin*, without too many nicks in her horn. Nevertheless, Miss Wells must be silenced. Permanently."

As soon as the men went back inside, Concordia climbed quietly down the ladder, legs shaking. They had to get out of here.

Chapter 45

Charlotte helped guide a trembling Concordia through the bedroom window. "That was close," she breathed.

Concordia groped her way to a chair. Her legs were shaking so badly she didn't know if they would hold her weight. "Luckily, his eyes weren't adjusted to the dark, and the balustrade blocked most of that side. Including the ladder."

"What did you learn?" Charlotte asked.

"Plenty, and none of it good," Concordia said. She fiddled with a suspender. Really, she could get used to such attire.

Charlotte listened with rapt attention as Concordia told her about Robert Flynn and the Circle's plans to set bombs at the candidates' rally tomorrow.

"Today, actually." Concordia drew a shuddering breath.

"But why?" Charlotte asked. "I hadn't heard of any threats against either candidate, as volatile as the interactions between the two have sometimes been. What benefit could be gained from such a despicable act?"

Concordia wondered that herself. Was it power? Money? *We're trying to get you elected,* one of them had said to Isley.

"I didn't hear any discussion of why," Concordia said. "I expect that ground has already been covered. It's clear that Flynn is running things."

Charlotte paced the room in her agitation. "What do we do?"

"We stop them," Concordia said flatly. And then to break the news to her mother, she added to herself.

Charlotte had gone pale. "Oh, no," she whispered.

"What is it?"

"A group of girls from the school plan to attend the debate, accompanied by Miss Pomeroy."

"We'll just have to get there first," Concordia said, with a confidence she didn't necessarily feel. "And the sooner we're gone from here, the better." She suppressed a shudder, remembering the message Flynn was sending to Hitchcock about another "job."

She stood, feeling more steady now. "Let's go."

As Concordia still wore Dean Maynard's clothes, she climbed down the ladder quickly. She held it steady for Charlotte, whose skirts hampered her progress.

"We need a conveyance," Concordia whispered, as they hurried toward the road.

"Well, we're not getting any of *those* carriages." Charlotte whispered back, pointing to the three vehicles in front of the house. Their drivers were standing idly beside them, smoking and laughing. "We'll have to ride Chestnut."

Concordia had hoped it wouldn't come to that. "Can he manage both of us?"

Charlotte nodded. "He's a big one, but it will be slower going." She pointed to the far pasture. "This way."

Chestnut whinnied softly as they approached. Charlotte rubbed his nose. "He was always my favorite at the school."

"Uh-huh," Concordia said doubtfully. The horse was looking at her with an equally skeptical eye. Perhaps he disapproved of ladies in male attire.

Charlotte swung easily into the saddle and grasped the reins. "Here, I left the stirrup open for you. I'll pull you up. Don't worry: he's gentle, really."

With a sigh, Concordia put her foot in a stirrup. At least it wasn't a side saddle, although how Charlotte managed to ride astride in her skirts was a question she didn't have time to ask.

Charlotte looked over her shoulder to make sure Concordia was in position. "Okay, just hold on. You'll be fine."

Concordia stifled a gasp and grabbed Charlotte's waist as they lurched forward. Charlotte kept the horse at a canter. Concordia glanced back toward the house, just visible through the trees.

Oh no.

Every light was blazing on the west side. Even worse, a dark shape was moving at speed down the drive toward them.

"I can't believe I'm saying this, but we need to go faster," Concordia said.

Charlotte took a quick look back. She touched her heels to the horse's flanks, and he broke into a gallop. Concordia clung to Charlotte for dear life, her hair coming out of its pins and whipping around her face.

The carriage wheels were audible now, and soon the vehicle itself was clearly visible. Concordia recognized Flynn's two-horse carriage. They were obviously outmatched. Chestnut was starting to tire from the extra weight. To make matters worse, they couldn't cut across the fields and leave the road-dependent carriage behind them. Low stone walls edged the road. The horse wouldn't be able to jump it with both of them on his back.

"I have an idea," she said in Charlotte's ear. The young lady nodded reluctantly, as Concordia described what they would need to do.

Charlotte slowed the horse as the vehicle caught up with them.

"Ah, Mr. Flynn, what brings you here?" Concordia called out as the carriage pulled up beside them. He couldn't see in the dark that she was carefully disentangling herself from Charlotte and making sure none of her clothes would catch on the saddle.

Flynn hopped out, face red with fury. "Dunna play games wi' me. Get down, now!"

The horse skittered nervously at the raised voice, and Charlotte Crandall patted his neck to quiet him down.

The driver climbed down to reach for Chestnut's bridle. He paused, eyes widening at the sight of Concordia in men's clothing. In one fluid movement, Concordia slid off the horse. "Now!" she cried to Charlotte.

Charlotte gave Chestnut a swift kick. The animal responded, and sped away at a gallop. Concordia ran in the opposite direction. She glanced back long enough to see Charlotte and Chestnut clear the stone wall beautifully and dash across the fields. Concordia kept sprinting for all she was worth. As long as Charlotte got away and reached Capshaw in time, that was all that mattered.

Flynn, stunned and slow to respond, gave a shout and chased Concordia as the driver stood in the middle of the road, mouth open.

Chapter 46

Maynard stared at the empty stall for a good long minute, as if willing the horse to reappear.

He gritted his teeth in vexation. Mischievous students again. Perhaps they were responsible for the note after all. But how were the two connected?

He had just awoken the stable hand and sent him off in search of the horse when he saw the Willow Cottage matron huffing down the path, bed-cap still clapped to her head, a shawl wrapped around her nightgown.

"Mrs. Hitchcock, what on earth are you doing out at this hour?" Maynard asked.

"Have you seen 'em?" she asked breathlessly.

"Seen whom?" Maynard asked.

"Miss Crandall and Miss Wells. They're not in their rooms. A critter yowling outside woke me. I checked all the girls' bedrooms since I was up. That's when I seen they were gone."

"Gone? For how long?" Why did he inevitably hear the name *Miss Wells* whenever there was trouble?

Ruby sucked in her lip as she thought. "They was goin' together to a dance or such-like. Left here just at lights out. I went to bed. Miss Crandall's ball gown is on her bed now, so she must 'a been back, but there's no sign that Miss Wells came back at all."

Maynard clenched his jaw. *A dance.* That was too much of a coincidence for his liking. And he didn't like what he was thinking now. "Chestnut's gone."

Ruby's eyes widened. "He's always been a favorite o' Miss Crandall's. Ya think she took 'im?"

Maynard was sure of it, but there wasn't time to explain. "I think I know where they are, but I need your help. Wake up President Langdon, and tell him what's happened—"

"Ooh, Mr. Maynard, they'll get in trouble, for sure!" Ruby protested.

"They're already in trouble," Maynard growled. Blast the woman. He'd never met a female yet who simply followed instructions without arguing over them first. "Tell President Langdon to telephone the police." Thank goodness the school had put in a telephone line last year. It would save time. "Have them meet me at my house in Cottage Grove. He knows the address."

"But he'll ask me why!" Ruby said. "What shall I tell him?"

"Tell him there's trouble. I haven't figured it out yet, but he'll trust my judgment," Maynard said. Without another word, he ran back into the stable to harness Ransom.

Chapter 47

*'tis a monster
Begot upon itself, born on itself.*

Othello, *III.iv*

As freeing as running in gentleman's clothing can be, Concordia's breath soon came in heaving gasps and her body trembled with over-exertion. She felt as if she were running through mud, her legs leaden weights. She heard Flynn close in behind her, his own breathing labored.

If he were going to catch her, she would at least make it painful. She stopped and turned abruptly just as he was about to tackle her, planting her feet apart and curling her fist, which she buried in his abdomen.

With a heavy *oomph* of pain, he was on the ground, bringing Concordia down with him. She winced as she fell on her sore shoulder. *Ow.* Her hand hurt, too.

No wonder ladies don't usually throw punches.

Flynn gave her a vicious slap that made her ears ring. He hauled her to her feet. "Egad, 'tis only one way to deal with *you*," he huffed, and raised his hand again. Concordia flinched.

"*Sir!*" came an outraged voice. Flynn's driver had caught up to them. "Hittin' a *lady?*"

Flynn lowered his hand. "Never you mind," he barked, keeping a firm grip on Concordia's arm and steering her back to the carriage. "Why didn't you go after the other one?"

The driver snorted. "And how was I gonna do *that?* The coach don't have wings, ya know. 'Sides, we'll be able to catch up wi' her. The creek borders the far side of the field about a mile fro' here, and wi' all the rain we've had, she won't be able to cross it. She'll have to double back to the bridge."

Concordia's heart sank. She prayed the man was wrong, and Charlotte would make it through.

Flynn nodded stiffly. "Turn the carriage around, and be quick about it. We're going back to the house."

Chapter 48

Driving along the quiet road at this hour of the morning would have been pleasant if Randolph Maynard wasn't so worried. As he tapped the reins along Ransom's flanks once more to urge him on, Maynard considered what had prompted Miss Crandall to take Chestnut in the middle of the night. None of the possibilities were reassuring. From what little he'd observed of Charlotte Crandall, he found her sober and intelligent, not given to reckless impulses like this. But at least they knew she'd returned to campus. What worried him most was that Miss Wells had not come back at all.

The side road he'd just turned on was darker and narrower. The houses here weren't yet wired for electricity. With only carriage lanterns for illumination, Maynard was forced to slow down.

He gritted his teeth at the slower pace. It would be at least twenty minutes before he got to the bridge, and another ten after that.

As Maynard squinted into the dark, he saw a glimmer in the distance. He slowed the vehicle, and listened. He was sure he heard the *clop-clop-clop* of another horse. Soon his lanterns picked out the white blaze of Chestnut's forehead.

"Miss Crandall?" he called out, not able to see, but his voice projecting into the stillness.

"Oh, thank heavens," came a lady's weary voice.

"What in tarnation did you think you were doing?" Maynard demanded, as he assisted a tired and muddy Charlotte, who was nearly falling off her equally tired and muddy horse.

"I've been trying to find help."

"These are summer residences along this stretch." Maynard led the fatigued horse through a pasture gate. "They haven't been opened yet for the season." He pumped some water into the trough, removed the saddle and bridle, and turned the animal loose.

"Will he be all right, just left here?" Charlotte asked anxiously, as they closed the gate and returned to the carriage.

"He'll be fine. This is Frank Pennington's place. He won't mind. Besides, it's only temporary."

"Now," he continued, after he had helped Charlotte up to the seat and grabbed the reins, "I assume we're heading back to my house to rescue Miss Wells. In the meantime, why don't you tell me what's going on."

"You're going to find it difficult to believe," Charlotte said wearily.

"Try me," Maynard said.

Chapter 49

Thou know'st we work by wit, and not by witchcraft.
***Othello**, II.iii*

With a sinking heart, Concordia saw the carriage drive was empty when they pulled up in front of the Maynard house. Except for the driver, she and Flynn were alone.

Flynn unceremoniously dragged her out of the carriage. "Bring the lantern," he called to his driver. He glared at Concordia. "I'll be putting *you* where you canno' cause me further trouble. There will be no window to climb out of this time."

Her new place of imprisonment looked to be far less congenial than Dean Maynard's bedroom. In the dim light of the single lantern, she could see they were headed for the root cellar. A wooden double door with a stout outer latch opened wide to a sloping entrance, stretching ten feet below ground.

"What are your intentions, Mr. Flynn?" Concordia said bluntly. She observed the driver, eyeing her uneasily. Perhaps here was a possible ally?

Flynn took the lantern from the driver. "Unhitch one of the horses and wait at the bridge for the other young lady. Dunna come back without her."

With a nervous tip of his cap, the man left. Flynn prodded Concordia toward the cellar opening.

"My intentions, Miss Wells? Why, your untimely demise, of course." He adopted a sorrowful look. "I grieve already for your poor ma. But ne'er fear. I'll be there to comfort her in her time of need."

She suppressed a shiver at the thought of no one else knowing who this man really was. Especially her mother.

But Concordia had no intention of meekly going to her Eternal Reward. She had to stall for time, hoping Charlotte would bring back help.

"But you'll have Hitchcock do your dirty work for you," she responded tartly. "As you did with Florence Willoughby."

"Aye, indeed—Florence," he said casually, as if she were an item he had misplaced and forgotten. "Quite careless of me to be givin' her access to the room where we stored our materials. To be sure, I didn't realize until too late that she had engaged in a nasty bit of eavesdropping as well." He scowled. "And then she had the audacity to extort money from *me*, no less! After all I had done for her: ball gowns, baubles, theater tickets." He shrugged. "'Eaten bread is soon forgotten,' as they say. God's truth, I did what I had to do."

"And was that the case with Eli?" Concordia asked contemptuously. "Following him back to the train, then having him arrested. No doubt you needed time to find out who he was and why he'd been following you, but why try to kill him? He's just a child."

Flynn gave her an unreadable look. "I learned he was associated with that policeman—Capshaw. I couldn't take a chance."

"It must have been quite a shock when you saw him alive in the Capshaw's living room," Concordia said coldly.

"The boy and Miss Hamilton were full of surprises," Flynn admitted. He gave Concordia a hard look. "She's not who she appears to be, is she?"

When Concordia didn't answer, he prodded her through the hatch.

Even as she inched along the dark, sloping dirt floor of the root cellar, Flynn at her back, Concordia tried to keep him talking. "You were sufficiently worried about Miss Hamilton to stage the 'accident' at the trolley stop. And when she survived that, you brought Hitchcock out of hiding in an attempt to silence her once and for all."

"Did I now? You have all the answers, don't you?" Flynn sneered.

Concordia ignored the jibe. "But you had to do some of the dirty work yourself, didn't you? Ben Rosen's murder. He wasn't garroted as Florence had been. You must have seen Rosen approach me at the luncheon, so you attacked him in the gardener's shed just before I arrived. What did you fear he would tell me? Had he learned of your connection to Florence? Possibly the identities of Inner Circle members?"

Flynn's brief look of surprise confirmed that Concordia's guess had hit the mark, but he merely grunted and prodded her toward the back wall.

Concordia continued on. "What I don't understand is how this is connected to setting bombs at the senatorial debate and getting Barton Isley elected."

Her words had the intended effect of stopping Flynn cold. "How in blazes do you know about that?" He hesitated. "Ah, the noise outside the balcony. Hmm, it seems that our lady professor has been engaging in some unseemly snooping. Well, well, aren't you a resourceful *cailín*."

"No matter what you told Isley, you know a great many people will be wounded or killed by the blast," Concordia pressed. "Have you no conscience? What do you hope to gain?"

"More than you, my dear, could understand." Flynn's face creased in a mock-paternal frown. "You modern women may well say that you know the ways of the world, but sadly deficient you are in seeing beyond your parlors and kitchens."

"Humor me," Concordia said, trying to keep the sarcasm out of her voice. "I may as well know the truth. I'm going to die, anyway."

Flynn gave her a wary look.

They were at the bottom of the cellar now, and Flynn released her elbow. Through the open hatch door behind him, Concordia could see the light of pre-dawn streak the sky. She leaned back against a bin, groping behind her in the dark for something, *anything*, that would serve as a weapon. A crowbar?

A spade? This time of year, the bins that usually held potatoes, carrots and other vegetables were bare.

Concordia persisted. "I already know about the Inner Circle. At first I thought that Isley was in charge, but it's clear they do *your* bidding."

Flynn puffed up in pride. "Indeed, now it serves *my* purposes, although it was Barton's creation. He had oh-so-high ideals when he formed it. Wanted to fight the corruption and inefficiency of our local government. He hand-picked a few men from the Black Scroll Order who professed the same ideals. Ironic, is it not? Such naïveté. I have shaped it into a more practical, effective entity."

"And the Black Scroll's general membership does not know of the Inner Circle's existence," Concordia said.

Flynn cocked an eyebrow. "Naturally. The Black Scroll Brotherhood would never approve. I want to keep the Brothers on my side; their oaths have proved eminently useful. The police turned a blind eye on several occasions."

"No doubt the investigators of the *Gascogne* explosion turned a blind eye, too?" Concordia asked, remembering what Miss Hamilton had learned. She continued exploring the bins behind her in the dark, her hands skimming along the surfaces.

Flynn scowled. "Apparently Florence passed on more information before her death than I'd anticipated. Or perhaps it was your resourceful Miss Hamilton who figured it out."

Concordia went on as if he hadn't spoken. "And because Lieutenant Capshaw was learning more about the Willoughbys in the course of investigating Florence's murder, you arranged for him to be removed from the case and replaced by someone less experienced, didn't you?"

Flynn gave her a mocking smile.

"Capshaw is out of my hair completely, now," he said. "He's been fired."

Concordia felt a twist of pity for Sophia, and fear for them all. How does one defend against a powerful few, working in secret, manipulating people to their will?

She couldn't despair. Somehow she would get out of this.

She heard a slight rustle outside. A night animal? Flynn's driver? Or perhaps it was Charlotte, bringing rescue? Flynn seemed not to notice.

She had to keep him talking.

"What about Barton Isley?" she asked. "Does he know you had Florence killed, and murdered Mr. Rosen yourself? Does he know of your attempts to kill Eli and Miss Hamilton?"

"Isley?" Flynn said derisively. "Of course not. He would never agree to such tactics, and I rely heavily upon his business acumen and considerable social connections. 'Tis a nuisance to cater to such a highly-principled fellow. Barton doesn't possess the steely resolve to do what needs to be done. We have a saying: 'Soft words butter no parsnips.'"

A very different saying had come to Concordia's mind: *Men's natures wrangle with inferior things, though great ones are their object.* The man whom Flynn considered "highly-principled" was part of the conspiracy to set bombs at a public function. If the situation weren't so dire it would be laughable.

"But he'll make an excellent candidate for the state senate seat," Flynn went on boastfully. "He was doing quite well before he withdrew from the race, to be bursar at your school. He has since regretted that decision."

"How does bombing the rally get Isley back in the race?"

Flynn smiled. "T'will appear to be an attack upon the Democratic candidate. We have arranged it so that blame falls solely upon Mr. Sanders—if he survives. Isley can step back in as the clean-cut, uncorrupted alternative."

Concordia snorted. "But the blast will *not* be harmless. He'll know you tricked him."

Flynn shrugged. "I doubt it. He believes what I tell him. I will express deep regret in being so mistaken, of course. 'Twas a pity…perhaps Johnny put in more explosive powder than he should? Barton's too embroiled in this business to pull out now."

"But why help Isley gain office at all, and by such extreme means?"

Flynn hesitated, then sighed. "As you say, you won't be leaving to repeat it, so I'll satisfy your curiosity. Once a state senator, Isley would be in position to be elected by the general assembly to the United States Senate. He knows I have the connections to make it happen. That sort of access would be invaluable." He snorted in derision. "I have grander plans than this little Nutmeg State of yours."

"I see." Concordia edged to her left, hands behind her back. There must be *something* she could use.

At last. She felt an object, metallic and claw-like. A hand rake. She curled her fingers around the wood handle, and subtly shifted her stance for better leverage.

"Well! As diverting as this little tête-à-tête has been, I have important matters to tend to," Flynn said briskly. "Johnny will be here in a few hours. You may as well make yourself...comfortable."

Flynn edged backward, shining the lantern in her eyes. Concordia inched forward blindly, fingers tightening on the rake handle behind her back.

This time, they both heard the rustling sound. As Flynn turned his head to look behind him, Concordia swung the rake, *hard,* at the lamp in his hand. It crashed to the ground and went out. Flynn gasped in pain as the weapon caught his hand.

In the midst of the confusion and darkness, another figure, quite tall and lean, leapt upon Flynn. Concordia yelled for help and crawled past the two as they rolled in the dirt.

"Concordia!" a voice shouted from across the yard. It was Charlotte Crandall, crouched behind the well. She pointed to the road. Against the sunrise-pink sky, Concordia saw three police vehicles, rattling at speed toward the house.

"It looks as if...the cavalry...has come at last," huffed a familiar deep voice behind her.

Concordia whipped around. Her eyes widened in surprise to see a panting, disheveled Randolph Maynard dragging a barely-conscious Flynn by his collar.

"How did *you* come to be here?" she asked.

He grimaced. "It's a long story."

In the brightening dawn, Maynard got his first good look at Concordia. His mouth hung open.

Finally, he found his voice. "Are you...are you wearing my *trousers*, Miss Wells?"

Chapter 50

By the mass, 'tis morning.

Othello, *II.iii*

Week 14, Instructor Calendar
May 1898

With the arrival of the police and a short explanation from Maynard, who then hurried into his house on an unknown errand, Flynn was promptly deposited in the prison wagon.

Concordia was pleasantly surprised to see Lieutenant Capshaw. In uniform, and...*without a mustache?* He looked like a youth of twenty. She tried not to stare. "I thought you'd been fired!" she exclaimed.

Capshaw grimaced as his gaze swept over Concordia. She knew she was a sight: rolled trousers held up by suspenders over a lumpy waist, shirt sleeves flopping over her wrists, feet bare.

An older policeman stepped forward. "No, miss. But it was a necessary subterfuge."

"Concordia," Capshaw said, "this is Police Chief Stiles." The man bowed.

Concordia frowned. This was the man who had succumbed to the Inner Circle's wishes? Who had fired Capshaw...but not really? Chief Stiles was now *helping* them? She gave Capshaw a puzzled glance.

"He's been investigating the Inner Circle for the past two weeks," Capshaw said.

Concordia folded her arms and glared.

The chief flushed. "I regret my part in this matter, Miss Wells. I didn't know. I should never have allowed myself to be so influenced." He glanced at Capshaw. "I've been trying to undo the damage ever since."

Capshaw nodded. "We're making progress. Hitchcock has been found."

"Where is he now?" Concordia asked.

"He's cooling his heels in the city jail," Capshaw said. "We were questioning him when we got word that something untoward was going on at Maynard's country house, and help was needed immediately."

Concordia breathed a sigh of relief. "So Hitchcock had no time to plant the bombs?"

Capshaw's expression was grim as he shook his head. "Unfortunately, we were too late for that. It's obvious he was making bombs at his hide-out, but the devices themselves are gone. He must have passed them to a confederate. And Hitchcock isn't talking to us."

Concordia remembered Flynn's mention of *someone local* who would be assisting Hitchcock. "Perhaps you can get Flynn to tell you the location of the bombs."

"We have a man on it now," the police chief said, looking over at the prison van, otherwise known as a "Black Maria," where Flynn was locked up.

"Are you taking him back to the station?" Capshaw asked.

The police chief shook his head. "I want him on the scene. Perhaps being a little too close to those devices will get him to talk."

Randolph Maynard approached the group. He thrust a pair of slippers at Concordia. "Put these on. I'd purchased them as a gift for my niece, but you are in more immediate need of them." He shook his head as he looked her over once more. "I have no female clothing to provide, unfortunately."

Blushing, Concordia murmured her thanks and slipped them on. They actually fit her quite well, and were a welcome relief to her sore feet.

Maynard turned to Chief Stiles. "I should return Miss Crandall to campus. And we have a horse to retrieve along the way. Isley is part of this bomb conspiracy, and he may be at the college. What should I do?"

"I'll send one of my men with you to the school to take him into custody," Chief Stiles said. He waved over a muscular, broad-chested patrolman, whose snug-fitting tunic jacket revealed a powerful torso and arms.

Concordia spoke up. "And you'd better arrest Mrs. Isley, while you're at it."

"Miss Crandall told me about the woman drugging your tea and keeping you confined." Maynard said, shaking his head in disbelief. "She seemed so harmless."

Lieutenant Capshaw guided Concordia to one of the carriages. "We'd better get going, too. You can tell us the rest along the way." He turned to the chief. "What time does the debate start?"

"There's a breakfast beforehand, hosted by the Ladies Civic Committee," the chief said. He checked his watch. "That starts in an hour. The outdoor debate takes place after that."

"Heavens," Concordia said, "it will take us at least that long to get there."

Capshaw's mouth tightened. "We'll make it."

The drivers pushed the horses as fast as they could go. Concordia, though grateful for their speed, had the misfortune to be riding in one of the older vehicles. There was at least one broken spring in the undercarriage, she was sure, judging by how often a rut in the road sent her lurching against the side, or into the laps of the carriage's other occupants, Capshaw and Sergeant Maloney.

After Concordia had given her full account of the previous evening, Capshaw shook his head and gave her one of his gloomy looks. "How you manage to survive these—" he struggled for a suitable word "—incidents...is a perpetual wonder to me, miss."

He turned his attention to the sergeant, who was looking everywhere but at Concordia's trousers.

"You'll be with me. The chief and the rest of the men will be occupied with clearing the area. We'll search the restaurant first for the devices, then outside, at City Hall Square. The restaurant seems most likely; it would be easier to hide a device with all of the furniture in the room, and avoid being seen."

Maloney nodded. "Any idea what we're looking for? I never laid eyes on such a thing."

"They are timed-detonation devices," Capshaw explained. "Which means they could have been placed hours ago."

"How big would they be?"

"We don't know," Capshaw admitted, "and Hitchcock isn't talking. An alarm clock would be used as the timer, so that part might be roughly the size of my hand. Then it would be connected with a brass wire to the fuse and explosive. It could be as small as a cigar box, but it could look like anything—a lamp, a box, a bench—made of wood, or perhaps iron."

"How do we shut off something like that?" Maloney asked.

"That's the tricky part," Capshaw said. "If they were in a hurry, the timer might be outside the bomb's outer casing. Then we can simply cut the wires. If they were more deliberate, then everything—timer, wires, fuse, and the explosive compound, which we believe to be nitrate—would be *inside* the casing. We'd have to open it up first, just to get to the mechanism."

Maloney swallowed.

"And remember," Capshaw added, "according to Miss Wells—" he gestured in her direction "—there are three devices."

"How do you know so much about bombs, Lieutenant?" Concordia asked.

Capshaw gave Concordia an unreadable look. "Miss Hamilton had a knowledgeable, though unsavory, contact who gave me a recent education."

Bless Miss Hamilton's pragmatic nature, Concordia thought. Even from a hospital bed.

Chapter 51

Lay hold upon him: if he do resist,
Subdue him at his peril.

Othello, I.*ii*

When the dean, Charlotte Crandall, and policeman arrived at the gate of Hartford Women's College, the men hopped out. "Can you see to it the horses are taken care of?" Maynard asked Charlotte. "We must get to Barton Isley at once."

"Of course," she said, taking the reins.

Maynard checked his watch. Seven-thirty. They'd made good time, even with checking the Isley house along the way. According to the staff, Isley had arrived home late and then left early this morning. Upon inquiring about Mrs. Isley, the maid had simply said she was not home and refused to say anything more.

Where was Isley now? Maynard passed a weary hand through his hair. Lord, what a long night. What day was it?

Friday. That meant Isley would be poring over the end-of-week invoices in his office.

"This way," Maynard said to the policeman, gesturing to the right. They hurried across the quadrangle to Founder's Hall.

Isley looked up in annoyance as Maynard flung open his door without knocking. "Randolph, what the devil?" He sucked in his breath sharply when he caught sight of the policeman in the doorway.

The dean crossed the room in two strides and grabbed Isley by the collar. "You miserable, no-account snollygoster! Drugging a defenseless woman and holding her prisoner?

Allowing that cur Flynn to do your dirty work for you, just to further your own gutter-rat ambitions?"

"Sir!" the policeman exclaimed, putting a hand on Maynard's sleeve. "A little restraint."

The color had drained from Isley's face as Maynard loosened his grip and shoved him back into his chair.

"Where is your wife, the poisoner?" Maynard sneered. "You both have much to answer for. She wasn't at your house, and the maid would not say another word."

Isley worked his lips together before speaking. "I don't know. She didn't come home last night."

"You don't know where your own wife is?" Maynard allowed his derision free reign.

"We know the Inner Circle has planted explosive devices at the debate," the policeman interjected. "Where will they be hidden?"

Isley put his head in his hands. "I don't know."

"Hitchcock has been captured, but the bombs are gone," Maynard said. "Who was going to place them? One of the other Inner Circle men?"

"I don't know."

Maynard gritted his teeth. They were getting nowhere with the man. It had to be someone from the Inner Circle setting the bombs. Except for Hitchcock, they didn't seem too trusting of hired help. Who was in the group? Maynard was sure, now, that the cuff links he'd been asked to order were for the Circle. Besides Flynn and Isley, who were the other three? No, four, he remembered. There had been a pin, too.

Whoever had set the devices must have nerves of steel, he thought. Bold and confident. And the pin....

He had a chilling thought. *No. It couldn't be.*

"Where is your wife?" he asked again.

Isley shrugged but said nothing.

The policeman took restraining cuffs out of his pocket. "Mr. Isley, I am taking you into custody."

Chapter 52

Strike on the tinder, ho!
Give me a taper! call up all my people!

***Othello**, I.i*

Week 14, Instructor Calendar
May 1898

At last, the police vehicles pulled up to City Hall Square. Even though the candidate's breakfast had not yet begun, spectators were already occupying positions outside near the speakers' platform, set up the evening before.

Capshaw and Maloney hopped out before the carriage came to a full stop. Capshaw paused and gave Concordia a stern look. "Stay here." Then he was gone.

Concordia, all too aware of her unsuitable attire, wasn't tempted to go anywhere. She did watch out of the window as the police began dispersing people. She saw Capshaw quickly cross State Street and enter the Long Brothers' Palace Restaurant and Hotel. She sighed and leaned back against the cushions.

Concordia awoke to the sun in her eyes. She sat upright and gazed out the window. *Mercy,* how late was it? She wished she had her watch.

The people, more of them now and lingering out of idle curiosity, had been moved farther back. She could see Capshaw and Maloney out in the square, crawling around the platform structure. What about the hotel? Had they found any devices in the breakfast room?

With people gathering in the square, she was having trouble seeing what was going on. Maybe she could get a *little* closer. She climbed out of the vehicle and closed the door.

"Miss Wells?" asked a high-pitched voice.

With a sinking feeling in the pit of her stomach, Concordia recognized that voice. She turned to see Miss Pomeroy, accompanied by Miss Lovelace and her friends. What she wouldn't give to be in a skirt right now.

Miss Pomeroy gave her a startled look over the tops of her spectacles. The young ladies smothered giggles behind their gloved hands.

Just a few steps behind Miss Pomeroy was David Bradley, looking even more startled than he had the day she had nearly run him down with her bicycle.

Concordia flushed. "It's a long story. I'll tell you about it once we're back to campus."

Miss Pomeroy nodded in her usual absent-minded way, but David was not so obliging. He looked her up and down, taking in the sight of her rolled-up trousers, over-sized shirt and jacket, bedraggled hair, and slippered feet. Concordia felt a hot flush creep up her neck and face.

"Why are you dressed like that?" he demanded. "And out here in public! This utter lack of propriety is uncharacteristic of you, Concordia." He peered more closely at her face. "And is that a *bruise* on your cheek?"

The students fidgeted, alternating glances between Concordia and David.

Concordia fought the conflicting sensations of wanting to crawl back in the carriage to hide and wanting to slap David's face. She settled for something close to the latter.

"It is indeed a bruise," she answered tartly. "Thank you for your concern."

David took a step back. Then his face softened and he drew closer. "Are you all right? What happened?"

Concordia shuddered at the memory of the past few hours and gave him a glare. "*Now* you ask? Which do you care more about, the propriety of my appearance, or my well-being?"

Miss Pomeroy put a protective arm around a trembling Concordia. "Perhaps it would be best if you leave us now, Mr. Bradley. Thank you for your escort. We'll see you back at the school."

"But—"

"Thank you, Mr. Bradley," Gertrude Pomeroy said firmly.

Tight-lipped, David turned on his heel and stalked off.

Miss Lovelace rummaged in her purse and pulled out a handkerchief. "Here, Miss Wells." Concordia wiped her eyes and blew her nose.

"Don't worry. We'll get it all straightened out later," the lady principal said to Concordia consolingly. "You have to admit—" her lips twitched in amusement "—your appearance *is* rather startling. Some gentlemen aren't as...well, shall we say, *flexible*...in their thinking. I'm sure it was a shock to the poor man." She gestured toward the square. "Why have the police blocked it off? What's wrong?"

"They believe there are bombs hidden at the site of today's debate," Concordia explained. She looked across the square to see Capshaw and Maloney quickly crawl out from under the platform structure and sprint in their direction. "I think he's found something," she said, excitement making her voice squeak.

"All of you...need to stand farther back," Capshaw huffed when he reached them. He caught his breath and turned to Maloney. "Doc Turbridge's is one block down Prospect. Striped awning. *Hurry.*"

Maloney ran for all he was worth.

"You've found one?" Concordia asked.

Capshaw shook his head. "We've found *two.*"

"Two bombs?" Miss Pomeroy asked incredulously.

One of the girls sucked in a breath.

"Are they the first you've found?" Concordia asked. "What about the breakfast room?"

"Nothing in the restaurant. We combed it thoroughly."

"So there isn't a third one?" Concordia asked.

"Just these two. I imagine Hitchcock ran out of time to construct a third," Capshaw said. He took a deep breath and cast a glance back at the platform. "Two is plenty," he added soberly.

"Can you dismantle them?" Concordia asked.

Capshaw pulled at his mustache distractedly. "We've already taken care of one." He pointed to a stand of shrubbery at the periphery of the square, where several policemen were gathered, one carrying a large bucket of water. "We found it there. The trigger mechanism was wired to the device from the outside. A simple snip of the relays took care of it, but we'll soak it, just to be sure."

"But the other one—" Concordia began.

"—is more complicated," Capshaw finished. "It's a much larger device, cleverly concealed beneath Candidate Quint's podium. Everything—explosive, fuse, timer—is contained within the casing. I've removed the access plate, but the opening is narrow. I don't have fine enough instruments to reach in, find the right wires, and cut them. Maloney's on his way to the dentist, to see if he has the tools we need."

Even as Capshaw was talking, the young ladies were whispering with great animation. Miss Lovelace pulled a familiar-looking canvas pouch from her reticule. Concordia recognized it as the improvised tool kit from their bicycle ride. Was it only last month? It seemed ages ago.

"Lieutenant," Miss Lovelace said, extricating narrow-nosed pliers and a pair of slim forceps, "will these do?" She handed them to an astonished Capshaw.

"Oh, and let's give him the long-handled jeweler's screwdriver we just added to our collection," one of the girls said. "That would be perfect for delicate work." She plucked it out of the bag and passed it to Capshaw.

"Oh, how I wish we could see this device up close!" another girl exclaimed.

Capshaw's look was unreadable. "Astonishing," he murmured. "Thank you, ladies. Now *please*, move back." He gestured to a patrolman standing beside the prison van.

The man hurried over. "I need you to assist me," Capshaw said. "It will take too long for Maloney to get back, and now I have what I need."

The policeman paled. "Me, sir? But I don't know anything about them contraptions."

"No need," Capshaw assured him. "You simply hold the lantern and hand me tools."

"But what about the prisoner?" The patrolman pointed a thumb toward the police van.

Capshaw glanced inside. Flynn was asleep, curled on the wooden bench against the wall of the vehicle. Capshaw shook the heavy barred door to make sure it was locked tight. "He's not going anywhere. Come on. There's no time to lose."

As the pair hurried back to the platform, the crowd that had gathered stirred restlessly, aware that something was about to happen. The police had their hands full, keeping people at bay.

"Oh, now I can't see!" Miss Lovelace complained, as several men pushed in front of them.

Concordia pointed to a small rise at the back end of the square, situated at a distance behind the platform. "We'll be out of the way up there, and still able to see." She turned to Miss Pomeroy. "Do you mind that we stay? I can explain everything later, but I need to make sure this turns out all right."

Miss Pomeroy nodded. "I must admit, I too am curious."

On the slope, the view was somewhat improved. Concordia could see Capshaw and his assistant crouching under the platform, although she couldn't see the device itself. She watched for a sign, any sign, that things were going well. Judging from the rigidity of Capshaw's back, and how many times the patrolman rubbed sweaty palms on his trouser legs, progress was slow.

Looking beyond the platform, Concordia saw Mr. Sanders and his Democratic opponent Mr. Quint chatting amiably with one another and the people surrounding them. Apparently, not even the threat of death or bodily injury was enough to stop politicians from drumming up potential votes.

"Look!" One of the girls pointed, and Concordia turned her attention back to the platform. "He's reaching for the wire cutters now. They must be nearly finished."

Sure enough, they soon saw Capshaw heave a sigh and drop his head as he sat back on his heels. The patrolman had a big grin on his face. He mopped his brow with a handkerchief.

"Thank goodness," Concordia breathed.

Miss Pomeroy touched her arm. "I'm taking the girls back to the school. Obviously, there won't be a debate today." She looked Concordia up and down and grimaced. "I would suggest that you accompany us, but your attire would cause quite a stir on the trolley. Do you have a way to get back?"

Concordia nodded. "I'll have the lieutenant arrange for my transportation. I'll see you soon." She smiled at the students. "Your help was invaluable today. It may very well have made all the difference in the outcome."

The girls flushed and followed Miss Pomeroy.

Concordia rubbed at her stiff neck. It would be good to get back to Willow Cottage, and sleep. She surveyed the thinning crowd along the square, wondering if Barton Isley had been arrested yet.

A figure moving at the periphery caught her eye. It was a familiar-looking youth. Where had she seen him before?

Of course.

It was the man she'd seen on a snowy, moonlit night, when she had gone to retrieve a scarf on Rook's Hill, and then again, weeks later, after the senior auditions. Concordia stood on tiptoe and craned her neck for a better look. Yes, it was the same slender build, the same tilt of the head, the same stride. Who was he?

The man turned his face in her direction, and she gasped.

Lily Isley.

It all made sense. The versatile actress, adept at costume and charade. Why *couldn't* she pass herself off as a man?

But why would she wear such a disguise?

Then she had her answer.

Just behind Lily, shouldering his way through the crowd, was Robert Flynn.

Concordia's mouth dropped open in shock. How had Lily freed him from the van, with all of these policemen underfoot?

Lily locked eyes with Concordia across the square. She nudged Flynn, and they both ran, Lily's cap coming off and her hair tumbling free down her back.

"Stop!" Concordia shouted. She called down to Capshaw. "Lieutenant! They're getting away!" Without waiting for a response, Concordia took off after the pair, pushing her way through the crowd.

Capshaw, heart still pounding from defusing two bombs, took in the astonishing sight of two trouser-clad women, one slipper-shod, running through the crowd. *What on earth?*

Then he saw Flynn. Muttering an oath under his breath, he got up and ran after them, leaving behind the open-mouthed patrolman.

Concordia had always taken the utility of sturdy shoes for granted, until today. Much was being asked of her poor feet; while pursuing Lily and Flynn, they hobbled her at last. She watched helplessly as the two got away. She bent over to catch her breath as hot tears prickled her cheeks.

Concordia felt a hand on her shoulder and turned around to see Chief Stiles frowning down at her. "Do you ever stay put, Miss Wells? My men are chasing them down. Let's get you home."

Chapter 53

O monstrous act!

Othello, *V.ii*

Week 14, Instructor Calendar
May 1898

Concordia returned to Willow Cottage to find an unexpected visitor, waiting anxiously in the parlor.

"Mother!"

Mrs. Wells started at the sight of her daughter in male attire, bruised, filthy, and weary. Nonetheless, she ran over and embraced her. Concordia rested her head on her mother's shoulder and held her tightly.

"How...when...." Concordia's muffled voice trailed off.

"Dean Maynard sent for me, dear." Mrs. Wells stroked Concordia's hair. "I'm so relieved you're safe."

Concordia wiped her eyes on Maynard's jacket sleeve. "You know what happened? Do you know about...Flynn?"

Her mother nodded. "Mr. Maynard and Miss Crandall explained it to me."

"I'm sorry he turned out to be—"

"Now, never mind about him," her mother interrupted briskly. "He's not worth wasting another thought on. I'll be fine. I'm a little too old for falling hopelessly in love, you know."

Concordia searched her mother's face. While some of what she said might be a bluff to spare her worry, Mother appeared composed rather than devastated.

Mrs. Wells looked her up and down. "I believe it's time for a bath, young lady." She grinned. "And take your time. I can wait."

It was sheer bliss to soak in the tub. Concordia took her mother's advice and stayed in it even as the water cooled. She wanted to forget the last fifteen hours.

But how could she forget? Flynn was without scruple or conscience. She shuddered to think what could have happened in that root cellar.

If not for Randolph Maynard. The man was a surprise, to say the least. He seemed to have softened toward her. Perhaps.

At the thought of David, however, her stomach tightened. After last night, all she had wanted was comforting words from the gentle man who loved her. Instead, she'd gotten shock and anger. *Mercy,* did he think she put on trousers for amusement? Why couldn't he see she'd been through a terrible ordeal? She was lucky to have come through it alive.

It surprised her how quickly he had jumped to recriminations. A concern for propriety. Would her married life be like that? Her life—normally—was respectable and ordered, where she could easily behave in the decorous fashion expected of her. To be fair, David had never wanted her to be a shrinking violet. He respected her intellect too much for that.

But could her conduct forever remain a model of propriety, without deviation…the product of a quiet, lady-like life? She wasn't so sure. It seemed that, time and again, she was drawn into other people's problems, dilemmas from which she could not simply walk away. She had to help. She had to *act.* Would David, once he was her husband, forbid it?

She had no answers, except to be grateful they weren't getting married right away. There were obviously more issues to sort out.

Concordia finished her bath, brushed and pinned up her hair, and dressed in a simple white pleated shirtwaist and lavender muslin skirt. How lovely to be wearing her own clothes.

Once she was presentable, she hurried back to the parlor.

Concordia found her mother chatting with Charlotte Crandall and Miss Jenkins. The infirmarian summarily pulled Concordia over to the sofa.

"Sit," that lady ordered. "I want to look at your injuries."

Charlotte joined Concordia on the sofa, a smile tugging at her lips.

Miss Jenkins gently probed Concordia's bruised jaw. "Nothing fractured. Any teeth loose...no? Good." She sat back on her heels and gazed searchingly at Concordia. "I was told it was Flynn who struck you. The man has much to answer for."

"I punched him first," Concordia said.

Miss Jenkins' mouth gaped. Mrs. Wells regarded her daughter as if she'd grown a second head. But Charlotte started to giggle, and soon they were all laughing and wiping their eyes.

"I'd better take a look at your hand, then," Miss Jenkins said, her lips still twitching in amusement. She experimentally flexed the fingers. "Does this hurt? How about this?" She pressed gently. Concordia winced.

"The knuckles are a little bruised and swollen, but that should subside soon," Miss Jenkins concluded. "So long as you don't make fisticuffs a habit."

The women giggled again.

"Where's Barton Isley? Did the dean tell you about him?" Concordia asked, as the infirmarian continued her examination, now removing Concordia's shoes and stockings and frowning over her battered feet.

"Eventually," Miss Jenkins said. "I thought my girls were talking gibberish when they told me our bursar had been taken away by a policeman. Quite disruptive to the routine, as you can imagine. But shortly before you got here the president called a staff meeting and told us the whole story."

Concordia leaned back against the cushions, relieved that she didn't have to recount her experiences of the night before.

She had just restored her stockings and shoes when a knock at the door brought Randolph Maynard and Lady Principal Pomeroy to the gathering.

"We wanted to check on you, dear, and see how you were faring," Miss Pomeroy said, glancing at the bruise blooming along Concordia's jaw.

"I'm feeling better than I look, really," Concordia said. She gave the dean a grateful look. "Thanks to you, Mr. Maynard."

Dean Maynard cleared his throat. "Glad to be of help. But you seemed to have the situation well in hand when I came on the scene." He nodded in Miss Crandall's direction. "Along with a strong ally."

Charlotte Crandall blushed. "Do you know if they've caught Flynn? Or Lily Isley?"

"No. But Capshaw just called. He says he has news. He's on his way."

At that moment, Ruby stuck her head in. "Do you mind fendin' fer yourselves for a little bit? It's time to take the girls over to supper."

"Of course, Ruby," Concordia said. "We can manage." No matter what events were going on in the world at large, students still had to be fed. She smiled at the normalcy of it. She'd missed that.

"There's a plate of sandwiches on the kitchen table, and hot water in the kettle," Ruby added.

Charlotte Crandall got up and smoothed her skirts. "I'll get tea started."

President Langdon and a somber-looking Lieutenant Capshaw arrived at Willow Cottage just as Charlotte came in with the tray. Although Capshaw looked ready to drop from exhaustion, his glance swept across the room and its occupants as usual, looking for that one clue he might have missed.

Additional chairs were brought in, and soon everyone was settled. It was getting crowded in the small parlor.

"Did you find Flynn and Lily Isley?" Concordia asked, trying to read Capshaw's expression. It didn't look to be good news. His lips were pale, and a muscle in his jaw twitched of its own accord. She pressed her hands tightly together in her lap. The thought of the two escaping was unbearable.

Capshaw sighed. "Yes. At Flynn's residence."

Concordia closed her eyes. *Thank heaven.*

"Do you have them in custody now?" Maynard said, leaning forward eagerly.

"They are both dead," Capshaw said.

This was met with shocked silence, until Concordia asked the question for everyone in the room. "How?"

"Mrs. Isley shot Robert Flynn, then took poison," Capshaw said grimly. He got up and paced as best he could within the confines of the room.

"But that wasn't the worst of it," he continued. "There *was* a third bomb, after all. Smaller than the ones we found in the square, but still plenty destructive. Mrs. Isley rigged it to go off when the front door was opened. Two of my men are in the hospital."

They all stared at him, horrified.

"Will they be all right, Lieutenant?" Miss Jenkins asked.

"They were fortunate. The door caught on a rug, and didn't open completely. So they were partly protected from the blast. The doctor expects them to recover."

"Lily had enough knowledge to set up the device?" Concordia asked.

Capshaw nodded. "Hitchcock coached her well." He rummaged through a pocket and pulled out two folded sheets of paper. "She left a note addressed to you." He passed it to Concordia.

With trembling fingers, she unfolded the pages. Mrs. Wells unabashedly craned her neck to read over her daughter's shoulder.

> *My dear Concordia,*
>
> *So here we are, in the final act of our little drama. How I wish I had known it would end as a tragedy for me.*
>
> *I was sorry to have to tamper with your tea last night, because I do like you, even though you are responsible for our plan falling apart. In fact, I've been trying to protect you all this time. I coaxed Robert to consider Miss Hamilton as the true danger to our plans and leave you alone.*
>
> *But you kept persisting, even after I left the flowers and warning note in your office. I never imagined a lady professor*

would concern herself with anything other than her books and her students.

I'm sure you see me as quite a scandalous woman, having a lover, plotting bold and violent deeds with unscrupulous men. Think what you wish; I don't care. You cannot know the boredom of my life before I met Robert.

By now you know that I set the bombs, disguised as a youth. You nearly caught me months before, as I practiced going about in my costume. I was sorry to lose my pin in the snow that night. As the only woman member of the Circle, I cherished it.

I had you all duped, didn't I? Everyone underestimated me.

After we escaped the police in the square today, we hurried back to Robert's house to get money and a few necessities to start a new life together.

But then he pointed a gun at me. He was going alone, he said, and didn't want any loose ends left behind.

Only then did I realize what a fool I had been. He had never loved me. I was a tool to be used and discarded when no longer needed. I was a "loose end."

But he underestimated me, too.

It is all over now. Prison is not for one such as I. The third bomb that I'd had no time to place will yet serve a purpose. I am leaving this note away from the blast. It will no doubt keep the stuffy society matrons gossiping for a good long time.

In the meantime, I wait for the tea—a different kind this time—to do its work. Good-bye Concordia.

~Lily

Wordlessly, Concordia passed it back to Capshaw. Her mind was a turmoil of conflicting emotions: shock, anger at Lily' betrayal and ruthlessness, sadness for the loss of life and the waste of talent.

She shuddered, and her mother patted her back reassuringly. "Be thankful that it's over."

Chapter 54

I pray you, in your letters,
When you shall these unlucky deeds relate,
Speak of me as I am.

Othello, *V.ii*

Week 17, Instructor Calendar
June 1898

"Here, let me get that," Concordia said, reaching around Miss Hamilton to prop open the door to Willow Cottage as they went in. "I'll make us some tea. And there may be some of Ruby's scones left," she added, leading the way to the kitchen.

Penelope Hamilton, wrist in a splint but looking otherwise whole, smiled. "That sounds lovely."

"I'm glad you could visit once more before you leave," Concordia said, putting the kettle under the tap. "Are you sure you're fit to travel?"

"I'll be fine," Miss Hamilton assured her.

"I imagine your family misses you," Concordia said. She set a plate of scones and a teacup within reach of Penelope Hamilton's good hand.

"My sister is the only family I have left," Miss Hamilton said. "Although she came to see me during my recovery, a hospital environment is hardly congenial for socializing."

"I don't know what we would have done without you," Concordia said, thinking over the events of the past few weeks. Lily Isley and Robert Flynn were dead, Hitchcock and Isley were in prison, each awaiting trial, and the police chief was facing disciplinary action for his part in obstructing the Florence

Willoughby investigation. The Inner Circle, without its leader, was broken up, powerless. Charlotte Crandall had told Concordia that her uncle, Sir Anthony Dunwick, had withdrawn his membership in the Black Scroll, along with Maynard and a number of other brothers. Accusations and blame were directed toward the powerful Willoughby family.

But it was over.

Miss Hamilton smiled. "I was happy to assist. A fascinating case. You did most of the hard work, however."

Concordia winced. The bruise on her jaw had faded, but the memories were painfully fresh.

"I haven't seen Mr. Bradley around lately," Miss Hamilton continued. "Miss Pomeroy told me what happened between you two at the square. I hope the rift has been mended?"

Miss Hamilton's directness was always a bit disconcerting. Concordia looked away, busying herself with steeping the tea to cover her silence. Forgiving David had been the easy part, but she'd found herself at a loss for words to answer any of his letters of apology. After a week of leaving his messages unanswered, she had received a terse note from him, saying that he was leaving for his parents' summer cottage and would be gone until the fall term. She wasn't sure whether she was angry, hurt, or relieved. She'd tried to push it out of her mind with work. Certainly the end of term had held plenty to occupy her: examinations, graduation preparations, letters of reference, dismantling the cottage household. Many good-byes were exchanged as the students scattered for the summer recess.

The good-byes were always the hardest part. Concordia would miss her girls, as impetuous, mischievous, and noisy as they were wont to be. Even Miss Smedley, who at last had settled down to be a fair student and planned to return in the fall.

But when Concordia wasn't busy—usually in the quiet of the night as she lay staring at the moonlight-bathed ceiling—she thought of David, and hoped she wasn't saying goodbye to him, too. She'd started four different letters to send, and had torn up each one.

Miss Hamilton was watching her carefully. Concordia finally met her gaze. "He's gone for the summer. And no—it has not been mended."

"Ah, I see." There was an awkward silence, then Miss Hamilton changed the subject. "I'll be starting my next assignment soon."

"Oh? What assignment is that?"

"It looks to be quite intriguing. It involves a cross-country railway trip. In fact, I was wondering…I'd need a companion for the journey. What do you think?"

Concordia's eyes widened. "*Me?* I already have a job. Shouldn't you find someone more—" she groped for a word "—professional?"

Miss Hamilton shook her head. "You underestimate yourself. Besides, you wouldn't do actual investigative work. I would merely need you to listen and observe. It would be helpful to have someone to talk to. Sometimes detection is lonely work."

Concordia nodded. She had felt that loneliness.

"You've just finished with the spring term," Miss Hamilton went on, as Concordia poured the tea. "The trip would involve only a few weeks of your summer recess. Besides, it might be opportune to get away from Hartford for a while. You could use a change of scene." She hesitated.

"There's something more to this," Concordia said.

"I'm also concerned about the Inner Circle," Miss Hamilton said.

"Why?" Concordia asked. "That has been broken up."

"We don't know the full extent of the Circle's influence, or if the remaining members might engage in some sort of retribution," Miss Hamilton countered. "Remember, we don't know the identities of the final three in the group."

Concordia sat lost in thought, gripping her teacup. When she had visited Sophia and Eli a few days before, she'd learned that Isley was still refusing to identify the other members. Did he fear them so? She'd tried not to think about those unknown men, possibly nursing a grudge against her.

Miss Hamilton waited in silence. The mantel clock ticked in the quiet.

The sound of the doorbell made them both jump.

They heard Ruby's footsteps in the hall, and then Capshaw's voice as he talked with Ruby. A couple of minutes later, the familiar stoop-shouldered man paused in the kitchen doorway. Concordia noticed he was growing his mustache again. It seemed to be coming in just as red as ever.

"I'm sorry to interrupt, but I have news."

"Of course, Lieutenant, sit down." Miss Hamilton gestured to another chair. "Would you like some tea?"

He shook his head. "I can only stay a moment. I came to tell you that Hitchcock and Isley are dead."

"What! Both of them?" Concordia cried. Her fingers felt suddenly chilled, and she gripped her teacup for its warmth. "How can that be?"

"Killed as they slept, and in different cells," Capshaw said dejectedly. "With a fatal dose of chloroform."

Concordia and Miss Hamilton exchanged glances.

"It looks like Ruby is a widow, once again," Concordia said.

Capshaw nodded. "I just told her."

Miss Hamilton grimaced. "The Inner Circle is alive and well."

Epilogue

What wound did ever heal but by degrees?

II.iii

Summer Recess
June 1898

Concordia sat on her suitcase to keep it shut as she wrestled with the buckle on the strap. It was at this inopportune moment that someone knocked on the door of Willow Cottage.

Drat. Since she was alone in the house, she would have to get that.

The man at the door was holding flowers. Concordia recognized both the flowers—prize-winning roses from President Langdon's garden—and the man.

"David?" Concordia stared at him, her hand gripping the knob.

He gave her a tentative smile, which dimpled his cheeks but didn't quite reach his brown eyes. "I couldn't stay away. Can we talk?"

Concordia took a deep breath. "Come in." She opened the door wider. As he passed her, she couldn't help but notice that his neck and wrists had been touched by the sun over the past few weeks, and the wavy black hair now curled past his ears. She resisted the urge to smooth it out of the way.

"Did Mr. Langdon let you take these?" she asked instead. She gestured toward the roses.

"He helped me cut them, actually—who knew there was so much involved in snipping a simple rose?—and sent me away with his blessing. For you," David said, handing them to her.

She closed her eyes for a moment and breathed in their gentle fragrance. "They're lovely. Come into the kitchen while I find a vase."

"Where's Ruby?" he asked, sitting at the well-worn table while Concordia rummaged in cabinets.

"Out shopping." Concordia pulled down a vase and soon had the flowers settled in. "Mr. Langdon certainly grows a beautiful rose," she murmured.

"Still, it's a poor expression of apology," David said soberly. He reached over and took Concordia's trembling hands in his. "Dean Maynard wrote me, and recounted the whole story of what happened that night. I had no idea. Even so, I behaved abominably in the square that morning, just at the time when you most needed strength and comfort."

Concordia swallowed back the lump forming in her throat. She would not cry. Again. She would *not*.

She could only trust herself to nod, pulling her hands away. She returned to shifting the flower stems in the vase, tucking them here and there, struggling to regain her composure.

"Am I forgiven?" David asked anxiously.

Concordia took a deep breath and met his eye. "Long ago. I should have answered your letters, but…I couldn't find the words. It was a difficult time." She touched the petals gently.

David nodded. "I understand that better now. At least we have this chance to talk before you leave."

Concordia's hands stilled. "You know I'm leaving?"

"Miss Hamilton wrote to say you're taking a trip with her."

"Oh. What else did she say?" She couldn't imagine Miss Hamilton telling David about the Pinkerton assignment, or the risk of revenge by the remaining members of the Inner Circle.

David leaned forward, lines of worry creasing his forehead. "Precious little, which makes me wonder. Knowing Miss Hamilton's line of work, I'm skeptical that this is the trip of leisure she implied in her letter."

Concordia looked past his shoulder, through the sunny kitchen window. She focused her attention on the wild daylilies outside, against the sweep of green grass. "Well, it's leisure for *me*. I need a change of scene."

David's frown deepened. "You know," he said mildly, "you never look directly at me when you're lying."

Drat. Concordia gave an exasperated sigh and met his eyes. "What do you want me to say? We have this argument again and again. You don't want me to 'get involved,' or 'take chances.' I've come to realize that I cannot live that way. I cannot simply be a bystander."

In her agitation, she stood and paced the room.

David stood as well. "Just be honest with me! Why are you going on this trip?"

Her back stiffened as she looked away. "The Inner Circle killed Isley and Hitchcock. In their jail cells, right under the eyes of the law. Lieutenant Capshaw and Miss Hamilton think it would be wise for me to leave town for a while." She turned back to face him, her eyes brimming with tears. "I kept it from you because I don't want you to tell me I'm in this pickle through my own fault, and that I should have listened to you." She tilted her chin defiantly. "Because, even now, I would make the same choices again."

David walked over and put his hands on her shoulders. She felt her neck tingle and her cheeks grow warm.

"Concordia," he said in a softer voice, pulling her gently toward him, "I promise, I will never again make you defend what you do. You have proved, time and again, that you are capable of taking care of yourself." He gave a shaky laugh and held her close. "I just want to take care of you, too. If you'll let me."

Concordia smiled through the last of her tears as David brushed them from her cheeks. "Yes."

She looped her arms around his neck as he brushed her lips with his, then deepened the kiss. They stayed like that for a long time.

Ruby Hitchcock, arms laden with parcels, glimpsed Concordia through the window and was about to knock to get help with the door. Until she saw the young lady professor being thoroughly kissed by Mr. Bradley.

Land sakes, it took him long enough. The matron smiled and walked around the path to the front door.

❧THE END❧

Afterword

It's a great time to be a historical author, with the wealth of digitized historical material available on the world wide web. For anyone interested in the background research that went into the writing of this book, I've shared some wonderful primary and secondary sources on my website, http://kbowenmysteries.com. I'd love to see you there.

I hope you enjoyed the novel. Should you feel so inclined, please consider leaving a review on www.Amazon.com or your favorite online book venue. Word of mouth is essential to help readers find books they will love, particularly those written by independently-published authors. Thank you!

To order other books in the Concordia Wells series, please visit: http://kbowenmysteries.com/books. Purchase links to all of the online venues are provided on that page.

CPSIA information can be obtained
at www.ICGtesting.com
Printed in the USA
LVOW13s2254270318
571425LV00010B/178/P